# Cravings

## by

## Brenda Huber

**Cravings**

Cover Art by *Rae Monet*

The Wild Rose Press
PO Box 706
Adams Basin, NY 14410-0706
Visit us at www.thewildrosepress.com

Publishing History
First Black Rose Edition, 2010
Print ISBN 1-60154-866-4

Published in the United States of America

**Kate O'Rourke extended her hand
and turned a heart-stopping smile on him.**
The floor slipped out from under his feet, and he fell head first into eyes the color of spring-fresh grass. Time spun out while every thought in his head deserted him.

Hers was a classical beauty, timeless and graceful. Pixie-like. Almost Faerie in quality. The top of her head barely came to his shoulders. Her hand was tiny in his. But she was all woman. The touch of her skin on his, warm silk, jolted through him like an electrical charge, nearly bringing him to his knees.

Awareness flickered in her stunning eyes.

He couldn't remember where he was. Couldn't remember how he'd gotten here...or why. He couldn't remember his own damned name right now, but there was no question in his mind. She'd felt the connection too. The darker, primitive side of his nature began to take over as he stared deep into her unblinking eyes. Images began to form in his mind...images of hot, sweat-misted, naked bodies writhing and straining on a tangle of red silk sheets. Hungry mouths. Greedy hands. Racing pulses. Skin on skin. He blinked, perspiration beading on his brow.

Judging by her dazed expression, those images had been unintentionally transferred to her mind. The fact that she'd been so quick to intercept those images only attested to the fact that the attraction was mutual. That realization fueled his hunger...and his thirst.

Her blood would taste so sweet...

# Kudos for Brenda Huber and *MINE*

"Ms. Huber splashes into the world of Vampyre romance with one amazing book. Mouthwatering, hot and not for the timid. The chemistry between Alex and Cole is electricity between the pages. These multi-dimensional characters will have you cheering in their corner and holding your breath for them to come together. The timing and pace of each scene is spot on. Ms. Huber is an author who makes every page look effortless. Paranormal romance lovers... are you listening? You do not want to miss this book!"

*~Catherine Bybee Blogspot*

"Ms. Huber composes a romantic vampyre ballad full of suspense. The chemistry between the hero and heroine is electric... I cannot wait to read Styx's story. That sexy Spaniard already owns a piece of my heart."

*~Coffee Time Romance*

"The writing is fantastic and the pace never relents."

*~Long and Short Reviews*

"I have to tell all the readers here today that if you like the vampire genre you're going to LOVE this book. The scene where Cole and Alex first lay eyes on each other snaps on the page and doesn't let you go to the very end."

~Catherine Bybee Blogspot

Dedicated to Joelle Walker...
Because "Thank You" isn't enough for all you do—
this one is for you...

"There are more things in heaven and earth,
Horatio, than are dreamt of in your philosophy."
~William Shakespeare, *Hamlet*

Prologue

He hung back several paces, biding his time while his little flower stumbled down the long, dark alley ahead of him. Streetlights blinked and died in the distance, casting the alley in gloom. An unnatural, smoky mist swirled around her ankles, skimming greedily up her toned calves. Her skinned palms left tantalizing smears of fragrant crimson along the shadow-blanketed brick wall. The alluring scent of her blood—blood copiously laced with fear and adrenaline—called to him like a siren's song. Her ragged breath heaving in and out, her staggering steps echoing in the night heightened his predatory instincts. He'd never been one to resist the excitement of the chase. And what a chase she had gifted him.

The magnitude of her efforts was humbling.

Her long dark hair—gleaming blue-black in the moonlight—streamed behind her like ribbons of luxuriant silk, beckoning him onward. Fragrant as the fragile petals of a newly blossomed rose, her skin had been baby soft beneath his adoring fingertips. He could barely hold himself in check. How she'd trembled at his touch. Soon. Very soon, he would touch her again.

Every few steps she darted a wide-eyed glance over her shoulder.

*Do not worry, amoura. I am still here.*

Once she tired—once she accepted her fate—he would close the distance and claim her for his own. He would not rush her. He was a patient lover...a patient hunter. He would not have to use *persuasion,* the hypnotic Vampyre gift of suggestion. She was meant to belong to him, as were the others.

Ah, but this one...this tiny, fierce female had surprised him—a rarity in and of itself, displaying great courage when he'd revealed his true self to her. His little flower had fought like a tigress, scratching and kicking and biting for her freedom. Fighting for this pitiful existence Humans called life. He could have overpowered her...easily. But he'd let her go. After all, he wouldn't want to undermine her self-confidence. She'd proven herself worthy. She would bring honor to his house.

He would call this one...*Layla*.

Yes, Layla was the perfect name, for she would be born of the night. His most treasured creation to date. He would bless her with eternity.

He could almost taste the delicate flavor of her blood on his tongue. So innocent. So sweet. He would teach her how to pleasure him. His blood surged in anticipation. His body hummed with excitement. He would educate her in all the exotic, sensual ways...the ways of his people. She was an intelligent creature. She would realize how lucky she was he'd chosen her. And she would be grateful. The tip of his tongue slid down the length of one long, razor-sharp fang. His lips curled upward.

*Oh, so grateful indeed...*

Bracing a hand against the wall, Layla bent slightly at the waist, panting heavily. She threw another wide-eyed glance over her shoulder and sobbed aloud.

*Have no fear. I will wait for you, little one.*

*We have all the time in the world...*

Up ahead, Layla lurched forward, stumbled, dropped to one knee. A bright burst of blood-scent exploded in the night. His nostrils flared. His eyes burned, casting an incandescent glow between them. Behind his lips, his fangs stretched longer, throbbing painfully, drawing forth trickles of his own blood. Her strangled gasp pricked his acute hearing.

Would she gasp the same way when he sank his fangs into her tender flesh?

Would she moan with pleasure?

Dragging in a long, labored breath, he shuddered as another wave of ravenous desire crashed through his taut body. The leash of his self-restraint snapped tight.

He would control himself. Soon she would welcome his ardor. At the moment, however, he had to remember to go slowly. He didn't want to frighten his radiant little flower—innocent that she was—with the depth of his passions.

*Not just yet...* An anticipatory grin curled the edges of his lips.

Battling to regain her feet, Layla pushed on. Admiration widened his smile. Oh, she was wonderful. A warrior's heart beat inside her fragile body. A few staggering steps later, Layla fell to her knees once more. There she remained. Chest heaving. Shoulders sagging. Head bowed.

A raw, defeated sob tore from her throat.

*Ah...at last.* Affectionate satisfaction swelled. He swept down upon her, gently catching her up in his arms, mindful of his overwhelming strength. He didn't want to bruise her.

"Let me go," she cried out, striking a small fist against his chest once, twice. She strained, pushing against him with all her might, but her efforts were feeble...and futile. Hers was the desperate struggle of a butterfly defying a desert *Simoom.*

Layla's voice was hoarse, her eyes wild. Her ragged breath raced across the flesh of his throat. Her blood—fresh blood, nearly impossible to resist—taunted him, and he was already so close to the edge as it was.

Too close, really.

"Shhh, *habibi*," he crooned softly, stroking the side of her damp, heart-shaped face. *Habibi*...his beloved. She'd proven far more precious than the others. So delicate. So unpredictable. So courageous. He would take extra time with her initiation, savor every moment. Layla had more than earned the privilege.

But he would not lose sight of his ultimate goal. This night he moved one step closer to regaining all that had been taken from him. Despite any interference by those bumbling, meddlesome TFRA agents. He'd heard they'd even taken it upon themselves to give him a name, of all the gall. The Collector. In a way, he supposed the name was fitting enough. After all, the acquisition of suitable brides certainly could be—however loosely defined— as collecting.

But the fact that the Task Force for Rogue Apprehension had gotten involved in his business in the first place was utterly ridiculous. How dare they consider *him* a Rogue, when the likes of that bastard Spaniard roamed the streets century upon century, free to besmirch honor and corrupt innocents without interference or consequence?

Well, no more...

Soon he would have retribution against the bastard responsible for his disgrace. He'd bided his time—studied his enemy, centuries spent plotting and waiting until the time was right. He was strong enough now; he'd mastered his abilities.

*Revenge was at hand...*

Jagged nails raked over his cheek, leaving trails of fire in their sharp wake. Jerking his head to the side, he hissed...and grinned. Even in the face of defeat, his little *habibi* showed true spirit. Predatory instincts took over completely, and he reveled in the power flowing through his veins.

Saliva surged. He opened his mouth wide. His

fangs ached, pulsing with the promise of life eternal. His little desert blossom had proven herself far beyond his expectations.

His Layla deserved a *Kiss*.

## Chapter 1

Sultry moonlight drenched the tropical landscape, accentuating the deepest, darkest shadows with shimmering hues of liquid silver. Muted by the gentle rush and ebb of the nighttime surf, the plaintive cry of a native bird wafted on the sensual breeze. The slow, seductive bump and grind of Stolen Innocence's latest chart-topper simmered enticement from hidden poolside speakers. Soft, strategically placed outdoor accent lights illuminated the floor-to-ceiling, heavily tinted glass walls of the decadent, ocean-side residence.

Preoccupied, Styx reclined on the doublewide chaise, surveying the sparkling mirror image of the full moon reflected on the serene surface of the pool. His fingers toyed idly with the strands of long blonde hair draped across his bare chest. The curvy little Human snuggling against him had sated him in more than one way this evening—yet restless energy lurked at the edge of his consciousness. The blonde— what was her name again? Ah, hell, what difference did it make—rubbed herself against his side, purring like a well-satisfied kitten bloated on a saucer full of decadent cream. The intoxicating effects of the Vampyre *Kiss* he'd bestowed upon her earlier obviously had yet to wear off.

Styx had always been affectionate and generous with his women, taking exceptional care of the females he'd taken to his bed. He always made certain they'd been thoroughly swamped with pleasure before he sought his own. Unfortunately, as of late, his blood hosts—each one as unremarkable as the last—failed to hold his attention beyond immediate gratification. He hadn't always been so dispassionate, so...so *detached* with his females.

Usually it took days before his interest faded.

What *was* this disconcerting apathy holding him in thrall?

To his chagrin, Styx caught his mind wandering once again to his friend Cole...or rather, to Cole's new *Bride* to be precise. Alexandra—Alex, for short—or Slim, as Styx had dubbed her at their first meeting.

It wasn't that he'd been entertaining inappropriate thoughts where Alex was concerned. Unashamed womanizer that he was, Styx wouldn't have been stupid—or crazy—enough to poach on that territory. Cole Gunnarrson, ancient Viking warrior, was one of the most ferocious warlords the Vampyre Nation had ever known.

And Cole was fiercely protective of his new mate.

In the five centuries they'd known each other, Cole had become the closest thing Styx had to family. They'd become as close as brothers. No, Styx's fascination leaned more toward what Alex represented. The perfect *Bride*. Blindingly beautiful. Highly intelligent. Amazingly open-minded. With a passionate zest for life and a deep well of absolute loyalty for those whom she loved. Alex had become the closest thing to a little sister he'd had since...

Gritting his teeth, Styx ruthlessly steered his thoughts to a safer, far less emotional path.

Over the last several months, he'd found himself holding Alex up as a measuring stick, so to speak. Sadly, all the women he'd surrounded himself with thus far had fallen short of the mark.

Far short, indeed.

Not so very long ago, he would've shuddered at the mere thought of tying himself to one female. His appetites, his friends had mercilessly teased him, were insatiable. Indeed, for as long as he could remember—even back while he'd still been Human—his personal motto had essentially been, "*so many women, so little time.*" Now, while a tiny part of him still scoffed at the idea of limiting himself to only one female, another part of him—a large part if he were being honest with himself— seemed to constantly wonder...*what if?*

What if he were given the opportunity to take a *Bride* of his own? What if there was a female out there as tailor made for him as Alex was for Cole? What if that female could accept him as he was...as Alex had accepted Cole?

What if he took the chance—accepted the risk— and the woman he'd chosen betrayed him?

What if *he* failed *her*?

Too many *what if's* for a rational conclusion.

Commitment seemed to be working out just fine for Cole...once he'd dealt with the Rogue threatening his Alex, of course. Cole was happy.

Happy, hell... Cole was so damned besotted, he all but glowed whenever Alex's name was even mentioned. And whenever she walked into the same room as Cole, anything combustible all but went up in flames in the wake of their palpable passion for each other. Styx wanted that for himself. Headstrong, supremely-feminine Alex had the fearless Viking conqueror wrapped firmly around her graceful little finger...except for when it came to her safety. Then it was Alex doing the bending. To say that Cole was a bit overprotective was a gross understatement.

Maybe he was a bit lonely. And maybe—just *maybe*—he was a little jealous. Not that he begrudged Cole his *Bride*. After eleven centuries of guilt and self-imposed emotional isolation, Cole had more than earned his happily ever after. But Styx couldn't help wonder sometimes what it must be like to have someone care so much they'd be willing to risk anything...give up *everything*...just to be with you.

Tucking a hand behind his head, he lifted his knee, swaying it side to side as the predictable press of restlessness surged once more. The salty tang of the warm Pacific breeze swept over him, rustling the palm fronds overhead, stirring the fragrant flowers scattered over the grounds around the house.

Styx shifted on the chaise, ignoring the blonde's disgruntled, drowsy grumble. She snuggled closer against him. Her breathing slipped back into a content, pre-sleep rhythm.

He should be content.

*¡Mierda!* He *should* be happy.

But he wasn't.

He'd like to tell himself this nameless apathy would pass, but he had the sinking sensation the assurance would be nothing more than a sad, wistful lie. It wasn't as if he didn't enjoy his current profession as drummer for the wildly popular American rock band, Stolen Innocence. He got on well with the rest of the band...rag-tag bunch that they were. He chuckled low in his throat. Two Vampyre, three Humans, and a Werewolf. Who would have ever thought it? And, as always, whenever Cole was around, there was never a dull moment.

Watching Cole's futile battle with fate before he finally succumbed to Alex's charms had certainly proven entertaining. Almost as entertaining as that time a few centuries back when he and Cole had inadvertently charmed and, subsequently, seduced a hotheaded desert sheikh's harem.

The *entire* harem.

All twenty-seven females.

His smile grew wide over that memory. They'd

barely escaped with their hides intact, but the sheikh's anger had been a small price to pay for the very thorough sexual enlightenment he'd received at the hands of the sheikh's women.

Styx stroked his trimmed goatee. *Oh, yes...worth every second.*

Over the long centuries of his life, Styx had amassed a substantial fortune, which, combined with his Immortal existence allowed him to do—or be—virtually anything he wanted. Thanks to his considerable charm and dark, wicked good looks, he'd never needed the Vampyre gift of *persuasion* to keep himself amply supplied with eager female companionship.

Nor had he needed his *other* special ability.

With Cole and Alex away on an extended honeymoon, Styx had plenty of time on his hands for relaxing and recreation...thus his current retreat to the bountiful islands of Hawaii. His appreciative gaze swept over the surrounding landscape, and his grin widened.

*The scenery wasn't half-bad either.*

The recreation part had been moderately enjoyable. The relaxing part seemed to be the problem. Then again, perhaps the very concept of time was the quandary. His grin slipped away on a heartfelt sigh.

Time was both blessing and curse for Vampyre. For any Immortal, really. Granting infinite possibilities for tomorrow and every day thereafter. Leaving in its unforgiving wake decade upon decade, century upon century, of memories...some—like his time spent with Sheikh Amir al-Rashid's harem—pleasantly recalled. His lips twisted suddenly on a pained grimace as other, darker images—images of deceit and betrayal, of innocent life frivolously squandered and lost forever—came to mind, unbidden, leaving a bitter taste in his mouth.

Some memories were definitely best left forgotten.

The rhythm of the nameless female's breathing slowed in time with the cadence of her heartbeat as she settled into a light sleep against his shoulder. Her warm, too-sweet blood slid languidly through Styx's veins. Her blood cells merged with his own, regenerating nerve and tissue, rejuvenating him. The musk of satisfying—albeit mundane—sex hung heavy in the air around her...increasing the hollow, restless ache in his chest. The breeze shifted, ever so slightly, and a new scent wafted on the night.

*Vampyre.*

Styx instantly tensed.

His preternatural senses dissected the night-enshrouded landscape, examining and isolating scents and sounds. The fine hairs on the back of his neck prickled as he confirmed the presence of another of his kind.

A familiar*, unwelcome* male.

Animosity churned deep in his gut. Bitterness boiled through his veins. Darting his focus to the female in his arms, he used *persuasion* to send her deeper into the realm of unconsciousness, his lips moving so quickly the Human eye wouldn't have been able to track the movement as he whispered the ancient hypnotic words.

In a flash, the change was upon him. His eyes burned, glowing with amber luminosity into the shadows. The skin on his face tightened. His fangs stretched, long and lethal. Styx instinctively snarled, warning the approaching male his welcome was precarious at best.

"Crispin," Styx hissed around a mouthful of fangs.

Crispin's presence didn't bode well for Styx...*whatever* the agent's business was here tonight. It was a well-known fact amongst the

Vampyre Nation, the TFRA didn't willingly take no for an answer.

The TFRA agent drifted from the concealing foliage and tread, utterly unperturbed, across the manicured lawns toward the placid surface of the pool and the nearby loungers. From their first encounter, Styx had been wary of the peculiarly emotionless agent. A healthy dose of anger now colored his opinion after the Task Force for Rogue Apprehension—the Vampyre equivalent of the Human FBI—had recruited both Styx and Cole to help apprehend a vicious Rogue targeting the Human music industry, only to leave them floundering on their own as the case swiftly deteriorated.

Crispin had been suspiciously absent the night the Rogue abducted and all but drained Alex. If Cole hadn't found her when he had, hadn't saved her by... Styx shuddered that thought away before it could take root. He couldn't bring himself to imagine what the loss of Alex would have done to his longtime friend. And that had been before they'd Mated...

Without a word, Crispin flipped his trademark dark trench coat out of the way and took a seat on a chaise near Styx. His bland stare flashed negligently over the sleeping female before settling on Styx's face. As ever, the agent wore his long brown hair in a ponytail at the nape of his neck, an incongruous paradox when paired with his expensive designer suits.

"Styx," Crispin finally deigned to reply, his deep voice flat. Emotionless as his eyes. Clasping his large hands, Crispin braced his elbows on his knees and leaned forward. "Nice place you got here."

Arching an ungracious brow, Styx waited. Although he held Crispin personally responsible for nearly getting Alex killed...and, by extension, Cole...Styx made the effort to temper the effects of his lingering animosity. After all, he was still sane enough to remember he couldn't attack a TFRA agent without serious repercussions.

"Stopped by Gunnarrson's place," the agent drawled in that slow, cultured tone Styx had come to loathe. "The Werewolf said Gunnarrson took his female on a trip to Norway."

"The *Werewolf* has a name, so does Cole's *Bride*," Styx spat out acerbically, quickly giving up on his self-admittedly weak attempt at civility. "Cole took *Alex* on an extended honeymoon. I'm sure *Zack* told you Norway's only one stop along the way. Alex is real big on postcards, got several of 'em so far. England, Brazil, Rome…"

Styx curled his lips and tossed out a few more countries for good measure as he made a mental note to call Cole later and give him warning to lay low for a while. The last thing he wanted was for the TFRA to track Cole down on his honeymoon. "If you're looking for him, you might wander around Transylvania for a while, maybe flash a little fang at a few of the locals…I'm sure they still have a few torches and pitchforks they'd be happy to dust off. Or, hey, better still, why don't you try a very thorough search of Siberia. If you look real hard, you might find him there."

"Actually," the edge of Crispin's lips curled upward at Styx's blatant jibes, "I was looking for you."

Styx muttered a less than complimentary comment about what Crispin could do with himself that should have brought some healthy emotion to the agent's eyes…had the agent been your normal Vampyre.

As it was, Crispin didn't even blink.

Disentangling himself from the oblivious female, Styx rose from the chaise and reached for the robe he'd tossed over the back of his seat earlier. Slipping his arms into the ivory silk, he loosely belted the robe around his naked body and paced a few steps away. Pivoting on his heel, he rubbed at the sudden knot of tension balling at the base of his neck and glowered at his undaunted, uninvited guest.

"What do you want?"

"We have another...situation." Sighing, Crispin pushed to his feet, but remained beside the lounger. Rocking back on his heels, he clasped his hands behind him. "We've encountered another Rogue with a...a puzzling agenda."

Styx didn't like the odd emphasis Crispin put on the word *puzzling*, nor did he appreciate the wry twitch of the agent's lips. The emaciated grin disappeared before it could achieve the status of a full on smile. Was Crispin afraid of betraying even that much emotion? Damned suspicious was what it was. A man who played his cards so close to his vest that he wouldn't even risk a smile couldn't be trusted.

"I don't give a damn about another one of your twisted psychos. Last I checked it was *your* job to round up Rogues, not mine...that makes him *your* problem. Not. Mine." He prowled along the edge of the pool, pausing at the far corner to shoot a scathing glare in Crispin's direction. "I'm not interested in cleaning up any more of your messes. The last one damned near got two good friends killed."

A muscle twitched along Crispin's jaw, but the rest of his features remained remarkably impassive.

*Damned, inscrutable bastard.*

Crispin cleared his throat and calmly informed Styx, "Ah, but there you are wrong. It seems this particular Rogue knows *you* quite well. In fact, he asked for you by name...in a roundabout way. That makes him your problem, too."

Styx growled, low and deep. He wouldn't give in

to such a blatant lure. His hands fisted at his sides as, unbidden, morbid curiosity burned through him. *¡Mierda!* It was just like last time, with boredom and curiosity working against him.

"*Gilipoya,*" Styx muttered beneath his breath. *Bastard.*

He was *not* going to ask.

He *wasn't.*

Styx snarled. "What the hell are you talking about?"

The corner of Crispin's mouth shifted—barely discernable, but movement nonetheless. Pushing his trench coat out of his way once more, Crispin settled on the chaise and folded his hands across his middle as his steady, brown-eyed gaze patiently followed Styx's progress across the cement. Styx itched to choke the life from the agent...if only Vampyre could be killed so easily.

"Our Rogue's been a busy boy." Apparently satisfied he'd snagged sufficient interest in the subject, Crispin reached inside his coat and pulled a familiar, small notepad free. Flipping the black leather cover open, he thumbed through a few pages before centering his attention on Styx. "Six hits in as many weeks running along the west coast of the U.S. stretching from San Francisco to Aberdeen."

"What's the matter, body count piling up too fast for you?"

"No bodies," the agent calmly replied, then amended, "at least, not directly."

"No bodies? Then how can you even—"

"He's turning them."

"*¡Los cojones!*"

Even as the harsh oath exploded between them, the frightening ramifications of the Rogue's actions flooded Styx. Stunned, he stopped pacing and sank down onto a vacant lounger. Vampyre law allowed its citizens—during the *entire* span of their existence—to change only two Mortals.

Absolutely no more than two.

For *any* reason.

If growth of the Vampyre Nation surged too quickly, the balance between Human and Vampyre could ultimately career out of balance, resulting in horrifying decimation of the Human population. If this wasn't contained—and fast—the other races, feeling they had no choice, would eventually step in. It would be full-scale war...apocalyptic. This Rogue had already turned six newborns...that they knew of.

*Six...*

Styx leaned back in his seat and stared, wide eyed, at the agent. Utterly at a loss for words. He could literally *feel* the blood drain from his face.

"He turns them," Crispin repeated. Then he drove the final stake home. "But he doesn't teach them the laws, doesn't teach them self-control."

"*¡Madre de Dios!*" Styx gasped.

He was off the chaise in a heartbeat, his bare feet eating up the distance along the side of the pool, from one end to the other and back. If the Sire wasn't—for whatever reason—sticking around to teach the newborn Vampyre the laws, wasn't helping them to master self-control, the fallout could be...

*Catastrophic.*

Appalled, Styx jerked to a halt, dragging his palms down the sides of his face.

Unrestrained, unnecessary killings.

*Killings, hell...* The attacks would be little more than feeding frenzies. Vicious and unstoppable. Unmindful of the presence of bystanders. Which would lead to possible—no, *certain* exposure of the Vampyre Nation. Human panic. Mass hysteria and unmitigated genocide.

Six untrained newborns in a centralized location, with the potential for heaven only knew how many more newborns...

No wonder the TFRA was desperate for help.

And the TFRA had to be desperate if they were coming to Styx for assistance, considering his current enmity. Particularly after the TFRA's humiliation at the hands of the last Rogue they'd squared off against. If Cole hadn't killed the Party Crasher, there would have been no telling how long that killing spree would have gone on unimpeded.

Crispin's mild stare followed Styx's unnerved pacing until he subsided once more onto a lounger. How could the bastard be so damned calm at a time like this? Styx raked his hair with splayed fingers. Bracing his elbows on his knees, he glared at the agent while a volatile mixture of resentment and anger seethed inside him. His chaotic emotions pushed the transformation in him up a notch. His fangs stretched taut. His eyes were on fire.

"Tell me the rest," he demanded in a harsh rasp.

Nodding, Crispin calmly folded his hands in his lap. "We're calling him the Collector."

"Isn't that cute," Styx snapped. "Does the TFRA have somebody specially assigned to come up with these ridiculous names?"

Ignoring his snide remarks, Crispin continued with his report. "His first hit—at least the first we are aware of—was just over six weeks ago, upper Washington state. The last hit was two days ago in Portland. All beautiful young women. No outstanding characteristics to define a potential mark. Ages vary. The oldest was thirty-five Human years. The youngest just seventeen. Hispanic, Caucasian, Asian, African American. Doesn't seem to have a preference...aside from the fact that all the women were extremely attractive...and very protective of their Sire. Apparently, he's very charismatic, judging by the lengths his progeny will go in order to protect him. We've...dealt with five of the newborns so far, with a solid lead on the last."

Crispin reached inside his pocket and withdrew a small, sheer scrap of material. Shaking it open, he held the fabric up between two fingers in the moonlight and offered it to Styx. Inexplicably filled with dread, Styx reluctantly accepted the handkerchief-sized swatch, fingering the sequin-edged material as some far off memory nagged the back edges of his mind. What exactly was he looking at here? He'd seen this before...or rather, he'd seen material *like* this. He was almost certain of that.

But *where*?

"The Collector's given each of his protégés a similar piece." Crispin fell silent as Styx twisted the fabric to a new angle, examining every frustrating inch. The trace scent clinging to the material was completely foreign...and no help at all. "The last newborn we apprehended indicated she'd been given a message from her master to be delivered specifically to you...and *only* to you."

"'Her master?'" Frowning, Styx lifted his gaze from the fabric in his hands. What an odd choice of words. For obvious reasons, Vampyre shied away from allowing emotional connections...especially with Mortals...because, once formed, those emotions were permanent. Extreme. Absolute. Most Vampyre only sired those they'd formed that deep emotional attachment to...either a mate, or one they chose to look upon as offspring of sorts. Although, it was possible to sire for the sake of slavery.

*Eternal* slavery seemed a bit like, well...overkill, but who was to say what went on in the mind of a Rogue.

"I believe the exact term she used was 'beloved master.' Her words, not mine," Crispin clarified. "The female is being held in our detention facility in Alberta. She calls herself Layla, but won't give us any further information."

"What about the others?"

"Others?"

Styx flashed an annoyed scowl at Crispin, remembering all too well how the agent had a tendency to overlook any details not directly related to furthering his case. He also hadn't missed the slight hesitation the agent had stumbled over just before he'd uttered the words *"dealt with."* "The other newborns? Have any of the others remembered anything prior to being changed that might help identify their Sire?"

"Ah...impossible to say," Crispin murmured. "The others were destroyed before questioning could take place."

"What!" Styx shot to his feet, towering over the still seated, bland-faced agent. A long string of heated expletives ripped through the harsh stillness of the night. On the chaise, the blond female flinched, shifting fitfully, but subsided quickly back into the depths of *persuasion* induced sleep. "Why were they destroyed?"

"They were too far gone with bloodlust, impossible to control. The first four had to be eliminated while still on the streets. The fifth newborn took out two agents before apprehension. Even then, she only allowed capture—we believe—because of the message her Sire demanded she deliver...only to you."

Styx resumed his agitated pacing, churning the information round and round in his mind. They were sucking him back in. Slowly but surely. Innocent women were dying, and he just couldn't stand by and do nothing. Damn the TFRA. Damn the Rogue.

Damn this weakness...this irrational, medieval need to protect the fairer sex.

He knew by now—perhaps better than most— that any female, given the proper incentive, could be more dangerous than the most deadly of predators.

If he had an ounce of sense in his head, he'd tell Crispin to go catch the next sunrise.

Crispin tucked his little black notepad away and pushed to his feet, all business. "We'd like you to come in, speak to her. Find out what the message is, see if you can get this Layla to disclose any—"

Rounding on the agent, Styx demanded, "And then what?"

"Excuse me?" Crispin stared back blankly, plainly confused.

"What happens to the female after I question her?"

"That's not your problem," Crispin stated flatly, his gaze slid to a point beyond Styx's left shoulder.

"The hell it isn't," Styx exploded. "If you think I'm gonna fly to Alberta and question her just so you can...so you can eliminate another loose end, you're out of your frickin' mind."

"What do you suggest we do with her?" Crispin's piercing, brown eyes swerved back to his. A muscle ticked in Crispin's jaw. At last, some real emotion. Too little, too late, as far as Styx was concerned. "She's been turned loose on the population once already. Would you like to hear where we found her? In the home of an elderly Human couple. It was a bloodbath. We were too late to help them...but we stopped her before she attacked the Human children's summer camp less than a mile away. She admitted that was her next stop, by the way...a midnight snack, I believe she said." Rare emotion flickered in the agents eyes. Frustration. Defeat. "What would you have us do, Styx? Let her go on her merry way? You may as well offer her a napkin and wish her bon appétit."

"Is there no hope for rehabilitation?"

"You know as well as I do, once a Vampyre has gone Rogue, they're beyond rehabilitation. It's too risky."

Styx caught the pointed innuendo. The last Rogue they'd taken out had been well beyond rehabilitation. And Cole had nearly paid the ultimate price...losing his precious Alex.

Once again, he cursed the TFRA. The female newborn's fate was sealed. He wouldn't be able to save her, but, by questioning her, he might be able to save other females from the same fate.

"From what little we've garnered, the Rogue is already on the hunt for his next victim," Crispin prompted. Translation...the clock was ticking. "The jet's gassed up and ready to go. They're waiting on us."

"You were pretty damned confident I'd meekly come along, weren't you, you cold son of a bitch," Styx snapped. He might be willing to lend his help in stopping this Rogue, but that didn't mean he was willing to let Crispin off the hook. No, they might have cornered him, but the TFRA was going to learn the hard way, he intended to be anything but accommodating.

"Styx," Crispin murmured. "Meek is not a word anyone would dare accuse you of being."

"You better get something straight, here and now. This is the last goddamned time. You understand me? Next time you find some other fall guy. This deal goes south, and I'll make sure I'm not the only one in the hot seat." Styx clenched his fists at his sides, his eyes burning with fierce determination. Crispin nodded tersely, his lips tightly compressed, his eyes flickered relief for a split second before blanking. Grim, Styx loped for the wide glass doors off the lanai. "I'll grab my gear. Let's get this shit over with."

Clearing his throat delicately, Crispin snagged Styx's attention. Inclining his head toward the slumbering female on the chaise, the agent suggested, "Perhaps you should do something with her before we go."

"*¡Mierda!*" Changing course, Styx scowled at Crispin.

One of these days, that damned *gilipoya* was going to bite off more than he could chew. Styx only hoped he was around to see it when it happened.

Chapter 2

Appalled, Styx observed the feral newborn through the one-way glass. She cowered in the corner of the tiny cell, snarling and hissing. From his vantage point, he'd studied her as one agent after another attempted to communicate with her. Attempted and failed. Some she ignored. Those had been the lucky ones. The last she'd attacked straight out, mauling him badly before his partner could wrestle him free and drag his limp body from the room.

The Collector definitely had an eye for beauty. Even disheveled—her clothes ragged and splattered with mud and blood—she was a knockout. Wide, almond-shaped brown eyes, tilted slightly upward at the outer corners, glowed like burnished gold in the dim lighting. Her dark hair fell loose around her shoulders, a tangled mess of jet black. Her full lips stretched back, revealing brilliant white, razor-sharp fangs.

Dried blood speckled her pale skin here and there. Human blood and Vampyre blood alike, he was sure. He couldn't tell if any of it was hers, though. He couldn't detect any injuries, but that didn't mean she didn't have them. Her battle with Agents Jordan and Hansgaard had been vicious. She was small in stature, but the womanly curves pressing against her torn garments left no doubt of her maturity. Her size belied her strength. She was inordinately strong with newborn bloodlust. In time, her strength would wane a bit, as would the bloodlust.

Provided she lived that long.

As far as he could see, her odds for survival weren't good. After witnessing the way she'd attacked Agent Jordan, Styx was beginning to agree with Crispin...though he'd rather have his fangs ripped out than admit it to another soul. Rehabilitation—training—would come too late for her. She was too far gone, too unpredictable to unleash on an unsuspecting Human population.

Even if the TFRA hadn't already determined she'd be destroyed after questioning, she probably wouldn't live to see another moonrise. Half-starved as she was, Layla was too volatile to allow near a blood host without the risk of killing the Human. Styx figured she had less than a full day before her body turned on itself, at best. Without nourishment her own blood cells would begin attacking and devouring each other. When that happened, she'd be well beyond coherent, little more than a driven, mindless killing machine.

If she wasn't that already...

Styx sighed. It was going to be a long, difficult night.

Gritting his teeth, Styx nodded succinctly to Crispin and trailed the agent into the interrogation room. Dark, suspicious eyes locked on them the moment they entered the room and followed their progress. Her nostrils flared as she dragged in their scents, her wary gaze bouncing back and forth between them. The female—Layla, he reminded himself—remained crouched in the corner. Tense. Ready to attack.

"Layla—" A vicious snarl cut Crispin's composed introduction short. Unmoved, Crispin continued, "I'm Special Agent Derrick Crispin with the Task Force for Rogue Apprehension." Baring her fangs, she hissed at Crispin. "And this...is Styx."

If he'd blinked, Styx would have missed it, so

swift was the change in her. Layla straightened to her full, if meager five foot two inches tall. Gone was the cornered, snapping animal. In its place stood a poised, sly creature with a smug smile on her lips and poisonous hatred burning in her eyes.

"You've come at last," she crooned softly. Derisively. "Are you afraid, Spaniard?" The pearl-white, lethal tips of her fangs edged into view as her smile widened. "You should be."

"Why should I be afraid?" He kept his expression and his tone carefully void of emotion. Unease slithered down his spine.

"My beloved master will soon replace all you have taken from him. He will destroy everything you hold dear. He will leave you with *nothing*," she boasted proudly. Her worshipful, malicious smile chilled him to the bone. "And then he will come for you."

****

Someone was following her.

She wasn't being paranoid. She knew it, deep in her bones. It was *him*. Kate picked up the pace, lengthening her stride as she weaved in and out of the heavy foot traffic on St. Charles Street. Darting around the corner by the newsstand, she dashed inside the first storefront she came upon. Her breath heaved in and out as she slipped between two bookshelves. Her heart hammered at her tonsils. She should have left work hours ago, when her shift had ended. But that last rush had come, and she'd been needed. Why hadn't she taken Jeff up on his offer to walk her home?

She knew the answer, even as she kicked herself for letting it matter. She'd recognized that look in his eyes and hadn't wanted to encourage him. It was over between them—the shallow, physical connection—and had been for months, but he just didn't seem to want to take no for an answer. Kate

25

drew a deep breath and pulled the edges of her coat closer together against the permeating chill that clung to the night air. Another twenty minutes or so, and she wouldn't even have been able to hide in here. All the stores along this street closed down at ten. If she hadn't been so damned noble, so damned *moral*, she wouldn't have been caught walking alone after dark.

With some creep tracking her every step.

Had he followed her inside? Cautiously, Kate peered between the rows of books, her anxious gaze sweeping the empty space near the front checkout counter.

It had to be him. No one else would follow her around like this. No one else had ever made her skin crawl like this either. She never should have accepted that first rose. She should have sent it back to him...whoever *he* was.

She'd told Elaine no good would come of it. But her friend had only scoffed at her dire prediction, claiming Kate had been married to her work for too long.

Poor, lonely Kate.

Poor, bright, responsible, *boring* Kate.

Elaine insisted Kate needed to take a walk on the wild side for a change. So, to prove everyone wrong, she'd gone along with the attention. She'd smiled and accepted the daily tribute of flowers, flushed with pleasure over the sweetly phrased cards, sighed over the decadent imported chocolates.

She'd ignored her instincts.

She should have known better.

But she was a woman, damn it. And what woman wouldn't be flattered by romantic gifts and mysterious, flirtatious notes.

The gifts had quickly grown more expensive, more...possessive. Costly bottles of wine. Exquisite jewelry. Beautiful designer dresses. Then the gifts had turned uncomfortably intimate. Daring negligees, imported perfumes, and an odd set of little finger cymbals, like those used by belly dancers.

Creepy.

Didn't it just figure? The first time she let her hair down and gave in to the allure of a potentially romantic encounter—not just the shallow gratification of physical needs—she ended up catching herself a damned stalker. Brilliant. Just wait until she got her hands on Elaine. Kate would wring her scrawny neck for goading her into this predicament.

The tiny bells above the door jingled, jarring Kate from contemplated murder. Panic trailed icy claws over the back of her neck. Standing on tiptoes, she rubbernecked for a better view. Dear God, why couldn't she have been blessed with a few extra inches? Here she was, five foot nothing, and couldn't see over some damned bookshelf. She'd tried not to let the height thing bother her. But times like this didn't help much. While Kate had gotten the brains of the family, her sister Maggie had inherited the height of a professional basketball player from their father. Wasn't being vertically challenged enough of a punishment? What had she done to earn the attentions of some whack job?

Finally catching sight of the newcomers, Kate sagged against the shelving. A woman with two small children. Nothing to worry about there.

*Get a hold of yourself, Katie girl. You're losing it.*

Straightening her spine, Kate ignored the suspicious glances the store's proprietor shot her as she slipped from the store. She wouldn't let some crazed nut-bag get to her. She paused at the corner long enough to cast a worried glance over her shoulder, though. It didn't hurt to be cautious, after all.

She didn't see anything suspicious, but the back

of her neck still prickled. As if someone were breathing on her nape. An icy, putrid breath. The hell with this. Tossing her hand out, she hailed a cab. Normally she would have walked the nine blocks home from work, but she just couldn't shake the paranoia any longer.

A short while later, as the cab pulled away from the curb, Kate sprinted up the steps of her apartment building, keys in hand. Her fingers trembled as she punched in the code for the main door, and she swore aloud. Glancing over her shoulder, she shoved the door open, scurried inside, then slammed it closed behind her. She avoided the stairs. It was her habit to take them, but, remembering that long ago self-defense training she'd taken back in college, she knew it would be all too easy for someone to ambush her there. The elevator seemed to take an eon, but at least she rode up alone. Inside her apartment, with locks firmly in place, she leaned back against the door and waited for the relief to set in.

It didn't come.

Odd, but even safely secured behind deadbolts and her apartment's security system, she felt...exposed. Vulnerable. She shook her head, disgusted with herself. Pushing away from the door, Kate dropped her keys on the island in the kitchen and emptied her pockets. It really would be so much easier if she just carried a purse like every other woman in America. But she had this unreasonable fear of losing it, didn't want to have to deal with the headache and worry of possible identity theft, and so she'd just made a habit of stuffing everything she might need into her pockets.

If it didn't fit, then she didn't need it.

Rolling the tightness from her shoulders, she made her way to her bedroom. She just needed a long hot shower, a strong cup of tea, and a decent night's sleep. Then she'd feel better.

*Hopefully...*

\*\*\*\*

Did she really think she could lose him so easily? He smiled benevolently. She should have more faith in him. He wasn't like one of the rare Human suitors she allowed herself. They were unworthy of her. His affections were not so fickle. Had he not devoted himself to her for these last few weeks? He'd given her much more time than he'd given the others. But she didn't know that, of course. She would learn to trust him. She would come to understand he would always be there, always watching over her.

Always in the shadows of the night.

He *was* the night.

His precious jewel. So graceful, so intelligent. A doctor, she was. Her vocation held little importance, though. Once he claimed her, she would no longer need to bury herself in her work. He would take care of her. He would give her the fulfillment she so desperately—so obviously—sought.

She was different, perhaps even more special than Layla...

No...no, that was being unfair. He should not compare his women, should not hold favorites. He should love them each as individuals.

*And yet...*

She had such a beautiful smile. She'd been radiant when she'd accepted his flowers. He'd taken great joy at her delicate blushes while she'd read the notes he'd penned. Though she'd shared the chocolates he'd given her with those other, worthless females she worked with, he knew she'd enjoyed them as well. The fact she'd given most of them away was only a testament to her admirable generosity. Her reluctance to accept his jewels bespoke of her humility. But she must have been flattered. After all, she hadn't made much of an attempt to return them...not that she would be able to find him. That didn't matter. He would always find her.

She was a treasure.

*His* treasure.

She worked too hard, though, spending nearly every waking moment at that Human hospital. Fighting a pointless battle against the inevitable. But she was a fine doctor, nonetheless, talented and committed to her purpose. How many lives had she snatched—albeit temporarily—from the clutches of death in that hellhole the Humans called the ER? In many ways, she was like him...giving weak Mortals another chance at life. Soon it would be her time. He would show her the way. He would pamper her. He couldn't wait to see her face when she found his next gift. He would treat her as the princess she was meant to be.

*His* princess.

His shining jewel.

Separating himself from the night, he settled back on his perch and watched as she undressed. Such an exquisite body. Built for seduction. Her long, red hair tumbled free as she pulled the clips loose. She was extraordinary. Such glorious hair. Like a flaming sunset. Bright and untarnished. Fiery, like her spirit. Like the sun he'd been denied by his very nature all these long centuries. She was small in form, as were the rest of his women. Her skin was pale, like milk—like alabaster—with a fine sprinkle of freckles. Cream and cinnamon. He couldn't wait to taste her. His body shivered with barely suppressed hunger, but he restrained himself, savoring the anticipation.

Soon, he promised himself.

*Soon...*

He had a few more details to see to first. He

wanted everything to be perfect for her initiation. And he had to pick a new name for her. *Kate* would never do for one so spirited, one so brilliant. She was far too precious for such a mundane, unimaginative name. But not to worry. Before he gave her a *Kiss*, he would pick something far more suitable. Her eyes were like the most precious of emeralds.

*Johara...*

*His jewel...*

Yes, Johara was far more suitable—just like her—for she would be the jewel of his collection.

Inside the apartment, she stepped through a doorway, concealing herself from his hungry view. He glided over the ledge and slipped inside through the cracked window. The scent of her was everywhere. Light. Whimsical. Like strawberries and cream. His footsteps made not a sound as he tread lightly across the thick carpet.

He paused for a moment near the head of her bed. Bending at the waist, he smoothed his cheek over her pillow. His nostrils flared as he dragged her scent in deep.

An infatuated lover.

A hunter committing the scent of its prey to memory.

The gentle cascade of her shower poured behind the adjoining door. He closed his eyes, imagining her standing beneath the steaming spray. His lips curled. Anticipation was almost as thrilling as the culmination of the chase.

He wandered through her room, carefully picking up, examining, and setting aside the trinkets she'd scattered over the top of one dresser.

Small, delicate figurines of ballet dancers.

Old photos. A faded picture of two little girls in matching tutus, wrapped in a tender maternal embrace. All three females had nearly identical features.

31

*Ah, how sweet...*

His little Johara was sentimental.

He fingered a tiny glass ornament, a prima ballerina soaring through the air in a Grand Jeté. So fragile. So graceful. He held the decoration up in the moonlight. Like a diamond, it caught the light and glittered, reminding him of Johara. Gently slipping the tiny figurine inside one pocket, he slowly drew a long swatch of red silk from the other pocket of his overcoat. He'd spent many hours selecting just the right offering for her. The sumptuous scrap of lingerie slipped over the comforter with a soft whoosh. He smoothed it flat, adjusted the shoulder straps.

Perfect.

Pulling a small gift card from his pocket, he placed it in the middle of the negligee, careful not to wrinkle the fluid perfection of the smooth silk. He'd spent nearly as many hours choosing and penning the perfect tribute to her beauty as he had in selecting the negligee. Turning, he traced the length of a fang with his tongue as he contemplated the adjoining door.

Dare he push the flimsy barrier open? Dare he slip inside the bathroom and observe her through the steam-covered glass as soap bubbles and water slithered down her skin?

She wouldn't even know he was there, imagining him a part of the steam that filled the room and seeped beneath the closed door.

A long, delicious breath shuddered out.

No. No, he dare not. He wasn't made of stone, after all. And it wasn't quite time yet. He wouldn't ruin his well-laid plans for one impetuous moment.

Turning back, he glanced around the room to make sure he'd not disturbed anything. His hand found the tiny statue in his pocket, and his fingers softly caressed the smooth, fragile ornament. His gaze fell to the negligee, and he smiled as power surged through him and he floated toward the open window.

*She would be so pleased.*

## Chapter 3

"Are you sure this is the right place?" Restless, Styx shifted in the plush passenger seat of Crispin's spotless Mercedes sedan. "We could be wasting our time here, you know?"

"Only lead we've got," Crispin replied. His deep voice held the tiniest bit of an edge. Was the waiting finally getting to the unflappable agent?

"She could have lied."

"She could have," Crispin agreed without batting an eye. "But, given her...disgruntlement over her Sire's abrupt, less-than-affectionate departure, I'd say the old adage is holding true in this particular case. Hell hath no fury like a woman scorned. And newborn number six definitely considers herself scorned."

"Just because the Collector was rude enough to express his disappointment in her...ah, performance—hearsay, I might add—doesn't mean she'd turn on him so readily." Styx heaved a troubled sigh and stared out the rain-streaked window at the large neon sign advertising Trinity Regional Hospital. "It could be a setup...or a wild goose chase." He waited a beat, then grudgingly conceded, "Hard for a woman to fake that kind of pissed-off, though."

"If he hadn't rubbed her nose in the fact he'd already picked out her replacement, I doubt we'd even have this much to go on."

"Number six...*Kalila*," Styx amended, silently berating himself for inadvertently falling in with Crispin's habit of emotionally distancing himself by using impersonal tags rather than an individual's name. "Kalila was willing to work with us. Suppose she'll get a shot at a second chance?"

Crispin remained frustratingly silent, and Styx clamped down on the scathing argument burning his throat. Arguing wouldn't do any good. As far as Crispin and the TFRA were concerned, the Collector sealed Kalila's fate the moment he sank his fangs into her.

Didn't mean Styx had to agree with their judgment...or like it.

But he also had no say in the matter either.

From their curbside parking spot, Styx had a clear view of the Emergency entrance. He glanced at the digital numbers displayed on the dash. Only a few sparse hours until shift change. Only a few hours until dawn. They'd be cutting it close. Close enough to keep a Vampyre's nervous eye trained on the eastern horizon.

Crispin's cell phone rang in his left breast pocket. Pulling the phone free, he checked the display before flipping it open. He tersely barked his name into the slim device, and didn't utter another sound as he listened to his caller.

He snapped the phone closed a few moments later. Without a word to Styx, Crispin tucked the phone away and pulled his infamous little black book from his pocket. He set pen to paper. Styx peered over his shoulder. He couldn't recognize a single word of Crispin's chicken-scratch shorthand. Glaring at the less-than-forthcoming agent, Styx waited, drumming his fingers on his knee. If Styx didn't ask every pointed damned question, he wouldn't know jack-shit about this case. The lack of willingly shared information rubbed him raw. Hadn't Crispin been the one to track him down? Wasn't he the one who'd asked Styx for help?

"Crispin," Styx growled. "Either you start giving

me everything you got as soon as you get it—without me having to twist your damned arm—or I walk right now. I'm not going to be any help if you keep leaving me out of the loop."

Crispin glanced up from his shorthand and stared at Styx for a long moment. The agent didn't betray an ounce of emotion, but Styx could all but see the cogs turning in his head.

"My sources indicate the target is most likely a Dr. Kathleen O'Rourke," Crispin finally responded. Styx made a less than polite noise in the back of his throat, prompting the agent to continue. He didn't know who Crispin's sources were...didn't want to know. The sooner they caught this perverted bastard, the sooner Styx could wash his hands of the dictatorial TFRA, the unnaturally emotionless Crispin, and Crispin's mysterious, creepily-accurate sources.

"Age 34. Red hair, green eyes, petite, of Irish descent. Prefers to be called Kate," Crispin read aloud from his notes. "Moved to Tacoma seven years ago. Worked Pediatrics the first two years before requesting reassignment to the ER. From what I've been able to ascertain, our Dr. O'Rourke is something of a workaholic. Brilliant, dedicated to her job. Father died when she was ten. Mother recently deceased. Only sibling is an estranged sister in Phoenix. Single...lives alone in an apartment a few blocks from here. Walks to and from work, rain or shine. Has a small group of friends, mostly co-workers. Socializes on occasion. Currently no intimate personal relationships."

"Keeping tabs on her is gonna be difficult. She comes in contact with too many Humans on a daily basis. Too easy for the Rogue to slip in and get to her. Lot easier if we could stuff her in a more controlled environment." Styx rolled the kinks from his shoulders. Confinement in the car was beginning to get to him. If she didn't come out of that damned hospital soon, he'd have to take matters into his own hands and go in after her. "Job's too public, too much exposure. Hours are too unpredictable. She's a walking bull's-eye."

"Wanna let him have this one and wait around to run surveillance on the next one, hope she's more convenient to tail?" Sharp sarcasm from Crispin caught Styx off guard, and his gaze snapped to the agent's face. Anger glowed in Crispin's eyes. Unmistakable.

Unexpected.

Crispin's discerning stare pierced through Styx's surprise. "You know who this guy is, don't you?"

His perceptive question took Styx by surprise.

"I don't know anything more about this guy than what you've told me," he hedged, shifting a deadpan stare out the opposite window.

"Bullshit," Crispin responded blandly, all trace of emotion buried deep once more. "I saw your face when Kalila described her Sire. Hell, even the first mention of her name startled you. Why did it bother you so much that he's apparently giving them new names?"

"It doesn't," he lied.

It bothered him all right. Not that the Collector had given them new names. It was the names he'd chosen that were the issue. Arabic names.

Vaguely *familiar* Arabic names.

Pieces of the puzzle were starting to click into place for him, and he didn't like the bigger picture. No. He had to be wrong. It was impossible. The wrathful, feudal bastard had died more than three centuries ago...

"Look, I know you don't want to be here. I know you hate the TFRA. And me. But don't let the Collector make any more prizes out of these innocent women." Crispin leveled a solemn, beseeching look at him. His deep voice lowered, urgent and guilty. "Don't let Dr. O'Rourke suffer for our...for *my* mistakes."

The desire to berate Crispin for his tight-lipped, unfeeling attitude during the last case they'd worked on together was hard to resist. He'd just made up his mind to give in to the urge, when Crispin suddenly tensed beside him and nodded briskly toward the windshield. Styx's gaze shot to the ER entrance. Near the sliding glass doors, a tall figure in a dark trench coat rose from a bench and nodded—nearly imperceptibly—in their direction before disappearing inside the hospital. Styx had noticed the coat earlier, but hadn't given him a second thought.

*¡Mierda!* Did the TFRA have spies everywhere?

A diminutive form in jeans, a pale green blouse, and a black leather jacket popped an umbrella open beneath the drive-up overhang not fifty feet from where they'd parked. A tight ponytail held her long, flame red hair in check. Her thin face was sharp featured, yet arrestingly soft around the mouth and eyes. Something stirred deep in Styx's gut. Shaking off the odd reaction, he narrowed his eyes and scrutinized her more closely.

The female darted a nervous glance right, then left. Then right again. She scanned the streets as though she expected a battalion of boogie monsters to ambush her from every shadow. Crispin started the car. He waited until she passed before shifting into gear and easing the vehicle from the curb. As she made her way down the sidewalk, she continuously cast darting glances over her shoulder, peering hard at every doorway and break between storefronts. A tall, male pedestrian brushed too close, and she jolted, arms reflexively lifting in an unmistakably defensive position.

"Bit jumpy," Styx commented, frowning.

"Wonder if the Collector's made contact somehow," Crispin murmured. His brow crinkled as he turned the steering wheel to slowly follow her progress.

"Maybe she's always like that."

"According to sources, Dr. O'Rourke is steady as a rock, not a skittish bone in her body. One of the most reliable, unruffled doctors in the ER."

"Something's got her spooked," Styx observed, leaning forward in his seat. He, too, scanned the shadows around her, his preternatural senses far more perceptive than her Human senses. Nothing stood out for him. No one on the virtually empty street seemed suspect. The shadows were empty. Leaning back in his seat, he commented, "I'm assuming you'll have someone on her twenty-four seven. How are you handling protection for her during the day?" He glanced again at the clock and added, "Speaking of...daylight's coming soon."

Crispin cut a short glance his way, then trained his eyes on the road, and the woman under discussion. "You're her protection."

"What?" Styx squawked. Once again, he wished—fervently—that he could strangle Crispin. It might not have the desired results, but the effort just might release some of the tension suddenly simmering through his system.

"We've arranged for you to stay in the apartment directly next to hers." Crispin's expression was oddly impassive. Why had that information sounded so ominous? They'd *arranged*. Better he not ask, he might give in to the urge to wrap his hands around the agent's throat yet. "From there you'll be able to keep an eye on her. Get a feel for her schedule. And you'll be able to watch for and deal with any uninvited visitors."

"What am I supposed to do when she goes out during the day?"

"We're working on enlisting a couple Humans for daytime surveillance. They'll probably have to stay with you, for convenience sake."

*"Enlisting..."* No, he *definitely* didn't like the sound of *that* at all.

"Like hell," Styx barked. "No Human is going to pose any kind of defense against this Collector. And I'm *not* living with any Humans I don't know."

"You got a better idea?"

Stroking his trimmed goatee, Styx settled back in the seat, his steady gaze never leaving the wary female. "As a matter of fact, I do."

**\*\*\*\***

"What the bloody hell did you get me into, you sodding bastard?"

Styx tugged the door farther open and motioned Zack inside the apartment. The Werewolf was beyond pissed-off and didn't seem to care who knew it. Two large Vampyre stood behind him, dressed head to toe in black, sticking out like the proverbial sore thumb.

*Dumbasses.*

When Zack didn't immediately accommodate everyone by obediently going inside, one of the agents reached a hand out to touch his shoulder. Within mere inches of contact, Zack whipped his head around and snarled menacingly. The sound was distinctly inhuman. The offending agent slowly lowered his hand and backed away several steps.

*"Que cabron!"* Styx snorted. "Will you quit snapping at those idiots like a rabid dog and get your ass in here?"

The tall, broad-shouldered male snarled at Styx now, but Styx ignored him. He moved clear of the doorway so Zack could enter, then slammed the door shut in the TFRA agents' faces.

"What's going on?" Zack strode through the living room of Styx's newly acquired apartment and

40

dropped onto the sofa. "One minute I'm entertaining a couple of nice young ladies poolside, and the next thing I know, I got five TFRA thugs breathing down my neck. They won't tell me a bloody thing, 'cept that you've *'expressed a need for my assistance'*."

"You don't know any *'nice young ladies,'* Zack," he countered, settling on the recliner across from the couch.

Zack's blue eyes narrowed, and he crossed lean, powerful arms over his chest. "Casting aspirations on my character is not the way to go if you want me to help your sodding arse out of whatever bind you've gotten yourself in."

"Okay, okay," Styx grumbled, tossing his hands up in surrender. Then a thought occurred to him. "Wait...you said five agents came for you. There were only two with you in the hallway. What happened to the other three?"

A wide, satisfied grin split Zack's face. Suddenly cocky, he leaned back and stacked his hands behind his blond crew cut. "You could say they'll be...*indisposed* for a while."

Giving an amused snort, Styx slid farther back in the recliner and propped an ankle on his knee. He started his explanation with Crispin's uninvited intrusion on his vacation, and ended with his current assignment as undercover neighbor/guardian to the unsuspecting Human doctor next door.

"Bloody ballocks," Zack whispered, shaking his head.

"So, as you can guess, I need a set of eyes and ears I can trust to watch over her if she leaves the building during the day. You onboard?"

Zack, always on the lookout for his next conquest, promptly inquired, "Is she hot?"

"She's not on the menu," he snapped. It might make things a hell of a lot easier if Zack kept her too busy in bed to leave the apartment, but—for reasons he couldn't fathom—the very idea left Styx distinctly troubled. "Keep your distance. Watch but don't approach. And for God's sake, keep your hands to yourself."

Grinning, Zack kicked his boots up on the scuffed coffee table between them, crossed his ankles. "My, my, that was *awfully* possessive."

"Possessive my ass," Styx grunted. "It's just a damned assignment that's complicated enough as it is."

He stood up and stalked to the small kitchen. Zack's smile was a little too knowing for Styx's piece of mind.

Jerking open the fridge door, he surveyed the contents. Bagged blood filled two shelves, just as he'd expected per Crispin's vague allusions. The rest of the fridge was empty. His gut churned. This was going too far. Bagged blood? Next they'd be handing him a bottle of sunscreen and a file for his fangs. The rotten bastards. He didn't give a rat's ass about the consequences. The next time that slimy bastard Crispin showed his face, Styx was gonna choke him senseless.

Scowling, he palmed the keys to his new apartment and stomped through the living room toward the door. "Hang out here for a little while, would you? I need to go hunt up something to eat before sunrise. Stay out of trouble."

"Don't I always?" Zack reached for the TV remote. ESPN flashed on the screen, and he called over his shoulder, "Hey, bring me back a couple pizzas or something. I'm bloody starving."

"You're always starving," Styx grunted, letting the door slam closed behind him.

## Chapter 4

*That rotten, worthless, pain-in-the-ass son of a bitch.*

Styx loomed at the end of the hallway, seething. His hands slowly crushed the large pizza boxes he'd carried up the stairs. Was it too damned much for Zack to follow the simplest of instructions? How goddamned hard was it?

Keep your distance.

Watch but don't approach.

*Keep your fucking hands to yourself.*

The hands in question were currently smoothing a strand of fiery red hair behind the dainty ear of a certain doctor Zack wasn't supposed to be anywhere near. The roaring in Styx's ears all but drowned out Zack's low, flirtatious murmur. Soft feminine laughter floated down the hallway. Zack shifted, propping a shoulder against the doorway, leaning intimately toward the female he was supposed to be keeping at a distance. The female smiled up at Zack. A tiny dimple flirted at the corner of her mouth.

Styx saw red.

That was it. He'd tear Zack limb from limb and ship the bloody pieces of his sorry ass back to LA in the cheapest damned freight he could find. He'd raid local Human law enforcement for tack-strips to wrap him up with instead of bubble wrap.

Styx stalked down the hallway, his steady gaze trained on the side of Zack's neck. His fangs began to throb. Zack suddenly tensed for a split second, his chin elevated almost imperceptibly as he drew two short sniffs of air. He glanced over his shoulder and perceptibly relaxed.

"Oh, hey...here's my roomy now." Zack straightened from the doorframe, shooting Styx an innocent grin. "And he brought pizza, bless his heart. Kate, this is Nick DeVaine. Nick, this is Kate O'Rourke. She's a doctor around the corner at Trinity Regional. Works the ER. Cool, huh?"

Gritting his teeth, Styx tore his murderous gaze from Zack's carotid and did his best to school his features into what he hoped was something less frightening than the look he'd given his "roomy." Kate O'Rourke extended her hand and turned a heart-stopping smile on him. The floor slipped out from under his feet, and he fell head first into eyes the color of spring-fresh grass. Time spun out while every thought in his head deserted him.

Hers was a classical beauty, timeless and graceful. Pixie-like. Almost Faerie in quality. The top of her head barely came to his shoulders. Her hand was tiny in his. But she was all woman. The touch of her skin on his, warm silk, jolted through him like an electrical charge, nearly bringing him to his knees.

Awareness flickered in her stunning eyes.

He couldn't remember where he was. Couldn't remember how he'd gotten here...or why. He couldn't remember his own damned name right now, but there was no question in his mind. She'd felt the connection too. The darker, primitive side of his nature began to take over as he stared deep into her unblinking eyes. Images began to form in his mind...images of hot, sweat-misted, naked bodies writhing and straining on a tangle of red silk sheets. Hungry mouths. Greedy hands. Racing pulses. Skin on skin. He blinked, perspiration beading on his brow.

Judging by her dazed expression, those images had been unintentionally transferred to her mind.

The fact that she'd been so quick to intercept those images only attested to the fact that the attraction was mutual. That realization fueled his hunger...and his thirst.

Her blood would taste so sweet, he somehow sensed instinctively. Not the *too* sweet stuff he'd been subsisting on for centuries, but just right. Like an aphrodisiac tailor made specifically for him and him alone. Her naked body would feel so perfect beneath his. She'd—

The sharp jab of Zack's elbow against Styx's ribs brought sanity flooding through him.

*¡Dios mio!* What was happening to him? He'd never lost control like this before.

"Nice to meet you, Dr. O'Rourke," he mumbled around a mouthful of throbbing fangs.

"Please, call me Kate," she insisted smoothly. But her eyes were strangely wary now, and she unobtrusively tugged her hand free of his lingering grasp. Could she sense what he was? He barely suppressed the shudder that worked its way through his system.

Did she have any idea how close she'd come to a Vampyre's *Kiss*?

"Kate," he acknowledged, oddly reluctant to release her. Clearing his throat, unfamiliar heat climbing in his cheeks, Styx thrust the mangled pizza boxes into Zack's midsection hard enough to gain a fast whoosh of air from his disobedient *"roomy."* "I'm sorry Z...ah, my roommate bothered you so early in the morning. It's barely dawn." He'd almost slipped, damn it. If Zack had given her a false name for him, it was hard telling what name he'd given for himself.

"Oh, it's no problem. Actually, I was just coming home from work. Colin tells me you're an artist?"

"*Colin* told you that, did he?"

"You've got to hear this...it's the funniest thing,"

Zack chuckled, shooting him a warning glance. "Kate here thinks I look like that hot guitar player from Stolen Innocence. Isn't that a riot?"

Becoming color blossomed in Kate's cheeks. Strange hungers began gnawing a deep, dark hole in his gut. *¡Mierda!* What was wrong with him? He'd just had a brunette. Though, granted, he'd only eaten. He'd been too preoccupied to deal with those *other* greedy appetites of his.

"Hilarious," Styx snapped, scowling once more at Zack before turning a benign smile to Kate. The way she studied his face had him quickly ducking.

Not quick enough.

"You know, come to think of it," she commented, an adorable little half-smile curled one side of her alluring lips. "You kind of look like their drummer. What's his name…Woody or something, isn't it?"

"Styx," he growled, running a disgruntled hand through his hair. "It's Styx."

*Woody. ¡Madre de Dios!*

"Yeah," Zack chimed in, eyeing Styx speculatively. "Now that you mention it, I see what you mean. But you know…I hear that dude's a real prick."

Styx cut Zack a sideways, narrow-eyed glare. "Yeah…but *I* hear that idiot guitar player doesn't have long to live."

Kate stood between the two of them, her puzzled stare following the conversational gambit back and forth like a tennis ball at the U.S. Open. A tiny wrinkle deepened between her slim, arched eyebrows.

Clearing his throat, Zack abruptly changed the subject. "I ran into Kate in the hallway. Invited her over for breakfast, but she turned me down flat. Can you believe it?"

That was a bit of a shocker. Women didn't just fall at Zack's feet. They catapulted themselves into his path with suicidal tenacity and prayed he didn't suddenly veer off in another direction.

"I pulled a double shift—third in a row—and I'm pretty beat. I probably wouldn't be much company right now anyway, not that your pizza doesn't look..." She glanced at the crushed box and quickly amended, "Ah, *smell* appetizing."

"Rain check, then?"

"Possibly," she hedged, stifling a huge yawn.

She looked ready to drop where she stood. Dark shadows smudged beneath her eyes. Styx suffered the worst urge to sweep her off her feet and tuck her into bed.

*His bed...*

"We'll get out of your hair so you can get some sleep," Styx offered, claiming Zack's elbow in a crushing grip. "It was nice meeting you, Kate."

"You, too," she replied, opening the door to her apartment. "I'll see you guys around."

"You better believe it," Zack quipped as his unabashed gaze wandered indiscriminately over her backside.

All but jerking Zack off his feet, Styx dragged him to the neighboring apartment. The moment they were safely behind closed doors, Styx wheeled on Zack. His eyes burned, glowing in the darkened hallway. He flashed fangs, snarling as he took a menacing step forward.

Zack held his hand up, palm out, and interrupted. "Hold on a minute. Let me explain."

"You got two minutes, *cabron*, then I shred you and ship you back to that miserable damn island you call home."

Shooting him an exasperated glance, Zack sauntered to the kitchen, flipping lights on as he went, and plopped the boxes onto the counter. "Look, if she sees us lurking around all the time—but we never introduce ourselves, never make contact—

sooner or later, its gonna freak her out."

Flipping the lid open on the top box, Zack leaned over and dragged in a soul-deep whiff of the cooling pizza. The grin curving his lips suggested he'd just glimpsed heaven...and would gladly live there for all eternity. He scooped a huge glob of cheese and pepperoni from the lid and popped it into his mouth, smacking his lips on his fingers with a muffled groan.

Talking around a mouthful of cheese and sauce, Zack mumbled, "This way, she'll be more relaxed around us. She'll get used to us, won't think twice about having us around all the time. Think about it...it'll be easier to protect her. Easier to pick up small bits of information here and there about her schedule...whether or not anyone strange has been coming around, that sort of thing," he added, tossing a shoulder as he scooped up a enormous slice and took a colossal bite.

Zack's argument was logical.

Styx still wanted to rip out his throat.

"Fine," he ground out between clenched teeth. Drumming his fingers on the countertop, he watched Zack inhale the slice of pizza. "But you play the part of unobtrusive neighbor...*without* benefits. Touch her again, you lose digits. *¿Comprende?*"

Zack eyed him, arched a golden eyebrow, and slowly took another bite. He chewed in silence, swallowed. "So it's like that, is it?"

Narrowing his eyes, Styx denied, "I don't know what the hell you're talking about." Spinning on his heels, he stalked from the room. At the doorway, he paused long enough to order over his shoulder, "Just keep your hands to yourself...don't push me on that, Zack."

\*\*\*\*

Kate flipped the deadbolt, slid the chain into place, and turned, leaning back against the door.

She wouldn't let herself run through the apartment, checking windows, testing locks. That bastard stalker had gotten in once, that didn't mean she had to live like some terrified victim. She'd reported him to the police, brought everything he'd given her in as evidence. Hopefully the police would find usable prints...or something. They'd promised they'd do all they could, but the reassurance hadn't helped much. All the same, she refused to live in fear.

Her coat slid from the crook of her arm and dropped to the floor, as a nauseating wave of exhaustion washed through her. The ER had kept her hopping last night, while worry over her unwanted admirer continued to nag the fringes of her awareness. Still, a small smile tugged at the corner of her mouth.

Her new neighbors were certainly entertaining. She'd been a little wary when Colin had first approached her. But he'd been so witty, so attractive, she couldn't help but like him. He was handsome...in a boyishly charming way. Tall. Blond hair and blue eyes. Muscular. The proverbial all-American jock...except for the sexy British accent, of course. But she wasn't fooled. Beneath that innocent exterior lurked the soul of a real heartbreaker. He was the guy your mother always warned you about. The type of man you flirted with, joked with...had shallow, meaningless affairs with...but never, *never* took too seriously.

His roommate, she'd gotten the distinct impression, was a creature of a completely different species altogether. Pushing away from the door, Kate snatched her coat up from the floor and juggled her keys as she forced her feet to traverse the long hallway through her apartment. Nick DeVaine. The name didn't really fit. Too generic.

Too...*shallow.*

His eyes hinted at far more depth than any

she'd ever seen.

He, too, had been tall. Then again, for someone vertically impaired like her, everyone was tall. Where Colin's unmistakable strength was whipcord lean, Nick's was brawny. Solid...and all muscle. She'd always felt small when standing next to most men. But standing next to him, she'd felt...distinctly feminine. He looked like he'd just stepped down off some billboard advertising designer underwear. There wasn't a Hollywood stud alive that had a thing on this guy. Unless she missed her mark, his black boots had been custom-made. His button-down shirt designer. The top three buttons had been left undone, revealing a deep swath of delectable bronze skin, his shirt-tails had been partially untucked.

And, holy mother, did the man know how to wear his jeans.

His hair was dark, silky sable, tugged back in a messy, short ponytail. The loose strands held just a hint of curl. Enough shine and curl that a girl would give her left arm to run her fingers through it, just once. Though not as pronounced as Colin's, she'd detected the accent in Nick's speech... unquestionably Spanish. His complexion was clear, dusky olive; his jaw was square and firm. A sexy, well-trimmed goatee lent him a wicked, almost diabolical air.

He looked like a Spanish pirate, bold and dangerous.

Sexy as hell.

But it was his eyes that had truly captured her. His stare had been unsettling. As if he'd been carefully examining her soul. A little frightening, and yet...thrilling too. So dark. So mysterious.

So *intense*.

She shuddered as she remembered the strange images that had suddenly popped into her head while she'd been standing there staring into his eyes. Never before had anything like that happened to her. It had been so...so real. And so *vivid*. Him. Her. Naked. Hot flesh on flesh. Steamy, soul-branding sex. And, oddly enough, red silk sheets. Strange. She didn't even own silk sheets—red or otherwise.

Stranger still, was the unsettling impression that—somehow—he'd known what she'd been thinking.

He was probably just used to that kind of reaction in women.

Shaking her head, she closed her eyes and groaned. She was just being silly. How could he possibly see what was going on inside her head? Drawing a deep breath, she brought his face to mind.

Definitely the brooding artist type. She'd taken one look at him—at his arresting eyes—and had completely forgotten to ask what his chosen medium was. His hands had been strong and lightly calloused, his knuckles scuffed. Wide of palm and long of finger. She'd bet her next day off he was a sculptor. She'd also be willing to bet those hands were good at handling far more than clay.

Kate opened the fridge door and stared dispassionately at the sparse contents. She needed to do some serious grocery shopping, not just buying the bare essentials as she'd been doing, but she just hadn't had time lately. Why bother, she scoffed. Who was she trying to kid. She couldn't cook her way out of a paper bag. Couldn't remember the last time she'd even turned on her oven. Probably just as well, she'd only end up giving herself food poisoning. Or burning the building down. Or both. How embarrassing would that be? She could see the headlines now..."*Local doctor found dead inside smoldering building, suspect in arson investigation, autopsy reveals self-inflicted food poisoning.*"

Snorting, she pulled a container of yogurt and an apple from the fridge, snagged a spoon from the drawer and skirted the island.

Flopping down on the sofa, Kate checked the expiration date. Close enough. She peeled the top off the yogurt, dipped her spoon. As she ate, her gaze wandered over her apartment. She hadn't done badly for herself. The apartment was nice, located in a good neighborhood...not far from work. Newly renovated when she'd first moved in, the space had a contemporary feel. Two bedrooms—not that she'd ever needed the second—with a full bath, and an open kitchen/living area combo. She'd converted the loft bedroom into a study of sorts. The apartment even had a nice roomy balcony where she'd set up a couple wicker chairs and a small, matching table...the perfect place to watch the sunset on those rare occasions she was actually home to witness one.

Tucking her feet up beneath her, she turned her blurry gaze to the window. The view up here on the eighth floor was fabulous. At night, the lights of the city reflected off Puget Sound. The city itself was wonderful, thriving. The third largest city in the state. Offering everything a modern urbanite could want. And for those times when she needed a retreat, needed down time, she took a short trip across the city to the Pointe Defiance Park Trails. 702 acres of tranquility. Hiking, nature.

Peace.

She couldn't ask for more.

Her gaze fell to the small, silver frame on the end table. The perfect family peered back at her. The flawless smiles of a man, a woman, and three teenage boys taunted her. The dog was just icing on the cake.

Her sister's family.

*Maggie...*

Sucking in a deep breath, Kate dragged herself

up from the couch and shoved thoughts of her sister from her mind. Maggie made her own decisions, and Kate had made hers.

Tossing the empty yogurt container and the apple core in the trash, she rinsed her spoon, washed the sticky apple juice from her hands, and, on the way to her bedroom, gave in to the urge to check her locks after all. Even so, it wasn't thoughts of her stalker—or thoughts of her sister, for that matter—that filled her mind as she wearily showered and dressed, crawled into bed and drifted to sleep.

Smoky amber eyes that seemed to see clear to her soul and a sinful quirk of sensual lips that turned her insides to mush followed her into the realm of exhaustion.

## Chapter 5

"Layla escaped?" Battling the urge to crush the cell phone in his fist and grind it into tiny particles of dust, Styx prowled the suddenly claustrophobic confines of the living room. "What the hell do you mean she escaped? When? How?"

"Shortly after you and I left Alberta," Crispin replied. The sound of rustling paper wafted over the phone line. Crispin's ever-present little black book, no doubt. "Three agents were assigned to escort Layla to the termination cell. We're not exactly certain what happened—security monitors were compromised, but we believe she had help breaking out. The three agents assigned to termination detail are now dead. Three more guards stationed in the lower hallway are also dead, as is one of the guards at the gate. The sole surviving guard—if he can be believed—claims a strange shadow-mist suddenly descended, and then everything went black." More papers shuffled, and Crispin added without any inflection, "Where is the target?"

*¡Mierda!* Biting back the urge to remind Crispin that 'the target' had a name—it wouldn't matter anyway, Crispin seemed to prefer keeping everything and every*one* on an impersonal basis— Styx shifted the phone to the other ear. He tunneled his fingers angrily through his hair and glared, unseeing, at the cheap reprint in an even cheaper frame hanging on the far wall.

"She spent the morning and early afternoon in her apartment, presumably sleeping. She left the apartment around five o'clock. Zack tailed her to a health club on Broad Street, then a homeless shelter on Eighth and Birch."

That seemed to grab Crispin's interest. "A homeless shelter?"

Styx gloated hollowly, "What's the matter, Crispin? You're sources didn't feed you that little tidbit of information? Apparently they're not quite as infallible as they would have us all believe, huh?" Crispin ignored the barb, and Styx snapped, "From what *my* source has discovered, she volunteers her time every Thursday night in the free clinic at Saint Mary's."

"The situation is more tenuous then I thought. This would all be easier if we could keep her contained," Crispin murmured absently.

"Excuse me...but didn't I suggest exactly that? Refresh my memory, but weren't *you* the one who wanted to use her as bait?" And why he'd ever agreed to go along with that half-baked scheme, Styx would never know.

"We're obviously dealing with a more complicated situation than we first assumed."

"Yeah, well, you know what they say...assumption is the mother of all fuck-ups. And just how, by the way, do you plan on containing her without letting her know all those horror movies Human's seem so fascinated with are a whole lot closer to the truth than she ever imagined—or that one of those monsters has painted a target on her back?"

Few Humans ever discovered the existence of the Immortal Nations. Of those few...even fewer were permitted to live with the knowledge. He understood the logic behind the mandate. But it still left a distinctly bitter taste in his mouth.

"We *could* bring her in," Crispin murmured thoughtfully.

"Would she be allowed to leave when this is all

over?" They both knew what he was asking.

Would Dr. Kate O'Rourke be allowed to *live* when it was all over?

A long, pregnant silence followed Styx's blunt question.

Styx didn't like Crispin's cagey tone when he finally responded, "That depends on a lot of factors. You know that, Styx."

"What I know is an evasive answer when I hear it." How could Crispin be so damned cold? "And you're *not* bringing her in," Styx ordered forcefully. He didn't quite understand the sudden, irrational drive burning through him to protect Kate O'Rourke. He didn't understand it…but he couldn't ignore it either. He shook his head, kneading at a knot at the base of his neck. These irrational instincts were motivated by nothing more than resentment over the TFRA's bumbling ways, that was all. The memory of sparkling green eyes marked the excuse for the lie it was. "You bring her in…you're on your own. I walk."

A long, resigned sigh slipped through the phone. "Okay. We'll do things your way…for now. But I'm warning you, Styx. If she becomes too difficult to manage, the TFRA would rather see her terminated than run the risk of the Collector getting his hands on her."

*Terminated.* Such a cold and impersonal synonym for execution. Stunned, Styx blurted, "The TFRA would kill an innocent? *¡Dios mio!* She hasn't done a damned thing wrong. She probably doesn't suspect that our kind even exists."

"If he changes her, she won't be innocent any longer. She'll be the same as the last six, unconscionable and ruled by bloodlust. How many Humans would she kill, how many would she change before we could stop her? Far more innocents would be spared by sacrificing the one."

Styx was still fuming over that last callous

remark, when Crispin figuratively pulled the rug from beneath his feet. "You know, this might be easier if we had some idea of what was going on inside her head...if we had some way to control her."

Again, he could read between the lines. Crispin was talking about something far more invasive than simple Vampyre *persuasion*. Styx stopped pacing as an icy wave of unease doused him from head to toe.

*Surely not...*

Crispin and the TFRA couldn't possibly have any idea of what he could do.

He'd been so careful never to reveal his abilities, never to use them once he'd learned the possible consequences. Consequences too terrible to contemplate.

Hell, even Cole didn't know what he could do.

"I think it's time for you to stop ignoring your gift, Styx." Crispin's voice dropped, as if he were trying to keep the conversation from someone standing nearby. Styx's palms went damp.

"I don't have any idea what you're—"

"Cut the bullshit," Crispin snapped in a furious whisper. Gone was the placid, emotionless agent. Fervor burned through the phone line. "We're running out of time, damn it. I'm sick to death of these bastard Rogues always being one up on us. You're a *dream walker*, Styx. You know it. I know it. Let's not waste time waltzing around the truth. You can get inside her head, figure out why the Collector has fixated on her. We need to know why he's spent so much time trailing this one Human. What's so special about her? Why is he courting her rather than just taking her straight off like he took the others?"

"Courting her? What the living hell is that supposed to mean?"

"The tips we've received indicate he's stalking her, sending her gifts and—for lack of a better term—affectionate notes. We haven't been able to confirm he's done that with any of the others, but according to number six that wasn't part of his routine. Dr. O'Rourke filed a complaint with the Human law enforcement." Crispin paused for one hesitant beat before grimly adding, "The Collector's been inside her apartment...while she was home. She was in the shower. When she came out, she found one of his gifts on her bed. A very pricy piece of lingerie. By the reports, she was nearly hysterical when Human law enforcement showed up at her apartment."

Styx exploded. The curses he shouted through the phone at Crispin were ripe and inventive. He hoped to hell and back he pierced the agent's eardrum.

Fully transformed, Styx prowled the confines of the apartment like a caged panther. The incandescent glow of his eyes cut through the dim room like lasers. Lethal fangs nicked his lower lip, drawing blood. The skin on his face stretched tight, bulged and puckered between his scowling brows as his explosive temper took firm control. Crispin might be tired of the Rogues having the advantage, but Styx was well and truly beyond fed up. Fed up with these nutcases that thought being Immortal meant a free license to prey on the innocent. Fed up with Crispin's detached attitude. Fed up with the TFRA's penchant for keeping crucial information under airtight wraps until it was damned near too late to be of any help.

And how the hell had the TFRA found out he was a *dream walker*? How long had they been watching *him*?

All Vampyre—upon turning—were gifted with certain preternatural abilities along with their Immortality. Inordinately heightened sensory perception, super-human speed and strength, and the power of *persuasion*...though some were more effective in that area than others—take Cole for example.

A very select few—for reasons still beyond anyone's knowledge—had attained uncommon...*special* gifts. Some acquired telekinetic powers. Others developed an unusual affinity for animals, the power to communicate with and control them. Some, he'd heard through very hushed back-alley whispers, could take on a shadowy, ethereal mist form. One Vampyre Styx stumbled upon a couple centuries back, had mastered levitation.

He'd even heard of the extremely rare *empath*. Imagine...a Vampyre with the unfortunate curse to feel every emotion his prey experienced. The poor, unlucky bastard. Styx shuddered at the thought. How awful would *that* be?

Vampyre with extraordinary abilities were careful to maintain absolute discretion—even from close friends—going so far as to promote the idea that such possibilities were no more than myth. The TFRA could be ruthless in their pursuit of information.

And *no one* wanted to end up a lab rat in some carefully tucked away TFRA observatory for the rest of his Immortal life.

Styx was a *dream walker*. One of the exceptionally uncommon breed who could deliberately send himself into a deep trancelike state and cross over into another's subconscious while he or she was asleep...a restricted form of astral projection, if you will. He could manipulate or guide the dreamer's subconscious, thereby directly influencing the individual's emotions and conscious choices if he so chose. He could, however, only walk in the dreams of those with whom he'd had actual physical contact.

His was an ability with great power.

And an ability with inherent risks...both to the dreamer and to the *dream walker*.

If the *dream walker* wasn't cautious enough, if he walked in the same persons dreams too often—tampered with memory too much—the dreamer could suffer deep psychological complications. If the dreamer suffered a mortal wound and died while the *dream walker* was inside his or her subconscious, the *dream walker* would be trapped on that ethereal plane with no way out. In addition, while the *dream walker* was in the requisite trancelike state, his own body would be defenseless, vulnerable to physical attack.

A risky endeavor all the way around.

His voice was deeper, threatening, when Styx demanded, "How did you find out about me?"

"My source—"

"Fuck your sources, you damned *gilipoya*—"

"I know you've gone well out of your way to keep your abilities off grid," Crispin hedged. "I give you my word, I haven't—and won't—let this information find its way into *any* TFRA paperwork. This will stay between you and me. I swear it to you. But Styx...there's no way I'm not gonna push this issue. We need all the help we can get, and I'm not pulling punches because you're squeamish about the possibility of negative side effects."

Negative side effects? *Negative side effects!* Only a heartless bastard would call the death of a beautiful, innocent, young girl a negative side effect.

"Styx, we have to stop this Rogue." A long moment passed in silence before Crispin somberly added, "Whatever it takes."

Without a word of confirmation or denial, Styx snapped the phone closed. Furious, he glared at the slim, silver device nestled in the palm of his hand. Pivoting abruptly, he hurled the phone across the room where it shattered against the far wall.

Stalking across the length of the room, he stood in front of the heavily tinted sliding glass doors overlooking the city and clasped his hands behind his back. The setting sun glimmered on Puget Sound, golden and entrancing. Searing UV rays seeped through the protective tinting, heating Styx's exposed skin, making it tingle. He ignored the uncomfortable sensations as he replayed his conversation with Crispin. Where had he lost control of the situation?

He hadn't even so much as considered *dream walking* again, not in six centuries.

*Not since Eliza...*

The mere memory of her name speared pain through his chest, deep and unerringly accurate.

She'd been such a sweet girl. So innocent and trusting. So lost after the death of her beloved older brother—and Styx's childhood friend—Thomas. He'd meant only to help her cope with the loss of her brother. Driven by guilt, he'd entered her dreams. He'd guided her subconscious passed the pain, into recalling those happier times with Thomas. Styx had become her best friend by day, offering her a reprieve from her grief at night. It was his penance. After all, if it hadn't been for him, Thomas would never have met Ava.

But the vengeful, jealous bitch had come back and taken even that small chance at redemption from Styx.

*Ava...*

Ava had sworn on the moon and stars above that her love for him was true. She'd seemed so sincere, so charismatic. So vulnerable. Appealing to Styx's protective instincts.

She'd seduced him.

She'd given him the unexpected, unwanted gift of eternity.

Then the cold, heartless bitch had betrayed

him...and murdered his best friend.

The flesh on his face and neck sizzled, erupting into raw blisters. Sucking his breath in on a sharp hiss, Styx swiftly drew away from the window, instinctively seeking succor from the shadows. His flesh immediately began to repair itself. Prolonged exposure to direct UV rays would—without a doubt—leave him nothing more than a smoldering pile of ash, but experience had taught him that after such brief exposure, while excruciatingly painful, not a mark would remain.

Unfortunately, the scars on his soul refused to heal so easily.

He should know. He'd been carrying those scars around for the last six centuries. Damn Crispin to hell and back for resurrecting those painful memories. Damn him for hinting that the very thing Styx had vowed never to do again might be the only way to stop this monster called the Collector.

Could he save Kate O'Rourke by slipping into her dreams?

Or would he kill her...like he'd killed Eliza?

\*\*\*\*

"Kate's coming over."

"What?" Styx was off the couch and across the room in the blink of a Mortal eye. No way was Zack going to drop that little bombshell and wander off on his merry way. "What do you mean she's coming over? *¡Dios mio! Why* is she coming over? And just where in the living hell do you think you're going?"

That wasn't panic in his voice. It was irritation, damn it. Absolutely nothing more than irritation. Why would he panic at the thought of spending time with Kate O'Rourke? All alone...in this tiny apartment. Kate...with her stunning green eyes that lured an unsuspecting male to sink in until he drowned, and translucent skin that begged to be touched and licked and kissed. Kate...with luscious lips that demanded to be tasted. A petite frame that made a male just want to tuck her inside his pocket and protect her, yet with curves so womanly all any male in his right mind would think about was seduction.

*Beautiful, innocent Kate O'Rourke...in this apartment...in this tiny, confined apartment...all alone...with him...*

"Let's see...'*Kate's coming over*'...pretty self-explanatory, I'd say," Zack called over his shoulder, interrupting Styx's increasingly uncomfortable line of thought.

Pausing by the door, Zack drew his wallet from his pocket and quickly scanned its contents. Styx caught a glimpse of several colorful plastic cards, a thick wad of cash, and numerous square blue foil packets. Evidently satisfied he was covered in any situation, Zack tucked the wallet back in his pocket.

"As to the why, I invited her over for a bite to eat. And just to clarify...that's *her* bite, not yours. Then again..." Zack cocked his head to the side, zeroing a thoughtful eye on the glowering Styx. "Maybe you *should* indulge. Lord knows your disposition has plenty of room for improvement. You've been a bloody bear to live with the last three days, I'll have you know." Zack took another step toward the door and paused to turn back one more time. "And as to where I'm going...since you took a certain delectable doctor off my menu...I, my prickly friend, have a date with the little hottie who works at the coffee shop across the way."

"You rotten son of a... What am I supposed to feed her," he growled. How dare Zack ambush him like this? Sarcasm dripped from his voice as he parroted, "Oh, hey there, Kate. Come on in. Care for a cup of O Negative? No? O Neg not up your alley? No biggie. I got a whole fridge *full* of blood. A Positive? AB Negative? Not a problem, take your pick."

He should have ripped Zack's head off last night in his sleep.

"Hey, no worries," Zack chuckled, shooting him a wide grin. "I took care of everything."

Before Styx could reply—or shred the Werewolf where he stood—Zack jerked the door open and cheerfully chirped, "Oh, hey there, Kate. Come on in." Zack shot Styx a devilish grin over his shoulder and stepped back, sweeping his arm toward the living room. "Care for something to drink?"

"Hello, Collin." Kate stepped inside the apartment, moved past Zack, and offered Styx an awkward smile. It took a moment for Styx to remember the roll he was supposed to be playing. *¡Madre de Dios!* What lame-assed name was it that Zack had given him anyway? Beneath the light dusting of freckles across her nose and cheeks, Kate's creamy skin pinkened, and Styx's mouth watered. "Hi, Nick."

Zack truly did have a warped sense of humor...naming a Vampyre Nick DeVaine. Ha. Ha. Hilarious. He hadn't gotten the joke at first, he'd been too furious at seeing Zack flirting with her. Once the pun had finally sunk in...well, he got the joke, but he still failed to see the humor.

Then again, perhaps it was the fact that Zack had unwittingly guessed closer to the truth than anyone else.

Nick...the Americanized, shortened version of Nicholas.

*His birth name...*

Plastering a welcoming smile on his lips, he prayed the tips of his fangs weren't visible. Why did he suddenly feel as if he were a deceitful spider beckoning an unwitting fly to come rest a while on his web?

"Kate. Please, come in."

"I ran into Colin at the supermarket again...funny how we kept bumping into each other today. Anyway, he wouldn't leave me alone until I promised I'd come over for dinner tonight. I hope you don't mind." Kate's gaze dropped to the bag in her hand.

Over her head, he flashed his fangs at Zack in a lethal, silent snarl. Oh, how the Werewolf would pay.

Grinning unashamedly, Zack shrugged and wiggled his eyebrows suggestively.

"I'm not disturbing your work, am I?" Kate fiddled with the plastic bag. Styx was quick to snap his mouth closed as she glanced up. "He assured me you needed a break, said your latest project was driving you up a wall." As if on cue, rather than closing the door, Zack stepped into the hallway. Clearly puzzled, Kate frowned back and forth between the two of them. "Did I get the night mixed up?"

"Nope," Zack reassured her. He glanced meaningfully at Styx and lifted both eyebrows. "Tonight is *definitely* the night." Turning his focus back to Kate, Zack poured on the charm and pouted, "I'm so sorry, Kate. I hope you'll forgive me. Something's come up and I have to run, but Styx assured me he'd keep you entertained this evening."

"Oh," Kate murmured, glancing sideways beneath her lashes at Styx. Deeper color stole into her cheeks, and heat punched straight to the pit of Styx's stomach. "I should go, too. I'm sure your very busy, Nick. I don't want to impose—"

"Nonsense," Zack blurted. Leaping forward, he all but shoved her into Styx's arms. Styx's hands shot out instinctively to steady her on her feet. Once he had his hands on her, though, he couldn't seem to make them let go. He barely registered Zack's next words. "Stay. *Eat.* Get to know each other better.

Have a *great* time."

Then Zack disappeared through the doorway, leaving Styx to stare, utterly hypnotized, into the most mesmerizing eyes he'd ever seen. Her arms were well toned beneath his hands, yet they felt so slight, so fragile, he was afraid to flex his fingers lest he snap her in two. Some dark corner of his mind cursed the obtrusive jacket preventing his greedy fingers from obtaining full contact with her skin.

She was so close, the heat of her body beckoning him closer still. His nostrils flared slightly as he detected the essence of strawberries and a unique, delicate scent he'd smelled only once before. With *her*. The distinctive scent of Kate O'Rourke slipped through his system like a drug, intoxicating and addictive. Her lips parted slightly. Moist and inviting. His gaze locked on her lower lip, lush and glossy coral.

Carnal hunger slowly tightened every muscle in his body.

Chapter 6

Unable to stop himself, he leaned closer, drawing her scent in deeper. His voice dropped to a hoarse growl he barely recognized as his own. "What scent are you wearing?"

"Ah..." She blinked up at him blankly. "I, ah... I don't...I don't wear perfume. I can't. I'm allergic to most of them, so it's just easier if I don't bother to put any on...you know, hives and all..." she rambled. Then Kate blurted, "Oh, the strawberries...it's just conditioner." The plastic sack in her hands rustled, and she glanced down, breaking the spell. "I, um...I...brought...um, desert. I brought desert."

Unable to speak in anything that would even remotely resemble a normal voice, Styx reluctantly released her and accepted the sack before moving stiffly away. The scent of her followed him into the kitchen, as did she, and Styx grappled with the fierce desire to swipe everything from the island, strip her bare, lay her across the pale laminate surface, and claim her in every way imaginable.

Clearing his throat—silently cursing because his voice was far deeper, far huskier than he could control—he muttered, "Have a seat. Can I get you something to drink?"

He set the sack on the counter and lifted a clear plastic carton of dark, rich brownies free. Ugh...what was it with Human females and this disgusting confection. Alex was forever buying, baking, or nibbling on something chocolate. Love of chocolate must be some strange, inherent affliction of the fairer sex. Not knowing what else to do, he

67

riffled through the cabinets for something to put the brownies on.

"Something to drink sounds great." Pulling one of the tall barstools away from the island, Kate asked, "What do you have?"

Kate flipped her unbound hair behind her shoulders, revealing the smooth, ivory column of her throat. Her skin was so pure as to be nearly translucent. He could all but see the vein throbbing in the side of her neck. He froze.

*¡Mierda!* The temptation alone would kill him.

Beheading wasn't harsh enough punishment for Zack for putting him through this. Drawing and quartering, perhaps. Or, better still, impaling...

Kate made to slide from the stool. "I can get it, you're—"

"No!" He dropped the plate and the brownie carton on the counter with a loud clatter and lunged for the fridge. Pressing his back against the door— his hands clamped on the handle behind him—he offered her a nervous grin. "Let me, please."

"All right..." Kate gave him an odd little half-smile, half-frown and scooted back onto the barstool. She tugged nervously at her hair, and cast her gaze over the open floor plan of his temporary accommodations. "I've never been in this apartment before. Your place is like a mirror copy of mine...only with a different color scheme."

Kate's gaze caught on the hideous, cheap artwork hanging on the walls, and the shadow of a puzzled frown darkened her brow. Her lips slowly parted, then pressed tightly together, as if she'd intended to say something, then abruptly changed her mind.

Turning around, careful to keep the bulk of his body where it would block her view of the contents of the fridge, he held his breath and opened the door. The heinous bagged blood was gone, praise the powers that be. In its place was a wide array of fresh and packaged Human foods. His breath slipped out on a relieved whoosh. Picking up one of the bottles of wine on the top rack, he turned to face her. Styx froze once more, whatever he'd been about to say wedged behind the hot ball of desire lodged firmly in his throat.

*¡Madre de Dios!* His control wouldn't handle many more of these shocks.

Kate was in the process of shrugging her arms free from her jacket. A vintage Guns N' Roses T-shirt stretched tight over high, firm breasts. The bottle shattered in his hands. Wine splashed over the tile floor, splattering the cabinets beside him, soaking his shirt and dampening his jeans. The pungent liquid dripped from his hands unheeded.

And still he couldn't tear his gaze away.

Those beautiful breasts... Oh, how he wanted nothing more than to cup them in his hands, strip them bare and worship them with his mouth. Rub his—

"Oh," she gasped. Hopping down from her seat, Kate tossed her jacket aside and rushed around the kitchen's small island. By the time he'd managed to stir himself, she'd already procured a towel and was mopping at his hands. "Are you hurt? Hold still. Let me see..." She caught the pink tip of her tongue between small, pearly-white teeth as she carefully examined every inch of his hands. Tiny grooves deepened between her brows. "I don't see any cuts. I could have sworn I saw the glass slice into your skin..." Her voice trailed away as she turned his hands over in hers, scrutinizing first one side and then the other.

Floored by his visceral reaction to her, he obediently stood still while Kate checked for injury. She bent her head over their joined hands, and the scent of strawberries intensified. He couldn't help himself. He lowered his head until his nose skimmed the silken strands. Closing his eyes, Styx inhaled, slow and deep. She smelled so damned good. Her touch was gentle, and warm.

*So damned warm...*

What he wouldn't give to have those small, competent hands running over his body, wrapped around his—

Styx barely managed to stifle the tormented groan working its way up his throat.

She glanced up. An amazed smile lit her beautiful features. "You don't have a scratch on you. I thought for sure you'd..."

Her words died away as her eyes locked on his face. She still held his hands in hers, but she no longer stroked them, no longer patted them with the towel. She simply gazed at his face as if she were as trapped as he was. Never before had Styx been so tempted to use *persuasion* to gain a woman's compliance...her *immediate* compliance. Never had he wanted a female's blood so badly. He was tempted now.

*¡Dios!* Was he tempted!

*Kiss me, Kate. Let me make love to you...*

It would be so easy. But not satisfying. The very thought of manipulating her will repulsed him. When this woman came to him, she would come of her own free will. He could see the desire clouding her eyes. He could all but taste it on the charged air between them. It was just a matter of time. But the waiting wouldn't be easy. Deep down, the primal beast lurking in the darkest corners of his soul shifted restlessly.

He'd never wanted a woman like this before. Irrationally. *Completely*.

Blinking, she stepped back and away. He nearly cursed aloud.

"I'll clean this up if you'd like to go change," she

offered, her gaze riveted to the puddle of liquid at their feet.

Change? Glancing down, he realized his shirt and jeans were drenched. He also realized the bulge by his zipper was unmistakable...and shockingly painful. He muttered terse thanks and hurried from the room. Once inside the bedroom, he leaned back against the door and dragged his hands through his hair.

Was he strong enough to resist this startling, unreasonable hunger for Kate? He'd never experienced raw need like this before—not in all his six centuries of existence, didn't know what to make of it...or how to handle it.

If he wasn't strong enough to rein in the darker side of his nature, would Kate survive the night?

The tinkle of glass rattling in the trashcan stirred him. He changed in record time, and, pulling the door open, he stepped inside the room. His control quaked, and he gripped the doorframe for support. The wood crushed and splintered beneath his grip. Kate was on her knees as she sponged a towel over the damp floor. Her shapely, blue jean-clad bottom wiggled in the air with her efforts, all but screaming for his undying devotion.

*Temptation, hell... This was nothing short of torture.*

Decade upon decade, century upon century, Styx had gleefully indulged his appetites—every last one of them—never once denying himself the pleasures of a woman's body. And now, the one woman he wanted above all others, he could not allow himself to have. There were too many complications for the pursuit of Kate. But he had no coping mechanism to combat this greedy hunger only Kate seemed capable of triggering.

She pushed to her feet and carried the dripping towel to the sink. The sway of her hips drew him inexorably into the room.

"Sorry about the wine," he choked out at last, coming up behind her as she rinsed the diluted red liquid down the drain. Tiny slivers of glass tinkled as they fell from the towel into the stainless steel basin.

"Maybe there was a flaw in the glass or something. You probably won't want to use this towel anymore...there could be a lot of glass still in the fibers." She offered a careless smile over her shoulder as she carefully squeezed the excess water out, then wadded the towel up and set it on the counter near the sink. She turned to face him, glancing down and to the side where the puddle of wine had been. "Oh, I missed a piece..."

Before Styx could move to intercept her, she bent down and swiped up the small, glistening shard of broken bottle. Her sharp gasp pricked his ears a split second before the heady burst of blood-scent swamped his senses. His vision blurred, then went acutely sharp, locking on the small droplet of blood welling on the pad of her forefinger. His entire body went rigid as a block of granite.

"Damn it," she muttered as she dropped the piece of glass in the trash and turned to the sink. Flipping the lever, she held her finger under the stream of running water.

"Apparently that bottle got the best of both of us tonight," she joked.

Styx stood immobile, his eyes locked on her injured finger. He wasn't sure how much time had passed since she'd cut herself. It couldn't have been more than a few seconds, a full minute at best. But it felt like at least a century...maybe more. He held himself tightly in check, holding his breath. He hadn't so much as twitched a muscle.

He didn't dare.

She tore a paper towel from the roll hanging

beside the sink and blotted the pink liquid from her finger. Then she pushed his control to the limit. With a clinical frown puckering her brow, she caught the tip of her tongue between her teeth and squeezed the pad of her finger until enticing beads of blood dripped, one after another, onto the paper towel.

Styx's eyes began to burn with a ferocity he was certain would light up the whole room. His stomach muscles quivered. Pain seared his gums as his fangs shot long and thirsty. Scrabbling for control—fiercely battling his natural instincts—Styx gripped the counter beside him and bowed his head, closing his eyes.

He'd never experienced this immediate, visceral reaction before. It stunned him. Saliva surged, filling his mouth. He forced a swallow. Swallowed again as he struggled to keep his breathing somewhat calm. But the scent of her blood filled his nostrils and need set his lungs on fire.

"Nick?" The warm concern in her voice—concern for him—was nearly his undoing. "Are you all right?"

He didn't reply. He couldn't. He didn't trust the sounds that might escape his lips. Instead, he squeezed his eyes more tightly closed and wobbled his head side to side.

"What's—" Kate paused, then gasped. "Oh…oh, I'm so sorry. I didn't realize…the blood," she said. "I'm so used to it I forget sometimes other people can be squeamish about the sight of blood."

*Please, Blessed Mother. Don't let her touch me. I don't know if I'd be able to stop myself from—*

A flurry of motion tickled his ears, then her painfully arousing blood-scent was muffled somewhat. Glancing up beneath the veil of his lashes, he watched as she mopped at the small splotches of blood on the floor beside her feet. She held a large wad of paper towels fisted over her injured finger.

"There," she reassured him. "All cleaned up—you can look now." Straightening, she twisted and tucked the trash can safely back beneath the sink and closed the cabinet door. It didn't help...he could still scent the blood. "It's just a small cut, no sutures necessary...but a Band-Aid might be wise. Do you have any?"

Strangled with the phenomenal effort required to keep from pouncing on her, his voice was hoarse. "Bathroom...maybe?"

"I'll be right back."

As soon as she disappeared down the hall and around the corner, Styx flew to the sliding glass doors. Yanking them open, he rushed outside onto the balcony. Styx gripped the iron railing as he threw back his head and dragged in one desperate breath after another. As the scent of Kate's blood slowly faded from his nostrils, control gradually returned. He'd never been so close to losing it before, not even when he'd first been turned. *¡Mierda!* What was *wrong* with him?

The answer came slowly, too astonishing to fully comprehend.

*His Bride...*

Was it possible? Could fate be so cruel as to send him a mate he wasn't sure he could protect? Even from himself?

Of course it could, he berated himself. Look at all Cole and Alex had gone through to be together.

Styx covered his mouth with his palm, stroked his goatee as he considered the ramifications of this unexpected revelation. Only a *Bride's* blood-scent—*his Bride's* blood-scent—should elicit that strong of a primal reaction in him. And he hadn't even tasted her yet. *¡Madre de Dios!* What would actually tasting her do to him? He trembled at the thought.

Hadn't he been wanting this? He'd been thinking about this very thing ever sense Cole had taken Alex as his *Bride*. But this devastating weakness...it was frightening. It was as if his instincts were at war with themselves. Part of him—the part that had scented her blood, the part that hungered for her touch—urged him to go back inside and claim her immediately. But the part of him that argued for self-preservation intuitively knew vulnerability like this could be lethal for an otherwise nearly indestructible Immortal.

He could be wrong. He clung to that thought desperately. Maybe he'd made a mistake. Maybe it had just been too long since he'd fed last, too long since he'd last taken a female to his bed.

He *had* to be wrong.

## Chapter 7

"I found a first aid kit in the vanity," Kate called as she crossed the living space behind him.

Styx nodded silently, dragged in another bracing breath. Small wonder she'd found any type of first aid kit given he and Zack literally had no need for one. Any wounds they might sustain—the small cut on his hand from the wine bottle earlier, for example—would heal virtually instantly. More serious injuries...anything short of a stake in the heart, decapitation, or a suicidal stint of sunbathing...would take only minutes for his body's preternatural abilities to heal. Well, his body's preternatural abilities and a bit of extra blood. The first aid kit must have been left behind by the apartment's previous occupants.

Trying hard not to think about those previous occupants—or what their fate might have been, given the TFRA's involvement—Styx slowly turned to face Kate. She stood in the doorway, smiling uncertainly at him.

She took his breath away.

"I'm told the fresh air helps," she commented, stepping out onto the balcony beside him. Tipping her head back slightly, she half closed her eyes and drew in a deep breath before turning her attention back to him. "Are you feeling better now?"

"Yeah," he replied, somewhat subdued.

How mortifying that she'd assumed he'd been squeamish over the sight of blood. Him. The Vampyre. But what bothered him more was the ridiculous fact that he *was* embarrassed at displaying a weakness—even an imaginary one—in front of her. Yet what was the alternative? To tell her the truth? To tell her that he'd wanted her blood so badly his control had slipped and his legendary charisma had failed him.

"I should have been more careful. I'm sorry," she murmured.

"Don't worry about it...none of this is your fault."

Clearly picking up on the unexpected note of regret in his voice, Kate changed the subject. "There's another bottle of wine in the fridge. Would you like me to open that one?"

Pushing away from the railing, still not trusting himself enough to touch her, he ruthlessly shoved the disturbing thoughts of *Brides* and fickle fate from his mind.

"Sure. You take care of the wine, and I'll get dinner started." Easier said than done when you took into consideration the person doing the cooking hadn't eaten Human food in six centuries.

"I'll gladly take you up on that offer. I must confess...I'm a failure in the kitchen. If it doesn't come already prepared, or with simple microwave instructions, I don't buy it."

The corner of his mouth lifted. "Then we're probably in trouble. Zack usually does all the cooking."

Grinning, Kate uncorked the wine and poured two glasses. "Life's an adventure, might as well extend that adventure into the kitchen."

Kate set one glass near the cutting board, propped a slim hip against the cabinet near him, and lifted the other glass to her lips. He watched as she savored the first sip. His vision blurred and his body quaked as the tip of her tongue caught a droplet of red wine lingering on her lower lip. Tearing his gaze away, he picked up a large knife with unsteady hands and hacked his way through a head of lettuce and several carrots. Laughing at his efforts with the knife, Kate found a bowl and scooped up the mutilated salad components. Her laughter, warm and husky, slid through his system, and he wisely set the knife aside. He didn't want to risk having to explain the reattachment of a digit sans extensive medical attention.

Seeking to divert his attention from the way she tilted her head when she laughed, he grasped at the first conversational straw that came to mind. "Why did you become a doctor?"

"Hmm," Kate murmured, popping a mangled hunk of juicy tomato into her mouth. She chewed thoughtfully for a moment as her steady gaze followed his fumbling culinary progress. "Shortly after my ninth birthday, my father was diagnosed with cancer. Lymphoma. We spent a lot of time in the clinic, a lot of time in the hospital. Mom did her best to keep things as normal for us—my sister Maggie and me—as she could."

He kept his gaze trained on the stream of water filling the pot, but the lingering traces of loss coloring her voice had snared every ounce of his attention. This conversation had gone far deeper, much more quickly than he'd anticipated. Never at a loss for charm around women, he didn't have the foggiest notion of how to proceed.

"Dad's doctors...one in particular...was always so kind to us. When dad's health took a turn for the worse, Dr. Shelby even made house calls. Dad didn't want to die in a hospital," Kate added quietly, then took a long sip of wine, her gaze distant. "Dr. Shelby became...almost a grandfather to Maggie and me. He was a doctor, first and foremost. But his compassion went well beyond the call of duty."

"He sounds like quite a generous man."

"He was. He paved the way for me at Tulane,

even though I insisted I wanted to do it on my own. He laughed and told me he was unnecessary...that my grades could have gotten me into any school I wanted."

"So you became a doctor because of him?"

"In a way, I guess so."

"And your mother?"

A sliver of time passed in silence as Kate chewed on her lower lip. "Mom was in a car accident eight months ago. She died."

Styx's gut wrenched at the pain shadowing her delicate features. Setting the pot aside, he turned toward her. "I'm sorry, I didn't mean to—"

"No, it's all right. You didn't know." She offered a thin smile and reached for the salad bowl, moving it from the work counter to the island.

"What of your sister...Maggie, was it?"

"Maggie lives in Phoenix with her husband Greg and her three boys."

At the mention of her sister's name, Styx noticed a subtle change in Kate's body language. Her shoulders were a little more rigid. Tiny grooves formed between her delicate brows, and a shuttered wariness darkened her lovely eyes. Crispin had mentioned Kate and her sister were estranged. Apparently, estranged wasn't a strong enough word. While he was dying to push for answers, it was more than obvious the subject of her sister fell firmly under the category of taboo, and was, therefore, off limits.

For tonight, at least.

Deliberately, he lightened the subject and turned their conversation to current events as the water began to boil. He opened a jar and poured red sauce into another pot. Setting the pot on the burner, he frowned at the knobs. After a silent internal debate, Styx shrugged and turned the dial to the high setting.

"Um, I think you're supposed to stir that a little," Kate interjected helpfully as she peered around his shoulder at the angry pot hissing and spitting water across the surface of the stove.

Blindly following her self-professed, inexperienced guidance, Styx glanced around and snatched up a long wooden spoon. Unable to focus on anything beyond the soft curves so close to his side, Styx mutely jabbed at the firm clump of pasta stuck to the bottom of the pan and gave it a couple of swishes.

"I've been meaning to ask, what is your medium, by the way?"

"My what?" He stared down at her, utterly lost. She smelled delicious.

The look she gave him clearly questioned his sanity. "Your medium...you know, oils, acrylics, water colors, glass, clay? Are you a sculptor? A painter? Do you make cute little paperweights out of modeling clay? Or are you the next Rembrandt?"

"Ah..." Damn Zack to perdition.

"Are you the temperamental kind, or will you let me see some of your work?"

"I'll think about it," he hedged quickly. *¡Mierda!* Now he was gonna have to put something together for her. Damn it. He hadn't sculpted in centuries. Did he still have the touch?

"You know," Kate murmured as she stepped away and reached once more for her wineglass. "This is probably going to make me sound like one of those brainless groupies—and I'm not, I swear I'm not— but I still can't believe how much you look like that drummer. Are you familiar with Stolen Innocence?" Before he could do little more than murmur a noncommittal grunt, she rambled on, saving him from having to choke on a bald-faced lie. "Of course you're probably familiar with them, what a silly question. Who alive *isn't* familiar with Stolen

Innocence? '*Taste of You*' was great. It's one of my all time favorites," she added, referring to one of Stolen Innocence's most popular chart-toppers.

A chart-topper that had been one of the few songs Styx had actually had a part in writing.

The song was edgy and seductive. Come-and-get-me erotic. A scorching, forceful bump and grind that overwhelmed the senses and set the blood on fire. The lyrics spoke of dangerous cravings and irresistible obsessions. Of carnal hungers too long denied.

Until now, he hadn't realized the song could have been written with her in mind. Her specifically. Perhaps, some deep corner of his soul—the corner that already knew she belonged to him, knew it before he'd ever laid eyes on her—had urged those words onto paper.

There he went again, he chided himself. Imagining she might be his *Bride*.

Styx forced a swallow as desire balled, hot and needy, in his gut.

*¡Dios! If it* was *true…*

Groping blindly at his side, his fingers closed mindlessly around the stem of the wineglass. Big mistake. Now she'd expect him to drink it. All these damned pretenses were beginning to wear thin. He felt like a heel, lying to her. But what else could he do without revealing the truth?

The *entire* truth.

He lifted the glass to his closed lips and tilted the glass, stopping just shy of dumping the wine down his chin. Kate turned away to examine the garlic bread packaging, and Styx hastily poured most of the contents of his glass down the drain. He snatched up a towel and blotted his lips. Dropping the towel to the counter, Styx set the now nearly empty glass aside as she turned to face him.

He was dead certain this was to be his

punishment for years of gluttony. Standing next to this woman, talking with her, smelling her...*wanting* her...and not allowing himself the gratification of taking. Torture on so many levels. For the last several months, he'd been wishing for something exactly like this—with someone exactly like her—being here with her gave him pause. She was amazing. Generous and kind. Quick witted and beautiful. With a quiet inner strength that enthralled him.

That old, time-honored phrase came back to haunt him. *Be careful what you wish for...*

Thanks to the TFRA and some demented Rogue with a twisted agenda, Kate was also a Mortal with not one but two targets as good as painted on her back. Storm clouds of blood and death loomed on her horizon, and she had no idea.

But he did.

The knowledge was tying him up in knots.

Yet every time she smiled at him, he melted. In fact, the more time he spent with her, the warmer he felt—there in that coldest part of his soul.

Ushering her back to her barstool at the island, he transferred the food from stove to counter and set about dishing up two plates. He'd diligently followed the instructions printed on the labels, but the pasta seemed inordinately clumpy. Maybe he should have added the noodles *after* the water started to boil. Did the order of preparation matter? The sauce smelled scorched, but then food in general usually smelled *off* to him. And the garlic bread—he laughed inwardly as he recalled the misguided myth about garlic and Vampyre—had turned a nice charred black on the top rather than the golden hue the instructions assured him he'd get after twenty minutes of broiling...or was he supposed to have baked it? What was the difference anyway? At least the salad seemed to have survived his inexperienced ministrations.

"This is a disaster." Dangling a misshapen, pasty clump of pasta from his fork, he grimaced. "I'm sorry."

Kate's eyes watered as she valiantly choked down a bite.

"No, no—" She forced another swallow for the same bite and downed half the wine in her glass. "It's not so bad."

Styx lifted a brow and eyed her dubiously over the rim of his glass. Her chagrined smile twisted his heart, and she finally admitted, "It's awful."

He found contentment in her laughter, and, for a time, the outside world disappeared. It was just the two of them...talking and laughing, sharing anecdotes about their youth and ambitions.

A tiny crease deepened between her brows as she unexpectedly scrutinized him over a forkful of salad. He shifted on his barstool, suddenly feeling as if she were peering through the layers of forced deception, clear to his soul.

"What's wrong?" The question popped from his mouth before he had a chance to weigh the wisdom.

She continued to stare at him for several long moments before she finally replied in a subdued, confused tone, "I just realized...I haven't really done this much talking with...well, with anyone before. I usually don't just dump it all out there, you know. I'm sorry for monopolizing the conversation."

Her puzzled gaze fell to her plate and, chewing on her lower lip, she absently pushed her clumpy pasta round and round.

Unable to resist the urge, he loosely captured her wrist, stilling her movement. Her wide, green-eyed gaze darted to his.

"Don't be sorry," he said softly. "You fascinate me. I like listening to you talk."

Color flooded her cheeks. Thick lashes swept

down, concealing her eyes as she addressed her plate, "You're very easy to talk to."

Her skin was so soft, her wrist so fragile in the large circle of his hand. Styx feathered his thumb over the pulse at the inside of her wrist. Her pulse skipped and pounded furiously. The knowledge he could affect her so easily, that she was susceptible to him—to his touch—was a heady aphrodisiac.

His blood surged, pounding in his ears. His groin tightened.

Startled by the intensity of his reaction to her response, Styx released her wrist. Without thinking, he picked up his wineglass and took a large gulp. His eyes flared wide. His stomach immediately clenched and heaved at the foreign liquid. Only by sheer dint of will did he manage to keep his expression placid and the noxious liquid down.

Relieved when she finally pushed her plate away, Styx stood and carried the dishes to the sink. He didn't know how much longer he would have been able to keep sneaking forkfuls of the toxic Human food into the drawer beside him before Kate noticed. The unplanned gulp of wine had been bad enough. One or two more bites of the pasta or garlic bread would have had him writhing on the floor in excruciating pain...if he didn't vomit it back up outright. He deposited the plates in the sink, food and all.

She made a clucking noise on the roof of her mouth, then nudged him out of the way with her hip. "You can't just leave them like that," she chided, carefully setting a fistful of silverware and the salad bowl in the basin.

"Why not?"

"Because it's disgusting, that's why." Kate picked up a towel and tossed it to him before she reached for a dishcloth and the small bottle of green liquid. "I'll wash, you dry."

Kate ran water in the sink and squirted a shot of the apple scented dish liquid into the basin. White foam immediately began to build, scenting the air. It was pleasant enough, but he'd rather be smelling the uncorrupted scents of strawberries and Kate.

"Next time I'll have something delivered." Where had that come from? He shouldn't even be thinking about, much less planning a next time. But he was planning, he realized. Candlelight and flowers. Soft music and seduction.

Kate stopped washing the plate in her hands and, gazing up at him, she squeaked, "Next time?"

He stared down at her for a long, intense moment. Slowly, he reached up and captured the stray wisp of fiery hair that had fallen across her brow and curled itself around beneath her chin. It was like silk, smooth and warm, between his fingertips. He drew it forward and inhaled the scent once more before gently tucking it behind her ear. Her lips parted, and Kate blinked bemusedly up at him. His stare dropped to her lips, lifted to pierce her eyes.

"Next time," he confirmed, slowly nodding. The resolve in his tone was unmistakable. Determined. Driven.

Her lips curled on a small smile, and Kate dropped her attention back to the dishes. "I kind of liked this...just the two of us, like this. I haven't...I haven't really let myself do this for a long time."

He stilled for a moment as her words registered. His instincts told him she hadn't been talking about washing dishes. Dropping the towel on the counter, he set the last dish in its place. Styx closed the cabinet door and turned to face her. He held her gaze as he slowly drew the towel from her hands and deposited it on the counter at his side.

Was he insane? Hadn't he talked himself out of doing exactly this? Getting involved with her in any way shape of form was a bad idea. A disaster waiting to happen. He shouldn't be even thinking about touching her, kissing her...claiming her.

But he was.

And there wasn't a force on earth capable of stopping him from reaching for her.

Nothing aside from Kate herself...and he wasn't even sure about that right now.

There would be no turning back after this, no second thoughts. It didn't matter. As if something greater than himself had taken the decision out of his hands, Styx gave up without a fight. Carefully, his movements deceptively calm, he slid his hand over the gentle curve of her hip, up and around her slim waist.

Unsettling doubt had tormented him all evening...no matter how hard he'd tried to ignore or deny the possibility.

The bottom line was...he needed to know.

"What shall we do now?"

"It's getting late, I should go," Kate whispered hoarsely.

He dropped his chin to his chest, tilting his head slightly to the side. His hand tightened on her waist, and he traced the contours of her cheek with the backs of his fingers. Oh, how the thought of *persuasion* tempted him. But he wouldn't. He couldn't risk influencing her. Right now, he needed pure, honest emotion. Emotion unhampered by—untampered with—Vampyre guile. The only way he would know the truth—know for sure if she were truly his *Bride*—was to allow this...this *thing* between them to play out naturally.

*Dios*, the need ripping through his system was killing him.

"You should stay," he quietly murmured, smoothly closing the slim distance between their bodies.

Kate's lips parted, her eyelids drooped half closed. At the base of her throat, the erratic thrum of her pulse raced beneath his thumb. Her breath puffed in and out on tiny, shallow gasps. She wanted him, too. Relief, anxiety, lust, fear, worry...a wild cocktail of emotion swam through his system.

How could a male feel the weight of the world pressing on his shoulders...and yet feel invincible at the same time?

The question floated away before it could take root.

It didn't matter. He'd been dying for a taste of her from the moment he'd taken her hand in his and looked into her eyes the night they'd first met.

It seemed so long ago. And yet, though he may not have realized it before this very moment, he'd waited the whole of his Immortal life for her.

His lips hovered over hers for a breathless moment. The warmth of her skin, the scent of her drew him as nothing else could. Something odd burst inside his chest. A strange, giddy sensation. An anxious, burning ache. It pressed against his lungs, making it difficult to draw his next breath. This strange, devastating vulnerability held his heart in a vise. He'd never felt this before. This unwavering certainty that if he didn't have this woman—didn't claim her for his own—he'd regret it for the rest of his unnatural life. He'd rather cease to exist that face another moonrise without her.

He didn't try to analyze it, couldn't focus on anything beyond the soft, alluring woman in his arms.

He gladly let himself sink.

## Chapter 8

Kate couldn't breathe. She couldn't move. He was going to kiss her. A tiny kernel of doubt niggled in the back of her overly analytical mind. He was too much for her to handle. She didn't have enough experience at this sort of thing. This was totally out of character for her, giving in to attraction so quickly and so easily. Then again, she'd never before experienced this level of attraction either. They'd only just met. She barely knew him...

None of her logical arguments mattered. The need coursing through her left her light-headed and confused...and longing for more. His body was so very large, so very hard against hers. So warm.

So very male...

He—everything about him—was so...so powerful. Raw. Too intense. No one had ever effected her so strongly before.

How could he make her burn with just one glance of those mesmerizing amber eyes? At this very moment, he looked as if he wanted nothing more than to devour her...as if every second that passed without touching her—kissing her—was pure agony.

Kate's knees trembled, and she flattened her palms against his chest. Pushing him away didn't even cross her mind. The searing heat of his flesh seeped through his thin cotton shirt. When the hard flex of his muscles moved beneath her hands, the mere act of thinking became an extreme struggle.

*Impossible...*

His lips feathered over hers, skimmed, nibbled,

and her mind went completely blank. Thinking was no longer an option. The large, warm hand at her waist urged her closer. Sprouting wings and taking to the skies would have required less effort than resisting. So she didn't even try. She registered the unyielding bulge pressing insistently against her stomach a sparse moment before he angled his head and deepened the kiss.

In that moment, she was lost. His tongue swept inside her mouth, bold and questing. He tasted like ambrosia. Like decadent sin. He was soothing comfort and erotic excitement and every degree in between. She met him parry for thrust, thrust for parry. His lips grew demanding. He moaned into her mouth, and the desperate sound shot a thrilling spear of desire through her core. She couldn't have been more stunned if a bolt of lightning had come down from the heavens and struck her where she stood. The hard wall of his chest crushed her breasts, easing the ache, stirring a new, greedier ache deep in the pit of her stomach. Her head swam and, sliding her palms up his chest and around his neck, Kate gave herself up to his kiss with a soft whimper.

A dark growl rumbled low in his chest the moment she yielded. His arms wrapped tightly around her, crushing her against him. The edge of the counter dug in to the small of her back as he bent over her, wrapping himself around her. The scent of him, spicy with a hint of musk, swamped her. His heat cloaked her, made her feel as if she'd floundered into the center of a raging volcano. Everything about him went straight to her head. She was drowning in the scent and heat and taste of him, and Kate couldn't imagine a better way to die.

Long, strong fingers tangled in her hair, dragging her head back. His sizzling lips cruised along her jaw, branded the side of her throat. His other hand, so large and so unbelievably hot, found its way beneath the hem of her soft T-shirt. His calloused fingers skimmed her stomach, and her muscles quivered. His hard palm closed over her breast, kneading, molding. She moaned, unable to keep the sound locked away. Her nipple pebbled against his palm, and he flicked it through the thin satin barrier of her bra. She shivered, moaned again, clung to him.

He suckled at the pulse pounding at the base of her throat. His hips surged against her. Once. Powerfully. Leaving no doubt in Kate's mind that he wanted her. Badly.

"Nick..." His name was a ragged plea upon her lips.

"*Querida mia*," he panted. His lips, hot and questing, raced up the side of her throat. His teeth tugged at her earlobe with countless, tiny stinging nips. "Let me—"

An insistent, high-pitched beep interrupted him, penetrating the haze wrapped around her brain. Her pager...

The harsh rasp of his breath against her ear, the lightly calloused hand kneading her breast, the hot lips suckling her earlobe were all-powerful incentives to ignore the call of duty. With a soft groan, Kate turned her lips into his and sank her fingers deep in his hair.

He angled his head deepening the kiss, deftly using his whole body to enthrall her. She'd never met a man who could kiss like this. Didn't realize it was even possible...

The cell phone in her back pocket began insistently ringing, and Kate's body cried rebellion. Never before had her job been a burden. Right now, she silently cursed the demands of her profession for all she worth. Reluctant, she tore her lips from his.

"I have to...I have to take this," she panted.

He didn't seem to have heard. He didn't move away from her, didn't spare her an inch of breathing room. He merely transferred his lips to her cheek, then feasted on the side of her neck. His wicked, talented tongue licked and swirled. His smooth, heavenly lips suckled. His warm, rough hands caressed.

Liquid heat pooled deep in her core.

Her hands trembled and she nearly dropped her phone. In a wobbly voice, she answered, "Y-Yes?"

"Dr. O'Rourke?" The feminine voice was faintly cautious, obviously confused.

"Hmm? Yes?"

He suddenly dropped to his knees before her, pushing her T-shirt up and out of his way. He caged her waist in his hands, and his hot, greedy mouth latched roughly onto her nipple. His teeth raked her through the thin swatch of satin and lace, and her knees nearly buckled.

"Oh…" Kate gasped softly.

A slight pause, and then the voice returned, obviously bemused. "Um, I'm so sorry to…ah, to interrupt you, Dr. O'Rourke." The vaguely familiar voice paused again, and the woman cleared her throat. "This is Mindy at the ER. Dr. Hooper instructed that I call you. We need you to come in stat. There was a bus accident, and we're swamped. We're calling in everyone available."

Somehow the clasp on her bra had come undone, and his hot mouth found her other breast. It took a few delirious seconds for her brain to begin firing on all cylinders again, but once the nurse's words sank in, Kate surfaced in a hurry. "I'll be right there," she replied shakily before ending the call and thrusting the phone back in her pocket.

Kate dragged in a long, ragged breath to steady herself. Not an easy thing to do with six feet of raw masculine strength on his knees before her, paying tribute to her breasts with his mouth. Against every instinct in her overheated body, Kate pushed gently at his shoulders.

He didn't budge. Instead, his arms slipped around her waist, his forearms running up her back, his hands splayed on her shoulders, tugging her closer.

"Nick, I have to go."

"You have to stay," he growled against her breast. Then he was on his feet again, towering over her, leaning into her. His lips found the pulse below her ear.

"No," she groaned, arching her back, bracing her hands against his heaving chest. Muscles leaped and bunched, and she forced a swallow.

*Whaa...*

"I have to go, that was the hospital. Nick, they need me."

"I need you," he disputed, chasing her lips with his.

"Nick. Stop."

He jerked back sharply and peered down into her eyes, though he didn't release her. His expression was befuddled to the point that laughter gurgled in her throat. Had no one ever told this man to stop before? He acted as if the very concept was completely foreign. His pupils seemed to retract and then grow before her very eyes, and her laughter died before it could burst free. His irises fairly glowed.

An odd chill coursed down her spine.

"You don't want to leave," he prompted slowly, enunciating each word as if the fate of the world, as if his very life depended on her understanding. "You want to stay. You want to make love with me." His voice slid through her like warm, rich honey. Enticing. Reassuring.

For a slim moment, Kate seriously considered

throwing responsibility—and her reputation—to the wind. For a slim moment, she contemplated giving in to the powerful pull of his eyes and the seductive allure in his voice. But images of the ER, swamped with frightened, injured patients filled her mind. The ER would be a veritable beehive of activity, her co-workers flitting from patient to patient, adrenaline coursing strong through their veins. They needed her. She couldn't let them down.

She wouldn't, no matter how badly she wanted to do exactly as he'd insisted.

"No," she firmly replied, shoving at his chest more persistently. "I need to go in. Step aside, Nick. Let me go."

He stared down at her, his expression undeniably shocked now. He blinked at her, once, twice. Three times. Then shook his head as if to clear his brain. He opened his mouth, then snapped it closed abruptly. Without warning, he dragged his hands from her and jerked back a full step.

"I'm sorry," he muttered hoarsely. He looked so disgruntled. So shocked and confused, she very nearly gave in and stepped back into his embrace to follow this madness wherever it led.

Instead, she struggled to right her clothes. "There was a bus accident. The ER is swamped. They need all the hands they can get."

"Sure, sure," he rasped, dragging a hand through his tousled hair.

She thrust an arm into her coat and jerked it on. Patting her pockets, Kate did a quick mental scan to make sure she had everything she needed. Keys, check. Phone, check. Pager, check. ID, check.

Good to go.

Then she glanced at the window. Pitch black. A raw nerve in the back of her mind twitched, and she bit her lip. Was *he* out there? Was her stalker lurking in some dark alley, waiting to leap out and grab her? She'd done a good job of pushing him from her mind, but now that she had to face going outside alone after dark, the crushing fear came back to terrorize her.

"What is it?" He laid a warm hand on her shoulder, detaining her. "What's wrong?"

"Nothing," she replied automatically, brushing his concern aside as she moved from under his hand. She was a big girl. She could deal with her own problems.

"Not so fast," he insisted, catching hold of her wrist when she would have walked passed him. This time she couldn't slip away as easily. "I saw that look. What's the matter?"

"It's just...it's..." She bit her lip again and peered up into eyes the color of smoky, smoldering amber. "Okay, some creep has been... Well, he's been stalking me."

His frown shifted to a scowl, and his jaw muscle tightened. Disappointment settled in the pit of her stomach like a cold rock. He'd back off now. Consider her too much of a headache, and give her the brush off.

After a curt nod, he snatched his keys from the counter and pocketed them, took a jacket from the peg by the door and shrugged it on. "All right. I'll go with you."

She was at a loss for words, and simply stood there, mouth agape. He stepped into the hallway leading to the door, then paused and half-turned to face her.

"You can trust me to keep you safe," he stated in a matter-of-fact way. Then he held out his hand. An invitation.

A promise.

Touched beyond explanation by that simple gesture, Kate swallowed the lump stuck in the back of her throat and stepped forward. She placed her hand in his and, as his long, strong fingers closed gently over hers, a warm sense of security filled her. For the first time since she'd begun receiving those unwanted, unsettling gifts, Kate felt hopeful.

As they hurried to the hospital, her mind began to race ahead, bracing herself for whatever she might find when she got there. Still, Kate was hypersensitive to the man keeping pace at her side. He'd refused to relinquish her hand and the warmth of his touch—the confidence he exuded—gave her a deep sense of peace. A strange feeling of rightness. She glanced at him from the corner of her eye and smiled.

Before Nick, she would have walked this route alone. Before Nick, she would have been constantly watching over her shoulder, jumping at her own shadow. Before Nick she'd *felt* alone.

How could one person change so much in such a short amount of time?

****

Sometimes life really sucked.

Two DOA's, a critically injured child, and an ER full of sutures, contusions, and fractures convinced Kate of that as nothing else could.

But then there were those precious glimpses of sunshine through the clouds of despair that made you keep going, made you put one foot in front of the other and trudge on. Like the tiny infant who'd survived the crash without a scratch. And the young man who'd suffered life threatening injuries, but, despite the odds, continued to hang on to life with grim determination.

She refused to consider her role in his recovery.

And then there was the miracle of Nick...

Kate dragged off her scrubs and stepped wearily into the hard spray. The tile in the shower was like everything else in the hospital. Cold. Sterile. She braced a forearm against the shower wall and heaved a sigh of relief, of exhaustion as the steaming water pounded against her skin. The night had been long and taxing. She had to work hard to keep one patient from blurring into the next tonight. Each was an individual. Each deserved to be treated thus.

And every time she'd gone out to the waiting room to speak to a patient's family, Nick had been there. Sitting patiently in the far corner. Offering her a bolstering smile each and every time. His presence, his wordless encouragement had stroked and eased some needy part of her she hadn't known existed. By the end of the night, every time she stepped through the waiting room doors, her gaze had unerringly sought him out. Before she'd even thought to call for her patient's family, she'd found him.

And after she'd delivered the stunning news to a grieving family that their teenage daughter had suffered a subdural hematoma and died, he'd slipped past the eagle-eyed charge nurse and found her in the blood-spattered, curtained cubicle where her patient had expired. She'd lost her patient there, and there she returned to steal a moment to regroup. Smoothing his hands up and down her rigid back, he'd wordlessly drawn her into his arms and simply offered his support. No one had ever done that for her before, ever taken into consideration what the loss of a patient did to the doctor who'd fought tooth and nail for his or her life.

Remembering again that young life cut so grievously short—seeing the faces of those who'd loved her and been devastated by the news of her passing—Kate leaned her head against her forearm and wept softly. Kate knew some might look upon her tears as a weakness she could not—should not—afford. She looked upon them as an affirmation of why she'd become a doctor. She looked upon them as confirmation that she was still human—that a doctor...a *good* doctor...should be, above all things, human.

Dashing the healing deluge of tears from her eyes, Kate finished her shower, toweled dry and dressed. Nick stood as she stepped back inside the waiting room for the final time that night.

Or, to be more accurate, that morning. Glancing at the large clock on the wall, she grimaced. Just after four a.m. Then, unbidden, a smile curled her lips. Just after four a.m. and he'd stayed.

For her.

Ignoring the speculative glances Nurse Mindy cast their way, Kate walked straight into his waiting arms. God, he felt so good. So solid and so strong. His deft fingers found the knot clenched tight at the base of her neck and kneaded, slow and easy. His warm lips pressed against her temple, gentle and undemanding. He nuzzled his nose into her damp hair, and she sighed as a low satisfied purr rumbled deep in his chest.

She'd sprung the information on him that she had a stalker. He'd responded with a simple pledge that he'd keep her safe. She'd been afraid to walk in the dark alone, and he'd held her hand. She'd had a long, difficult night in the ER. And he'd stayed...he'd waited, for her. She wasn't so naïve as to believe every promise she heard...especially not one given so quickly by a stranger. Yet, for reasons completely beyond her understanding, she believed him... unconditionally. He'd meant every word.

His compassion wrapped itself around her like a warm, fuzzy blanket, and Kate was as good as sunk.

She'd never believed in love at first sight. In fact, she'd scoffed openly at the very notion. Yet here she was—an intelligent, independent, practical woman—suddenly dreaming of castles in the sky and dashing, bold knights with smoldering amber eyes riding to the rescue. She'd known this man for less time than it took her to decide if she liked the feel of a new pair of shoes, and she'd already begun envisioning a future with him.

No, cynical Dr. Kate O'Rourke did not believe in love at first sight.

But she'd fallen anyway.

Chapter 9

Styx stood on the balcony, bare feet spread wide on the cold grate, scanning the shadows lurking on the street below. The sun would rise in a few short hours; its approach as tangible as the ticking of a clock's hands, thanks to the innate intuition all creatures of the night possess. Instinct urged him indoors, out of harm's way, and yet he resisted, gripping the wrought iron railing in white-knuckled fists as he focused his senses...all of them...on the night around him.

The night had been home to him for so long now, not that he'd had much choice. Eventually, after the first few bitter years had passed, he'd come to terms with his existence. He'd found succor in the darkness. Solace in the stillness.

Now darkness held the threat of death.

And the stillness was ominous, an uneasy calm before the storm.

In the alley, just around the corner, a Human vagrant rummaged through trashcans, muttering to himself. His unappealing scent—stale sweat and cheap liquor—wafted on the night. Thirsty as Styx was, the smell turned his stomach. It had been a long, long time since he'd been that desperate, hopeless enough to rely on one of those poor, bedraggled creatures for sustenance. He shuddered with distaste at the unpleasant memory...and not just the memory of sour, corrupted blood.

No, Styx shuddered at the sad state he himself had been in when he'd first realized the truth of his existence.

His loathsome, desolate, Immortal existence...

Forcefully diverting his focus, he listened carefully to the wind...the voice of the night. A tomcat sat patiently near the questing vagrant, grooming himself with loud, reverberating purrs, eagerly anticipating the aromatic feast he was hopeful of sharing. A block over, the rev of a diesel engine and the honk of a car's horn punctuated the steady hum of a sleepy, thriving city. Just up the street, a car alarm pierced the night, annoying and repetitive, until the vehicle's grumbling owner tromped outside to kill the alarm and inspect for damage.

Cool wind rushed over the choppy waters of Puget Sound, battering against Styx's bare chest and stomach. His loose shirttails flapped madly around his waist. Tipping his head back, nostrils flared, he drew the scents of the night deep into his lungs. It would rain before dawn, a torrential downpour judging by the scents the wind carried and the underlying rumble far off in the distance. He could detect no essence of eminent danger, and yet he couldn't let his guard down. Too much was at stake.

His gaze slid to the neighboring balcony only a short distance away. No distance at all, really, for his Vampyre reflexes. The glass doors were closed tight; the room beyond the filmy drapes dark. Was she sleeping? Was she lying in her bed, even now, soft and warm and thinking of him...and of the kiss they'd shared? His body throbbed like a live wire, taut with need. Aching for physical contact.

Contact he adamantly denied himself.

If he went to her now...if he touched her...he would take more than she would willingly—freely— give. He would take everything...

And she deserved so much more. She deserved the right to decide her own future...not have it chosen for her. She was amazing. He'd known she was a doctor. He'd thought he'd understood what the profession entailed.

He'd been so wrong.

Watching her interact with her patients' families had shed new light on another facet of Kate. She was good at what she did. And, much more than that, she *felt* for each and every patient, each and every family. She cared for her patients...she cared *about* them. It was impossible to *not* be touched by her. From the moment he'd taken her hand in his and stared deep into her bottomless eyes, he'd been fighting the inevitable.

Complications aside, Styx could fight the truth no longer.

A dark, enticing voice in the back of his mind— absolutely certain in its conviction—prodded him, goading him to claim what he knew in his heart to be his. Kate O'Rourke was destined to be his *Bride*. Hadn't he been wishing for this, wishing for her?

Why, then, did she scare the living hell out of him?

His conversation with Crispin came back to him, taunting him. Dare he walk in Kate's dreams? What would he find there? Would he uncover the answers they needed to end this monster's hunting spree? Did Kate unwittingly hold the key?

Would he find himself there in her dreams?

Or would he find memories of another?

Would Kate O'Rourke be his salvation...or his damnation? There were so many things about her that he wanted to know, so many mysteries he longed to unravel. Why did she drive herself to the point of exhaustion to provide free medical attention at St. Mary's after putting in grueling shift after grueling shift at the ER? Why did Kate and her sister no longer speak to each other?

Why did she always catch the tip of her tongue between her teeth whenever she concentrated fiercely on a task?

Satisfied the threat of immediate danger didn't hover just outside her window...at least for the moment...Styx released the rail and retreated inside the apartment, where he prowled the confines of the living area like the caged predator he was.

*Dream walking...*

Did he dare?

The question gave him pause. He hadn't intruded on another's dream in centuries. He hadn't dared, fearful Ava would come back. Fearful she'd somehow find out and senselessly end another innocent's life the way she'd taken Eliza from him. How had she known what he could do? He hadn't told another...not a single soul. Maybe it was the connection between them, Sire to progeny, which had given away his secrets. He had no idea, could only guess.

Why hadn't he just killed the vengeful, jealous bitch when he'd had the chance...when he'd had his hands wrapped around her slim throat, his fangs hovering above her tender flesh?

The answer haunted him, even now.

*Because he was too chivalrous to harm a female...even if she deserved it, more fool he.*

But then, how many innocent lives had she ended since Eliza? That thought, too, had haunted him from the moment he'd released his grip on Ava's throat and ordered her to never come near him again. How many innocents had died because he'd been too weak to slay a female? It was but yet another mark on his long, long lists of regrets.

Perhaps this uncertain guilt was his punishment...his own private hell on earth.

If so, he deserved every fiery moment.

No, there had to be another way to access Kate's memories. Something less chancy. No way would he risk bringing Kate to Ava's attention. A sudden, fierce need to protect burned through him. Obsessive. Fanatical.

Stronger than any he'd ever experienced before.

Styx glared at the pale sage-colored wall a few feet from his face. His eyes began to burn. His gums throbbed as his fangs pushed, long and hungry, against his lower lip, drawing fine trickles of blood. His forehead bunched, the skin over his cheekbones stretched tight.

The object of this violent need to protect, this insatiable hunger to touch lay on the other side of these paper-thin walls. With a slight flick of his wrist, an infinitesimal twist of his hand, he could easily punch a hole through plaster and lathe, through wood and brick. In his hand, two by fours would splinter like toothpicks. Brick pulverize to dust. He could tear a hole in the wall large enough for him to slip through faster than a Human could blink in surprise.

He could slip soundlessly across her apartment and into her bedroom. He would pull the sheets back slowly and run his hand down the length of her sleeping body, over every curve and valley. Her clothing would prove no barrier, slipping away to leave the silk of her flesh exposed for his hands, and his lips...and his fangs.

Styx blinked, startled, as plaster caved, lathe cracked. Staggering back a step, he jerked his hand away from the wall and watched, surprised, as a puff of white dust floated innocuously to the floor at his feet.

*¡Mierda!* He'd come so close to losing control. So close to becoming the very thing he sought to protect her from...a demon of the night.

Dragging a trembling hand over his goatee, he tottered back another step, then another, sucking in a ragged breath. Sweat beaded on his brow, dampened his chest. With a vicious oath, he swung around and stomped across the apartment, storming inside the bedroom he'd claimed for himself. He slammed the door, as if the addition of that flimsy barrier might shield her from his hungers...from his thirst.

The joke was on him.

*A demon sent to protect the angel...*

Right now, he was probably more of a threat to Kate than the Collector was.

And he was trapped in this apartment. Trapped between the razor sharp cravings he had for this one, unsuspecting female and the threat of oncoming dawn. He should have left when he'd had the chance. He should have fed. He should have called Zack back to watch over her so that he could have put a little space between them...a little space between him and the indelible scent of Kate—a scent that lingered on the fringes of his awareness, unwilling to grant him the meanest sliver of peace.

Not bothering to remove his jeans or shirt, Styx threw himself across the bed and forced himself to take deep, even breaths as he stared at a minute crack in the ceiling near the darkened light fixture. He ruthlessly channeled his energies into calming the raging hunger, the searing thirst ravaging his control.

No, *dream walking* with Kate was definitely out of the question. Especially now. Never mind Ava...there was no telling what *he* might do to Kate.

Closing his eyes, Styx sought oblivion—however temporary—in the arms of slumber. Never had it been so difficult to slip into sleep for him. Never had he fought this hard for control. At last, once the edges of need dulled, the soft wings of his dreams lifted him gently into the soothing release of slumber.

*Warm Mediterranean breezes pulled him through the orchard. The scents of citrus and sea wove themselves around him like a well-loved cloak, inviting and irresistible. Through the deep-green leaves overhead, stars twinkled bright, like handfuls of brilliant diamonds scattered wildly over a black velvet backdrop. Bright, silvery moonlight lit the well-known path, guiding his reluctant feet to a destination he'd visited a thousand times before.*

*High, girlish giggles floated on the breeze, followed, nip and tuck, by a deep baritone laugh. Styx's gut twisted painfully at the unforgettable sounds. Sounds time and distance could never erase. No, no...he would go no farther. He didn't want to see this, couldn't bring himself to gaze upon their welcoming faces, their happy smiles.*

*Yet his feet continued to move forward, his pace to quicken.*

*This was the dream he both sought, and the nightmare from which he'd tried desperately to hide. Would that he could change what he knew to be inevitable.*

"I see you, midget," Thomas taunted.

"You cheated," cried Eliza, doubling over in another fit of giggles as her brother poked her in the ribs.

*Unable to resist the sweep of his dreams, unable to divert the oncoming nightmare down another less painful course, Styx stepped from behind a tree, into the bright pool of moonlight. But something was different. It was more a feeling than anything tangible. Yet the feeling was powerful, and it gave him hope. Hope he'd not had since the night the dream had been reality. This wasn't the same dream he'd had countless times before. But he couldn't quite determine what had changed.*

"Tell him, Nico..." Eliza gasped, twisting away from tickling hands. "Tell him he cheated. He didn't cover his eyes..."

"It serves you right, sweeting," Styx cajoled her,

*falling effortlessly into the dream, savoring the sounds of their voices, the vivid colors of their hair and eyes and clothing as a drowning man knowingly—hopelessly—savors his last gulp of air before the churning sea claims him for all eternity. "You're too old to play those childish games anymore."*

*The words were the same, the actions and the sounds and the smells were the same. But the pain wasn't as sharp, the memories not quite so bitter.*

*Why?*

*"He's right, midget," Thomas agreed, sending a shower of fragrant petals into the air above her head. "You should go home and get a good night sleep. You have a long day ahead of you tomorrow."*

*Eliza's pretty bow of a mouth twisted on a grimace, and she crossed her arms petulantly. Dark brows drew together over eyes the color of melted chocolate. "Don't remind me."*

*"Come on, sweeting, it can't be so bad."*

*"If you think that, then you go in my place. Just once, I'd like to see you get poked and prodded with needles and pins. Señora Mendoza is a demon. She does not stop until she draws blood. I wish Mama would find a nicer seamstress."*

*"But she is the best in the city. And you want the most beautiful dress at the party, don't you?" Thomas dusted pale petals from Eliza's unbound hair. Her long tresses, glistening blue-black in the moonlight, bounced back in curly disarray. Slinging an affectionate arm around her slender shoulders, Thomas pecked a fond kiss to the crown of his sister's head. "The birthday girl must always have the most beautiful dress."*

*"Soon she will no longer tag after us, Thomas," Styx predicted with an unexpected pang of sadness. "Soon she will be too busy with her suitors to pay us any mind at all."*

*Eliza's adoring gaze turned his way, glittering brightly with the reflection of moonlight and years of childhood worship. "I will always have time for you, Nico." Then her gaze turned a bit too wistful for Styx's comfort. "And I will be saving a dance for you...don't let me down."*

*"I'll be there," he reassured her. But that wistful smile upon her lips—a smile that hinted her childhood hero worship might turn to something more mature—urged him to tease, "After all, Thomas and I must approve your dance partners first, eh? We can't have our little pest associating with bad influences, can we?"*

*Rolling her eyes, Eliza planted an elbow in her brother's unprotected stomach and pushed away from his loose embrace. With a feminine grace that surprised Styx, she twirled in and out of the pools of moonlight.*

*"Thomas will be too busy trying to catch Catalina alone in some corner without her duenna," Eliza predicted, balancing her arms in the air, as though she waltzed in a lover's embrace. "And you, Nico..." She twirled and swayed in time to a delicate melody only her ears could hear. "You will be too busy hiding from Ines and Filipa and Vanesa and all the others...leaving me free to find my prince without you two meddling busybodies interfering."*

*Styx slapped a hand to his chest as though mortally wounded. "She cuts to the quick, Thomas. She is truly becoming a woman before our very eyes."*

*Eliza giggled, pirouetting into the shadows. Dark mist suddenly—insidiously—swirled up from the ground, wrapping itself around Eliza's feet, crawling up her legs. It snaked out, engulfing Thomas, obscuring the trees and the moonlight. Darkness crept in around the edges of Styx's vision.*

*All of a sudden, Thomas was gone.*

*The orchard evaporated.*

*And yet somewhere on the periphery of his conscious, a calm, soothing presence lurked. Just out of reach. Just beyond his sight.*

*But there nonetheless.*

*No. No, this was what he'd sought to avoid. He didn't want to see this. Couldn't witness this disturbing vision...this nightmarish re-enactment. Not again.*

*But the clawing, choking fear, the furious rage, the paralyzing panic...they had all diminished. Somehow, Styx sensed, the unseen, soothing presence had dispelled the devastating emotion that always gripped him whenever this dream came upon him. He didn't understand it...or where the presence came from...but the faint hint of strawberries tickled his nostrils, calming him.*

*A shadowy form materialized near Eliza, stepping into her embrace, sweeping her up in unforgiving, treacherous arms. Long hair, dark as the night, straight and smooth as silk fluttered, slithering around the girl as the shadow curved over Eliza's suddenly limp form.*

*"No," Styx shouted, struggling through the fog, desperately trying to rush to Eliza's rescue. But the fog pushed against him, resisting him. It was like wading through hip deep water, water with a strong current fighting in the opposite direction. "No, Ava, don't... She's too young. Stop!"*

*Eliza's lifeless body slid lethargically to the ground at the shadow's feet. There it remained. Motionless. Slowly, the shadow turned to face him. Ava's lush lips, coated bright crimson with fresh blood, curved up in a benevolent smile. The tip of her tongue skated along her lips...bottom first, then the top, licking the crimson away. Then she lifted her hand and lapped red droplets from the back of her wrist, like a greedy cat grooming cream from its coat.*

*Finally, the fog abated and Styx staggered*

*forward, dropping to his knees at Eliza's side. Gently, overwrought with anguish, he scooped the lifeless girl up in his arms. He cradled her to his chest, his head bowed until his forehead touched hers. Her skin was cold and pale. Her melted-chocolate eyes open and lifeless...already beginning to cloud in death. Hot tears spilled down his cheeks, splashing on her frozen face like raindrops from grief-filled clouds.*

*Eliza...so innocent and sweet.*

*Eliza...dead.*

*"Why?" He turned an agonized gaze up to Ava. Distraught, he cupped Eliza's head in one hand, pressing it gently to his shoulder. "How could you do this? She was innocent."*

*"She was Human," Ava sneered. "I did you a favor, Nico."*

*Stunned, Styx stared up at her. His confused gaze slid to the girl in his arms.*

*No, no, there had to be a way to save her. Perhaps it wasn't too late. If he gave her his vein...*

*She would become a monster, like him...like Ava.*

*But how could he not do all he could to keep her alive. How could he let her go...the way he'd let Thomas go? Could he change her? He didn't know how, not really. He could only do his best, and pray...*

*The change ripped through his system. His fangs stretched so quickly, his gums bled. His eyes teared anew at the searing burn. He set fangs to his wrist, brutally rending his own flesh. His blood—Vampyre blood—flowed from his veins, gushing forth, splattering on Eliza's marble-white skin. He pressed his fingertips to her jaw, forcing her mouth open, and held his wrist to her parted lips.*

*"Please, sweeting," he pleaded. "Please, drink, Eliza. Drink from my vein, help me save you..."*

*Cold laughter pierced his ears.*

*Ignoring Ava, Styx gently shook Eliza, pressing his wet, burning wrist insistently against her lips.*

*Already he could feel his flesh mending, and yet she did not respond. Her head rolled back on her shoulders. Her eyes stared up at the night sky, unblinking. Crimson stained her lips, smeared across her cheek, splotched her neck. And there, just below her ear...two tell-tale, damning puncture wounds.*

*No, please...it couldn't be too late. Not little Eliza...*

*"You're wasting your time," Ava taunted. "It's too late for her. She's gone. I felt the last beat of her heart with my tongue. But she was delicious...the innocent ones are always the freshest."*

*The last wisps of mist swirled madly as Styx released Eliza's body and lunged at Ava. His hands closed over her throat, squeezing. His fangs grazed her flesh, poised to tear away flesh and kill the vicious, treacherous creature. The very creature that had cursed him with life never-ending...*

*"You vengeful, jealous bitch," he snarled.*

*Ava gasped, blinking up at him with wide, doe-brown eyes. Her gaze turned patently innocent. Her hands, cold and bony, clutched at his wrists. "Doing you...favor," she rasped.*

*Roaring his rage, Styx tightened his grip and shook her like a rag doll. The tips of her shoes scuffled across the dirt. She clawed at his hand, raking her nails across the backs of his hands until blood flowed. He welcomed the sting, fueled his anger with it.*

*"Hear me...out," she pleaded between gasps.*

*Narrow-eyed, Styx relaxed his hands only enough for her to draw the barest wisps of air. And he waited, nostrils flared, fangs bared.*

*"Mortal's die," Ava insisted. She sucked in a long gasp of air, her hands clutching his wrists. "You cannot become attached. Old age, illness, accidents...they all die, Nico. All of them eventually—"*

*"Liar," he screamed, shaking her roughly. "You were jealous of an innocent girl."*

*"You endangered us all, Nico," she railed, changing tactics. Apparently, she realized he wasn't buying the innocent act from her, and so she tried going on the offensive. "You walked in her dreams. You could have exposed us all and then—"*

*"You know nothing," Styx denied, shaken to the core at her accusations. How could she possibly know?*

*He tightened his grip once more, shook her hard enough that, had she been Human, he would have snapped her deceitful neck. Styx howled his grief and his rage, but when he looked at her again, he couldn't seem to look beyond her gender...though he knew her to be anything but a helpless female.*

*Oh, how he longed to tear her throat out. How he longed to rend her to pieces and fling those pieces into the sea.*

*But he couldn't do it.*

*Damn his pitiful soul, he couldn't kill her.*

*"She was no threat...to you, or to any of us." Shoving her viciously away from him with a dark growl, he turned back to Eliza. Ava's presence crept closer and Styx snarled over his shoulder. "Don't come near me, Ava. You stay the hell away from me, or the Devil help you I* will *tear you limb from bloody limb. I never want to see you again. Understand me well," he vowed. "If I see you again...I. Will. Kill. You."*

*Ava disappeared as abruptly as she'd arrived. Styx continued to kneel beside Eliza's body. His tears drenched her bodice. He clutched her hand to his cheek, rocking back and forth. He'd failed her. Just as he'd failed her brother.*

*Even the mere memory of that cursed day brought bile to the back of his throat and twisted his guts in tortured knots. He'd come to this very orchard in search of Ava, the enthralling seductress that had lured him into Immortality. And there he'd found her, kneeling over the limp, bloodless corpse of his best friend. She'd glanced up at him, as if she'd been awaiting his arrival, and she'd smiled. Thomas...dead. His lifeblood staining her sensuous lips...*

*His body jerked. It was as if he'd been touched with the brightest of lights. As if lightning had arced from the heavens and made contact with his shoulder. Warm. Frighteningly soothing.*

*Damp eyes wide, he stared over his shoulder.*

*How could this be?*

*Kate...*

*In his dream? How?*

*His thoughts a jumble of confusion, Styx blinked up at her, slowly turning to face her as he stood. Carefully, fearful she would vanish before his eyes, Styx reached up to touch her face. Was this real? Was she real? His fingertips stroked her temple, brushed gently down the side of her face. Her skin was silk beneath his fingers, warm and alive. And real. Gone were the wounds he'd inflicted upon himself. Gone was the blood, both his and Eliza's. The mist evaporated.*

*They were alone.*

*Desperate need swamped him. Not the searing thirst. Not the lustful desire he'd battled whenever he was in this woman's presence. This desperation was so much more elemental. It was a need for comfort. A need for understanding.*

*The need to reaffirm he was still alive...in whatever capacity.*

*Kate stared up at him with wide, bewildered eyes. "Nick?" She glanced around them, and his gaze followed hers. "What's going on, Nick? I, I don't understand..."*

*The room was foreign to him, the contents*

*feminine. Across the room, the top of a dresser was filled with tiny figurines and small, framed photos. The shades were drawn tight against the encroaching sunshine. The scent of strawberries...and the very essence of Kate...filled his senses.*

*"Nico...call me Nico," he insisted. He wasn't sure where that baffling demand had come from. He hadn't allowed anyone to call him that name since Eliza's death, preferring the moniker he'd dubbed himself—Styx, like the rivers of death, for that was how he'd viewed himself since that long ago day. And yet, he needed to hear his name—his real name—tumbling from Kate's perfect lips. A balm to sooth his damaged soul.*

*She blinked up at him, a deep crease between her brows, before she glanced uncertainly around the room once more, as if she imagined she might be tugged against her will to another location in the blink of an eye.*

*"Say it," he demanded, grasping her shoulders, pulling her attention back to his face. "Say my name."*

*"Nico..." She breathed, clearly puzzled by the odd demand.*

*"I need you, Kate," he rasped, cupping the back of her neck in his hand, drawing her steadily closer. "I've been waiting so long for you."*

*Her brow crinkled again, and her lips parted slightly. Styx captured her lips with his before she could form the questions shining in her bright eyes. Her mouth opened beneath his kiss, and he swept his tongue inside her mouth, catching her up in an unrelenting embrace. Her flavor surged through his system, devastating his defenses. She was so small against him, and yet she fit so perfectly. He swept a hand down the front of her silk nightshirt. Buttons flew, spraying across the bed, dropping on the carpet at their feet with soft, nearly indistinguishable thumps.*

Her warm arms wrapped around his neck, her fingers tunneled through his hair as she tipped her head back. A soft moan purred through her throat, vibrating the skin beneath his questing lips. Kate pressed her hips closer to him, cradling the bulge of his rigid, painful erection against the smooth, soft flesh of her stomach. She tugged his shirt down off his shoulders with greedy hands.

Styx tore her nightshirt from her body, his movements becoming rough, unsteady. He was so close to the edge, so close to losing control. And her eager cries drove him on. His eyes burned, glowing in the darkness between them. Releasing her long enough to kick off his jeans, he glanced up and stared in mute wonder. She stood before him, clad in nothing more than the thin lacy scrap of her panties. The full creaminess of her bare breasts beckoned him. With a feral growl, he lurched forward, jerking her back into his arms. In seconds, he had her pinned beneath him on the bed. He tossed the shreds of her panties onto the floor.

Fisting a hand in her hair, Styx dragged her head back as he licked and nipped his way across the curve of her shoulder and up the side of throat. His hips surged back and forth; the pulsing, aching length of his shaft slid back and forth along the hot, wet cleft of her womanhood, tormenting them both. Kate gasped and writhed beneath him, tilting her hips up as if begging for his possession. The sting of her nails dug into his shoulders.

"Oh God, Nico, please..." She tugged at his shoulders. Her eager hands swept down over his back, and she gripped his buttocks, urging him to end the agony.

Styx rocked his hips back as he repositioned himself between her soft thighs. The tip of his shaft slid through her damp curls, slipping ever closer to *the raging heat of her core. He opened his mouth wide, saliva surged, and he gently lowered his fangs to her skin.*

*The instant his fangs began to penetrate her flesh, a split second before his pulsing shaft pushed inside her, Styx's ears began to ring. The tiniest hint of her blood blossomed on his tongue. He'd never tasted anything so perfect in all his existence. Thirst slammed through him. The ringing grew insistently louder. Where was it coming from? The low, distracting hum of a vibrating pager joined the ringing.*

Suddenly Styx was all alone, lying face down on his bed, with a mouthful of pillow. Sputtering, he spit the pillow out and rolled over, gawking around the darkened room. He was alone. And yet, the faint essence of strawberries clung to the air around him...clung to his skin.

A dream...

Nothing more than an empty, wistful dream.

Groaning, Styx swiped a shaking hand over his face and rolled to the side of the bed. He sat up and glanced to the bedside table. Six o'clock glowed red on the face of the digital clock. How long had he been trapped in the dream this time? Thirst twisted his insides in an unforgiving grip. Pushing to his feet, Styx realized he was naked. He paused, frowning. He'd crawled into bed with his jeans and his unbuttoned shirt *on*...hadn't he?

He shook his head. Maybe he'd kicked them off in his sleep. He just needed a long, hot shower to wake up properly. Styx sauntered toward the bathroom. Then he stepped on something. Something small, and hard, and round. Crouching down, he picked the object up, and stared in confusion.

*A button?*

A pink button with a small bit of matching silk

still attached. His focus slipped beyond the button in his hand to the carpet around him. Where had the button come from?

Slowly straightening, he pivoted to stare at the bed. His gaze slid over the tangle of sheets, dropping to the floor near the foot of the bed. His eyes widened, and the breath caught in the back of his throat. Bending at the waist, Styx scooped up the shreds of pink lace.

*¡Madre de Dios!*

Styx staggered to the bed and dropped heavily on the edge as he stared in dazed confusion at the mangled pink panties...or what was left of them...in his hands. What had happened this morning? Licking his lip, he caught the smear of blood across his lower lip. Addictive flavor shot through him like lightning. His mouth fell open, his wide-eyed gaze shot to the pillow, and images raced through his mind.

Reaching out, he gingerly picked up the pillow, as cautious as if it were a poisonous snake—and he still a Mortal. Turning the pillow over in his hands, he caught a whiff of blood-scent. And, sure enough, there on the soft pillowcase...a smear of blood. Human blood.

Kate's blood.

*Not possible...*

He'd never heard of anything like this before. *Was* it possible? Had he somehow pulled Kate into his dream without realizing it? Or had he somehow slipped into hers? That would explain the dream...

But not the physical evidence. Never before had he ever been able to transport objects through the dream realm into the physical plane.

*What had he done?*

Chapter 10

Kate woke in a tangle of sheets, naked and aching with feverish need. Ragged breath ripped from her lungs. Panting, she bolted upright in the bed, her wild-eyed gaze darting madly about the room. Familiar furniture lurked in the shadows of the darkened room. Slivers of dying sunlight sliced around the edges of the thick drapes hanging from the windows, forming a broken pattern of warm gold on the dark blue, well-worn carpet.

*Whoa...a dream... Only a dream...*

*But, man, what a dream.*

Too bad the phone had disturbed her. She wouldn't have minded following that dream all the way to conclusion. Sighing, Kate pushed the tangle of hair from her eyes with a trembling hand and glanced at the digital clock on her nightstand. Six pm. She'd slept most of the day away, and yet she felt sluggish...almost intoxicated. Shaking her head, she reached for the insistent phone at her bedside.

"Hello?" Kate croaked as she fumbled the phone open. Damn it, she sounded as if she'd swallowed the proverbial frog. Clearing her throat, she tried again. "Hello?"

"Dr. O'Rourke?"

"Yes," she answered automatically. She didn't recognize the voice, but that didn't necessarily mean anything. If the ER was overflowing, it was hard telling whose hand they'd shove a phone into.

"There's been a bad accident, doctor. We need your help in the ER...ah, *STAT*."

Frowning, Kate focused harder on the voice.

117

Blurting *STAT* like that, the woman sounded like a nervous actress in some poor imitation of a TV medical show...uncertain of the term. Odd.

Shaking her head at her own fancifulness, Kate replied, "Dr. Jennings is on call today. Have you—"

"We were unable to reach him," the woman interrupted impatiently. "Please, Dr. O'Rourke, we need all the help we can get."

Heaving a sigh, Kate ground a palm against her gritty eye. "Okay...I'll be right there."

The line abruptly went dead.

Kate's brow wrinkled as she blinked at the phone. *How strange...*

Shaking her head, she dropped the phone back on the nightstand, jumped from the bed, and hurried unsteadily toward the bathroom. Halfway there, she stumbled to a halt, stiffening. Why on earth was she naked? She *never* slept naked. Turning, she spied her pink silk nightshirt balled in a heap near the foot of her bed. Buttons littered the floor.

*Good grief...*

That must have been one hell of a dream.

She vaguely recalled bits and pieces, yet the whole picture remained frustratingly elusive. Her brow puckered as she suddenly recalled a strange wispy fog, and an unfamiliar scent in the air. Like citrus...and sea air. Echoes of a young girl's giggles, light and whimsical, had beckoned her closer, but— inexplicably—a deep sense of fear had filled her. A beautiful face swam in her memory...lush dark hair, wide brown eyes—and blood-stained lips.

And her handsome neighbor had flitted here and there throughout the dream...a constant, tense presence. First, he'd affectionately teased the girl, as one would a beloved younger sister. Then, filled with frightening fury, he'd threatened the woman. The next few moments of the dream were strangely— maddening—hazy, and yet, Kate was oddly reluctant to dredge the memory into the bright light of day, certain something horrible had happened to that beautiful young girl...

The final moments of that dream were disturbingly, vividly clear, however. Nick had been there, in her room.

And the things he'd done to her...

Heat climbed her cheeks as she scurried toward the bathroom. A nice, long, cold shower was definitely in order. Too bad she didn't have time for one. She couldn't remember ever having had such a sensual...explicitly erotic...dream before. Goodness, how was she to look the man in the eye the next time she saw him?

*Pull it together, Katie girl. You don't have time for this.*

Unsettled, Kate rushed to the bathroom and splashed water on her face. She blotted the water from her skin with a towel and dropped the damp cloth on the side of the sink as she pulled an elastic band from the top drawer of the vanity. With a quick economy of motion, she quickly jerked her hair up into a ponytail. As she reached for the toothpaste, a red smear on the damp, white hand towel caught her eye. Blood?

Puzzled, Kate picked the towel up with one hand as she examined her face in the mirror. Had she scratched herself last night in the midst of her wild dreams?

Her face was clear of any marks.

Hmm...where had the blood come from?

She turned her face from side to side, and then she caught sight of the marks on her neck. Lifting her hand, she lightly brushed the tips of her fingers along a set of red welts just below her left earlobe, flinching at the sharp sting. The welts were small, no longer than an inch each, spaced about the same distance apart. Both were bright red...with just the thinnest shallow line of broken skin trailing down the center of each welt.

*Weird...*

Kate held her nails up in the glaring florescent light, examining them carefully. No blood lingered beneath her carefully trimmed nails. Had she unwittingly washed it away when she'd rinsed her face? Frowning, she dropped the towel back to the sink and rushed from the room.

Grabbing her pager and phone from her nightstand, Kate tottered from the room, dragging her clothes on as she headed for the kitchen. She scraped her keys, IDs, and a small wad of cash from the counter, stuffing her pockets as she staggered down the hallway toward the door. Pausing long enough to grab her coat from the hanger beside the doorway, she jerked the door open and lurched through the doorway as she pushed one arm into a coat sleeve.

Her leather jacket hung from one arm as she reached to tug the door closed behind her. Kate fumbled her keys, snatching them seconds before they tumbled to the floor. Cursing beneath her breath, she thrust them into her left hip pocket as she spun around to race to the elevator, grabbing blindly behind her for her wayward coat.

Kate crashed headlong into a solid wall of warm muscle. The absurdly familiar scent of Nick coiled itself around her, even as the man himself wrapped powerful arms around her to prevent her from toppling to the floor at his feet.

*"Say it," he'd demanded, grasping her shoulders. "Say my name."*

The phantom voice of her dreams slipped up on her from out of nowhere, catching her by surprise.

Kate gasped, involuntarily whispering, "Nico..."

Nick froze, like a solid block of granite encasing her. Heat swam up her neck, gushed into her cheeks as she slowly lifted her stunned gaze to his.

"Oh," she gasped again, breathless. The expression on his face was unfathomable. "I didn't mean to... I don't know why I said that, Nick. I'm, I'm sorry, I—"

"Please," he interrupted, his large, warm hands slid across her back to her shoulders, glided down to cup her elbows. "It would please me if you would call me Nico. My family..." he paused, cleared his throat, "my family used to call me that," he added quietly.

"I, um, all right. Nico..." Her voice trailed away as she slipped effortlessly into the depths of his mesmerizing amber eyes. Heat swam through her veins.

"Where are you rushing off to?"

"Huh?" She blinked rapidly, stirring herself. Good grief, what was wrong with her? "Um, the ER. I have to go in to the ER. There was another accident," she mumbled. His chest was hard as stone beneath her palms. And the warmth radiating through his thin shirt was...*amazing*. Oh, how she'd like nothing more than to burrow in and—

"You barely just came from there," he protested, frowning down at her. His breath feathered across her cheek. Sensual lips—lips designed with the sole purpose of a woman's pleasure in mind—were so close. So very close...

"From where?" Why was it so difficult to follow such a simple conversation?

His head tilted ever so slightly, and the hint of a smile winked at the edges of his sensual lips revealing the faintest trace of a dimple in his left cheek.

"From the hospital," he explained slowly, drawing each word out. His voice rasped over her, and she shivered, desire pooling deep in the pit of her stomach.

Her gaze locked on his mouth as he swept the

tip of his tongue across his lower lip. The way a starving man licks his lips before diving headlong into a tempting feast. A low moan tickled the back of her throat. The sound...the vibration startled Kate, snapping her back to her present circumstances. Lord, could he tell how badly she longed to throw herself into his arms and wrap herself around him, kiss him senseless? Another wave of heat swept up her neck, rushing clear to her hairline.

*Well...it was all his fault, damn it.*

Irrational as that line of thought was, she latched on to it like a lifeline. How dare he come rushing past her door when she was in such a hurry to leave? How dare he look so damn...*edible*? His shirttails hung free from the waistband of his jeans, a few of the buttons were misaligned. His eyes were heavy-lidded, and the prickly shadow of a beard darkened his cheeks. His dark hair was loose around his shoulders, tousled as if he'd just rolled from bed...as if he'd just rolled from her dreams.

Her face went up in flames. And, strangely enough, with this latest wave of heat across her face, his expression went oddly taut. Her lips parted slightly, and she frowned, watching in confusion as he visibly forced a swallow. His eyes narrowed, and his pupils seemed to dilate right before her eyes. His lips compressed into a thin line, a thin line that sort of...well, *bulged* at the edges.

The room around her began to spin, and Kate sucked in a deep breath, quickly filling her oxygen-starved lungs. How did he manage to keep doing this to her? Reducing her to a mumbling, bumbling idiot? She was an intelligent, independent, self-assured woman. Why, then, did he make her feel like a starry-eyed teenager in the throes of her first crush?

As if he could somehow read her thoughts, his grin suddenly widened...though his lips remained firmly closed. His grip tightened on her elbows, drawing her inexorably closer.

Mortified, Kate blinked rapidly and dropped her gaze to one of the misaligned buttons on his shirt. She'd never seen him so poorly put together. Without giving it a second thought, Kate tucked the tip of her tongue between her teeth as her fingers mechanically worked the buttons free, matched them up to the proper holes, and re-fastened them. As the last button slid home, she came to her senses.

Dear heavens...what was she doing?

She needed to get to the hospital, and here she was, all but undressing her sexy neighbor...and in a public hallway of all places.

"I'm sorry," she muttered, dropping her hands to her sides as she jerked out of his hold. Her wide-eyed gaze darted around them. Suddenly that old phrase, *deer in the headlights*, began to hold new meaning for her. "I, I have to go."

"Wait," he called, trailing behind her as she rushed to the opening elevator doors. "I'll go with you."

"No, don't be silly, Nick—*Nico*." Flustered, Kate bolted through the doorway. There, just across the threshold, she pivoted to face him, effectively denying him entrance to the elevator. Offering him a wobbly smile, she blindly reached to her side and stabbed impatiently at the lobby button on the glowing control panel. "You were there all last night, and there's no telling how long I'll be needed today. I couldn't possibly ask you to wait for me again."

"But you can't—"

"I'll be fine," she assured him, forcing a bright, cheery edge to her smile as the doors slid closed between them.

The moment the steel doors snapped closed, Kate staggered back a few steps and sagged against the far wall of the elevator with a loud groan. Squeezing her eyes shut, she dropped her chin to her chest and pressed the palms of her fisted hands to her forehead. She'd barely been able to maintain eye contact. Had he been able to tell? And she'd never blushed so much in her entire life. Had she been an open book? Her thoughts—her dreams—etched plainly there on her face for him and all the world to see?

*Concentrate, Kate.*

Heaving a deep sigh, she pushed away from the wall and straightened her jacket. She couldn't worry about Nico now...couldn't worry about this startling, unsettling attraction that seemed to have taken control of her body. She needed to focus. The ER wouldn't have called her in today unless there had been a major crisis. The elevator dinged off floors as the corresponding number flashed above the door. At last, the lobby button lit up and the elevator doors slid open. Kate bolted through the doors, belatedly remembering to zip up her jacket as she jogged through the apartment's main lobby.

Cool wind slapped at her face as she rushed out onto the sidewalk. Fall had come early this year, leaving an abnormally sharp nip to the air. Her long, heavy ponytail bounced against her back as she glanced first one way, then the other, searching in vain for a cab. Never one around when you actually wanted one, was there? Then again, until recently, she'd never really relied on them much. Perhaps it was normal they didn't circle this block looking for fares.

Thankful she'd put on her sneakers, Kate dashed down the street. At times like this, she actively regretted not having a car of her own. This, she supposed, was the price she paid for deciding years ago that she really had no need for one...that, and parking was nothing short of a migraine in the making. She rounded the corner at a flat out sprint, narrowly dodging a woman walking a small dog. The little terrier yipped a ferocious warning as it cowered between its mistress's feet. Calling a hasty apology over her shoulder, Kate darted along the sidewalk, zigzagging around a trashcan and a large planter overflowing with struggling greenery.

"Help me! Somebody...please, help me!"

Kate skidded to a halt, throwing a hand out to brace herself against the rough brick corner of a building. Her chest heaved in and out as cool, damp evening air seared her throat and lungs. She stood still for a moment, straining to filter the sounds around her. In the background, car horns beeped amid the hum of traffic, indistinguishable voices chattered, dogs barked.

"Help..."

Kate's head whipped around, and she peered down the length of a long, dim alley to her left. Puddles of grimy water covered quite a bit of the filthy ground. Left over rainwater from this afternoon's storm, no doubt. Dingy brick walls rose up on either side of the narrow lane, the naked framework of fire escapes clung to the side of one of the buildings like a network of magnified, uniform spider webs. A short way down the alley, a trio of overflowing Dumpsters lined up along the wall on the right. A tangled mass of discarded boxes littered the ground at haphazard intervals. The musty scents of damp trash hung like a cloud in the air.

"Please, someone," came that insistent voice once more. Feminine. Desperate. "Help me..."

Fingers of apprehension tickled her spine, but Kate bit her lip and slowly crept into the alley. The call for help was a siren's song to her doctor's soul. Irresistible. Nevertheless, she remained alert, tense, prepared to flee should the slightest threatening movement catch her eye. Kate pressed close to the wall with the least amount of debris, and edged her way onward. Shooting a wary glance behind her to make certain no one followed her into the alley, she sucked in a sharp breath, praying she wasn't making a mistake. Kate hopped silently over another puddle, then eased around a pile of small, mangled cardboard boxes.

"Is anyone there? Can anyone hear me?" The trembling voice was a bit louder now. She had to be getting close.

Kate peeked around the side of one of the Dumpsters. Her heart gave a little lurch inside her chest when a stray cat bound from a broken crate some way down the alley and darted into the shadows. Pressing a palm to her chest, dragging in a long, shuddering breath, Kate edged around the Dumpster.

A small form huddled on the ground near the second Dumpster. A long tangle of dark hair obscured the woman's features. Then again, it might have been an adolescent girl, so small was she. Her clothing was ragged, her skin grubby. Kate shot one last suspicious glance over her shoulder, searching the shadows, before she spoke.

"Hello? Do you need help?"

The huddled figure went absolutely still for a moment. And then, by slow degrees, the woman lifted her head and rocked back on her heels to peer up at Kate through the thick curtain of her wild hair. Pale golden eyes gleamed in the darkness. Compelling. Feral.

Kate drew back a step, instinctively preparing to pivot and flee. Something was not right here.

Indeed, something was very, *very* wrong.

The next few seconds moved past in a blur. Feeling as if she were moving in slow motion—and everything else around her had suddenly been fast forwarded, Kate shifted her weight, turned her foot, and lunged toward the entrance of the alley. A gust of wind blew around her. And suddenly that feral, crouching street urchin was standing before her. Her expression was smug, and ominous. Kate blinked, astonished at the speed in which the woman had moved.

Not possible, her mind denied, even as her eyes confirmed the truth.

"Too easy," the bedraggled creature whispered, clucking her tongue as if disappointed.

"What," she forced a swallow, "what do you want?" Kate demanded, straightening to her full, if meager five feet. Chin up, show no fear, she reminded herself.

By her best calculations, she and this strange woman were nearly evenly matched. Though she'd never been put to the test in quite this way before, Kate was confident in her abilities. She could handle herself if it came down to it. Still, she'd rather not engage in a back alley brawl if she could avoid it. She'd seen too many people rolled through the ER...and too many bodies passed on to the morgue...who'd probably thought the same thing.

Perhaps this woman could be reasoned with. "Look, I only have a small amount of cash on me...but you can have it. Just step aside and let me pass. No one has to get hurt here."

The woman met her suggestion with a cold, mirthless laugh, sending an alarming chill racing through Kate's body. It was, quite possibly, the most frightening sound Kate had ever heard.

"I don't want your money," the woman informed her at last, sneering disdainfully.

"All right," Kate said, lifting her hands in a placating gesture. "You called for help. I can get help for you. Just tell me what you need. What's your name?"

"You want to help me?" Her voice was like silk now, silk with the hint of a knife's edge just beneath it. Deceptive. Lethal. Her smile grew wide, and she began to pace, slowly, sinuously, from one side of the alleyway to the other, all the while her unblinking gaze never left Kate.

"That's right. I can help you." Kate drew a calming breath. It wouldn't do her any good if she lost her head and panicked. She'd dealt with far more stressful situations than this and survived. Just now, she couldn't bring any to mind, but she was sure she had. She just had to keep a level head. "I can get you warm clothes...food. A safe place to sleep. What's your name?"

In silence, the woman prowled across the alley twice more. Cocking her head to the side, she licked her bottom lip. A lump of fear lodged in the back of Kate's throat. Nico had licked his lip almost exactly like that earlier...and yet her instinctive reaction couldn't have been more opposite in the extreme. How could such motion look so ominous...and so *hungry*? Kate glanced nervously over her shoulder to make certain no one was sneaking up on her from behind, then she snapped her gaze back to the pacing woman a few feet in front of her. This woman was toying with her. The way a cat toys with a mouse before it moves in for the kill. Kate just didn't understand why.

The end of the alley seemed so terribly far away all of a sudden. If she made a mad dash for it, could she make it, or would this bedraggled creature catch her first?

As the woman indolently pivoted to move in the other direction, she murmured, clearly amused, yet a hint of curiosity lingered in her eyes, "You want to know my name."

Kate's gaze followed the woman's progress, but she didn't respond. Unease had settled around her like a cold, damp mist. She had to get out of this alley. *Now.*

Her hands began to tingle. Her heartbeat sped,

thrumming in her ears until she feared she'd pass out. Her skin prickled as the swell of ozone crackled around her. Her own body's unexpected reaction frightened her almost as much as this woman's threatening behavior.

Maybe even more so.

*Oh, God. Not again...*

"My name," the woman said softly as she fully turned to face Kate. Her eerie eyes glowing jarringly in the dim alley, "is Layla. And *I* don't want you..." She leaned slightly forward, the crouch of a predator waiting to spring. "But my master does."

## Chapter 11

With one arm raised to shield his face from the dying rays of blistering sunlight, Styx raced down the street, cursing fluently beneath his breath, unmindful of the incredulous stares following his progress. He was moving much faster than he should be, considering all the Humans nearby, but he couldn't help it. He hadn't expected Kate to duck out on him so quickly. And he'd certainly never expected her to get so far ahead of him so quickly. If he didn't know better, he would have sworn she was half-Faerie.

He stumbled as the thought snagged in his mind. *Faerie...*

No...no, surely not. He'd have been able to tell, beyond the shadow of a doubt.

*Wouldn't he have?*

Bottom line, it was hard to say. In all his long existence, he'd had only the most limited contact with the Faerie Nation. They were a race that kept strictly to itself as a rule, only mingling with other races when they had no other recourse. They were an ancient and powerful race, self-righteous in their pursuit of noble bloodlines and borderline narcissistic in their magicks. But, as always seemed to be the case, with great power came great vulnerability...thus their preference to stick close to their own kind.

Surely, it was impossible. She'd told him both her parents had died. Her father had suffered disease. Neither of which would have been possible for an Immortal. He'd held her in his arms, tasted her Human essence. And yet, the alluring scent of her...and the flavor of her blood on his tongue—pure ambrosia. Unique.

Kicking his speed back up, he forced those disturbing thoughts to the back of his mind. He'd sort it out later. Her fading scent trail suddenly grew stronger as he rounded the corner. Adrenaline, fear, and trace amounts of anger tinged her scent. His own pulse hammered in response. The scent of Vampyre hit him like a sucker-punch to the gut. He recognized that scent. It had permeated the air inside that small interrogation room in Alberta.

*Layla...*

Human witnesses forgotten, Styx flew to the entrance of the alley. The sight that met his stunned gaze struck terror clear to his heart. His precious Kate faced off against the wild-eyed creature he'd faced in that interrogation room. Layla crouched, poised to strike. A rabid snarl pulled at her lips. Her eyes glowed, unnatural and wicked, in the dusk.

Kate stood fast, chin elevated, eyes oddly unfocused. In the split second that Styx paused to assess the situation, the air around Kate suddenly pulsed with life, as if an electrical charge had abruptly coursed through her small, taut body, zapping the air around her. She held her arms at her sides, slightly away from her body, fingers splayed, palms pointed forward toward her adversary.

Before Styx's stunned gaze, wind abruptly snapped through the alley, gusting into a sudden, ferocious whirlwind...a force of nature that whipped and swirled around Kate's fragile body. All around them, debris rose into the air, tossed and caught by the churning wind. The tips of her hair lifted, swaying slightly as if touched only by the gentlest of breezes. And the expression on her face remained serene...almost as if she'd fallen into a deep trance.

He, apparently, wasn't the only one surprised by

Kate's sudden ability to master the elements. Layla fell back on her haunches, lifting an arm to defend her face from the flying projectiles swirling in the wind. But she didn't hesitate long. Hissing, Layla pushed to a crouch once more, albeit visibly wary now.

Without warning, Kate's eyes drifted closed, and she lowered her chin to her chest.

Layla, seeing Kate's focus unexpectedly diverted for the moment, snarled and leaped to attack. With a wild roar, Styx launched himself forward as the shift in his body ripped through him. Muscles bunched, tightening painfully. His claws curled, preparing to tear into the Rogue female. Blood gushed in his mouth as his fangs shot forth. Searing pain lanced through his eyeballs as his pupils shifted. His irises glowed, cutting through the encroaching darkness like laser beams.

Some inner sixth sense honed in on Kate, even as he sailed through the turbulent air. Power seemed to be building around his female, gathering like a tangible ball of steel. All of a sudden, Kate's head wrenched back on her shoulders, her delicate body jerked, and a surge of power exploded around her, shooting out from her core.

That surge hit him like a freight train. An invisible wall of energy slammed into him, throwing him backwards. From the corner of his eye, he watched as Layla, too, hit that energy wall. Mid leap—caught in mid-air—she was hurled swiftly backward, where she crashed against the brick wall behind her like a mistreated ragdoll. Brick and mortar cracked loudly, caving and crumbling around her as she slowly slid to the filthy ground.

The alley went instantly, eerily silent. The wind vanished as quickly as it had arrived. Trash seemed to hang suspended in the air for a moment, then benignly tumbled to the ground. Kate gave a low moan, her hands fell limply to her sides, and she swayed on her feet. Dragging in a breath—the harsh, ragged sound echoed in the alley around them, Kate staggered to the side.

And then she collapsed on a soft whisper of breath.

Styx's heart froze. And for one terrifying moment, he couldn't move. Paralyzed with fear, he stared at Kate's motionless form. Her name ripped from his throat, torn free by the acid claws of despair. His body, tingling and strangely weak, fought his will as he struggled to his hands and knees. Across the alley, Layla laid unmoving, silent, eyes closed.

Panting, he crawled toward Kate.

*Madre de Dios, why wasn't she moving?*

The delectable, sweet scent of her blood grabbed him by the throat.

"*¡Mierda!*" Styx gasped. "No, *querida*, no..."

Sharp pebbles bit into his palms. Broken glass sliced his flesh. Damp, muddy earth soaked his jeans. And the few short yards between them felt more like endless miles, but still he pushed on, determined to get to his female's side. He couldn't wrap his mind around what he'd just witnessed...what he'd just experienced. The only thing that mattered was Kate. She had to have survived. If she'd been killed—

He couldn't hear her pulse above the raging tide of his own blood pounding in his ears.

"Kate," Styx rasped hoarsely. Hand over hand, he dragged himself closer. Currents of electricity still thrummed through her body with alarming, sporadic jolts.

*Please, querida, wake up...*

*So...close...*

He was only a few short feet away from reaching her, when the alley erupted into a second wave of violence. The Rogue female snarled as she, too, pulled herself to her hands and knees and began scrabbling toward him...toward Kate. Protecting Kate—protecting his female—became his sole reason for being. Utilizing every dwindled ounce of strength he could summon, he crouched—a weakened, yet single-minded defense—between Kate's fallen, vulnerable form and Layla's fury.

From out of nowhere, a dark mist descended, swarming between Layla and him. Before Styx's narrow-eyed stare, the mist solidified. He sucked in a sharp, startled breath. The unmistakable scent of another Vampyre filled Styx's nostrils. Rage darkened the newcomer's countenance...a face Styx hadn't seen in centuries. The face of a man Styx had believed long dead.

The Vampyre closed the distance between them, ignoring the hissing, snarling female behind him. That cocky swagger brought back a rush of memories. Desert sands. Exotic pleasures.

Vicious jealousy and unbelievable cruelty.

How was this possible? The sheikh had been Human when Styx and Cole had escaped the fiend's clutches. How had he come to this? A Vampyre. All the fears Styx had been denying, all the disquieting clues the evidence foretold came to life before his eyes. He knew this killer, the vicious Rogue the TFRA had dubbed the Collector.

*Sheikh Amir Kazim al-Rashid...*

The sheikh's venomous gaze darted to Kate's inert form, cut back to Styx. "You will take no more women from me, Spaniard," al-Rashid spat. Poison dripped from every syllable. "She will belong to me, and I will finish you...you and that bastard Norseman...once and for all."

A feral hiss rent the silence, and al-Rashid bared his fangs lunging toward Styx. At the same moment, Layla surged to the side, trying to dart around Styx's defenses, her goal the woman Styx guarded with his very life. Smashing a large fist into al-Rashid's midsection, delivering a brutal uppercut to the jaw, he drove the Rogue back. Whipping around, he grasped a handful of long, dark tresses. Twisting his fist in the cold lash of Layla's hair, Styx yanked viciously, jerking her off balance and away from Kate.

Layla let out a blood-curdling scream and turned her wrath on Styx. She launched herself at his back as he twisted to fend off al-Rashid's attack. Wiry legs wrapped around his waist from behind. Claws dug into his scalp tearing wildly at his hair, and fangs sank into his shoulder, just at the crook of his neck. Pain blazed through his body, and yet he forced his trembling legs to carry him farther away from Kate. He couldn't risk her becoming collateral damage. Growling, he snapped his fangs and slashed at the sheikh with one hand as he reached over his shoulder, tugging uselessly at the infuriated female on his back.

Al-Rashid grunted and went down to one knee as Styx connected a firm kick to the side of his leg. Hot blood gushed forth as the female's fangs ripped at Styx's flesh. Slamming her back against an overflowing Dumpster, he finally managed to dislodge her. Al-Rashid lunged for Kate. Styx flew at him, wrapping his arms around al-Rashid's waist, letting his momentum tumble them both to the ground. In the blink of a human eye, both males sprang to their feet.

Lunging at Styx, Al-Rashid growled. His lips pulled back, revealing glistening, lethal fangs. His eyes were luminous, his claws poised to strike. Styx braced himself for the assault, his mind racing as he tried to figure out the best way to protect Kate from both these vicious Rogues.

The attack never came.

Sheer seconds before al-Rashid would have tackled Styx to the ground, two hundred pounds of formidable, snarling Werewolf came flying from out of nowhere. The jarring force of impact knocked the sheikh back, just as Kate's energy blast had repelled both him and Layla earlier. With massive elongated jaws snapping and wickedly sharp claws slashing, Zack threw himself at al-Rashid.

Styx caught the scent of Vampyre blood a sparse moment before the Rogue disappeared in that menacing cloud of black mist. Before either Styx or Zack could react, the mist slithered across the ground, shielding Layla from them. When the mist rose into the air and shot around the side of the building, Layla was gone.

Styx's knees nearly buckled with relief. Not that he didn't think he could have held his own—because, beyond a doubt he would have...somehow—but, whatever Kate's energy blast had done to his system still had yet to wear off. He was weak as a babe.

Zack threw his head back on his shoulders and howled his disappointment to the night sky. He'd had the Rogue in his clutches...had Vampyre blood on his teeth...and he'd lost him. His great chest heaving, Zack slowly turned to face Styx. The expression on his transformed features was ferocious.

Styx held his hands up, palms out. Body tensing, he took a shaky step to the side, placing himself squarely between Kate and danger once more. The only thing that might well rival a Vampyre protecting his mate...was a pissed-off Werewolf.

And Zack was defiantly pissed-off.

"Whoa buddy," Styx cajoled. "Calm down, man. It's over...they're gone."

The last thing he wanted to do right now was tussle with Zack. Especially not in his weakened condition. A Werewolf fully *morphed* was a danger to anyone around him, friend or foe. Logic fell by the wayside, reason was nearly nonexistent as Were instinct took over. And, to make matters all the more precarious, Werewolf bites were as good as poison to Vampyre. At best, the wound would fester painfully, becoming severely infected, causing debilitating weakness for an indeterminate amount of time. At worst...given the severity of the attack...a long and excruciating death. Indeed, shy of beheading, a stake to the heart, or full exposure to the sun's lethal UV rays, Werewolf attacks were about the only other option for killing Vampyre.

Zack flexed his hands, lethal claws clacking, as he took an intimidating step forward. Styx half-crouched, preparing himself for another battle...without trying to *look* like he was preparing for battle. *Dios*, he needed to get to Kate, needed to get her to safety. Make sure she wasn't seriously injured. He did *not* have time to be playing at calm the Werewolf. Glancing over his shoulder, he stole a fleeting glimpse of Kate. She had yet to move. Damn it.

He eyed the opening of the alley. More than likely, he could snatch her up and flee with her before Zack realized what had happened. Given how his knees wobbled though, he wasn't altogether certain if he'd be able to get far enough away before Zack caught up to them. And then there was the complication of innocent Humans. A *lot* of innocent Humans. Humans who had absolutely zero defense against an enraged Werewolf...and would be directly in Zack's line of fire should Styx attempt to whisk Kate to safety.

Running was out of the question.

*Okay...calm the Werewolf it is.*

"Zack, man, it's me...Styx." He sent up a silent prayer to the Holy Mother. *Please...let this work.*

"Zack, you have to calm down. You have to focus...the threat is gone."

Zack paused, shook his head, scowling. He blinked at Styx, pressed a massive fist to his temple, and shook his head again as if he'd somehow been dazed. And, for the first time since six and a half feet of towering, bulked-up, pissed-off Werewolf turned his way, Styx began to hope. "That's right, Zack. It's me. It's Styx. Come back to us, man."

By slow, harrowing degrees, Zack gradually regained control of himself. The wild, animalistic characteristics steadily receded, until Zack once again stood before Styx in Humanlike form. His clothing hung in tattered shreds from his chiseled body.

"You okay?" Zack's weary gaze traveled quickly from the top of Styx's head to the tips of his toes. Then his gaze shot to Kate. His eyes widened, horror filled his countenance. "Bloody hell, I didn't—"

"No, man," Styx rushed to reassure him. "You didn't do this to her. You got here just in the nick of time. Much as it bites to say this...you saved my ass, Zack. I owe you one, man."

Zack mumbled something as he turned away, shoulders hunched, head bowed, fists pressed to his temples. He'd once told Styx that Were instinct was nearly impossible to resist. Especially after he'd *morphed* back from Were form, it was still difficult...at least initially...not to give in to the urges ravaging his body. Urges to maim. Urges to kill. Urges that sometimes left the always rational, always controlled Zack shaken to the core...and sickened with self-disgust. When in the Were state, there was no black and white, no defining line between good and evil, innocent and guilty.

No conscience whatsoever.

The guilt always came later.

Setting his worry for his friend aside, albeit

temporarily, Styx hurried back to Kate. With infinite care, he cradled her body and gently turned her over. A fine trickle of fresh blood seeped from one nostril. The sight of that blood, the smell of it sent a shudder of need through his injured body. But he fiercely suppressed the natural impulse tearing at his control. The compulsion of a wounded Vampyre in need of blood to heal. The overwhelming hungers of a mate whose *Bride's* blood called to him on a wholly fundamental level. He'd nearly lost her tonight...lost her before he'd even had the chance to claim her as his own. Somehow that knowledge took the edge off his hungers and brought sanity to the beast within.

Her skin was beyond pale...almost chalky. But she didn't appear to have a scratch on her. Straining his senses, he focused acutely on her physical well-being. Her pulse was still faint, her breathing much too shallow for his liking. Why hadn't she regained consciousness yet? What he wouldn't give to be able to reach her on a subconscious level right now.

"Kate," he called softly, scooping her up in his arms. Resting her head against his shoulder, he cupped her cheek in his palm, ran the pad of his thumb tenderly over the lush fullness of her lower lip. *"Te necesito."* *I need you.* "Please, *querida*, wake up for me."

Still her eyes remained closed. Not so much as a flutter of lashes. Desperation swelled. What if she never woke up again? What if the energy she'd somehow summoned...the power she'd somehow unleashed...had damaged something inside her? What if she never came back to him? Never smiled at him...never laughed again? Never caught the tip of her tongue between her pearly Human teeth while she concentrated fiercely on something...anything?

Styx went utterly still as he stared down at her face, floored by what he'd just discovered in himself.

*¡Estoy enamorado!* That one simple sentence

circled in his brain like a swarm of bees. *I am in love.*

Stunned, he pulled her closer, holding her as if he'd never let her go. How was it possible that he'd existed all this time with nary a glimpse of that sweet emotion? Oh, lust he'd had aplenty. But love— the love a man feels for his woman, that rare and most precious passion—had eluded him century upon century. In such a short space of time, this one delicate female had turned his world upside down.

*But was it truly love? Was she really the Bride he'd been praying for?*

*Yes,* his heart immediately chided him.

*Would he lay down his life for her?*

*Without a second thought,* his soul vowed.

*Would he kill for her?*

*In a heartbeat,* the beast inside him pledged.

*Now that he'd found her, could he continue to exist without her? Would he even want to try?*

Stealing one of Zack's more favored exclamations, his being as a whole replied, *Not bloody likely.*

A fierce wave of tenderness washed over him as Styx half-smiled, half-scowled down at the woman in his arms. His female...

His *Bride.*

Chapter 12

Disoriented, Kate squeezed her eyes tightly closed. A soft moan escaped her lips, and she cringed as the sound reverberated through her brain like the crash of a gong. What happened? She struggled to piece all the fragments of her treacherous memory together as a killer migraine from hell threatened to shred what was left of her brain. It was as if someone were raking nails over a chalkboard inside her skull. Hell, her skull *was* the chalkboard. And the nails were forged from pure steel.

And yet, for all the pain, her body hummed with a perplexing, restless energy. She felt as if she could win the Boston Marathon just now. As if—were she not being held so tightly—she might well fly through the air.

Those strong arms holding her shifted, and Kate had the fleeting sensation of vertigo. The world tilted around her for a moment, then she was gently cradled against a rock-hard, warm chest. Fighting down an unexpected wave of nausea, she tentatively squinched one eye open. Where was she? What had happened?

Glimpses of images, flashes of lingering emotion pulsed through her mind, faster and faster.

*A woman...*

Yes, there'd been a woman...a mysterious woman with bizarre, wild eyes. The woman had threatened her. Layla... She'd said her name was Layla. And fear. She'd been so afraid.

*And the wind...*

Her lips parted, and she sucked in a shaky

breath as she recalled the wind, and the surge of power. She didn't know where it had come from, didn't know how she'd controlled it...or if *it* had controlled *her*...but, somehow, the power had been there all the same.

Just as it had on that long ago day when her father had died...albeit much, much stronger this time.

Resolutely pushing that chilling thought from her mind, Kate focused her tactile senses. The air was chilly, and damp. And yet soothing warmth wrapped itself around her. No, wait...the warmth was familiar. She'd recognize that warmth...and that scent...anywhere. *Nico*... Nico held her in his arms. The night was oddly quiet, except for the harsh breathing near the top of her head and the pounding thud of a racing heartbeat beneath her ear.

And erratic, labored pants from a short distance away.

"Nico?" She sounded weak, even to her own ears, and yet she couldn't seem to harness that restless energy thrumming in her muscles in order to level her tone.

All motion abruptly ceased.

That ragged panting continued.

"Kate?" Nico's tortured voice washed over her in shades of anxiety and relief, anger and...and something far more tender.

Then, beneath her cheek—and all around her— his body tensed. An explosive string of Spanish spewed forth, stabbing at her sensitive eardrums like ice picks, and she winced. Her Spanish was rusty at best. However, she was reasonably positive she'd never learned *those* particular words in a classroom environment. Cool air rushed by her once more. Why was he running again? The bouncing jarred her stomach, which, in turn, threatened to rebel at any moment.

"Stop...running..." she gasped. Then Kate clapped a hand over her mouth and squeezed her eyes tightly closed. Motion abruptly ceased once more. Damn it...these sudden stops and starts were seriously messing with the steely self-control she prided herself on when faced with even the most gory of medical emergencies in the ER.

The strange ragged panting caught up with them. Nico's furious Spanish mutterings lowered in decibel, but continued on without missing a beat. When she lowered her hand from her mouth and nodded, in control once more, the motion resumed, albeit at a slightly less hectic pace. The ragged panting trailed behind.

What the hell was that anyway? *Who* was it?

New sounds filled her ears. Doors opening and closing, the murmur of voices, the ding of an elevator. Light and shadows shifted and danced behind her closed eyelids. Movement shifted from forward motion to straight up, and still she didn't dare open her eyes. She refused to even try until he'd put her down. Then, at least, if she got sick, she stood a reasonable chance of not barfing all over him.

The elevator dinged again, doors slid open, and forward motion resumed. More doors opening and closing, and then motion changed. Down she went. Soft cushions met her descent. And still Nico's warmth remained, his scent never left her. He held her hand now in one of his while his other hand softly brushed the hair back from her forehead, feathered over her cheek. His hand left her hair and fingers pressed against the racing pulse at the side of her throat.

At last, she screwed up her courage and forced her eyelids open.

Nico's handsome, worried visage hovered

directly above her face. Troubled amber eyes scanned her face, then his burning gaze bore into hers. "Kate? Are you all right? Talk to me, damn it. What happened out there? Why the hell did you rush off like that? Do you know what could have happened to you? Do you have any idea how much danger you put yourself in?" The furious Spanish tirade started all over again.

Cringing, Kate closed her eyes.

"Damn it, woman, open your eyes. Don't you leave me again! Talk to me," he ordered.

"She might try if you shut your bloody mouth for one damn minute," interrupted a hoarse voice from somewhere on the other side of the room.

Collin? Collin was here? Had *he* been the source of the ragged panting?

Opening her eyes again, she blinked up at Nico's now scowling face.

"Talk to me, *querida*," Nico pleaded.

*Sweetheart...* Her heart did a little stutter step inside her chest. She knew enough Spanish to interpret that word. *He'd called her sweetheart.*

"I'm, I'm okay...I think." Better. Her voice didn't shake that time.

"What were you thinking? Rushing off like that?" Anger again. Disappointment settled like dead weight on her chest. She should have known better than to read too much into that endearment.

And then the reason she'd rushed off in the first place came flooding back. The ER...

"Oh, hell..." She struggled to sit up, but Nico gently pushed her back down on the sofa. She blinked, scanning the shadow-enshrouded room. His apartment. "I have to go...the ER..."

"Fuck the ER," he exploded again, raking an unsteady hand through messy hair. That was when she finally noticed all the blood drenching his shirt, the violent scratches scoring the side of his cheek, and the nasty gash on the side of his neck.

"Oh, my God!" Adrenaline shot through her veins. She surged to a sitting position, knocking his hands away when he would have restrained her again. She swung her legs up and around, planting her feet firmly on the floor as she reached relentlessly for him. "You're hurt, Nico. Let me see your neck," she demanded evenly. At last, she'd mastered her control. It seemed a medical crisis always had that effect on her.

"I'm fine," he muttered, pushing irritably at her questing hands. He scrambled backward, then sprang to his feet. She followed him every scrabbling step.

His pupils appeared to be slightly dilated, but, then again, the room was dark and she didn't have a penlight to check for certain. Kate stretched two fingers toward his neck, but he ducked away like a prizefighter. If he'd just hold still long enough maybe she could get an accurate pulse. He'd lost a lot of blood by the looks of his shirt. His complexion looked a little pale. Kate clapped a hand to his forehead. Clammy. He dodged her hand again, but she caged his face between her cupped hands, careful of his injuries. Drawing his head down and to the side, she peered intently at the scratches on his cheek. Bleeding...but superficial.

*Perhaps a topical to prevent infection... Hard telling what that creature had had under her nails. Definitely a topical...and oral antibiotics as well.*

That gash on his neck was far more troublesome.

*Definitely needs sutures and an injection of—*

"Stop it," Nico barked, shrugging away as she peeled the edge of his torn shirt from the seeping wound. She flat out ignored the deep, hoarse chuckles emanating from the far corner of the room, making a mental note to speak to Nico's roommate later about his lack of compassion.

"Damn it, Kate. Leave it alone..." Twisting to the side, Nico pulled away once more. "It's nothing more than a scratch."

Like hell it was nothing more than a scratch. She'd caught more than one fleeting glimpse of his ravaged flesh. Losing her patience, Kate snapped, "Hold still, you big baby."

Collin's roar of laughter echoed in the apartment as he settled himself on the recliner. He wasn't looking so hot himself, come to think of it. His clothes were freshly pressed, as if he'd just pulled them on, but his hair was mussed and he, too, sported scratches on his face. Unlike Nico, Collin's complexion was flat out ashen. Well, he wouldn't be laughing for long. As soon as she finished with Nico, he would be next on her proverbial exam table.

Kate shot him a warning glare. The two of them were behaving like a couple of little boys. One bent on avoiding medical treatment for a booboo, the other taking childish glee at his friend's cowardice. Catching the tip of her tongue between her teeth, she relentlessly followed Nico across the room. Honestly. She'd seen five year olds who'd face needles with more courage.

Which immediately brought back her responsibilities.

*Damn it...*

Kate pulled her cell phone from her pocket and flipped it open, temporarily giving up the chase. Before she managed to punch in the first number, she realized the phone was dead. What on earth? The battery had been fully charged when she'd left the apartment. Of that she was sure. She always made a point of checking the charge before stepping outside the apartment.

*Huh...*

"I need to borrow a phone," she said to the room

at large. "Mine's dead."

"Why?" Nico's suspicious question caught her off guard.

"Well, for starters, I need to call the ER and tell them I won't be in…at least, not right away—"

"Not at *all* tonight," Nico disagreed. "You've been through enough. They can find someone else to help out this time."

The look she shot him clearly contested his domineering order, but she wasn't about to get into a debate right now. "I also need to call the police."

That brought an immediate end to Zack's laughter. He came to the edge of his seat. Nico, too, responded oddly. He snatched the worthless phone from her hand…as if he feared it would suddenly regain a charge from out of the blue. "You don't need to do that."

"Yes," she contradicted. "I do. That psycho is still out there somewhere. She might hurt someone else."

Nico remained strangely quiet for a moment. She could all but see the cogs turning in his mind. Then he calmly replied, "Okay, look. You can call the ER…tell them you can't come in." His gaze cut to Zack, who immediately settled back in his chair. "I'll call the police."

"But I'm—"

"You were passed out cold most of the time. I saw more than you did. I should be the one to call them."

Heat swamped her cheeks. How much *had* he seen? She chewed her lower lip in indecision for a moment before relenting. "Fine."

"Zack, give her your phone." Nico stared at her phone for a moment, then frowned up at her. "You shouldn't be walking around with a dead battery. It's not safe. If I hadn't come along when I did, you wouldn't have been able to call for help."

His censure pricked her temper. Did he think she was scatterbrained? Incompetent? He couldn't have offended her more had he accused her of sleeping on the job. "I always keep it charged," she replied hotly. "It was fully charged when I left the apartment earlier."

"Well, it's dead now."

"Maybe the battery's going bad."

Scowling, his gaze dropped from her to the phone in his hand, then lifted to her once again. Then, like a riotous rollercoaster ride, his facial expressions ran a gambit of emotions. The slow build up of confusion, the interminable cresting of consideration, the wild drop of tumultuous speculation. And the final, gentler slopes of revelation.

Uncomfortable with the assessing stare he now leveled at her, Kate turned away to accept Zack's offered phone. The sooner she put this call through, the sooner she could take care of Nico's wounds.

And this time she wouldn't take no for an answer, wouldn't put up with his childish behavior.

She stepped away and placed the call. A few moments later, however, she returned the phone to Zack with a troubled frown. Nico had left the room while she's dialed the ER, presumably to make his own phone call to the police.

Nico came back inside the room just as Zack's curious gaze locked on her face, and he asked, "What's wrong?"

Kate gnawed on her lower lip, confused.

Nico stepped closer. His large, warm hand settled proprietarily on her lower back. "Kate?"

"I, I'm not sure..." She turned a puzzled stare to Nico. "They never called me in."

"What?" He thrust his own phone back into his pocket. He'd changed his shirt and cleaned away the blood from his face and neck. Good grief, she hadn't realized she'd been on the phone that long...

*Not more than a few minutes, at most...*

"What do you mean they didn't call you in?" Zack rose from the chair, thrust his hands in his back pockets and rocked back on his heels.

"Mindy said no one from the ER called me. She even double-checked with the other nurses on duty. No one called me. She said there'd been no accident as far as she knew...in fact, the ER was abnormally quiet for a Saturday."

"Then who called you?"

"I have no idea."

Nico looked as if he thought about saying something more, but he seemed to change his mind. Curious as she was, Kate was hesitant to probe, fearful that if she were to start asking more questions, he, in turn, might begin to ask questions of his own. Questions she was unable to answer...at least not without sounding completely insane. So she let the matter drop. Her gaze fell to the red welts on his cheek.

*Wait...those had been scratches before, with broken skin. Hadn't they?*

Without waiting for permission, she quickly reached up and tugged the spotless collar of his shirt down and away from his injury. Bright red, raw grooves marred his golden flesh. Her eyes flared, and she gaped up at him. Where were the deep gashes she'd seen earlier?

Those wounds should have required sutures. She knew what she'd seen, trusted her earlier diagnosis. Blinking, she staggered back a step. Had she been seeing things that weren't there? Had it finally happened?

She'd lost her mind.

Cracked.

Gone round the loony bin.

That strange woman's eerie eyes...had they only

been an illusion cooked up by Kate's over-worked mind? And the wind... the inexplicable power surge in the alley...nothing more than a figment of her imagination? But she'd never misdiagnosed a patient before.

*Or had she?*

What about that boy in the accident just last night? She'd pushed the incident ruthlessly from her mind, buried it down deep. But now she couldn't pretend any longer—couldn't act as if it hadn't happened, like she'd vigilantly ignored all those *other* inexplicable occurrences over the years.

She hadn't believed the boy would survive those first few harrowing moments when they'd placed him on the table in front of her, no matter what she did. With bleeders to numerous to count, and organs damaged beyond repair she'd counted him among the bodies to be forwarded on to the morgue. For a split second, she'd been daunted by the sheer magnitude of his injuries. He had been so young...too young to die. And she'd seen so many die already. Weary, she closed her eyes and dipped her head, her hands hovering over his gaping chest for a split second.

That strange hum in her veins had been there that night too. Not as strong as in the alley, but, elementally it had felt much the same.

Suddenly—without any viable, logical explanation—the boys vitals had spiked, his bleeders suddenly stopped without aid. Wounds that were irreparable before she'd closed her eyes suddenly required only a few stitches. She'd been too stunned to do more than shift into autopilot and let her training take over. Hadn't that been a misdiagnosis of sorts? Or had she just been so tired that she'd—

No. She knew better than to pick apart every decision she made on shift. Many a good doctor had fallen prey to self-doubt and second-guesses.

"You're neck—"

"It was just a scratch...like I told you before." Nico self-consciously tugged his shirt back into place. Clearing his throat, he moved farther away. "I called the police. They'll send someone over later...to take...ah, statements." Nodding to himself, he plugged her phone into the charger on the counter. "Why don't you go in and lay down for a little while. I'm sure you could use the rest."

Grimacing, she glanced down at her grungy clothes. "I'll go back to my place. I could use a shower."

"You can take one here."

"Don't be ridiculous. I don't have any clean clothes. I'll just—"

"No, you won't. You will stay here," he growled. Why was he suddenly staring at her with such a fierce...intent expression? Did he think glaring at her would change her mind?

Shaking her head, Kate opened her mouth to argue, but, with an oddly frustrated expression, he cut her off. "I'll worry until we speak to the police. Please...just stay here for now. You can shower here...I'll go next door and grab a change of clothes for you...and then you can rest in my room while we wait."

She didn't really want to be alone right now anyway. Why was she arguing so much?

Conceding with a slight nod of the head, Kate followed Nico into one of the doors in the hallway. The bedroom smelled like Nico. Spicy. Pure male with a capitol M. Heavy drapes were pulled tight over the windows, leaving the room cloaked in darkness. He flipped on a light switch dispelling the shadows.

"Bathroom's through there," he informed her, indicating another door to her right. "You should be able to find whatever you need. I'll be right back with your stuff."

And then he disappeared, leaving her to her own devices. Fatigue hit her like a brick wall. On trembling legs, Kate stepped inside the bathroom and closed the door behind her. Operating on pure instinct alone...instinct that had kept her going through the typical sleep deprivation of a medical education and career...Kate stripped down and stepped beneath the steaming spray of hot water. Shivering the chill from her bones, Kate straightened her arms, braced her palms on the shower wall, and dropped her head forward, sighing gratefully as the water pounded her flesh.

As always, she used the shower as therapy of sorts, washing away the strains of the day. Even so, the lingering fatigue refused to leave her. She was drained, all the way to the core. The scent of Nico's soap and shampoo lulled her senses, and a strange warmth seeped through her body, originating somewhere in the middle of her chest.

Feeling human once more, Kate turned off the water. Stepping from the shower, she dried off and then wrapped the huge, plush bath towel around her body, leaving her damp, tangled hair loose around her shoulders. As she picked up her dirty clothes, her key ring tumbled from her pocket, clinking against the tile floor.

*Wonderful...*

She'd forgotten to give him her keys. Well, she'd just wait in his room while he went to her place to get her clothes. But she wasn't going to lay down and take a nap as he'd ordered. She needed to speak to the police, give them her statement.

And she needed to figure out who in the hell had called her, claiming to be from the ER. Had it been a prank? If so, how had they gotten her unlisted number?

The disconcerting questions jumbling in her

mind promptly dissipated as she returned to the bedroom and found a clean change of her own clothing neatly piled on the foot of Nico's bed. Stepping forward, she lifted the familiar, tatty sweatshirt she still had from her time at Tulane. Beneath that was her *Def Leopard* T-shirt...God how she loved those old, big-hair rock bands...and a pair of worn jeans. Typical man that he was, he'd completely bypassed the sports bra and plain panties she preferred to wear on her days off, and went straight for the Saturday night special. Black silk and lace. She picked up the scraps of silk, and her cheeks flushed. He'd been in her underwear drawer. How embarrassing.

*How intimate—*

Abruptly killing that train of thought, Kate dropped the panties and bra back on the pile of clothes.

*Oh...*

He'd even brought her own hairbrush and deodorant. His thoughtfulness touched her...until she glanced at the keys still lying in the palm of her hand.

*How in the world had he gotten into her apartment?*

Chapter 13

He rocked back on his haunches. Pain sliced through his body as he gingerly lifted his tattered shirt from his shredded ribcage. Pale moonlight filtered down through the dense treetops over head, illuminating the ragged wounds. The claws of his left hand dug into firm soil. His fist clenched down hard on grass and dirt as he bore down against the agony. The wounds, coated with Were saliva, throbbed worse than any other combination of injuries he'd sustained in the three long centuries of his life.

*Damn his distraction...*

*Damn the Werewolf...*

Dropping his head back on his shoulders, he let out a furious roar. The few nocturnal, woodland creatures that had only just made a tentative return to their hunting grounds, promptly fled in a rush of muffled sound. Vegetation quickly fell silent in their wake.

*Damn Layla, this was all her fault...*

How could she have been so foolish? Why hadn't she waited for him to return? Why had she taken it upon herself to attempt to procure Johara for him? He should have known better than to trust a female to follow directions. They were an impatient and greedy lot.

*Should have left her in that alley to face the Werewolf alone...*

As soon as that thought crossed his mind, he choked it back. Remorse swelled, competing with bitter disappointment. Layla had just been eager to please him. She was young and hadn't realized the danger she'd placed them both in.

And he would have regretted it if he'd left her behind.

Perhaps he'd been too indulgent with her, granted her too much independence. Even though his Layla was different, a rare lily among a bouquet of roses, he needed to remember that she—like the rest of the females he'd kept—needed a firm, guiding hand. The others—the ones who'd let him down—hadn't been worth the time or the effort to guide. How disappointed he'd been that they hadn't lived up to his expectations.

But really, those disappointments were trivial. More a nuisance than anything...time lost hunting, time lost choosing, and the gift of Immortality wasted—thrown back in his face. Ungrateful wretches. He wouldn't focus on any of that now though. After all, in the greater scheme of things, the successes far outweighed the failures.

Human females were notoriously difficult to change. Something in their chemical make-up, no doubt. Oh sure, in the beginning he'd struggled, just as others had done. Failure was a necessary part of perfecting a skill. Like a science experiment, if you will. His lips twisted in a wry grimace. His Johara would appreciate that analogy. She herself was a scientist, wasn't she? Didn't *she* have a hunger of her own to hold power over life and death? In essence, wasn't that what she did every time she entered that hospital emergency room? Did she not look death in the eye and sneer? Did she not fight to lengthen her patients' lives with her knowledge? Their ambitions were one and the same. To give life to those who would otherwise cease to exist. How happy she would be when he granted her that ultimate power.

As far as he was concerned, *he* hadn't failed. He just hadn't known what to look for in the females early on. And those that hadn't survived the change...well, they just hadn't been worthy. Where other Vampyre without the thirst and the drive to reach out and take what they wanted had given up...or been too timid to try in the first place...he'd persevered. Now he knew what to look for, what combination of traits provided the best probability for success. His dedication was certainly commendable, his numerous triumphs surely a sign of divine blessing.

He would have to teach Layla her limitations though. Clarify that *he* was master, and that she *would* follow his instructions from here on out. Much as he hated to do it, he would have to punish her. After all, disobedience could not be tolerated. Disobedience undermined authority...set a bad example for the others.

Grimacing, he removed the rest of his torn, soiled shirt and settled on his knees near the gentle stream. Lingering like that when he'd been so severely wounded—even if only in mist form—to conceal Layla while she'd made good her escape had sorely taxed his strength. He would have been severely displeased had he lost her though. Unfortunately, as in any time while in mist form, he'd been unable to inflict injury to the Werewolf, or to that bastard Styx. Indeed, while in mist form, he could do little more than observe and, like in the alley with Layla, conceal.

Upon his arrival, he had been shocked—and not a little curious—as to why Layla hadn't already taken Styx out. As a newborn, she certainly possessed the strength and the speed. While he undoubtedly appreciated her restraint—he so looked forward to feeling the Spaniard's blood gush over his own fangs as he tore the bastard's throat out— survival instinct alone should have overridden her control. Then again, maybe she'd already sensed the

Werewolf's approach.

Allah knew he lacked the strength to track her down just now. She may have gone off to lick her wounds alone, but she would return to him. Sooner or later, they always did. But once she returned, Layla would have a substantial number of questions to answer. Beginning with how she'd come to be in that alley with his enemy—and his beautiful Johara—in the first place.

Tonight had been an exercise in disappointment. He'd certainly not expected to find Styx with Johara...defending her as if she belonged to *him*. The Spaniard's arrogance new no boundaries.

He should never have left her alone for so long. Going north to claim the last female could have waited. He'd wanted to give Johara more time to adjust. And in doing so—in stepping outside his normal way of doing things—he'd put her in danger...exposed her to Styx. Well, not this time. He'd be damned before he let Styx dishonor his harem again. Styx would die first. He couldn't blame Johara. She didn't know any better. She simply didn't know what Styx was.

*The corrupt, womanizing, deceitful bastard...*

Bending to dip the unshredded portion of his shirt in the stream, he hissed as pain lashed through his side. Again and again, he repeated the torture. He had to remove as much of the Were saliva as he could before it soaked in to his system. The wound would be bad enough to deal with as it was. No sense risking an even worse infection. Unlike any other flesh wounds which didn't even require cleansing— and regardless the amount of blood he consumed— these wounds would take days to fully heal. More time lost to Styx.

More risk to his Johara...

The pain was excruciating. He could already feel Were saliva eating away at the soft tissue at the edge of the ragged wound like acid. Allah, what he wouldn't give for a vial of Wolfsbane brew. This was what he got for not anticipating every possibility. Nonetheless, while both races were on amiable terms, who would have ever guessed that a Werewolf would put himself at risk in defense of a Vampyre?

Dip the shirt. Ring the water out. Wipe. Bear down. He used the image of Johara to center himself through the difficult process. He would save her. Surely, Styx hadn't had time to ply his deceitful ways upon her innocent soul yet.

Dare he risk seeking out a witch to obtain a vial of Wolfsbane extract? Could he afford more lost time?

Dare he not?

He no longer had the luxury of time on his side now. The wooing of Johara had officially been cut short. One more thing Styx had taken from him.

One more thing for which Styx would pay.

And that, perhaps was the bitterest pill to swallow. Styx's tainting of Johara's initiation into his family. In many ways, Johara reminded him of his first wife Kali. So gentle. So beautiful and delicate. She'd been the sunshine in his day. Her smiles and laughter had always been a comfort to him. And she'd known her place. She'd been among his most favored. Even after nearly a decade of marriage, she'd always left him well sated in the bedchamber, and content with every other aspect of her presence. Few of his other wives could boast the same. Oh, how it had devastated him to learn of her dishonor. He'd never known such torment, such emotional turmoil.

But honor came before all else.

Ending Kali's disgrace—killing Kali—had been the hardest thing he'd ever done.

Resentment boiled like caustic acid through his veins. Just as quickly, his vision blurred and a wave of dizziness washed over him. He needed to feed...badly.

There would be no more time to replace the women Styx and that bastard friend of his had taken from him. No more time to find suitable females for his harem. He would find no rest until that abomination that called himself Styx no longer walked this earth.

Shifting into mist form once more took far greater effort than he could ever have imagined. He shot across the wooded landscape—an unnatural shadow that sent intuitive creatures scurrying for sanctuary—until the natural forests yielded to the concrete jungle. He found his nourishment quickly, without fanfare or deference. Cold and unfeeling, he claimed the first vein he came to in the shadows of a dirty alley similar to the one in which he'd faced off against Styx and the Werewolf.

Injured so critically, one vein wasn't enough. Only as the third lifeless body slid to the pavement at his feet did he begin to feel the searing burn as cells merged and flesh mended. And still it wasn't enough. Vengeance stoked to life inside him, flaming through his body. Stepping over the lifeless vessel—a vessel good for nothing more than nourishment—his eyes smoldering, fully transformed, he strode into the night in search of more prey to sate the unquenchable thirst burning in his belly like wildfire.

He would not rest now...not until he had Vampyre blood dripping from his hands.

****

Styx's nostrils flared. Without a glance in Zack's direction, he paced across the living area, down the hallway, and jerked the door open. Crispin hadn't knocked yet, but Styx would recognize the familiar scent anywhere. The agent stood motionless on the other side of the portal, hands thrust deep in his pockets, his trench coat thrust back over his hips and out of the way.

Without a word of acknowledgement or welcome, he spun on his heel and stomped back down the hallway, Crispin close on his heels.

"Where's the female?"

"Kate's in the shower," Styx snapped, annoyed beyond reason by Crispin's stubborn refusal to acknowledge Kate as an individual. "She'll be out soon so we won't have much time. She thinks you're with the local police force...here to take her statement."

Crispin grunted in response and made himself comfortable on the recliner. He drew a silver pen and the slim black notepad from his inner breast pocket and flipped the cover open. Across the room, Zack set an empty beer can down on the kitchen counter and cracked the top on another, lifted it to his lips without a word. The crazed look had left his blue eyes, thank heavens. But his hands still shook, and he kept rubbing at his temples, grimacing with pain every now and again.

Styx could hear Zack's stomach growling from clear across the room, and he stifled the urge to shake his head. Hell, at least *he* wasn't personally footing the Werewolf's food bill. The way that boy ate could decimate the life savings of even the most affluent of Immortals.

"Your Collector is Sheikh Amir Kazim al-Rashid," Styx barked without preamble.

The TFRA agent arched a brow but remained silent as he continued to pen his notes.

"And he's a shade."

That got Crispin's undivided attention...Zack's too. Their stunned gazes whipped to Styx. It took a long, long moment for the imperturbable agent to contain the look of alarm swimming in his deep brown eyes.

Drawing an uneven breath, Crispin lowered his notepad and his pen to his lap. "You're sure?"

"Kinda hard to miss," Styx snapped, then turned away to gaze at the shadows on the street below. "I don't have any idea who his Sire is...or where he's been all this time. But he's definitely a shade...of that I have absolutely no doubts whatsoever." Styx quickly recounted the incident in the alley—glossing over the surprising revelation of Kate's powers—up to and including the moment al-Rashid shifted into shadow-mist and all but blinded them as Layla made good her escape.

The sound of muffled running water abruptly ceased, and Styx's gaze darted to the still-closed bedroom door. Did he dare trust his suspicions about Kate being half-Faerie with the agent? Crispin knew his own secrets...and, thus far, had proven trustworthy. But revealing something so crucial about his female to someone of Crispin's chosen profession set his teeth on edge.

And yet, who better to get the answers he needed than this male who seemingly had a source for any and every situation?

"There's more..." *God help Crispin if this came back to bite Styx in the ass.* "Kate's half-Faerie."

"*Buggar me,*" Zack gasped. Beer sprayed across the work surface of the kitchen's island as he fumbled his beer can and coughed, pounding on his chest.

"What?" Again, that uncharacteristic, alarmed expression from Crispin. Damn, two for two. This night was just chock full of surprises.

The apartment door rattled beneath the weight of a fist, breaking the sudden tension choking the room. Crispin glanced at the door, his nostrils flared slightly, and he tensed.

"About goddamned time," Zack muttered as he prowled down the hallway. He returned a moment later, two large pizza boxes stacked on his palm, and Crispin subsided back in the chair. The scent of sausage, pepperoni, and double cheese filled the room. Styx watched as Zack flipped the lid open on the top box, scooped up a steaming slice, and all but shoved the whole thing into his mouth.

"I'm sure about Kate, too…or reasonably confident." Crossing his arms over his chest, Styx braced his feet apart and drew a deep breath. "She manipulated the winds tonight…called down some kind of electrical storm and knocked both me and Layla on our collective asses."

"I was wondering what the bloody hell was wrong with you when I first got there," Zack mumbled around a mouthful of food.

"I don't know how it affected Layla, but Kate's little energy blast threw me for a loop. It was all I could do to get my feet back under me, much less fight."

"Well this certainly complicates things, doesn't it?" Crispin's gaze slid to the bedroom door, his expression assessing.

"I don't think she has any idea about what she is. She didn't seem to have much control, knocked herself completely out there at the end."

And that didn't sit well, either. She'd been completely vulnerable. If he hadn't been there—

"I'll do some digging. See what I can find."

"Keep it quiet," Styx ordered. "The last thing I need right now is some controlling, conceited Faerie clan showing up trying to claim her."

*Dios*, he wouldn't even let himself consider *that* horrifying prospect.

Crispin grunted, nodding agreement, his expression inscrutable. "About what we discussed on the phone…" He darted a brief glance at the otherwise occupied Zack, then leveled a serious look at Styx. "Have you given it anymore thought? I really think it would be helpful. If fact, given all these unexpected complications, it might be the wisest course of action."

*Dream walking...*

Easy enough for Crispin to suggest. He didn't know the dangers Kate might face. Then a niggling question formed in the back of his brain and refused to go away.

"With Kate being a Halfling...is it even possible for her to be changed to Vampyre?"

"I honestly don't know if it would be possible or not. For all we know, she could already be Immortal. A Vampyre Faerie...a Vampyre with the ability to control and manipulate the elements—call down an electrical storm, Christ Almighty...who's to say how that scenario might unfold." Crispin shifted in his seat, tucking the notepad and pen back inside his pocket. "Then again, I've never heard of any Faerie consorting with a Human before either. So I guess anything's possible. As to the Immortal theory, shy of inflicting a life-threatening wound—" Styx's abrupt, venomous snarl cut the sentence short. Crispin continued on in a slightly more reserved tone, "Her blood should be the best indicator."

"Her blood is Human," Styx admitted, then conceded uneasily, "for the most part."

Crispin arched a brow and tilted his head to the side, as if struggling to decide which point he'd rather deal with first. The issue that her blood wasn't completely Human...or that Styx had firsthand knowledge of that fact.

He settled on the former.

"What do you mean...for the most part?"

"It's...it's like..." Styx trailed off, shaking his head, unable to put into words the heady, intoxicating addiction he felt for something he'd only tasted in a dream. No other Human had ever tasted so— "Forget it," he finally muttered, turning away from the disconcerting pair of rapt gazes centered on him. "Just see what you can come up with. And keep it under the table."

Crispin pushed to his feet and adjusted his trench coat. "I'll get right on it," he promised.

"She's going to be expecting to talk to you when she comes out," Styx reminded him.

Crispin stared hard at the bedroom for a moment, then turned back to Styx. "Interrogating her right now...isn't advisable. Tell her I was called away on official business. Tell her I took your statement and that's enough for now. If she insists on calling the police again, or going downtown to give her statement, use *persuasion* to dissuade her."

"Persuasion doesn't work on Kate," Styx admitted grudgingly.

Crispin's brows elevated slightly, but he remained impassive. "Give me a call then...we can always play out the charade if necessary."

He started down the hallway, then stopped and turned back. "Oh, and Styx... If she is a Halfling, you'd better treat her with kid gloves until we can get a handle on her powers. It sounds like she's just beginning to *phase*. You know as well as anyone, the Faerie Nation keeps to itself. Getting information about her parentage...hell, getting information about what to expect as far as her powers go...is going to be next thing to impossible. That power surge in the alley could be an anomaly. Or, it could be just the tip of the iceberg." His gaze slid to the bedroom door again, and he peered hard at the wood panel, concentrating with acute precision. "She needs to eat. She needs to rest now. She's drained, confused."

Styx frowned at Crispin's retreating back. The way he'd said that last bit, it was...eerie.

As one door closed, another opened. Pushing up the sleeves of her sweatshirt, Kate stepped into the living area. Though she smelled of his soap, her essence still punched him straight in the gut. Saliva surged in his mouth, and his fangs lengthened as thirst gnawed at his self-control.

His hungry gaze raked over her, from the top of her head to the tips of her toes. Her hair was still damp, curling in big, loose curls around her shoulders and down her back. Her skin was flawless, the light dusting of freckles only adding to the perfection. As his gaze continued its downward descent, he recalled the black scraps of nothing he'd pulled from her drawer.

His vision blurred for a moment, then sharpened painfully. As did his fangs.

The length of the room separating them disappeared, and suddenly her skin was beneath his fingertips. Warm. Soft. Compelling.

His gaze returned to her face, and his breath caught in the back of his throat. Crispin had been right. One had only to look into her eyes to see the emotion. Wary confusion. Exhaustion. Vulnerability.

With eyes glassy and bewildered, she looked like a lost orphan. Dark shadows smudged her eyes.

"You're too pale," he accused, frowning down at her. How had Crispin known?

"I'm fine." Even her voice trembled.

It was all he could do to keep himself from sweeping her off her feet so that he could tuck her into bed. *Kid gloves...*

"Did I hear voices out here? I didn't miss the detective, did I?"

"Actually, yes. He came in, I told him what happened, and then he received a call and said he had to leave. Official police business..." He'd never made a habit of lying to women, but neither had he shied away from stretching the truth to fit his needs when it came to females. Why then was it that with one glance of those gem-like eyes of hers, he had the worst urge to spill his guts? Confess all and plead forgiveness?

So this was what Cole had meant when he'd said Alex made him want to be a better male.

*Dios mio...this was going to take some getting used to.*

"Are you hungry?" Not waiting for her response, he glared at Zack just as the Werewolf reached for the second box of pizza. "She's hungry. Give her the pizza."

Kate laughed aloud as she crossed to stand at the counter beside Zack. "I certainly don't need all *that*! A slice or two would be nice though."

Grinning, Zack slid the box in front of her and the two of them ate in companionable silence until Kate noticed Styx had remained near the sofa. "Aren't you going to grab a bite?"

*I wish...*

"No...I'll," he cleared his throat and growled, "I'll grab something later." *Someone flavorless and ordinary when compared to the taste of you...*

As Kate polished off a second slice, Zack passed her a napkin. Thanking him, she dabbed at the corners of her delectable mouth and then wiped the grease from her fingers.

"Luv, you look exhausted," Zack informed her as he flung an arm over her shoulders. But his gaze was on Styx, his smile taunting. Did the Werewolf not realize he was courting death and dismemberment here?

A dark, threatening growl rumbled in the back of Styx's throat. His suddenly burning eyes narrowed.

"I'll be fine." Kate shrugged, but the color had yet to return to her cheeks.

"Don't be ridiculous," Zack replied, his voice dropping a seductive octave. "You should let me tuck you into bed."

The loss of life and limb obviously meant nothing to the idiot.

"That will be awfully difficult for you to do...without any hands," Styx warned. "Besides, she'll be sleeping in my bed. If anyone gets tucking privileges..." The grin he turned to Kate was utterly shameless. "It will be me."

Kate's brows lifted, and her gaze darted back and forth between Zack and him, much as she'd done that first time they'd met her. Lifting her hands, palms out, she half-smiled, half-frowned at each of them in turn as she stepped away from Zack and remarked, "There will be no tucking at all." Then she turned to Styx. "And I'm not sleeping with you...I mean, I won't be sleeping in your bed...with or without you..."

Color exploded in her cheeks. He hadn't realized it was possible for a Human...Halfling or otherwise...to flush that deep of a shade of scarlet so quickly. She was flustered.

*So adorable...*

"Yes, you will." He closed the distance between them once more and took her chin between his fingertips. Ignoring Zack's loud guffaws as the Werewolf retreated to his own room, Styx peered deep into her eyes. He focused hard, trying once more to use the voice of *persuasion*. "You will sleep here...in my bed."

"No, I won't," she insisted, pushing his hand away.

Scowling, Styx stomped after her as she crossed to the balcony. "Yes, you will. It's not safe for you to return home alone. Whoever called you and lured you out to that alley obviously knows enough about you to find you. I won't risk them finding you alone. I won't allow it."

She gasped, whirling around to face him, planting fists to hips. "You won't allow—"

"No, I won't allow it." He squared off with her, toe to toe...nose to nose. "Now, either you go back in there," he jabbed a finger toward the bedroom door, "and get some sleep. Or I'll come with you back to your place. But either way, I'm not leaving you alone." *Not ever again...*

"Why are you being so difficult about this?"

"Because keeping you safe has become my number one priority." He'd never meant anything more.

There was nothing more important to a Vampyre than his *Bride's* safety and well-being, her happiness. A Vampyre would give his life to defend his mate without a second's hesitation. If she thought for one minute he'd allow her to put herself in danger, she had another thing coming.

Kate stood motionless, staring at him with a bewildered expression. She sputtered for a moment, then whispered, "Why?"

Styx stared long and hard at her. How could she miss the emotion raging through his system. The unreasonable urge to shield and protect her from any and all possibilities of danger. The driving need to claim her. The overwhelming yearning to cherish and worship her.

*Dios*, he felt ready to explode with it.

Kate closed her eyes, bowed her head, and lifted a hand, pressing a palm to her temple. She swayed on her feet, and Styx's heart lurched inside his chest. Between one heartbeat and the next, he swept her off her feet and carried her back inside his bedroom.

She struggled to sit back up as he laid her down, but Styx would not be denied. With gentle insistence, Styx pushed her back on the bed.

"I'm not bending on this, *querida*." He drew a blanket from the foot of the bed and tucked it around her, ignoring her feeble sputtering. "You are ready to pass out. Sleep. You can yell at me when you wake up."

With one last token argument and an angry huff, Kate settled back on his pillow.

His scent surrounded her, making it nigh on to impossible to be angry for long.

"There now," he murmured, adjusting the blanket. "That's not so bad, is it?"

That earned him a healthy scowl. Ignoring it, Styx leaned forward and pressed a soft kiss to her forehead. Then he stood up and padded quietly to the door. He stole a quick glance over his shoulder to make sure she stayed where he'd put her, then he shut off the light and slipped from the room, closing the door behind him.

*Madre de Dios*, what it did to him to see her there in his bed...

The next time he got her there, he'd make damn sure she was in the kind of condition that allowed him to take advantage of the situation.

## Chapter 14

Styx paced the limitations of the living area. It would be dawn soon. Damn, he hated this forced confinement. He wanted to get out there, try to pick up some kind of trail. He needed answers...answers he wouldn't get sitting here spinning his wheels.

He also needed to feed. It had been longer than he cared to remember since the last time he'd gone out hunting, and being near Kate when he was this thirsty was far more difficult than he could ever have imagined. Dangerous. Logically speaking, she'd be safe enough with Zack. The Werewolf was more than capable of protecting her. And, given the fact that Zack had confirmed he'd sunk his teeth into the Rogue, the likelihood of the Rogue making an appearance any time soon was pretty slim.

But the very thought of drinking from someone other than Kate was, quite frankly...well, repulsive. No, he couldn't...wouldn't...leave Kate. The pull to stay close to her was just too damn strong.

Styx tensed midstep. His nostrils flared, and his gaze whipped to the doorway. He drew another long breath, and relaxed...minimally. A moment later, Crispin entered the apartment.

"Why are you back so soon?"

Crispin tapped a manila folder in his hands. "I got that information you requested."

*Already?* Still as a statue, Styx's gaze locked on to that envelope, and he waited for the other shoe to drop.

"Pulled a few strings to expedite things." Crispin sat down on the recliner and dropped the folder on the coffee table in front of him. "And, before you tear out my throat, yes...I kept it hush-hush."

Styx swiped a hand down his goatee. He licked his lips as he crossed the room and dropped onto the sofa. All the while, his gaze remained on the envelope, and yet he couldn't bring himself to reach for it. A cold sweat covered him from head to toe.

When the moment stretched on and Styx didn't move any closer to the folder, Crispin blandly informed him, "Kate's biological mother is the Human female that raised her. Her name was Beth O'Rourke née Dupree. Died eight months ago, victim of a drunk driver. Kate has a younger half-sister, Maggie McClain née O'Rourke of Phoenix. Her step-father, Duncan O'Rourke, as you already know died of lymphoma.

"Now, here's where things get interesting. Two years prior to Beth's marriage to Duncan O'Rourke...and Maggie's subsequent birth...young Beth met one Aaron O'Callaghan of the northern Faerie clan of dioane Sídhe."

*¡Madre de Dios!* Dioane Sídhe were the most dangerous of all the Fae. The royal guard. They were tall, well muscled, and physically perfect...and notoriously lethal with any weapon. And the most deadly of all their weapons...their bare hands...or rather the magicks those hands wielded.

*What the hell had a dioane Sídhe been doing with a Human?*

Crispin settled farther back in his seat and stretched out his legs. A deadly predator sprawled in a deceptively blasé slouch. "By all accounts, Aaron was a bit of a wild card. The Tuatha Dé's own legendary black sheep with a dangerous streak and a deadly temper. It seems the delicate Beth soothed the beast within. Aaron concealed his magick from Beth. She had no inkling of what he really was, but she was completely taken with him. And, despite his clan's...ah, shall we say *severe* disapproval—not to mention the Faerie's strict edict of no intermingling with outside races, Aaron became absolutely enamored with his little Human."

Styx could literally feel the blood drain from his head as he leaned back against the cushions. It didn't take a road map or GPS to see where this was going. A garden gnome could do the math.

Human plus Faerie equals Halfling.

While, more often than not, Halflings were Mortal—at least when other races mated...as Crispin had mentioned before, there'd been no prior precedent to a Faerie/Human mating—there were those rare few who actually *phased*, coming fully into their powers as they transitioned from Mortal to Immortal. That, in and of itself, was a dangerous concept. A Mortal with the powers of an Immortal...without the full measure of inherent control all full-blooded Immortal offspring possessed.

"You sure you want me to go on?" Crispin eyed him speculatively. "You don't look so good."

Gritting his teeth, the muscle in his jaw ticking a rapid staccato, Styx nodded tersely. His unblinking stare remained rooted to that benignly colored paper.

"Beth and Aaron had a few happy months together before Aaron's clan stepped in," the agent continued on stoically. "Apparently the clan elders decided Aaron's place was with his own kind, and they summoned him home. There they trapped him. He was sanctioned to never again leave the Isle of Fae, never see his Beth again. And, to add insult to injury, his magick was bound. Beth was led to believe he was killed in a freak accident, but by then it was too late. She was already with child...your Kate.

"Aaron was a dangerous Faerie before he met his Beth. Once he was denied his Beth, his fury new no bounds. The only thing that kept him from seeking revenge—the only thing that kept him from returning to his precious Beth—was the threat of a death order for Beth should he step out of line. If Aaron finds out that Beth is gone, it's hard telling if the elders will be able to keep him contained...if that's even possible at this point."

"You're sure about all of this?"

Crispin merely nodded, expressionless.

Pushing to his feet, Styx prowled to the sliding glass doors and thrust them open, emitting the sounds of a city at rest. Cool air rushed inside the room, but it couldn't chill the uneasy, acidic fire burning in his belly. He stood there, palms braced on the doorframe, head bowed.

He wouldn't lose her.

He wouldn't let them take her away.

"And her father...her clan? Do they know about her?"

"They do now."

"What?" Styx rounded on Crispin with a feral snarl. "I told you—"

"I had nothing to do with them finding out about her. Did you really think Kate's phasing...or her power surge in the alley, for that matter...would go unnoticed by the Tuatha Dé Danann? The only race among us with the ability to control the elements? The very race that sired her? The moment she used her powers, she as good as flipped the switch on a homing beacon. What's more, now that Kate has begun to *phase*, it's going to be difficult for the elders to keep her existence a secret from Aaron any longer."

"*¡Christo!*" Styx dragged a hand across the back of his neck. "You mean he didn't know Beth had been pregnant? All these years, he had no idea about Kate at all?"

"No knowledge whatsoever." Crispin leveled him

with a pointed look. "Sanctioned or not, do you really think even Fae elders could keep a Faerie male from his offspring?"

The fire in his stomach turned to a solid block of jagged ice. "But Aaron is still under sanction? His magick is still bound, right?"

"As far as my sources were aware, yes. At least for now." Just as Styx began to breathe easier, Crispin swept the rug out from under him. "But Kate has a half-brother—a full-blooded dioane Sídhe—and *his* magick is, most definitely, *not* bound. His reputation is every bit as bad as his father's, if not more so. If I were you, I'd prepare myself for a family reunion. Half-brother or father, either way, I'd be willing to bet it won't be long before one or the other of them comes looking for her."

"*¡Mierda!*"

"You need to tell Kate. Everything, Styx. She's of our world, and she needs to know...before her long lost family pops into her life." Crispin leaned forward, propping his elbows on his knees as he clasped his hands. "She could be a valuable asset in fighting the Collector, after all. If they *shimmer* in and take off with her, we could lose a significant advantage."

"Damn it, Crispin. She's not a weapon."

"That has yet to be determined."

"I won't let you use my female that way, Crispin. I won't allow you to deliberately put her in harm's way."

Crispin's expression turned enigmatic at Styx's possessive claim, and he leaned back tilting his head, but he didn't push his point any farther. Instead, he turned the focus. "You better call the Werewolf. We've got more trouble to deal with."

*More trouble than a possessive clan of dioane Sídhe?*

*Not bloody likely...*

Not trusting the agents effortless capitulation where Kate was concerned, Styx left the room long enough to wake Zack and summon him to the living area. As he passed the door to his own room, he paused, straining to hear beyond the barrier of wood. Kate's deep, even breathing ran over him like a soothing hand.

*I'll keep you safe, querida...no matter what it takes.*

"So now what do we get to 'deal with'?" Zack kicked his stocking-covered feet up on the coffee table and crossed his arms over his chest. His handsome face was haggard. "The seven plagues? Pissed off Faeries? Demented Warlocks? A Demon horde from the nether realm?"

Styx dropped onto the sofa beside Zack, and Crispin shot him a speaking glance. "Well, you're probably partially right there."

"Buggar me, I was only—"

"But I'll leave Styx to fill you in on that point. Right now, I'm more concerned with the trail of bodies the Collector...this al-Rashid...is leaving in his wake."

"Bodies? Bloody hell, I thought you said he was changing these women."

"Mostly, he is. His success rate is unusually high. But he's still losing a few here and there. And those bodies are beginning to turn up all over the city."

"Wait a minute, what do you mean 'mostly'?" Zack turned a puzzled gaze from Styx to the TRFA agent and back again. "And if this bloody bastard is trying to re-establish his harem, why is he killing the women?"

"The change doesn't always take in females," Styx offered with a shrug. "No one knows why."

"From the trace scent on the corpses and the

lack of complete exsanguination, Layla is responsible for several of the fatalities. And changing wasn't her goal." Crispin drew a deep breath. "She was feeding."

Again, Zack's gaze swung to Styx. "Hey...wait a sec. I thought you guys could feed without killing."

"We can. The vast majority of us do. Layla, apparently, chooses not to," Crispin offered, bringing Zack's gaze back to his face. "As I'm sure you can imagine, the TFRA is growing understandably concerned. The number of bodies in a centralized location is going to spark more questions than we can gloss over...even with *persuasion*."

Crispin flipped the top folder over, and, for the first time, Styx noticed a second folder beneath the first. The agent opened the cover, then spun the folder around so Zack and Styx could have a better view. Leaning forward, dropping his feet to the floor, Zack thumbed through the stack of papers and photos. Newspaper clipping reporting an increase in regional murder rates. Speculation of a possible serial killer. Glossy, color photos of young women lying pale and lifeless on pavement, their throats all but shredded.

The sight of one particularly violent attack pushed Zack back in his seat with a dark expletive.

"More disturbing," Crispin intoned, "are the things that the TFRA *did* manage to cover up. Bodies suddenly and inexplicably disappearing from the morgue. Clear puncture wounds on the throats of some of the deceased." He paused, shifting his gaze from the pictures on the table to the males on the sofa. "Clinically dead women suddenly sitting upright on the morgue table and attacking medical examiners. We've had to post operatives in Human morgues now to control collateral damage."

"There's one thing I don't understand." Zack crossed his arms over his massive chest again and tilted his head. His brow drew together. "Why would Layla attack Kate if the Collector's earmarked her for his harem?"

"We don't know," Crispin muttered. From the rare, dissatisfied expression on the agent's face, Styx guessed that particular admission was a bitter pill for the agent to swallow.

"So much for the Rogue's happy little family," Zack smirked. "Apparently he hasn't taken into consideration that the female mind isn't always predictable...or malleable enough to willingly share the object of their affection with another female."

If anyone would know that fact, it'd be Zack. He'd majored in female psychology and earned his Masters at the University of Seduction.

"So, not only is Kate in danger from the Rogue...but now Layla has set her sights on Kate, too?" *Dios, could he not get a break? Just one?* "Is she going after Kate to take out a rival for her master's attention...or is she trying to acquire Kate as a present for al-Rashid?"

"I don't think we'll have the answer to that question until she attacks again, which, given the situation, I'd say is only a matter of time." Crispin arched a brow. "We can still take Kate into custody."

"No," Styx immediately denied. The thought of being separated from Kate was more than he could bear, and there was no telling where the TFRA might place her. No, she was far better off with him. "Hauling her in won't prevent al-Rashid from taking another in her place. He's already proven he hasn't stopped hunting. Hell, Zack wounded him tonight...he's probably out there hunting right now for all we know."

"I'd say that's a given." Crispin's calculating gaze slid to the bedroom door. "Have you tried—"

"No," Styx snapped, leaving Zack blinking in confusion.

"What's he talking about?"

"Butt out, Zack," Styx ordered.

"Look, Styx...bloody hell, man, if there's something I should know about—"

"Zack, I said—"

A soft gasp from the doorway turned every male head in the room. Glittering, furious emerald eyes pinned Styx to the spot.

****

Styx...not Nico?

Zack...not Collin?

What was going on here? And who was that other guy? Dressed somewhere between a mobster and a government agent, the sight of him sent a chill of apprehension skittering down her spine despite his captivating, handsome face and entrancing, gentle brown eyes.

One thing was crystal clear—they'd lied to her.

"Would someone care to explain what the hell is going on here?"

Nico...Styx...whatever the hell his name was...dropped his head back on his shoulders, closed his eyes, and groaned aloud. Collin...no, Zack...Zack's eyes widened, and his mouth fell open. The stranger simply stared at her, no emotion flickering across his face whatsoever.

God, she'd seen more emotion on a cadaver.

"Styx? Is that really your name?" Kate clenched her hands into fists at her sides. She'd been such an idiot. *You look just like that drummer...,* she'd told him the first time they'd met. She wanted very badly to crawl into the nearest hole. She must have sounded like some naïve bumpkin. How humiliating! "You know, forget it. I don't care anymore."

Furious, Kate stomped across the living area. She grabbed her mud-splattered jacket from a stool near the island in the kitchen as she headed for the door.

"Damn it, Kate," Nico/Styx growled, leaping to his feet and rushing after her. "Wait...I can explain."

"Oh, I'm sure you can," she called over her shoulder, her hand stretching for the doorknob. "I'm sure you've got all sorts of neat little excuses all lined up and pegged out for every occasion. Well save them for someone who gives a damn. I'm finished here."

Kate jerked the door open and plowed through, Nico/Styx breathing down her neck. Well, he could just go to hell. If he couldn't be honest with her about something so basic as his name, then she didn't need to waste another second of her time on him.

"Kate—"

"Damn it," she hissed as her keys tumbled to the floor. Bending, she scooped them up and jabbed blindly at the lock on her apartment door. "Just go away. You've had your little joke at my expense. I don't have to stick around to hear the laughter. Run along back to your buddies."

"Will you just listen to me for a damn minute. I'm trying to—"

"I already told you I don't care...I don't want to hear anything you have to say." She whirled on him, gouging a finger into his chest. "Let me make this perfectly clear. I don't want to see you again, don't want to speak to you ever again. I don't need your help...I don't *want* your help. I don't want you anywhere near me, *ever again*. Go. Away."

Turning away, she twisted the doorknob and pushed the door open.

"The hell I will," he growled, pushing through the doorway right after her.

"What do you think you're doing?" she demanded, sputtering as he drove her farther down the hallway.

He slammed the door behind him. "Shut up."

Kate gasped, outraged. How dare he push his way into her apartment? How dare he tell her to—

"Get out!" she exploded.

"I'm not going anywhere, and you *will* listen to me."

"Like hell I—"

A frustrated, animalistic growl erupted from deep in the back of his throat, cutting off. Stalking forward, he scooped her up and tossed her over his shoulder like a sack of feed. Gasping, snarling, she pounded her fists against his back, kicking and squirming for all she was worth. Ignoring her indignant struggles, he strode through the apartment and into her bedroom, where he flopped her onto her back in the middle of her bed. Before she could master her indignation and regain her breath, his weight covered her, pinning her to the mattress.

Kate opened her mouth to rail at him, but a large hand clapped over her mouth. Her eyes went wide. *Oh no, he did not just...*

"Shh," he demanded. "Listen."

She huffed out a breath through flared nostrils, narrowing her eyes, and shoved against his chest. With a wry twist of his lips, he captured both her wrists and pinned them above her head in one of his large, strong hands, then clapped his other palm over her mouth once more.

"Fine," he hissed, caging her thrashing legs between his, effectively holding her completely immobile. Completely at his mercy. "We'll do this the hard way."

"Mmmmph..." Of all the nerve. Just wait until he let go of her. Then she'd show him *"the hard way."*

"Yes, my name is Styx. At least that's the name I've gone by for the last...well...that's another conversation. Let's go at this one step at a time. Yes, I am Styx. Yes, I'm the drummer for Stolen

Innocence. But I didn't lie to you...my real name *is* Nico. Nicholas Diego Esteban Montega y Cordoza, to be exact, but no one's called me that in...well, a long time. And Zack...*Collin*, Collin is Zack. He's part of Stolen Innocence, too."

A suspicious scowl pulled at her brows. "Mmmmphmmh..."

"His name is Derek Crispin. You could say he's a...a law enforcement official."

"Mhuh?"

"What?"

Impatient, she jerked her head from side to side to dislodge his hand. He tentatively removed the offending appendage, sliding it up to join their hands above her head.

"What is going on, *Styx*?" Kate demanded. "Stop jerking me around and give me the truth for a change...or else you can just get the hell out right now."

"Nico," he corrected.

"*Styx*," she countermanded angrily. "Nico implies a level of intimacy, and I don't know you at all, now do I?"

He ground his teeth. "Fine...but *that* discussion is far from over."

"I'm waiting," she reminded him.

"All right," he replied. But the expression on his face suggested he'd far rather be sitting in a dentist's chair right now rather than having this discussion. "Okay. Zack and I are...we're helping Crispin with a case."

Her eyes narrowed again. Did he really think she was going to buy, for one damn minute, that he was suddenly some kind of undercover agent? Next, he'd be trying to get her to believe he was an alien from some other damn planet.

"What case?"

His gaze searched her face, and he drew a deep

breath. "Have you noticed anything strange in the ER? Victims coming in with...severe blood loss? Strange wounds? A higher number of mortalities passing through the ER, particularly young, attractive females. Have you heard any strange stories coming from the morgue?"

That caught her attention, and she peered hard into his eyes. Rumors, gossip around the nurses' station suddenly came back to her. "What are you trying to tell me? That there's a serial killer slashing his way through Tacoma? Some kind of monster tearing his victim's throats out like a rabid animal?"

As soon as she said the last, her eyes widened. That's exactly what he was trying to tell her. She could see it in his eyes.

"That woman that lured you to the alley—"

"No—" she gasped, shaking her head. Impossible.

"Yes," he argued. "She's involved."

"My God," Kate whispered. If her hand had been free, she would have instinctively clutched at her own throat.

As if he'd read her mind, Styx nodded and pressed a gentle kiss to the tip of her nose, then dropped his forehead to hers.

"But...why you? Why would the police ask you and Zack for help?"

"You could say we have...prior experience with this sort of thing." He smiled wryly down at her, lifting his head from hers. "Not too long ago, we had a similar...problem...in L.A. Cole and I were in a position to help identify the Rogue and—"

"Rogue?"

"Ah...the killer. We had the perfect cover, as the Ro...the killer had targeted the Hu...the music industry." Closing his eyes, Styx shook his head, then refocused on her face. His expression grim. "This killer seems to have fixated on you."

"The stalker..." A fresh wave of chills crashed through her. "Oh my God, I didn't...I didn't connect them...I assumed..." Panic welled in the back of her throat, cutting off her words. Cutting off her supply of air.

"Shh," he whispered, pressing soft kisses to the corner of her mouth, her cheek, just below her ear.

As distractions went, that worked quite effectively. The scent of his skin, the warmth of his lips pushed heat through her veins, dispelling the chill that has settled bone deep.

"I swear to you, *querida*. I will keep you safe." His lips returned to hers, brushing light as a butterfly's wings. "Trust in me." His legs released hers, and one powerful thigh slipped between hers. Instinctively, Kate lifted her knee, allowing him to settle farther into the cradle of her thighs. He caught her lower lip between his teeth, then gently suckled. "I will protect you with my life, *querida*."

God help her, but she believed his impassioned pledge. What kind of fool was she? He'd lied to her once already.

*Maybe he'd thought he'd had no choice...*

Kate lifted her head from the mattress, seeking his lips with her own.

His mouth settled over hers, hot and greedy. Above her head, his hand released her wrists, and he linked his fingers with hers. Slanting his head, his tongue thrust past her parted lips and plundered her mouth, stealing her breath. Grinding any second thoughts to dust. Smashing through any hesitancy. Demolishing her defenses.

Kate lifted her knee higher, hooking her calf over his thigh, tilting her hips to rub at him in an unmistakable, timeless invitation. Styx groaned low in his throat and bucked his hips against her. He released her hands. One large, warm palm found its way to her breast, where it cupped and kneaded with desperate determination. His other hand slipped beneath her head, his fingers tangled in her hair, cupping the back of her head.

"*Mi corazón,*" he whispered fervently between kisses. His scorching lips blazed a trail of fire from her lips to her ear. "*Quiero hacerte el amor.*"

That wonderful, wicked mouth licked and nibbled down the side of her throat, turning her limbs to jelly. Kate caught her breath as he suckled hard at the pulse racing at the base of her throat. He mumbled something else against her skin, but she couldn't make out the words. His voice was deeper, hoarse...saturated with need...and it resonated through her body, striking an unfamiliar chord deep, deep inside. She could happily spend the rest of her life simply steeping herself in the textures of his voice.

The heat of his palm dipped beneath the hem of her sweatshirt, skimming up over the sensitive flesh of her stomach, and, in a flash, her bra came unhooked. Slightly abrasive, deliciously warm skin covered her breast, seducing her with friction. Weighing. Molding. Kneading. Caressing. Desire pooled, hot and moist, low in the pit of her belly. Kate grasped at his broad shoulders, frantic to get closer.

Her fingers pushed up his neck, sinking deep into his hair. She gripped his skull, pressing him closer still. In a flurry of movement, he whisked the sweatshirt up and over her head. She had no idea where it landed, couldn't have cared less. Her bra soon went the way of her shirt, and Kate's breath left her completely as his sculpted, smooth chest settled heavily atop hers, crushing her in an avalanche of decadent sensations.

His lips seized hers, possessive...intoxicating. His hard hands gripped her hips, dragging her up tight against him as he ground the thick, hard length of his erection against her. Her jeans were too tight, her panties chaffed. She squirmed, groaning into his mouth. God, she needed more friction. Bare skin on bare skin. Hot. Wet.

*So much heat...*

*More...*

She tugged eagerly at the back of his loose shirt, dragging it from his shoulders as his tongue swirled through her mouth, capturing her tongue and drawing it into his mouth. She needed him naked. Now. Needed to feel his heat sinking deep into her, filling her. Claiming her. His greedy mouth dipped to pay homage to her breasts, worshiping each one in turn, then moved back to her throat, sending goose bumps skittering over her flesh. Blistering, open-mouthed kisses branded her flesh. Tiny points of pain suddenly mingled with the pleasure. Mindless, Kate tossed her head to the side, begging for more.

His fingers dipped to her waistband, tugging at the button on her jeans.

"Nico...oh God, please..."

Electrical energy crackled through the air, tickling the fine hairs on the back of her neck, and the whispery scent of ozone—that irresistible, fresh scent that proceeds a summer storm—wafted through the room.

"Leech...you have exactly one second to get the hell off her," came a dark, deadly command from the shadows. "And then I'm going to fry you where you stand."

## Chapter 15

Like a bucket of ice water, that precisely enunciated threat cut through the haze of passion clouding Kate's brain. Time seemed to spin out...and yet the next few moments flashed by in a whirlwind of confusion. Wide-eyed, panting, Kate strained to peer over Styx's suddenly stiff shoulder. There, in the corner of her bedroom towered one of the most beautiful men she'd ever clapped eyes upon. He was exceedingly tall. His long, white-blond hair was stick-straight, his skin fair. Thin, incongruously dark brows formed an angry slash above smoldering sapphire eyes perfectly set in a breathtaking, grim face.

Eyes shining with the promise of death.

At first glance, he appeared slim...almost lanky, but the cut of his strange garb left little doubt as to the whipcord strength packed onto his lean frame. A silky white, long-sleeved tunic with strange Celtic symbols emblazoned in gold across the chest stretched tight over his well-formed shoulders. Tan leggings encased his long, muscular legs, and unadorned, butter-soft, moccasin-type boots covered his feet, stretching up to mid-calf.

Orlando Bloom circa *Lord of the Rings* came swiftly to mind. Orlando Bloom with a lilting accent straight out of the *Highlander* series...only the inflection was *different*, more melodic. Like a hybrid mixture of Scots and Irish and British. Absolutely beguiling. The man's carriage bespoke nobility, an inherent grace no amount of training could mimic. This man, however, was the very epitome of danger.

Calculating and lethal as a demon, with the deceptively luring face of an angel.

Brazen. Staggering in his sensuality.

Hazardous to the health of any who crossed him.

He didn't appear much older than she was, but she got the unsettling impression that she was in the presence of an unstoppable force of nature, timeless. Ancient.

Something far beyond her understanding.

"Dinna ye ken me, blood-sucker," he hissed, his growing anger thickening his brogue. His inflections altered slightly, r's rolling seemingly of their own free will. "Get your fangs off her. *Now.*"

It took her a moment to get around the brogue, but once she had, she was well and truly baffled.

*Blood-sucker? Fangs?*

*What the hell?*

Kate gasped aloud as the man stretched his hands out at his sides, palms facing forward. Concentrated—*controlled*—twin points of energy glowed to life in the palms of his hands. Throbbing, shining, pale purple. The very tips of his silky, nearly waist-length hair lifted as if charged by static.

And his eyes...his beautiful, mesmerizing blue eyes...began to blaze brightly.

Styx vaulted to his feet so quickly, he was little more than a blur of motion. Jerking her up, he thrust her behind him. Her alarmed stare glued to the intruder, Kate frantically snatched up her sweatshirt and yanked it over her head, shoving her arms into the sleeves as she did her best to conceal her bare chest.

"Move away from him, wee one. I've no' wish to harm ye, even by accident."

As if her safety were somehow important to him? Who in the hell did he think he was?

And why did he keep calling her that...as if he

knew her?

"You were not invited here." Styx held his arms out at his sides, semi-crouching in an obviously protective stance. She strained up on tiptoe to peer over his shoulder.

"I need no invitation to protect my clan, leech," he asserted coldly. "'Tis you who trespass here."

*How was he* doing *that with his hands?*

"I am exactly where I belong," Styx countered, his voice a harsh rasp. "She is my mate."

His claim so surprised Kate that she nearly missed the look on the stranger's face.

"Och, lassie, what has he *done* to ye?" Clearly horrified, his already pale complexion abruptly lost what little color it had. His stunning eyes widened, then narrowed—glittering brighter, if that were possible. Then, without warning, his lips curled back on a wounded snarl. Explosive energy sizzled in the air around him. "I will no' believe she willingly accepted the likes of you as her consort." The cold fury in his voice cut through the room like thousands of razor-sharp knives.

"Did I force you to accept me, *querida*?" Though he didn't look at her as he asked the question, Kate could easily read the tension in Styx's stance, knew...somehow...that her answer was vital.

"I am with Styx of my own free will," she immediately answered, her voice filled with incontestable conviction as she met the intruders glare.

One would have thought she'd reached out and slapped him, so stunned was his expression. Just as quickly, his face became a mask of calm determination. "It matters naught. She doesn't *belong* with you, leech. She will come with me."

"Who *are* you?" Kate nervously pushed the wild tangle of her hair from her face with trembling hands, tossing it back over her shoulders. Her shaking hands settled on Styx's tense shoulders, as much to draw strength as to calm both herself as well as him. "How did you get in here? What do you want?"

The stranger ripped his wary gaze from Styx to dart a glance at her, then his gaze whipped back, as if he expected her protector to pounce at any moment. His chin elevated with unmistakable pride. "I am Cian O'Callaghan son of Aaron of the northern clan of dioane Sídhe. And I have come to take you home, lass."

His word wrung a strangled oath from Styx, startling her.

Did he know this man...or know of him?

"I *am* home," she squawked. And still she couldn't tear her gaze from the energy orbs hovering at his palms. Her thoughts slipped out on a whisper, "*What* are you?"

This time his blue eyes lingered on her. Pride gleamed in his eyes. "I am Tuatha Dé Danann. As are you, wee one. Och, but 'tis the spittin' image of your mother ye are, lass."

Her throat went dry, and she could barely force the words past the sudden lump in her throat. "How do you know my mother?"

"I have seen da's memories, wee one." His answer left her as lost as if he hadn't spoken at all.

Perhaps more confused even.

Her blank expression must have finally registered. His confidence faltered for the first time since he'd intruded, and he demanded incredulously, "How can you no' know of us, lass?"

"I haven't had a chance to explain any of this yet," Styx interrupted.

Cian O'Callaghan's angry glare snapped back to Styx at the same moment Kate blurted, "Explain what?"

The energy orbs in Cian's palms pulsed angrily.

Ozone crackled thicker in the air, building, throbbing. "You will explain *nothing*, leech," Cian sneered. "Kate will learn all she needs to know from her clan."

"You aren't taking her anywhere, O'Callaghan," Styx snarled. "She stays with me."

"My clan...I, I don't...what the hell are you talking about?" Kate's fingers dug into the corded muscles of Styx's shoulders. "And why do you keep calling Styx names? You don't even know him."

"I need no formal introduction to know what he is," Cian spat.

*What...not who.* He spoke in riddles, this Cian O'Callaghan son of Aaron. Whoever *that* was. How was she to figure anything out when he insisted on speaking around her rather than giving her direct answers? Her temper pushed to its limits, Kate demanded, "How did you get in my apartment?"

"I *shimmered*," Cian replied shortly, never taking his wary gaze from Styx. *Oh, of course. That explained so much...not!* "And she goes with me, parasite."

Those pulsing orbs were growing ever brighter by the second. Part of her mind rebelled, denying the truth of her vision. And yet, unsettling emotion tugged at her. Familiar. This strange energy...pulsing with a life of its own...was *familiar*. She was positive it should have frightened her, should have terrified her to the soles of her feet. But the scent, the charge was oddly comforting. Like...

*Home...*

"Step aside, lass," he commanded her. "Now."

Beneath her hands, Styx's tense back muscles bunched and rippled, and he seemed to grow before her very eyes. As if trying to make himself into an even bigger target.

*A bigger shield...*

Now true fear shot like lightning through her

veins. She wouldn't let Styx get hurt for her. Power coiled tight inside her, swelling, pushing outward. Her nerves tingled, her pulse hummed. Her vision seemed to sharpen, and every tiny detail in the room—right down to the miniscule particles of dust floating in the air—came into sharp relief. Her body seemed to vibrate from within. Her skin suddenly felt too tight for her frame. Her breathing went fast and shallow. Her gaze locked on those pulsing orbs in Cian's hands, and Kate's instinct to protect Styx dwarfed all else.

The muscles in Cian's shoulders and arms flexed as he began to lift his hands. Kate darted beneath Styx's arm, planting herself firmly between them with inhuman speed. Seemingly of their own volition, her hands shot up in front of her, and a wildly uncontrolled pulse of light exploded from her palms. Cian sailed through the air, crashing into the far wall where he dropped to the floor with a solid thump. Framed pictures dropped from the wall all around him, glass shattered.

His expression stunned, Cian slowly righted himself and stepped forward...palms pulsing with emerging energy once more. His wary gaze now slid back and forth between Styx and Kate, as if she'd suddenly become a factor...whereas before she'd only been a bystander.

Behind her, Styx snarled a harsh expletive. His hands circled her waist as if to push her behind him once again. But the moment his hands touched her, he jerked them back with a sharp hiss, as if he'd unwittingly grasped live, super-charged electrical wires. Kate refused to budge. She faced off against Cian. He was going to have to go through her if he wanted a crack at her man.

Wait...*her* man? Where had that come from?

Gahh... She didn't have time to think that one through right now. Now she had to protect Styx.

"You will not hurt him." Chilly resolve battled the onset of shock. She didn't know how she'd just managed to knock Cian back, but, if it meant keeping this...this unnatural *person* from harming Styx, then, by all that was holy, she'd damned well do it again.

"Kate," Cian warned, cautious now. The energy orbs in his palms slowly vaporized, and he held his empty hands up in a placating gesture. "You have no control yet. You must be careful while you *phase*, or you could damage yourself and your magick."

"Then back off, damn it."

Cian shot a fulminous glance over her shoulder at Styx, then slowly lowered his hands. Once more, that mask of utter calm slipped into place, and he stared at her with a soothing, concerned expression. His tone became that of a patient teacher with a struggling student. "Take a deep breath, Kate. Call back the power. Slowly lower your hands. Focus, lass. Tame the *quickening*. Feel the power ebb. Och...that's right, it is a part of you, lass, stop fighting it. You *can* control it...don't let it control you." He took several steps closer, ignoring the dark warning growl rumbling from the man behind her. "That's right. You're doing verra well." He held his hand out to her. His burr became soft, coaxing. Enchanting. "Take my hand, wee one. Let me help you."

"Don't touch her, O'Callaghan. I'll tear you apart before I let you *shimmer* off with her."

Kate eyed Cian suspiciously. Her battle for control momentarily forgotten as alarm slammed through her. "Can you do that? Can you disappear and take me with you?"

Cian glared at Styx, reluctantly admitting, "Aye."

"Only if he's touching you," Styx added.

Anger flared, as did the energy inside her, and

Cian's eyes widened. "Breathe, lass. Control it."

*Yes...yes, control it...*

Controlling the energy consumed her, pushing all else aside. The *quickening*, he'd called it. Somehow, having a name for this momentous force surging through her body seemed to help her leash the beast.

*Control it...must contain it...*

She didn't take his hand, but she did as he'd previously instructed, focusing on her breathing and on controlling the energy coursing through her body, though concentrating was difficult. After a long moment, she felt the power seep from her. Too much. This was all too much, too fast. And none of it was logical. Weak-kneed, she sagged toward the floor, unable to summon enough strength to keep herself upright.

Cian immediately lunged for her, but before he could lay hands upon her, Styx snatched her back. His arms slipped around her waist, lending her support as he cradled her gently against him. Kate glanced up at him, wanting to make certain she hadn't somehow harmed him when she'd driven Cian back, but Styx turned his face away, and she couldn't see anything more than the lower edge of his cheek.

The tiny muscle running the length of his jaw flexed and strained.

A new kind of fear knotted in the pit of her stomach.

What had she done? She'd been forced to use that horrible power she'd denied for so long. The power she'd kept buried for the better part of her life. It had only gotten the better of her twice before. But never like this. Never so violently. And now he'd seen it. Surely he must find her...what? Repulsive? Abnormal?

God, help her...a freak?

"What business have you here, leech?"

"There will be no more of that," Kate snapped, aiming a cautionary, albeit shaking finger at Cian as her temper flared. "You will be civil, or you will leave. He has a name. It's Styx. Use it."

It was getting more difficult to focus, harder to concentrate. Her hand trembled, and the room around her blurred for a moment. God, she was so weak.

Gritting his teeth, Cian tilted his head with regal concession, though his eyes remained defiant...and wary.

"I already told you once, O'Callaghan," Styx growled, his voice low, his stare intense. "My place is with my mate. You see...that's the difference between your kind and mine. Absolutely *nothing* is capable of keeping one of *us* from our mate."

Again, the talk of a mate. He spoke as if she belonged to him.

And again, that warm flutter deep in the pit of her stomach.

Oh, now was a fine time for him to be talking like this...giving her unreasonable ideas. What was wrong with him? Or was this some kind of act for Cian's benefit? She didn't know what to believe anymore. Was too drained to try to make sense of it.

Cian's lips pulled back in a frightening sneer over his perfect teeth. Ozone crackled.

All this talk of mate's and "*your kind*" and "*my kind*" had her head swimming. Intuition told her there was suddenly an entirely deeper conversation going on...way above her head. Lord knew Cian had just reacted as if Styx had grievously insulted him.

"Allrighty then," she interrupted, eager to diffuse the resurgence of unpredictable tension holding the room in its volatile fist. Dragging in a shaky breath, she dredged deep for strength and forced herself to straighten. "Let's go to the living room and try to sort all this out, shall we?"

Cian offered Kate a stiff nod of assent.

She couldn't bring herself to glance at Styx. What expression would be on his handsome face? Repugnance? Disgust?

Brutal uncertainty twisted like a rusty blade in her belly. Why had this had to happen this way?

But her gaze connected with Cian's, and she couldn't look away.

Dear God, could he give her the answers she needed? Could he tell her what was happening to her body? Tell her why strange things occurred to the environment around her whenever extreme emotions of fear or pain swamped her.

And, perhaps more importantly, could he tell her how to control it?

Again, his head dipped in a regal nod. His steady gaze held hers. The nod...the narrowing of his eyes...seemed to hold deeper meaning.

*Good grief, could he read minds, too?*

Or was it just her mind that was open to him? He didn't seem to have much confidence in anticipating Styx's responses.

Cian's expression was carefully impassive as he turned away to precede her into the living room, but for a moment there, she could have sworn one corner of his mouth had quirked upward in a wry twist.

Styx kept his arm anchored firmly around her waist as they made their way into the living room. Kate took small comfort in that. At least he wasn't pushing her away. Perhaps he was willing to give her the benefit of the doubt. Grateful, she leaned on him, not trusting her legs to traverse the short distance safely.

"Please, have a seat." Kate indicated the furniture in her living room with a wide sweep of her hand, then waited for Cian to choose a place to sit.

He perched on the edge of one end of the

loveseat; as if he worried the cushions might suddenly come to life and attempt to devour him. His decidedly unfriendly glare landed on Styx, and he ordered tersely, "She needs water."

More concerned with unraveling the confusion surrounding her uninvited guest, Kate frowned and shook her head. "I'm fine."

The movement left her slightly lightheaded, but she fought to ignore it.

"Nay, you are no'," Cian disagreed forcefully, his burr thickening once more. Then he drew a deep breath and the burr dissipated. "You need water. In the phasing process, each time you give in to the *quickening*...especially so recklessly and without instruction...your body will become weakened, dehydrated. We draw a measure of our strength from the elements."

"*We...* You say that as if...as if you believe I am the same as you."

"I speak only fact. Search your feelings, Kate. You know I speak true." He paused for a moment, as if waiting for the obvious to sink in. Then, when she neither agreed with nor disputed his claim, he went on, "If you use too much power too quickly—and without control—you will become disoriented. You might even pass out...or worse. You need water." He turned that angry, electric-blue glare on Styx once more. "*Now.*"

"Fine. Just keep your hands to yourself, O'Callaghan," Styx warned. Ever watchful of Cian, Styx went to the kitchen and retrieved a large bottle of water from the fridge. He cracked the top and twisted the lid off as he crossed the room. Handing it to her, his probing gaze searched her face as if to assess for himself the measure of her strength. His expression became oddly resigned, and he grimly demanded, "Drink."

Exasperated, Kate complied. Neither one of

them looked as if they were about to bend on this issue, and the sooner she got the drinking out of the way, perhaps she could get some questions answered. Styx sat down on the opposite end of the sofa as Cian and pulled her down beside him, tucking her against the protective shelter of his body, wrapping a possessive arm around her waist. When the bottle was half empty, she set it aside. Without conscious thought, her hand sought his, and she entwined her fingers with his. The heat of his palm pressing against hers, the solid strength of his arm around her gave her something stable to hold on to as the world as she'd known it came apart at the seams, becoming a swirling vortex of insanity she couldn't seem to deny or escape.

The water *had* helped. At least, she wasn't shaking like a leaf anymore.

"Okay, let's start at the beginning. You're name is Cian O'Callaghan?"

"Aye," Cian replied simply.

"And you are from the northern tribe—"

"*Clan*," he corrected with a great deal of smug pride. "The northern *clan* of the dioane Sídhe."

Styx's arm tightened around her, his body went taut, but she pushed on, irrationally desperate for answers. Fear and confusion clotted in the back of her throat, making the words difficult to form. "And this clan of dioane Sídhe are…"

"We are the Tuatha Dé Danann."

"And that is…"

Looking slightly appalled at having to explain, Cian replied, "There are a number of different clans of the Sídhe. There are the áes Sídhe, banshee, leanan Sídhe, sluagh, the fairy host…an slua Sídhe, Sídhe who shift shape at will, there are the guardian Sídhe of the lakes of both Ireland and Scotland, and many more.

"We are of noble bloodlines, lass. We are the

*People of the Goddess Danu.* You and I are of the dioane Sídhe. We are the warrior class of the Sídhe. The royal guard. I realize the Druids were a secretive lot, and the Veil between the Human world and the world of the Sídhe vigilantly maintained, but surely your Human bards have told the tales of us?"

"Sorry..." She shook her head, shrugging helplessly.

"You've no' heard the tales of the High Kings of Ireland..." He frowned at her, plainly taken aback. "Bres, Nuada, Lugh? Delbáeth, Fiacha? Mac Cuill, Mac Cecht? Mac Gréine?"

Again, she shook her head, feeling almost apologetic for the look of disbelief on his beautiful face. Druids...and bards? Those were terms of long ago...she'd studied her share of history. In fact, ancient history had been a passion of hers at one point. But she'd never delved much into mythology. The way these obviously revered names rolled off Cian's tongue was distinctly appealing, yet struck no chord of familiarity.

"Och, lass," he tsked, clearly horrified at her lack of knowledge. "What of the Four Seelie Treasures? Dagda's Cauldron, the Spear of Lugh, the Stone of Fal...or the Sword of Light of Nuada? Please tell me you've at least been taught of those even here in this place they call Tacoma? Surely you've heard *something* of our people?"

*"This place they called Tacoma..."*

Dear Lord, he spoke as if he were from another world...another time.

"Again...sorry?"

"We are Faerie, lass," he charged indignantly. As if her lack of knowledge of these strange names had somehow offended his senses.

"Faerie?" Kate frowned at him, unwittingly scooting farther into the sanctuary of Styx's arms.

Much as she wanted to humor her uninvited guest, she couldn't keep the skepticism from her voice. "Like Tinkerbelle?"

Cian blinked at her, plainly clueless. Beside her, Styx's body convulsed, and a sharp bark of laughter burst from his lips. As soon as the word left her mouth, she shook her head. She should have known better. She pinned Styx with a withering glare until he regained control of his misplaced humor.

*Think, Katie girl. Think before you speak. You don't want to offend him.*

*Not until you get some answers...*

No way was Cian...in any way, shape, or form...related to that tiny, green-clad figure she'd come to associate with children's tales, the one who gaily went about sprinkling pixie dust on inquisitive children. No, this specimen before her was raw male. Momentous, intimidating, in-your-face male, brimming with copious amounts of testosterone.

He'd doubtlessly left broken hearts by the legion in his wake. Perhaps her lack of caution was because her heart didn't flutter when he turned his steady gaze on her. Not the way it did whenever she'd intercepted one of Styx's smoldering glances. Well, she supposed that had to be something. At least she wasn't attracted to the crazy guy. Score one for her. In a way, that knowledge offered comforting reassurance.

Ever since she'd first taken Styx's hand in hers and gazed into his eyes at their first meeting, her hormones had shot through the roof like a roman candle. Dear heavens, she all but detonated whenever he kissed her. Her lack of control where he was concerned had, quite frankly, worried her. At least now, she knew her body's overblown reactions seemed isolated to Styx alone.

*No...don't go there right now. Stay focused.*

Had this Cian broken out of some insane

asylum? Was he demented?

Dangerous?

*Of course he's dangerous, Katie girl. Weren't you paying attention to what he was doing with his hands just a short time ago? Normal men just couldn't do things like that.*

*Quickening...*

But, fast on the heels of that thought came another, equally frightening thought. *She* could do that with her hands, too.

What then, did that make *her*?

Her frown deepened. Yes, she'd seen Cian's...powers. She could hardly ignore the proof, could hardly pretend she hadn't watched that power shape and grow.

*Perfectly controlled power...*

*Quickening...*

And, what's more, he seemed to know what she was capable of...maybe more so than even she did. That knowledge was both blessing and curse. Frightening...and yet oddly comforting.

"And you said you've come to take me home with you?"

This time Styx clasped her so tightly, she nearly squawked aloud. Placing her hand on his knee, she gently squeezed, silently reassuring him. She had no intention of going anywhere with this man. Whoever he might claim to be.

*Whatever* he claimed to be...

"Aye," Cian responded calmly. As if the matter were already a foregone conclusion.

"Why do you think I'd be willing to go anywhere with you?"

"Because I'm your brother, lass." Cian's unblinking stare held hers. "And you belong with your clan."

****

Broken shards of moonlight filtered down

through the looming, thick cloud cover and the hodge-podge of rooflines, forming a fractured pattern of liquid silver on the stained pavement. Al-Rashid stared down at the lifeless, bloodless form at his feet. Her heart was silent inside her motionless chest.

Apathy swam through his veins along with her blood. Why didn't she change? What was wrong with her? Had he misjudged her?

*Impossible.*

No...she could have survived had she wanted it badly enough.

This was the female's failure...not his.

She lacked Johara's vibrancy. Dissatisfied, he thrust his hands into his pockets, stepped over the corpse, and sauntered down the alley. His side ached, but it had already begun to heal. Allah save him from another of these excruciating wounds. Anything less than a Were bite, and he would have already healed and exacted retribution by now. As it were, he'd need another day or two before he'd be ready to claim Johara for his own. Such a long time...and yet he didn't dare go after her in his weakened condition. Not with all these unknown factors that had suddenly swarmed around her.

Shifting into the mist, al-Rashid glided over the pavement, sweeping up above the rooftops. He longed to see Johara, to breathe her scent. But he didn't dare. In mist form, no one could touch him, but the Werewolf might still be with her, and...should he see Styx...it was hard telling if he'd be able to control his temper and maintain mist form. Confident as he was in his abilities, he was also a realist.

Restless, disgruntled, he hovered high above the city. In the distance, a bright neon sign taunted him. Was she there? Was she working?

Was she thinking of him?

*Soon, little jewel. Soon you will be right where*

*you belong...*
*With me.*

\*\*\*\*

Kate stared at Cian in blatant disbelief. The tale he'd spun of a father she'd never known...a father, he'd claimed, that hadn't known she'd even existed until only a few short hours ago...had been too surreal to believe. He told her of a fantastical, star-crossed romance. Oh, nothing as epic as *Romeo and Juliet*...and yet tragic all the same. Then, he'd gone one step farther, weaving for her a world of mystical powers and compelling magicks. He'd related to her tales of her clan...kinsmen and kinswomen with inherent powers that could control and manipulate the natural world around them, as well as other, mind-boggling powers. He'd also regaled her with stories surrounding the Isle of Fae...an isolated place so tranquil, so beautiful that the majority of his race never stepped foot off its cherished shores.

And through it all, Styx had remained at her side. Silent. Impassive. His arm firmly anchored around her. His hand clasped hers. Yet he sat still as a stone. Rigid. Poker-faced.

And his reaction...as with the rest of this astonishing tale...left her utterly baffled.

Why wasn't he horrified? Why hadn't he reached for the phone to dial 9-1-1 to have both her and this man who claimed to be her brother off to the nearest sanitarium?

She could little fathom any of it.

"So you expect me to believe that you are my long lost brother, and the only reason you found out about me is because..." She had a hard enough time wrapping her mind around the very idea. Her tongue flat out refused to form the words.

"Because you *quickened*, lass," Cian supplied. Somewhere in the middle of his tale he must have determined the sofa offered no threat, because he'd settled back, even going so far as to prop his ankle on his knee. "When you began to *phase*...the physiological transformation from Mortal to Immortal—Human to Faerie...your power called out to us, particularly to Da and me, as our blood runs through your veins."

Her hand shook as she reached for the water bottle. This was too much. She'd wake up any minute now. Realize this had all been one long, distorted dream.

A horrendous nightmare.

*Any minute now...*

Water slid down her throat. Cold. Wet.

*Real...*

"If I am so important to your father...then why did you come for me, rather than this Aaron?"

*And if this Aaron really is my father, why did no one ever tell* me *the truth?*

"Your father, too, lass," Cian reminded her, gentle but steadfast. "He is still bound, though how much longer the elders magick with hold him is anyone's guess."

Cian leaned forward, dropping his foot to the floor. He held his hand out to her, palm up, and slowly, gently smiled. Warmth seeped through her, spreading languidly through her limbs. Calm acceptance eased through her mind. His relentless gaze pulled her toward the edge of her seat. Drawing her closer to him, like an invisible tether. A soft voice in the back of her mind, so muffled as to be nearly incoherent, cautioned her to resist.

But it was just...so...hard...

"Would you like to meet him, Kate? I can take you to him. I can show it all to you. All you have to do is—"

"No," Styx exploded, wrapping both arms around her, tugging her hard against him once more. "You will use no Faerie *guile* to trick her. I told you,

O'Callaghan, my mate stays with me."

Kate blinked, feeling as if she'd just tumbled headlong from a hazy, enthralling fog.

"Damn it," she gasped, glaring at Cian. "Stop *doing* that. You will not...*shimmer* me anywhere. You got that?"

"Soon, there will be no need. You will be able to *shimmer* yourself, lass, once you've fully *phased*," Cian informed her. "I can teach you how." He smiled again. "I can also teach you to block your mind to the *voice*. I can teach you how to block your mind from all outside intrusion," his suddenly seething glance slid to Styx, "including *persuasion*."

*Persuasion...voice*? What on earth did any of that mean? To her, it all sounded the same. A weak point of semantics...but essentially—in either case—mind control. Invasive. Intrusive.

Sinister.

"Our clan can teach you much, wee one. All you have to do is say the word."

At her side, Styx snarled. If he kept squeezing her so tightly, she'd be one big, walking bruise from hip to shoulder. She'd be lucky to walk away with anything less than shattered bones. Shaking her head at Cian, she rubbed Styx's knee, breathing a sigh of relief when his grip relented...even if only slightly.

Cian gradually leaned back against the cushions, his expression an odd mixture of bemusement and irritation. "Why do you interfere, le—Styx?" he hastily amended at Kate's narrow-eyed scowl.

Kate twisted around to stare up at Styx. His actions...his *reactions* were suddenly suspect. Frowning, she studied his face. Why was he so calm? Anyone else would have run screaming from the apartment.

But then, he, too, had seen what Cian could

do...he'd seen what *she* could do...why was he behaving as if this were all perfectly normal?

*Unless...*

"Do you believe him?" His shuttered expression sent an icy chill coursing through her veins. "Did *you* know about all this?" She turned farther in the circle of his arms, peering more closely at his face. "Did you know about all this before *he* came here?"

For the first time since this bizarre conversation had begun, Styx finally showed a glimmer of emotion. Guilt.

He wore it like a banner.

*Oh, yes. He'd known...*

"You knew?" Kate pulled away from him, but he refused to release her completely.

"*Querida*...there's more that you need to know." How dare he sound so anguished?

"You knew, and you didn't tell me?"

Angry, she jerked her hand from his and stood up. Ozone crackled in the room, but this time it wasn't coming from Cian. She caught a glimpse of his self-satisfied smile before she pivoted and began pacing the room.

"Lass, much as I'd like to watch you turn your leech into a smoking lump of coal, I would see no harm come to you. You must be careful. The *quickening* can become as a hungry beast if loosed to freely or too often. It can consume you."

*Deep breath. In. Out. Control it.*

"Kate, let me explain the rest...please."

She rounded on Styx and studied his face. Lips compressed, she gave a terse nod.

"Ask him to leave, Kate." Styx shifted on the sofa, leaning forward, tense. "We need to talk...privately."

Torn, her gaze flew to Cian. She needed to hear what Styx had to say. But she also had questions for Cian.

So many questions...

"If you wish it, little sister, I will go...for now," Cian said gently. Could he somehow sense the turmoil of her emotions? "I will return anon. Or, better still, you could come with me back to Fae...let me help you sort all this out there." His tone turned hard as his agonistic gaze swung toward Styx. "I do no' like the idea of leavin' you here alone with *him*."

His concern warmed her, despite the fact she was still having trouble processing all he'd claimed. But his dislike of Styx was a palpable thing, and she had only his word that he was who he said he was.

She couldn't say why, couldn't isolate any one particular reason, yet, she trusted Styx. Instinctually. Elementally.

And if there was one thing she'd learned from life as well as her profession...she trusted her instincts.

*Better the devil you know...*

"Please...just for a little while, Cian." Kate resumed her pacing, wringing her hands before her. "I...I have to hear him out. Please understand."

From the foul grimace tightening the lines of his face, she could tell he wasn't happy with her request. But in the end, Cian granted her one of his regal nods. "I will always be close by, little sister. All you need do is call out for me, and I will come." Then Cian's cold gaze locked on Styx. "Harm her no', leech, or I will see that you pray for sunlight."

*Pray for sunlight? What an odd threat...*

"Wait a minute..." Her gaze swept past Cian and lingered on Styx. "So, if Faeries really do exist, how many other...mythical creatures are real? You know, Werewolves and Trolls and unicorns and all that?"

"Trolls and unicorns, nay. Werewolves," Cian responded with a decidedly sour expression, "aye...nasty, appalling creatures they are. No self-control whatsoever. But I'll leave it to Styx to sort out those other, *darker* creatures. After all, he's much more of an expert there than I..." And with that last, enigmatic verbal jab, Cian melted away on a fresh burst of ozone...like a wavering desert mirage boiling in the heat of the Sahara. There one moment, gone the next.

*Hmm...so that's what shimmering is.*

Blinking, calling herself back to the present, Kate turned to face Styx. The length of the room separated them, and yet, inexplicably, it felt more like miles.

*Why hadn't he denied any of Cian's wild claims?*

So much in her world had tipped upside down in the space of a few short hours. Things that utterly defied every basic Human view of reality. Monsters that ripped their victim's throats out. Grown men literally popping in and out of rooms in a flickering mirage. A stranger who claimed her very identity was suspect...the very same stranger who claimed to be her brother. Her brother of all things... Energy orbs that defied the laws of science...or religion...or...God help her, she didn't even know *how* to classify that one. *Quickening...*

But this unfathomable distance between she and Styx bothered her more than anything else. Her brain ran circles around all that she'd heard tonight. Then she froze in her tracks as one of Styx's comments came back to her.

"What did you mean when you said...*one of* my kind?" She faced him, searching every nuance of his face as a tight ball of dread lodged itself painfully in the middle of her chest. "What, exactly, is *your* kind?"

## Chapter 16

Styx dragged his hand down over his goatee and stifled a groan. She *would* have to start there. Kate stared at him as though he'd suddenly sprouted another head. As though he were a stranger and not the male she'd been on the brink of giving herself to.

"You know who I am," he whispered softly, rising from the sofa. Restless energy pushed him to pace the room.

"I didn't say *who*, I said *what*." She tucked a lock of hair behind her hear and crossed her arms over her chest in an emphatically defensive stance. "You know what I mean."

"You're not ready for this, Kate," he hedged, easing closer. "Let's deal with this one thing at a—"

"Cut the bullshit, Styx," she snapped. Temper danced in her brilliant green eyes. Her fiery locks cascaded down her back and around her shoulders.

*Dios*...she looked every bit the enraged goddess.

He shuddered with need. His hands reached for her. Ozone sizzled, filling the room. His own eyes went wide, and he came to a halt, remembering the stunning jolt that had seared his palms when he'd tried to remove her from the threat of Cian earlier. She'd all but electrocuted him. She clearly wanted the truth...all of it, and yet, he feared pushing her too far. She'd been forced to face too much all ready. How much more could she handle?

Hell, floating in a swimming pool brimming with gasoline as he toyed with a book of matches suddenly seemed much, much safer.

"Okay..." Dragging his palm across the back of

his neck, he paced haltingly away, then stormed back, fists clenched at his sides. "You have to promise me that you will hear me out...all of it."

Ozone slowly receded.

"You think, after what Cian told me...after what I've seen with my own eyes...that anything you have to say could possibly shock me?"

"I'm not worried about shocking you," he muttered beneath his breath as he thrust his hands deep in his pockets. "I'm more worried about frightening you." Her brows drew together, and she opened her mouth to speak, but he quickly interrupted. "Shh... Just...just bear with me...all right?"

Lifting a brow, Kate pinched her lips together and nodded.

"I don't ever want you to fear me, *querida*. I'll never hurt you, Kate," he began. *Madre de Dios, let her believe him.* "I swear to you I'll never harm you. You know that, don't you?"

She stared at him for a long moment, and he nearly changed his mind about telling her the truth of his existence. At length, though her frown remained, she nodded once more. "Yes. I believe you."

His breath slipped out on a long relieved sigh. "Cian told the truth when he said other races exist."

"Other *races?*"

"Yes. But I'm not talking about something so simple as Hispanic or Asian. I'm speaking in bigger terms...Werewolves, for example."

Kate suddenly shook her head, a mocking smile curling at the edges of her lips. "Yeah, like I'm supposed to be Faerie... If you're going to try and tell me that *you're* a Werewolf—"

"Halfling, *querida mia*...you are a Halfling. And no, I'm not Werewolf." He laughed hollowly, though there was little humor in him now. "Kate, you need to understand that other races do, indeed, exist. And, despite what popular fiction might proclaim, those races work very hard to co-exist...even with Humans."

"Okay." Her rapt gaze fixed on him as she sat down on the sofa. Tucking her legs up beneath her, she pulled a throw from the back of the sofa and wrapped it around herself. "I'm not going to like this, am I?"

Styx joined her on the sofa. Unable to resist the urge to touch her, he claimed her hands and peered deep into her eyes. Where best to start? What was the best way to ease her into the truth of what he was? "Each race has its own strengths, as well as its own weaknesses, as you've already begun to discover." He drew a deep breath and plunged on. "You are Faerie, Kate...on your way to becoming Immortal."

"Immortal?" Kate spit the word out as though it had burned her tongue.

She began to shake her head in denial, but he squeezed her hands tenderly and nodded. "Yes, you are. You can't...and I won't...deny it any longer."

*Christo*...she looked so lost, so damned vulnerable curled up like that, wide-eyed and pale. He wanted nothing more than to scoop her up on his lap and hold her. Wanted to reassure her that he would never let anything or anyone hurt her. That he—and he alone—would keep her safe. Funny that. In the end, she—in all likelihood—could potentially be more powerful than he was.

It didn't matter. He would give his life to keep her safe.

In all fairness—and in spite of his naturally protective nature where she was concerned—Kate deserved to be treated as an equal. As such, she warranted all the facts.

Or as many as he was capable of giving, at the

very least.

"Since you brought up Werewolves...that seems as good a place as any to start." She murmured consent, and he searched her eyes, breathing a silent sigh of relief that she appeared to be granting him the benefit of doubt. "I know O'Callaghan may have left you with the impression that Werewolves are...less than perfect, shall we say. To a point, he does have some facts correct. They do have deplorable self-control." A small grin tugged at his lips when he considered Zack's tendencies to overindulge in food and women. To be fair, at least as far as food was concerned, Zack had little choice. A Were's metabolism was the highest of any species, demanding near constant appeasement. Zack's inclination for constant female companionship, on the other hand, was an entirely different kettle of fish all together. "But...they are loyal to a fault when they make a commitment."

"And the moon thing?"

"Myth."

"A Werewolf bite...can it turn others into..."

"No. Again, myth," he explained. "Werewolves...breed. They don't—can't—further their race by biting Humans. But it takes a very *special* female to mate with a Were, to successfully breed with a Were."

She appeared to be puzzling over that one, but she didn't press for more. She was taking this better than he expected, and Styx began to relax somewhat. He settled farther back against the sofa and drew her unresisting form into his arms. His fingers toyed with the silky ends of her hair, and, as she nestled her head onto the crook of his shoulder, he pressed a soft kiss to her forehead. The scent of strawberries tempted him to take more, but now was not the time.

"Werewolves are probably considered more,

well...shape-shifters, I'd guess you'd say. There are numerous societies within the Werewolf race as a whole, too many to go into now anyway, just like the Faerie. Hell, probably more than I'm even aware of. At any rate, I don't want to confuse you, so we'll just keep it basic for now."

"You speak as if you know Werewolves quite well...yet you say you aren't one of them. I got the impression from Cian that the Faerie keep mostly to themselves on this...this Isle of Fae? Is that true of all the races? Do they all keep to themselves?"

"No...the Faerie are a race unto themselves. They are the only race with the ability to control and manipulate the environment around them. But I'm told each particular individual, for lack of a better word, *specializes* in one particular element, be it wind, water, fire, etc. As such, they view their magick as...well, as next to godliness. Most have the mindset that any other type of magick...any other *power* is unnatural." He ran his hand up and down her arm, from shoulder to elbow and back, bracing himself to soothe her should she become upset by his next revelations. "And I am quite familiar with Werewolf abilities...I live with one."

A moment passed before she went rigid in his arms. Twisting around to frown up at him, she squeaked, "Zack?"

Styx nodded, waiting for her to assimilate that bit of information.

"But he seemed so...so *normal.*"

"He is normal." Well, as normal as any two hundred plus pound male who could transform himself into a living, breathing nightmare complete with claws and fur and fangs.

Then again, Zack probably thought the same of him.

Minus the fur, of course.

"That's not what I meant," she grumbled,

subsiding back into his arms. "I just thought...I don't know. That he'd be more... I don't know—just forget it. Go on."

Smiling, he settled her into his arms again. He let a long moment pass in which he stroked her hair, her arm, breathed in her scent, and simply savored the warmth of her cuddled close to him. Never had he been so content with the straightforward process of just holding a woman. Always there'd been demands. Expectations. Seduction and nourishment had been the driving factors.

This was different.

This was effortless.

*This* was...peace.

"There are Warlocks and Witches...Demons and Angels. Banshees and Nymphs. Goblins, Mermaids, Valkyrie, and Muses...and Vampyre..."

"And they all live among Humankind?" Her fingers traced lazy patterns on his jean-covered knee, distracting him. "Out in the open?"

"Most do, yes."

"So, where do you fit in to all this?"

*Ah...the million dollar question. His kingdom for a simple answer that wouldn't send her frantically searching for the nearest wooden stake.*

"I am Vampyre."

Dead silence. She didn't move a muscle. She wasn't even breathing. *Dios*, but her heartbeat had taken off like a racehorse fresh out of the gates. The sound of it thundered in his ears. He held himself still, rigid, waiting for her to jump from the sofa and streak for the door, shrieking every step of the way.

*¡Mierda! Please, don't let her scream for Cian.*

"Come again?" she croaked.

"Vampyre, Kate. I am Vampyre."

Slowly, cautiously, she pushed herself up and out of his arms. Just as slowly...*Dios*, was she afraid sudden motion might trigger some predatory instinct?...she turned to gape, wide-eyed at him.

"Vampyre?"

He nodded, careful to keep his expression as non-threatening as possible.

A deep breath shuddered from her. "Like, like Dracula?"

*Christo...again with the movies...*

She was as bad as Cole's Alex. Well, he supposed he had it coming after she'd compared Cian to Tinkerbelle and he'd laughed. Their keyboardist Devon was forever lecturing him about Karma. He supposed this would be a perfect example of what goes around comes around.

"No...yes...well, ah, sort of."

She frowned at him, demanding, "Well, which is it?"

Wow, *that* hadn't been the reaction he'd been expecting. Not at all...

"Oh, come on." Kate blew a loose strand of hair from her eyes, settling the blanket around her shoulders once more. "After all I've seen and heard tonight, I've given up being surprised. I think I'll just claim shock." Once she had the blanket where she wanted it, she leaned her shoulder against the back of the sofa and regarded him with a steady gaze. "I suppose I can always check myself in for a psych eval tomorrow if these delusions persist."

Frowning, he leaned forward, deadly earnest. "Kate this isn't a delusion. You really are—"

"I know," she assured him softly. "I'm just trying to deal with this all as best as I can. I guess it was a poor shot at humor. Sorry."

Come to think of it, she did look a little dazed.

"Maybe you should rest for a while. We can talk about this more after you've had some sleep."

"Don't be ridiculous. Might as well get this over with. I'll just reserve the right to scream my head off for tomorrow if that will make you feel better." He was at a loss for words. Had she finally succumbed to nerves?

Ever inquisitive, Kate plied him with question after question. Some of them so astute as to be frightening. Did he, in fact, exist on blood. *Yes.* Could he eat Human food? *Not advisable.* Could he drink without killing? *Yes.* Was he able to drink from his hosts without changing them? *Yes.* Were there willing hosts, or did he require some kind of mind control in order to feed? *Yes, there were willing hosts. But most Vampyre chose not to risk exposure, therefore they nearly always exerted at least some level of* persuasion. Was he the "undead?" He lifted her hand and placed it on his chest, directly over his beating heart.

Some questions were so bizarre, so comical he had trouble maintaining a straight face. Did he sleep in a coffin? *No.* Could he change into a bat and fly? *Eww...that didn't even justify a response.* Still, he did his best to answer each and every question in a straightforward and concise manner.

"You mentioned that some...Immortals," she tripped over the word as if she still found that particular term unbelievable...Faerie and Werewolf and Vampyre she accepted without batting an eyelash, and yet Immortal seemed to leave her reeling, "have special powers."

"Um-hmm," he murmured, stroking the back of her hand with his fingertips. He couldn't seem to be around her anymore and *not* touch her.

"Do you have any of these...powers?"

His fingers stilled on her skin. Again, he felt he was walking along a precipice. Century upon century he'd kept his ability a secret. And now, in a matter of days, it was as if the whole world knew...or was about to find out. But he couldn't keep this from her...not from his mate.

"I do," he said quietly, peering deep into her

eyes. How would she react? "You have to understand, those of us with special talents go out of our way to keep them secret. There are some beings out there who would...*exploit*...these abilities. Just like in the human world, those with special talents are considered...abnormal. Even among our own kind, we are looked upon as mutants or freaks of nature."

"But that's just ridiculous," Kate burst out, shaking her head and frowning. "You can't help how you're...made."

A slow smile stole across his lips, and any lingering tension seeped from his body. He should have known his Kate wouldn't look at the situation as others might. He slid his arm around her shoulders, drawing her closer again, needing to feel her secure in his arms.

"Nevertheless, it is true." He rubbed his cheek against her hair, savoring the scent of strawberries. "I am a *dream walker*. I can send myself into a trancelike state and enter the dreams of anyone I've physically touched."

She seemed to ponder his words for a time, then she twisted her head around to peer up into his eyes. "Have you ever *dream walked* with me?"

The vivid memories her question brought to mind, stirred carnal hunger in his veins.

"Not intentionally," he assured her, then he admitted, "But, yes, I believe I did once."

Color swamped her cheeks. Quickly she ducked her head, but she made no more comments on the subject as she toyed with a button on his shirt.

At length, she eyed him speculatively. "You don't have fangs."

"I do." Why did it feel as if she'd just insulted his virility?

"I don't think I would have missed something like that, Styx." Wry sarcasm dripped from each word. "Show me."

*¡Madre de Dios!* She *had* lost it after all. She wanted to see his fangs. The very idea, however, sent a ripple of lust coursing through his veins.

Stunned, he stared down at this amazing woman in his arms.

Bit by bit, he let the change overtake him. His eyes began to burn. The skin on his face tightened, bunching between his brows. His gums throbbed as his fangs stretched, long and razor sharp inside his mouth.

Her eyes widened in an unmistakable expression of bemused fascination as he opened his mouth for a lethal display of fangs. Kate's lips parted, but no sound came out. As if in a trance, she slowly lifted one hand, finger extended, and unhurriedly traced the length of one fang with her fingertip. Styx groaned aloud. She may as well have rubbed herself all over his cock. Coming from this particular female, the sensation was nearly the same.

Without warning, Styx captured her wrist in his hand, holding her immobile with his fixed gaze. Canting his head down, he stared up at her from beneath his brows, letting the full measure of his desire for her—and all those things he longed desperately to do to her, do *with* her—shine in his glowing eyes. His tongue swirled around that dainty fingertip, drawing it into his mouth, laving it. Kate sucked in a sharp breath. Her eyes shot wider, dilated.

He gently nipped at the tip of her finger, and her breath rushed out on a ragged sigh.

Blinking, she visibly forced a swallow. "You said..." She forced another swallow, cleared her throat. "You told Cian..." He could all but see her train of thought evaporate as he rasped his fang across the pad of her fingertip.

The dazed look in her eyes effected him more potently than any sensual caress of the most experienced female he'd every been with. Releasing her finger from the suction of his mouth, he trailed the backs of his fingers along the column of her neck, down, down, down over the tantalizing curve of her breast. Her nipple puckered against the soft cotton, and his mouth watered. His hand slipped around her waist, drawing her ever closer.

"Yes?"

"Ah..." Kate cleared her throat again. "You told Cian I was your mate. What did you mean by that? Was that just for his benefit?"

"I meant every word, *querida*. You. Are. My. Mate." His free hand cupped the back of her neck, pulling her closer. Until his breath mingled with hers. Until the tip of his nose brushed hers. His gaze bore into hers with an intensity that left no room for doubt, no chance for misunderstanding. "You are my *Bride*."

"Bride?" Breathless. Her gaze locked on his mouth. Never before had an invitation been so obvious...or so irresistible.

No. He couldn't kiss her. Not yet. He needed to explain it all...before he lost his head completely. Reluctantly, he allowed space between them.

But not much...

"It's said, for every Vampyre, there is one true mate. One female whose blood calls to him like a siren's song. She affects him more strongly than any other before...more potently than any other ever will again. She becomes his life, the center of his universe. He would die to protect her. Do anything, *anything* to possess her...do anything to make her his *Bride*. And, once they form the blood-bond...once they take the *Vows*...nothing can separate them."

"Vows?" Kate tilted her head. A tiny frown puckered her brow as she followed his description.

"Blood-bond?"

"When a Vampyre takes a Bride, three elements combine to form the Sacred Rites. Blood, spoken vows, and sex. As the Vampyre claims his female—while they make love—he drinks from her vein and pledges his devotion for all eternity. She, in turn, does the same...takes his vein and pledges herself to him. From that moment forward, their souls merge, become one. Throughout time and space, he will be drawn to her. He will be physically unable to draw nourishment from any other. If she is Mortal, then she will periodically drink from his vein to sustain youth and vitality. Vampyre blood is as good as a fountain of youth for a Human.

"But, as I said...their souls become one." His gaze pierced hers as he willed her to fully understand. Understand and accept. "Literally. If one dies, so dies the other."

"And you think...you believe that I'm your..."

"My mate...my Bride," he supplied. *Go time...* It was all or nothing now, and so he laid his heart bare for her. "I *know* you are. You call to me on every level imaginable, Kate. I can't stay away from you. I have no other explanation for it." His lips feathered over hers, lingered, rubbed. The taste of her surrender brought an ache to his heart, a throb to his soul. *"Quiero estar contigo para siempre,"* he whispered against her mouth. *I want to be with you forever*, he'd told her. *"Te necesito." I need you*, he'd promised.

She trembled beneath his hands. Her lips parted, and he moved in with unhurried, sensual determination. Her hands slid up his chest, and a purr of pleasure rippled through him. Her arms twined around his neck, and she pressed against him in seductive abandon. Tilting his head, he gently deepened the kiss, dragging her inexorably into the tide of desire cresting through him. Shifting, he cradled her in his arms as he twisted, pining her beneath him on the sofa.

She sighed as he settled his weight atop her, the satisfied purr of a woman exactly where she wanted to be. Her eager fingers tunneled into his hair, tugging it loose of the band he'd used to confine it. Tumbling around their faces, his hair formed an intimate curtain that she hungrily clutched with both hands. Kate slid the arch of her foot over the back of his calf, stretching sinuously beneath him. A conflagration of passion raged in his bloodstream. But he was determined to go slowly. Anxious to savor every moment of their joining.

His hands slipped beneath the hem of her shirt, easing it upward as he flexed his hips, gently, insistently, pushing his painful erection against her.

*Dios, to be buried in her heat...deep, deep inside...*

He shuddered, groaning aloud, as he fought the urge to tear her clothing from her and ravish her with a wild, reckless lack of restraint that bordered on dangerous.

Ozone snapped in the air a split second before an affronted voice hissed, "Och, leech...can you no' keep your bloody hands off her for one damned minute. I swear you're no better than a bloody Werewolf."

"Faerie, so help me... Is your kind incapable of knocking on a damned door?" Growling like a rabid beast, Styx rolled away from her and sat up. "If you keep popping in like that, it's your own damned fault if you get an eyeful of something you don't like." Then, eyes-narrowed, he jabbed a finger toward the bedroom door. "And stand warned, O'Callaghan. Shimmering into that room is strictly off limits from here on out. You enter there at your own peril."

Beside him, Kate scrambled to an upright position. Becoming color rapidly blossomed in her cheeks, and Styx's throat was suddenly parched. Thirst bore down on him, hard, and his eyes began to burn.

*Christo...he'd been so close to—*

"No...no, it's all right," Kate murmured. "I'm glad you came back."

"I told you, little sister, you have only to call my name to summon me."

"I have more questions for you...I think, I...um..."

She shook her head, as if slightly muddled, and a surge of smug male satisfaction washed over Styx. He'd done that to her, scrambled her wits with a simple kiss.

Well hell, it was nice to know he wasn't alone.

"Don't you have somewhere else to be, Vampyre? Someone you could be sucking dry?" Cian leveled a hard stare at Styx. Styx snarled, but Cian continued to push, his expression cool disdain. "After all, isn't one of *'your kind'* running rampant here, decimating the Human population of this Tacoma?"

"*'Your kind'?*" Kate's eyes flared, her gaze snapped to Styx. "That monster killing those women is...is Vampyre?"

Cian's sensual lips stretched wide on a superior smile. "Astute choice of words, lassie."

"Enough, Cian," she barked without taking her gaze from Styx.

*Mierda*...the way those two slipped easily into squabbling...it was as if they'd known each other from the womb. It gave Styx chills of apprehension. Was he to deal with *this* for the rest of his life?

*Ah, Dios...daily doses of Cian...for all eternity...*

Styx shuddered...and this time it had absolutely nothing to do with passion.

"Well, is he?"

Cursing the arrogant Faerie pain-in-the-ass to perdition and back, Styx tersely nodded. "He is."

"And I suppose that's the '*special experience*' you spoke of before."

"Partially."

"So, as I said, Vampyre," Cian repeated, the word Vampyre rolling off his tongue like a poisonous curse. "Don't you have someplace *else* to be?"

"I'm staying." Styx stared the Faerie down, and, wishing to high heaven and back that *persuasion* would work on this spiteful nuisance, he envisioned Cian taking a nice long stroll on an iceberg somewhere far, far away. "You better get used to that right now."

"Well then," Cian murmured, dropping to the loveseat with a vainglorious smile. He poked curiously at a throw pillow and propped his ankle on his knee, lacing his fingers across his midsection. "I'll no' be going anywhere either, Vampyre. Someone must make certain you aren't corrupting our Kate with your filthy Vampyre ways." All pretense of innocence vanished in the blink of an eye as his smile turned downright Machiavellian. "So...'tis movin' in I'll be."

A small, bemused smile curved the edges of Kate's delectable mouth. Styx glowered, too furious—too appalled—to utter the irreverent string of curses filling his mind.

## Chapter 17

Less than twenty-four hours into their new living arrangements—Zack, too, had moved in as it was no longer necessary to keep up the pretense of two friendly bachelors from the neighboring apartment—and Kate was ready to pull her hair out by the roots. Her life had become a whirling vortex of insanity that threatened to suck her under at any moment, and she had no choice but to go with it.

If Cian wasn't *shimmering* in and out at odd hours—though thankfully he seemed to have taken Styx's warning about the bedroom being off limits to heart, he constantly antagonized Styx with mercenary determination. Zack, Cian dismissed outright with an apathetic, finely arched eyebrow. Zack blatantly ignored Cian's condescending attitude. Charming and sexy, he continued his flirtatious behavior, which only seemed to inflame Styx all the more.

A fact of which Zack seemed to take great pleasure.

Cian, too, seemed mildly amused by this turn of events. Though he made no bones about preferring that the male flirting with his little sister was of the Fae race, he turned a blind eye to the Werewolf's amorous comments and affectionate gestures.

In short, anything that got under Styx's skin was fine by him.

And, last but not least, she met Derek Crispin...the enigmatic, FBI-type agent she'd first caught a glimpse of the night of the Rogue attack. He'd been polite, but distant. When she'd offered her hand in greeting, he'd simply stared at her with a strange smile and went on speaking, his own hands firmly buried deep in the pockets of his black trench coat. He was an odd duck, all right. Attractive...but odd. Didn't anyone else notice that he went out of his way to never, *never* touch anyone? If they had, no one mentioned it.

Styx, for the most part, remained sullen and quiet. Until Cian *shimmered* out. Then, it was as if a light switch had been flipped. Though he was always attentive, the minute Cian left, he became downright solicitous. And when Zack, too, took off for parts unknown...and they were alone in the apartment...his attention was nothing short of dangerous.

During those stolen moments, he constantly sought out one excuse or another to touch her...then again, the lack of an excuse didn't seem to make all that much difference either. A brush of the hand across hers as he passed her something. The proprietary slide of his hands over her body as he'd helped her with her jacket. The protective claim of his palm at the small of her back as they walked together in the moonlight to the 24-hour convenience store a few blocks over. The delicious nuzzle of his nose and the feathery press of his lips at the sensitive curve where her neck met her shoulder as she'd perused the store's selection of fresh fruits.

And the kisses he'd stolen throughout the day were utterly devastating. Quick, nibbling pecks caught her completely off guard. Light, feathery slides of soft, supple lips absconded with her wits. Slow, deep, erotic possessions melted her defenses. Hard, desperate, devouring kisses left her panting and aching for more. No matter the depth or breadth of contact, Styx was a master at kissing. A connoisseur. The touch of his lips was like a highly addictive drug. Satisfying her hunger, and yet each stroke built up the irresistible craving for another.

He'd just devastated her with another of those long, leisurely possessions, only to leave her hanging with a smile on his sensual mouth as he steered her to a stool at the island in the kitchen. He'd insisted on preparing a late lunch for her. His efforts touched her. Though it was more than apparent the directions in the recipe book frustrated him to no end, he persisted without complaint. He'd given her a large glass of icy-cold chocolate milk—claiming milk was good for her bones, of all things—and kept up a steady, engaging flow of conversation, periodically asking what one cooking term or another meant, though he'd refused to let her lift one finger to help.

As he placed a heaping plate of French toast, scrambled eggs, and bacon on the counter before her, the smile curving his lips was an adorable mixture of uncertainty, pride, and eagerness to please. In the face of that smile, Kate promptly decided she'd choke down every last bite with a happy smile...no matter how awful it tasted...even if it killed her.

"You didn't have to do this, Styx. But it smells delicious," she assured him, smiling brightly.

And it *was* true. Her mouth had actually been watering for the last ten minutes or so.

So far so good.

He remained silent, watching her closely as she picked up her fork.

Just as she lifted the first bite of egg to her lips, Cian *shimmered* onto the stool beside her, vanquishing Styx's smile. The pleasure in his eyes was quickly shuttered away, and tension instantly roiled in his body. Disappointment settled in the pit of her stomach like a cold, hard stone. He'd been so relaxed, so...so *at ease* this last little while. To see him poker up like this actually caused a physical ache in the middle of her chest.

"What are you trying to do, Vampyre? Poison her?"

Without a word, she reached across the countertop and covered Styx's stiff hand with hers. "Cian," she scolded, "be nice. Styx was thoughtful enough to make a late lunch for me. And it smells delicious. I was just about to take the first bite, so, if you don't mind…"

"Shall I have the emergency number for a healthcare provider ready then?"

Kate gently squeezed Styx's hand and, ignoring Cian's taunts, she scooped a hearty bite of eggs into her mouth and tentatively chewed. A little bland, but very edible. Smiling, she nodded at Styx and scooped up another bite. The bacon was a little crispier than she normally preferred, but she'd rather die than criticize—especially in Cian's presence.

"The French toast is perfect," she praised between mouthfuls, and, despite his stony expression, she could tell her words had pleased Styx.

"Any moron can make French toast," Cian grumbled beside her.

"And even a Ghoul knows when he's not wanted," Styx shot back.

"So what's *your* excuse then, leech?"

"If it weren't for the fact that you're her brother, Faerie, I'd—"

"Oh, for heaven's sake," Kate exclaimed, setting her fork down on the side of her plate. Her fed-up glare skated back and forth between the two of them. "Can't you two give it a break? Just for a little while? You're driving me—"

Her pager danced across the counter near the phone charger. With an angry huff, Kate slipped from the stool, skirting Cian on her way to the small black device. One glance at the number sent her straight into her doctor mode. Without another word to either of them, she began filling her pockets. ID...check. Phone...check.

"What are you doing, lass?"

Pager...check. "I have to go to work."

"Now? You just sat down to eat," Styx argued.

"It's not safe for you to go out right now, Kate," Cian spoke over the top of Styx. "You've begun to *phase*. You're powers are too vulnerable, to unpredictable. You need to train. You need to learn to harness the *quickening*."

"Yeah, well..." Cash...check. "I don't have time to do either right now." Debit card...check. "I have to go."

*Keys...where were the damned keys?*

Spying the glint of silver, she shoved the cookbook aside and snatched up the keychain.

Keys...check.

The glance Styx and Cian exchanged was mutually irritated. If she hadn't been so worried about getting out the door without missing something, she might well have stopped to make some pithy comment over their choice of common ground.

"Kate, you're *not* going in," Styx ordered. "Al-Rashid is still out there—"

"And whose fault is that, I wonder?" Cian pinned Styx with a snide sneer. "Too busy playing Julia Crocker to worry about—"

The harsh roar erupting from the back of Styx's throat was decidedly not Human.

Exasperated, Kate laid a restraining hand on Styx's forearm and glowered at Cian. "It's Julia *Child* and *Betty* Crocker, not that it matters. Just lay off, all right, Cian?"

"You say you're worried about her safety, Vampyre? Then send her with me. I can take her to the Isle of Fae...I can—"

"Trap her there like your precious elders trapped Aaron? *Never*."

"Stop it you two!" She shoved her arm into her jacket, blanketing the room in general with a fierce scowl. "I don't have time for this."

"Kate, you—"

"No!" She jerked the coat up on her shoulders. "Cian...get it through your thick Faerie skull...I am not going to go to the Isle of Fae with you. Not now...maybe not ever."

"But lass, Da wants—"

"Your father, Cian. *You're* father," she enunciated. "Bottom line...he's a stranger to me. And, it may sound selfish, but right now, his wants aren't real high up there on my list of priorities. I don't—" She broke off, shaking her head. "I need time to think about all that. And, in the meantime, I won't be pressured into some kind of relationship. Yes, I will train...eventually...and you can teach me what I need to know. But any training will be done right here, on my terms. And you..."

She ripped the pager from her waistband, thrusting it up into the air a scant few inches from the tip of Styx's nose. "I've accepted who you are...accepted *what* you are. This is who *I* am, Styx. I. Am. A. Doctor." She re-attached the pager to her jeans, her motions jerky. "If *you* want to be with *me*, then you're going to have to deal with that." She turned one last heated glare to Cian and snapped, "and so do you."

Styx glanced quickly at the slivers of late afternoon sunshine winking around the heavy drapes, his face a roadmap of anxiety. "At least wait, let me call Zack back..."

"Just because you can't leave the apartment, doesn't mean that she can't. Or that she should have to rely on a *dog* for protection." Cian's chilling gaze scolded Styx. "*I* will keep my sister safe." Cian held his hand out to Kate, "I can *shimmer* us there. It will be your first lesson."

Kate glanced at Styx. If he turned any redder in the face, she feared he'd pass out. Taking pity on him, she shook her head. "This time...we'll walk."

But that was the only concession she'd be making for Styx's peace of mind right now. She turned away and strode toward the door. She made it two steps before Styx hooked her elbow and tugged her around, straight into his arms. She had no time to do little more than gasp is surprise as his arms wrapped around her, and his lips captured hers.

And, just like that, she slipped under the enchantment of his kiss.

For a few precious moments, his hot, hungry mouth slanted over hers...as his unyielding arms crushed her against the hard length of him, the world melted away. Her fingers slipped into his hair, and she yielded.

At length, Cian's groans of revulsion broke through the fog. Slowly, Styx released her. Dazed, she staggered back a step, and he smiled down at her. She stared dumbly back up at him.

*Gahh...he turned her mind to mush.*

His grin turned downright wolfish. "Changed your mind?"

God help her, but for the life of her, she couldn't remember a damned thing about what had happened just before he'd laid those magnificent lips on her. "About?"

Behind her, Cian snorted, plainly disgusted.

"You were on your way to work, Kate," Styx reminded her gently.

"Work?" The haze evaporated. "Work! Damn it!"

Whirling, she raced from the apartment, Cian dogging her heels.

\*\*\*\*

Styx closed the door of the dishwasher. Piling the dishes inside had vaguely reminded him of a jigsaw puzzle, where every piece would eventually fit...if you could only figure out exactly where. He'd dropped the two-sided detergent tablet into the machine as he'd seen Zack do. Now all he needed to do was start the damn thing.

Why were there so many damned buttons? Frustrated, he randomly jabbed a finger at the control panel a few times until the whooshing sound of streaming water met his ears. With a satisfied grunt, he paced to the living area. Just because he'd cooked for Kate...and washed the damned dishes...did not make him Julia Child, or Betty Crocker...or Martha frickin' Stuart.

*Damn idiot Faerie...*

This waiting was driving him out of his mind. Never before had it chafed to be away from one woman. Then again, maybe it was just the not knowing that was driving him crazy. He'd called the ER at least half a dozen times, just to make sure she was all right. From the moment she'd walked out that door, he'd had a bad feeling. That bad feeling had persisted for the better part of two hours...in fact it had grown exponentially. But each and every time he'd called, he'd been told Doctor O'Rourke was with a patient and unable to come to the phone. And, so far, she hadn't returned any of his messages.

*Dios*, he was beginning to feel like a jealous wife.

And far be it for that damned Faerie to carry a cell phone. Well, that was about to change. As long as Cian was going to lend his protection for Kate, he could damn well carry a phone like the rest of the civilized world.

Styx wanted to climb the walls, wanted it so bad he could taste it. *¡Mierda!* Nightfall had never taken so long before. At least at Cole's estate, there'd been things to do. A fully equipped gym to work out in. His laptop. The studio...

He toyed with the idea of trying his hand at writing another song. The last one had been a chart topper, after all...hell why not? With that goal in mind, he went in search of a notepad and pen. In his quest, he stumbled upon an old photo album. Some of the pictures were faded, yellowed with time. Intrigued, he carried the album to the sofa.

Styx traced the path of Kate's life through those photos. From the first one of a beaming fresh young mother—so acutely similar in looks to Kate that they could have passed for twins—as she sat in a wheelchair cradling a newborn baby in her arms, straight through to Kate's high school graduation. Opening Christmas gifts and hunting for Easter eggs, losing her first tooth and learning to ride a bike. Dance recitals and Proms.

Each and every picture only strengthened the conclusion Styx had come to.

Not only had Kate been loved...but she'd also been cherished.

Nevertheless, one thing puzzled him. In all the pictures with Kate's younger sister, never had there been a glance of animosity. Never a glimmer of jealousy or spite. Not one. Kate even had a framed photo of her sister and her sister's family on display in the living area...though he'd heard her flat out refuse to speak of it when Zack had questioned her about it earlier.

Why was there such an irrevocable estrangement?

Clearly the discord between them caused Kate a great deal of pain.

Could he, in good conscience, encourage her to mend this rift, when, in all likelihood, she'd only be forced to sever contact in a few years at best? What would losing her sister a second time do to her?

Could he somehow—

The front door opened and closed.

*Dios*, he'd been so lost in thought, he completely lost touch with his surroundings. A dangerous slip-up, even in the best of times.

Of which these definitely were not...

His nostrils flared, and he dragged in the scent of Werewolf. Zack was back. In a blur, Styx shot across the room and tucked the photo album back inside the drawer. Things were touchy enough right now without Kate finding out he'd invaded her privacy.

And Zack had a big mouth.

"Hello, darling, I'm home," Zack called in a singsong voice. The rattle of plastic bags in the kitchen was a pretty good indicator of where he'd been, so Styx didn't bother to ask.

Still morose over this latest conundrum...to encourage reconciliation between Kate and her sister, or to leave well enough alone...Styx prowled to the kitchen island and sat down.

Zack immediately frowned. "Where's Kate?"

Styx hadn't stretched the truth when he'd claimed Zack was loyal. For all his carefree, bad-boy attitude, once Zack made a commitment there was no turning back. And he'd committed himself to finding the Rogue and helping to protect Kate. Both of which Styx was supremely grateful. Every day, while Styx—and presumably the Rogue—were stymied by the light of day, Zack was out there on the streets, tracing scents and following leads. And he'd guarded Kate on the extremely rare times when Styx was forced to leave her side to hunt for food and answers of his own.

And that had become another sore point.

He was going to have to feed again. Soon. He'd put it off as long as he could, but his body was beginning to rebel. Each time he took Kate in his arms, it was becoming harder and harder to resist the call of her blood.

The last time he'd gone hunting...

He shuddered at the memory. He'd found a perfectly clean, relatively young female. With a little *persuasion*, she'd fallen willingly enough into his arms. But her curves were...wrong. Her flavor...wrong. The sound of her soft, euphoric cries as he'd swiftly drank his fill—forcing down every abhorrent swallow—had been...wrong.

At this rate, he may as well start relying on the bagged stuff. *Dios* knew, everyone else had lost their flavor since he'd met Kate.

"Styx?"

He cleared his throat, forcing himself to focus on the conversation at hand. "She got called in to the ER."

Incredulous, Zack paused to stare at Styx, a thick package of steaks in one hand, a frozen pizza in the other. "Buggar me. And you let her go alone?"

"You don't *let* Kate do anything," Styx rumbled beneath his breath. Then, louder, he added, "And she's not alone. The Faerie is with her."

Zack didn't look any less shocked. "You trusted *him* with her?"

Styx's wry gaze shot to the fading rays of sunlight seeping around the curtains. "Didn't have much choice."

"You could have called me, you know." Great, now Zack was offended. "I would have come back."

"She wouldn't wait."

"You could have done your little Vampyre woo-woo mind trick."

*If only it were that easy...* "*Persuasion* doesn't work on Kate."

"That's right, I forgot...bloody fabulous," Zack thrust a gallon of milk into the cram-packed fridge and burst out laughing. "That's gotta be a bite in the shorts."

Zack snagged a family sized package of bakery brownies and a six-pack of soda and crossed to the sofa, his laughter trailing behind him. Plopping down on the sofa, propping his feet up on the coffee table, he cracked open a soda can and tore into the brownies with the manners of a castaway fresh off the island after years of subsisting on coconuts and bugs.

He watched Zack down the chocolate and sugary drink with a sour stomach. How could he eat that stuff and not puke?

"Man, I've never seen you so twisted up over a female before," Zack commented after washing down a particularly large mouthful of chocolate goo. He grunted, got up, sauntered to the kitchen and returned with an enormous bag of potato chips. "I mean, you're always so cool...always in control," Zack continued on, as if the conversation hadn't ever been interrupted. "Your reactions to Kate are..." he tossed a broad shoulder and popped another chip, before deciding on the proper term, "extreme."

"None of the others mattered," Styx answered quietly...honestly.

Zack cocked his head to the side, a chip suspended a few inches from his lips. "Buggar me... She's the one, isn't she? She's your *Bride*."

Styx nodded. No words were necessary. Zack had seen—firsthand—the bond between Vampyre and Bride.

"Bloody bullocks," Zack breathed. "Does *she* know?"

"I told her," Styx leaned back against the sofa cushions, absently rubbing at his chest. *Ah, the ache just thinking about her...* "She just hasn't completely come to terms with it..." He shot Zack an indomitable grin. "Yet."

"Bride, huh? The poor girl," Zack murmured. He

tossed the chip into his mouth. Washed it down. "Then again, if Cole and Alex are anything to go by, maybe I should be offering *you* my sympathy." Zack's grin grew wide, and laughter burbled up, breaking free. "A Faerie *Bride*...you are so screwed."

Styx shot him a fulminous scowl, and Zack only laughed harder.

"You know, Styx, I'm thinking I need a holiday."

"Why?"

"'Cuz you blooming gits are dropping like flies, and I'm beginning to think it might be contagious."

## Chapter 18

A crackle of ozone gave Styx only a moment of warning before Cian *shimmered* into the room.

Alone.

"Where's Kate?" He was off the sofa and at the Faerie's throat—fangs bared and eyes burning—before Cian had time to blink.

"I've been summoned," Cian replied tersely. He gritted his teeth, staring Styx down with an impressive display of courage given that he had two hundred plus pounds of enraged Vampyre literally in his face. "I will take you to Kate."

"Where is—"

"Time is of the veriest, leech," Cian ground out. "We must go *now*."

"Zack—"

"The dog will have to follow on his own four paws. I have no' the time to *shimmer* the both of you." Cian's hand—strong as a band of iron—clapped onto Styx's elbow.

The world shifted before Styx's eyes. In a wavering fog, Kate's apartment superimposed itself upon the darkened interior of a hospital janitor's closet. Two separate images, one laid over top the other, both wavering in disconcerting Three-D visual effects. Then Kate's apartment fell away, and blackness engulfed Styx. As soon as he felt solid ground beneath his feet, he lurched a step away from Cian and pitched forward, crashing into a shelving unit piled high with rags and rolls of plastic garbage bags. His stomach churned, his head spun. A myriad of swirling pinpoints of light swam before his eyes on a canvas of shadow, and he blinked, struggling to focus.

"Bastard," he gasped.

"Kate is through this portal and to the left, two portals down on the right."

"Portals?" Styx braced a hand on the wall, struggling to mentally keep pace with Cian's directions. Doors? Did he mean doors? Why couldn't these damned Faeries talk like everyone else?

All of a sudden, Cian stiffened, canting his head slightly to the side. His gaze seemed to go vacant for a second, before his shining blue eyes snapped to Styx. "I must go."

"Wait, does she..." He was speaking to thin air.

Hands shaking, Styx dragged a palm over his goatee. His knees felt like jelly, but at least he no longer wanted to vomit at the slightest motion. Gritting his teeth, he eased the door open and ducked his head out into a long, empty, brightly lit hallway. The antiseptic scent of hospital assailed his hypersensitive sense of smell. Then other unfamiliar scents took hold. Unfamiliar Humans. Chemicals. Stale sweat and fear.

Blood...

Saliva surged as predatory instincts attempted to engage, but he swallowed it. He was not here to feed. He was here to protect his female.

It took a moment to sift the scents, a moment to isolate Kate's essence. But it was there, calling to him like a beacon in the dark. Slipping from the closet, he staggered down the hallway, trying his best to appear normal—like he hadn't just had his guts ripped out twisted around and shoved back inside him—should someone chance upon him. He'd never *shimmered* before, and he was quite certain he'd rather take a stake in the heart than ever do so again. The horrendous weakness that had engulfed his entire body was slowly receding, but that didn't matter. For a Vampyre to be so weakened—even momentarily—was unacceptable.

Unacceptable, hell...it was just *wrong*.

And it chafed even more that Cian had witnessed his debilitating vulnerability. Maybe, somehow, Cian had done something to him, made the *shimmering* process more stressful than normal...the slimy, vengeful, twisted bastard.

With a string of muttered expletives trailing in his wake, Styx made his way to the door Cian indicated on unsteady legs. Kate's scent was stronger here. From through the closed door, he heard her voice unexpectedly call out, "Clear."

An odd click-whoosh-pop followed her command.

He eased the door open and gazed through the crack. Several men and women crowded the small room, all dressed in similar fashion. Kate hovered near a gurney; blood spattered the disposable gown that covered her scrubs. She'd tucked her beautiful hair away beneath a small tight cap the same dismal teal-blue color as her scrubs. Protective glasses shielded her eyes, and latex gloves covered her hands.

She held strange looking paddles in her hands, paddles that were hooked by long cords to some kind of machine on a rolling cart. Her hopeful gaze was riveted to a small monitor with a straight line running across it. The monitor emitted a steady, high-pitched tone.

"Damn it," Kate hissed. She stood for a moment longer, staring at the semi-naked man on the table. He looked to be in his late thirties, early forties. Blood seeped from large gashes across his chest and abdomen, pooling on the floor at Kate's feet. His right arm was mangled, and his eyes were closed. Plastic tubes ran from his arms up to clear bags suspended from metallic posts, one containing clear fluids, the other contained blood. A positive. Torn paper and plastic wrappers littered the floor, as did blood-soaked gauze pads.

It was a battlefield, if ever he'd seen one. The war waged against death.

And Kate, the defeated general, stalwartly held ground zero. Battered but not broken.

He was in utter awe, even as her shoulders sagged, and her breath seeped out.

"Time of death..." she glanced up at the large clock on the wall, "six thirty-six p.m."

Though he didn't know the man on the table, had never laid eyes upon him before, Styx's heart ached at his loss, for he instinctively knew that every patient Kate lost affected her deeply. That same instinct urged him to go to her immediately, to comfort her loss. To sweep her into his arms and whisk her away from all this blood and death.

His hand clenched on the door handle.

*"This is who I am, Styx. I. Am. A. Doctor."* She'd told him. *"If you want to be with me, then you're going to have to deal with that."*

Bowing his head, he released the door handle. He would not interfere. He would let her do her job.

He could still offer comfort...just *later*.

Slipping back into the hallway, Styx turned toward the waiting room. And, without warning, through the hospital scents came another essence. Strong. Unmistakable.

Vampyre.

Razor sharp crystals of ice raced through his veins. Impossible.

He *had* to be wrong. *Please*...let him be wrong.

*Ava*...

He'd not scented her in nearly half a millennia, but he could not mistake her for another. She'd sired him. Her essence, however abhorrent to him now, was a fundamental part of him. No matter how he wished it otherwise. Tensing, he followed her trail down one hallway after another. There, just at the juncture of another corridor, he caught the soft ripple of dark silky hair, the edge of a deep crimson skirt.

She was running from him.

The fool...how dare she come this close in the first place.

Then he nearly stumbled over his own feet. *Why* had she come here? The answer slapped him in the face. The dream he'd shared with Kate. That could be the only reason. He'd put Kate in danger without even trying. The very thing he'd been resisting...*dream walking* with Kate...and he'd slipped up *once*. How could fate be so cruel?

He'd kill Ava.

He would tear her limb from limb, female or not, if she so much as glanced Kate's way. Fury shoved caution aside, and he vaulted forward at phenomenal speed. He caught Ava by the arm, jerking her around to face him. Though she bared her fangs at him, he saw no surprise in her eyes. With an angry growl, he pushed her inside the nearest room. Thankfully, it was empty.

"What are you doing here, Ava?" His claws curled, digging into the flesh of his palms. Oh, how he longed to rip out her throat. Never again would this malignant creature taint another innocent.

Never again would she cause him or anyone else pain.

"Come now, by beautiful Nico...is that any way to—"

"Never call me that again," Styx snarled, grabbing her by the throat, squeezing, cutting off whatever lies she'd been about to spout. Her pulse fluttered beneath his palm; her eyes shot wide. Licking her lips nervously, she gently grasped his wrist and shook her head slightly.

"Wait," she mouthed.

His eyes narrowed. "Why? Give me one reason I shouldn't sever your head from your shoulders and rid the world of you?"

"Mean no harm," she gasped, the gurgle of her words vibrated against his palm.

Her wide, exotic brown eyes pleaded with him, and, cursing himself for a fool, he released her with a violent shove. She flew across the room, crashing onto an empty hospital bed in an undignified sprawl. Slowly righting herself, she smoothed her designer clothes, ran a hand over her long, smooth hair, and smiled at him.

*Actually smiled...the treacherous bitch.*

"Haven't you forgiven me yet, Nico? Come now, it's been so very, very long..."

"Styx," he grated. "My name is Styx...like the Rivers of Death."

"As you wish," she murmured with a submissive nod.

Again, his eyes narrowed. He didn't buy the subservient act for a second. That was all it was, after all. An act. He didn't trust her any farther than he could spit.

"I'm going to ask you one last time, Ava... Why are you here?"

"A number of reasons, actually," she demurred. Casually, as though the threat of death didn't hang over her head like a guillotine waiting to draw first blood, Ava rose and wandered the perimeter of the room, idly tracing a finger over a windowsill here, a shelf there. Her stilettos echoed sharply in the silent room.

"My patience grows thin, female," he growled.

"Always so hot-blooded," she purred, turning to face him, her movements a sinuous, erotic flexing of toned muscle. "I've always loved that about you." Her gaze tracked its way slowly down the length of him, and he fought the urge to shiver in revulsion.

How could he ever—even for one insane Human moment—have thought this creature beautiful? How could he have been so stupid?

His expression must not have been what she had been expecting. A frown puckered her smooth brow, and her sensual lips twisted bitterly. "Still carrying a grudge, I see."

Hatred raged through him. His nostrils flared. His fangs lengthened. His vision narrowed to the pulse beating at the base of her throat. But, unlike his fixation on Kate's pulse, the only desire he felt for Ava, was the desire to destroy. How dare she make light of what she'd done to Thomas? To Eliza?

"Okay, okay…" Folding her arms across her ample, well-showcased breasts, she tapped long red nails on the dusky skin of her elbow. "One would have thought, after all these centuries, that your disposition might have improved, even minutely. Especially given your new pet."

A sly smirk slid across her lips when his eyes flared. She'd hit pay dirt with that catty remark, and well she knew it.

"You'll have to forgive my curiosity, but I just couldn't resist. I had to see with my own eyes the female who finally snared my brawny Spaniard. After all, you've gone all these years ignoring your…*talents*. Fighting them. And, at long last, the great Nico…oh, excuse me…" she sneered disdainfully, "the great *Styx* finally caved…and for a helpless little Human female no less. Such a shame—"

In the blink of an Immortal eye, Styx was across the room, his hand clenched tight on her neck once more, claws digging into her yielding flesh.

Ava gasped, genuinely shocked judging by her unmasked expression.

"Kate is my *Bride*," he hissed.

Ava's mouth fell open. Her eyes rounded in

shock. For a split second, her hands went lax around his wrist. It was the one...and probably only...rule of the Vampyre code that was ingrained in every Vampyre from rebirth...the one rule no one in his or her right mind ever tampered with. Never harm a Vampyre's *Bride*. Unless you had a death wish, of course. Tiny, quick nods rippled her hair around her shoulders. He eased his grip, but this time he didn't let go completely.

"She will come to no harm by my hand," Ava vowed quickly. "I swear it by Amun-Ra."

Swearing by her Egyptian gods was probably as close as Ava would ever get to honesty.

He still couldn't find even the tiniest kernel of trust for her.

"I have come to regret a great many things, Styx," Ava alleged. "I am here to try to correct one such mistake."

"That being?"

She licked her lips again and gently, carefully pried his hand from her throat. With a narrow-eyed warning, Styx let his hand fall to his side. Trails of crimson trickled from the wounds his claws had carved into her skin.

There was no remorse in his heart. Only hatred.

"The Vampyre you hunt...I can help you find him."

His scowl slowly shifted to a confused frown. "How?"

"A Sire can find all her creations," she whispered. And she waited.

The venomous jolt of her claim sank through him, and Styx staggered back a step, sickened. Horror-stricken. "You?" The bitter taste of bile rose in the back of his throat. "It was you? You changed al-Rashid?"

She might just as well have taken ownership for the Black Plague; he could scarce wrap his mind around her confession.

"Yes. It was I. You see, I was so very...*peeved* with you, my darling. At first, I couldn't believe you would actually cast me from your life. And then, later, I was shocked that you would truly stand by your threat. I was really quite put out with you, Styx. And changing Amir seemed a good idea at the time," she offered with a careless shrug. "After all, who else did I have to commiserate with over your deplorable behavior?" Then her finely shaped brows drew together, and her lips quirked ruefully. "How was I to know the ungrateful wretch's anger could possibly be so great? His need for revenge turned him to bloodlust almost from the first."

Incredulous, Styx gaped at her, "And so you loosed him on the world?"

"Don't be ridiculous," she scolded. "I'm not that stupid. Those miserable busybodies at the TFRA would have been pounding down *my* door. Besides, that was nearly two full centuries ago."

His frown deepening, Styx tilted his head, scouring her face for some sign of treachery. He found none...for a change. "Then where has he been all this time?"

"Confined, of course."

"Confined?"

"Confined," she quipped. "You know...locked up, in the can, behind bars..."

"Where?" Was it really possible she'd sired al-Rashid, then kept him imprisoned all this time when she'd realized he'd gone Rogue?

"Oh, darling, I have this lovely little villa in Italy, complete with its own dungeon." Her eyes lit up, and she slithered closer, trailing a pointed nail down the middle of his chest. "It's right on the sea. When the moonlight shines down on the water just so, even the most hardened of hearts can think only of romance. You really must come see it. The things

I could—"

"Al-Rashid," he reminded her pointedly, knocking her hand aside.

A small muscle at the corner of her eye ticked in irritation, but she withdrew across the room and perched on the edge of the hospital bed. "Well," she replied pertly, crossing her legs as she examined her cuticles. "I never imagined he'd decide to replace his harem...you know, he killed every last one of those poor girls after you and your friend escaped?"

"What?" Styx staggered to the adjoining bed and sagged to the mattress.

"Mm-hmm," Ava confirmed, inclining forward at the waist. Her avid expression was far more suitable for gossiping at a beauty salon rather than to be relating the heinous acts of a psychopath. "Every last one. Phhit," she drawled, drawing a finger across her throat. "Even that pretty one...I believe she was his first wife. Dear me, what *was* her name? Marci...Carly...no, no that's not right." She shrugged indifferently, adjusting the hemline of her skirt.

"Kali," Styx whispered, the name dredged up from some long forgotten memory.

"That's it...Kali," Ava chirped. "And that other one...um, Layla, I think he called her. He killed her, too. And she'd been with child, from what I heard. Shameful behavior...but he kept ranting on and on about tarnished honor. I swear, all you males think about is honor," her smile grew wicked, "and sex. You were always an expert on that subject, darling. Oh, how I've missed you. However, I digress. Yes, indeed. He killed them all with his bare hands. How many of them were there in all, do you know?"

"Twenty-seven." He could barely get the words out for the thick acidic bile in the back of his throat.

Twenty-seven females. All dead.

All his fault.

Even an unborn babe...

*¡Madre de Dios!* What had he done?

Never mind that al-Rashid's women had welcomed him and Cole to their beds like returning heroes. Never mind that he'd not forced a one of them.

Guilt sliced him to ribbons. He'd been so damned self-righteous, condemning Ava all these centuries for the deaths of his friends...two innocent lives...when he'd been, however unintentionally, responsible for twenty-seven—twenty-eight...ah, how could he forget the babe?

One night of passionate education. One night of earthy, erotic bliss.

One—innocent, he'd thought—night of passion.

The price? Twenty-eight innocent lives forever lost.

Dear God, *he* was the monster.

\*\*\*\*

Kate stepped out into the hallway, fatigue dragging at her. It would be hours before she could go home, and yet all she could think of was a nice soft bed...and Styx's warm arms. She regretted being so harsh with him, regretted parting the way they had, and yet she felt justified. He had to get it through his head that just because of all this other...insanity...she wouldn't stop being a doctor, wouldn't stop trying to save lives. *This* was who she was, damn it.

Kate turned down the long corridor to her office. She needed a few minutes to regroup, particularly after that last patient, and she knew better than to waste a lull in ER activity. Grab a rest while you could. You never knew if you'd get another chance all night.

It always hit harder when they were young...*had been* young. Past tense.

Closing her eyes, she dragged the surgical cap from her head and pushed the door to her office open. Weary to the bone, Kate flipped the light switch on as she stepped inside the room. She made her way across the small space and cranked the window open. Leaning her palms on the ledge, she closed her eyes once more and dragged the clean fresh night deep into her lungs. Breath after breath, the tension gradually melted away.

Being a doctor was all she'd ever known. All she'd ever wanted to be.

But reality refused to be ignored.

She was also Immortal...or would be soon, if Cian and Styx were correct. How long could she keep up the façade of a normal existence? How long did she have before people started wondering why she never got a single gray hair? Why she never wrinkled, never got sick, never aged?

Then what would she do?

The blare of a siren cut through the stillness. The strobe of ambulance lights shot adrenaline through her system. *Incoming...*

Uncertainty for the future was thrust to the back burner. She had responsibilities *now*. Wounded to heal, lives to save.

Whirling on her heel, lifting the surgical cap to her head, Kate lunged forward, only to screech to a halt. Her eyes went wide, and her hand instinctively covered her throat as she backpedaled.

The woman from the alley...only she wasn't a woman. Her eyes were wild, her skin unnaturally pale. And she had fangs.

*Definitely not Human...*

A Rogue, Agent Crispin had called her.

*Oh God, Oh God...*

Her gaze slipped past the woman's shoulder to the closed door behind her. If she screamed for help, would anyone hear her?

If she screamed for help...would that just give this Rogue more victims?

Tamping down the urge to bolt...she'd seen this woman move before, and knew it would be useless...Kate dropped the surgical cap to the floor and let her hands fall to her sides. Loose.

Ready...

"What do you want?"

*Don't panic, don't panic. Focus. Channel the energy.*

The Rogue slowly shifted to the balls of her feet. She canted her head, her deep brown eyes turning amber...glowing. The smile knifing across her features send paralyzing fear through Kate like a bolt of lightning.

"I want you dead," the Rogue hissed.

Kate's nerves began to tingle. Her pulse sped up, her breathing turned fast and shallow. Just as it had back in the alley. Right before everything slid out of focus and went completely black.

*No, not like this...focus, Katie girl. Leash it. Contain it. Control the quickening...*

She drew a long, deep breath. Forced another. And another.

And felt, clear to her soul, the moment the power ebbed and flowed at will. At *her* will.

*"Och...that's right, it is a part of you, lass, stop fighting it..."* The memory of Cian's voice filled her head. She could do this.

The Rogue's wary gaze dipped to Kate's hands, widened. Kate followed her gaze and was amazed to see twin points of purple light dancing on her palms. Just like Cian's.

*Cool...*

The energy orbs fluctuated, and she immediately chastised herself for loosing focus. This Rogue wasn't here for a magick trick. She was here for blood. Kate's blood.

Well...if Kate had anything to say about it, she wasn't going to get any.

In the blink of an eye, the Rogue lunged across the room. Kate forced the power outward, and those energy orbs burst from her palms, missing the Rogue by scant inches. In fact, the tips of her flying hair smoked. The energy orbs blasted against the far wall with a loud crack, just above the doorway, leaving charred, round holes where they'd connected with sheetrock.

Framed degrees and medical certifications danced on the wall as smoke curled away from the blackened surface. Another energy orb shot free of her palm, flying wildly through the air, and burst against the door. Charts and paperwork shot into the air and scattered across the floor as the Rogue dodged the second attack and crashed into Kate's desk.

Firing energy orbs willy-nilly, Kate managed to herd the Rogue far enough from the door that she could make good an escape. Wrenching the door open, Kate shot out into the hallway like a missile. Her mind raced half a step ahead of her feet. Dare she run to a more crowded area of the hospital and pray that causing a scene might put the Rogue off? Would she only create a mass panic as the Rogue went on a killing spree?

*Where in the hell had Cian gone?*

God, why hadn't she waited until Styx could have come with her?

A broken sob caught in the back of her throat as Kate skidded over the polished tiles, rounding the corner at an all out sprint. Crying wouldn't do any good. Only running. Running faster. The vacant nurses station flew by. Past the gift shop she ran. Down the hallway she raced. Pictures on the walls, numbered doorways streaking by in a blur. Her heartbeat pounded in her ears, drowning out any possible footsteps that may or may not be following her. Her lungs strained inside her chest, threatening to burst at any moment. Away from the crowded ER she ran. Crisscrossing the hospital hallways on the first floor. Fortunately this floor was seldom utilized for inpatient use, but there still should have been some staff present. Where had everyone gone?

And still Kate ran. She didn't dare stop. Yet, she knew she couldn't keep running indefinitely. Damn it, she should have let Cian *shimmer* her earlier...should have grilled him ten ways from Sunday about all the ins and outs of that particular method of Faerie travel. If she survived this nightmare, Styx was just going to have to put his reservations aside. No way in hell was she ever going to leave herself vulnerable and trapped like this again...like some damned lab rat in a maze.

Tossing a glance over her shoulder, she slowed a bit. No one was following her...yet. She had to calm down, get her bearings. Where the hell was she anyway?

Oh, shit. She'd passed this nurses station once already.

Definitely needed to get her bearings. At this rate, all the Rogue needed to do was sit back and sharpen her fangs as she waited for Kate to run straight back into her open arms.

Chest heaving, Kate slid to a halt. Her gaze flew from one end of the long hallway to the other. Okay. Down that way was...the Lab, X-ray, waiting rooms...all should be empty by now, or nearly so. And the other way...hospital rooms...and helpless patients.

Heading back toward the X-ray sign, Kate peered cautiously around the corner. No sign of the Rogue. Had she lucked out? Had she somehow managed to confuse the Rogue with her wild flight?

She hoped so. She'd certainly done a good job at confusing herself there for a moment. The hallway was empty, so she slipped around the corner and hurried toward the end of the hallway. Just around the next corner was the hospital entrance to the ER. Maybe she could blend with the crowd, get to a phone, call for help.

Kate slowed long enough to reach for the door. Twisting around to glance one last time behind her, she jerked the door open and darted through the doorway, gaze still locked on the hallway behind her, vigilant for any sign of the Rogue. The hallway remained empty as the door slowly slid closed.

Dropping her chin to her chest, Kate braced a palm against the cold metal door. Relief swam through her in dizzying waves. Safe. She was safe. She had to get out of here. Get home somehow. Styx would know what to do.

Steel bands clamped painfully around her, crushing her, hard and unforgiving. A chilly breath feathered over the side of her neck. Icy lips brushed her ear.

"Tag...you're it."

Raw, searing pain sliced into the side of Kate's neck, burning her all the way to her toes. Her body convulsed, rocked by agony, paralyzed by shock. The metal door before her blurred. Oh, how she tried to focus, tried to summon the quickening. But the pain was just too much. Too...much...

The brightly lit corridor grew dim. The pain grew distant. The loud whooshing in her ears slowed to an alarmingly lethargic tempo. And then she was floating, free of the pain as darkness closed in.

\*\*\*\*

Styx stiffened. A jolt of fear arced through him like an electrical current, dragging him up from the depths of guilty despair.

*Kate...*

He didn't know how he knew...or why. He didn't even know where she was. But of one thing he was suddenly and unmistakably certain.

251

His Kate was very, *very* afraid...

Styx bolted from the room, Ava completely forgotten. Fear pounded through his veins. Rounding the corner, he raced toward the ER. And then he caught the scent trail and fear became sheer terror. Layla was here. Blood permeated the air here, making it difficult to focus, but one thought had him clinging to sanity. Kate needed him. Cutting through the ER, moving faster than a Human eye could detect, he raced onward, dodging medical staff and patients and medical equipment.

Where was Kate?

*"Nico..."*

It was as if the voice—Kate's voice—had spoken aloud. And yet, he knew...knew deep in his gut...that she was communicating with him somehow through the connection they shared. Her voice was heavy...as though drugged.

*"Help..."*

*Querida, I'm coming. Help me find you.*

As if his plea had been answered, he slammed through another door and turned a corner and there she was. Caged in Layla's arms.

Limp.

His heart lodged in his throat, even as the enraged roar tore free. Layla's head jerked up, and her blazing eyes met Styx's. Her lips—lips liberally coated with fresh blood—turned up in a feral sneer. Kate's head listed to the side, exposing the ravaged flesh at the side of her throat.

Her eyes were closed.

She didn't move, didn't struggle. Didn't so much as twitch a muscle.

*Oh, Dios mio...*

Grief ripped through him. Grief and mindless fury. Layla released Kate...opening her arms in a taunting gesture...and Kate slowly crumpled to the floor. There she lay, motionless. Black rage consumed him. He flew at Layla. The impact sent them both crashing through the door and into the hallway on the opposite side. Layla was fast and strong with bloodlust, wiry. A real scrapper. Hissing and spitting, fangs gnashing, claws slashing, she instantly went on the offensive. Her claws shredded his ribs. Her fangs sank into his bicep.

He didn't feel a thing. He was beyond the pain, beyond reason.

His mate was gone.

Driven by grief and fury, Styx fought back with deadly intent. They rolled across the floor, crashing into the wall in a shower of sheetrock dust. Framed pictures tumbled to the floor, scattering broken glass over the shining tile. Strong and fast as she was— even with the added strength of newborn bloodlust and a fresh feeding pulsing through her veins— Layla didn't stand a chance in the face of Styx's counterattack.

Warm blood splattered across his chest, coating his hands. Vampyre blood dripped from his fangs. Slowly, he pushed to his feet, staring dispassionately at his hands as he uncurled his fingers and flexed his hands open. Layla's head tumbled to the floor with a sickening thud and rolled a few feet down the floor's incline.

*Kate...*

He started toward the door separating them, dread dragging at his heart, when he heard the faint inhalation of breath behind him. Spinning around, tensed for an attack, Styx froze.

*Ah, Cristo.*

Never lose track of your surroundings, and never...*never*...leave witnesses. It was part of the Vampyre creed. And he'd just failed on both accounts. A tall, heavy-set woman stood in a doorway not fifty feet away, clutching the doorframe for support. Her dark skin contrasted sharply with the white nurse's uniform she wore. Her glazed coffee-brown eyes darted from Layla's decapitated body to Styx and back again. Her hand lifted to clutch her throat, and she opened her mouth. A silver-plated nametag flashed in the bright light. Elsie Chapman, RN.

Cursing, Styx leaped over Layla's body and clamped his hand over the nurse's mouth. Her pulse hammered at his ears, and thirst bore down on him. His eyes, already burning from his battle with Layla, zeroed in on the rapid flutter of her pulse at the base of her throat. It would be so easy to give in, take as much as he wanted. Gorge himself. What was one more innocent life wasted when he'd already taken so many—however unwittingly—already?

He opened his mouth wide, long fangs drenched with blood. The claws of his left hand curled, piercing the flesh on his palm. He wouldn't even have to come up with an excuse for the TFRA...not that he really gave a damn anymore. He'd just blame Layla for the nurse's death. The female whimpered. Her eyes dilated, and she trembled beneath his palm.

Why not...it wasn't as if he had anything left to lose?

Kate was gone.

*Kate...*

A fresh wave of grief nearly doubled him over.

*Kate...*

Kate was all about saving lives...*had been*...had been all about saving lives, he corrected. To take this woman's life in the very place Kate had worked tirelessly to heal and save others was a desecration.

He couldn't do it.

Wide-eyed, the nurse stared up at him, paralyzed. Her breath puffed in and out in rapid succession through flared nostrils.

Dios, if she didn't calm down, he wouldn't have

to worry about leaving a witness behind...or killing her. She'd keel over from a heart attack, saving him the hassle of wiping her memories.

Forcing himself to concentrate, he gazed deep into her eyes and used *persuasion* to erase the last few moments from her mind. Implanting the suggestion that she turn around, find the nearest restroom, and clean herself up, then go on about her business, Styx released her. She blinked up at him from her stupor. Slowly, she turned and went back through the doorway without a peep. Heaving a deep sigh, Styx glanced back at Layla. Damn it.

Digging in his pocket, he pulled his phone free and dialed Crispin. The moment the agent answered, he barked, "I need clean up at the hospital. Layla is no longer a problem."

With that, he snapped the phone closed, shoved it back into his pocket. Though the distance to the door dividing the hallway was only a few short feet away, it was the longest walk of his life.

## Chapter 19

Pushing the door open, Styx stepped through the doorway and froze, his heart clamped in a vicious, spiked vice. Tears coursed down his cheeks, unheeded. A sob clogged his throat, and he couldn't breathe.

Dropping to his knees beside her, he gently scooped Kate's limp body up and cradled her tenderly to his chest. Head bowed, he rocked slowly back and forth. A low, keening wail echoed in the hallway. Only when he stopped to drag in another breath did he realize the desolate, wounded-animal sound came from him.

"Ah, *querida*, no..." He pressed his lips to her temple, squeezing his eyes shut tight.

Empty...

He was so empty. So cold.

He should never have left her alone. Should never have let Ava lead him away from her. How could he have been so stupid? So blind to the danger? She hadn't had time to fully *phase*...hadn't been Immoral when Layla had attacked. An Immortal might have stood a fighting chance...maybe. But a Mortal? A Mortal would never have stood a chance against a Vampyre's lethal fangs.

His precious Kate...

He doubled over her, torn to the very depths of his soul by anguish so keen, so devastating, he could only think of one thing.

The dawn...

His mate was gone. His Bride dead. He couldn't

face the thought of a future...an empty eternity...without her in it.

"*Te necesito,*" he whispered, anguished. "*Te amo...*"

A slight puff of air whispered over the sensitive skin of his throat. Styx sucked in a sharp breath, his gaze shot to her face, and he held his breath. Too afraid to hope. Movement. Just the tiniest bit of movement as her chest laboriously rose and fell. Once... An eternity passed. Again, that minute lift and fall. He strained to listen. Her pulse was so slow, so feeble, that he could only hear it by pressing his ear to her chest.

She lived!

Euphoria as he'd never known blossomed in his chest, spreading warmth and hope through him. Had she gone far enough into the phasing process to recover from wounds as extensive as these?

But reality came close on its heels.

She'd lost so much blood. *Human* blood. And her wounds continued to trickle more of her strength away...not mend. Swiftly bending over her, he let saliva surge inside his mouth and quickly licked her wounds, sealing them closed. Her blood sent a shiver of primal need coursing through him, but her health, her safety held top priority...even to the greedy beast within him.

Glancing swiftly right, then left, he sought a private haven where he could see to her without the chance of discovery, or interruption. He carefully picked her up and hurried to the first door he came to. It was a small office, dark but empty. Not bothering with the lights, he sank to the middle of the floor, cradling her on his lap. Without giving it a second thought—for her feelings on the matter, or the bond it might forge between them—he set his fangs to his wrist and pressed the gushing wound to her parted lips.

His blood filled her mouth, seeping from the corner of her lips.

"Please, *querida*," he begged. Why wasn't she swallowing? "Drink from me, angel. I can heal you...just please, please drink."

His tears fell upon her cheeks, glistening in the silvery moonlight peeking in through the uncovered window like diamonds upon her pale skin.

Her throat convulsed.

"Yes," Styx gasped as her lips slowly latched on to his wrist.

Another teardrop slipped free of his control...a glistening glimmer of hope.

The drag of her tongue over his skin speared desire to his loins even as it fed the hope raging in his heart. Her brow wrinkled slightly, but the suction of her mouth increased. The erotic sensation of Kate's mouth suckling his flesh...the very thought that his blood was, even now, bringing her back from the edge of death...was a heady, primal aphrodisiac. His jeans grew painfully tight over his straining manhood, but he wouldn't shift her to readjust himself to a more comfortable position. Wouldn't risk that she might stop feeding and not continue when she so desperately needed his blood.

"That's it, *querida mia*. Drink. Live."

At length, the room around him began to spin. Lethargy spread through his arms and legs. His vision blurred around the edges. He didn't care. He'd willingly let her bleed him dry, if only she would heel.

If only she would survive.

Abruptly, her mouth released his wrist. Dazed, it took a moment longer for him to realize she no longer drank from his vein. With great effort, he lifted his wrist to his lips and sealed his wound.

Though she remained unconscious, healthy color had returned to her cheeks. Her breathing had eased back to a normal tempo. The strength of her pulse reassured him. Heaving a sigh of relief, Styx scooted sideways, bracing his back against the wall. He drew Kate up against his chest, nestling her head into the crook of his shoulder.

*So cold...*

He'd gone too long without feeding, and the additional loss of blood had weakened him, dangerously.

*Just need...to rest...a moment.*

His muscles quivered; his stomach twisted and knotted painfully. A cold sweat broke out on his brow and upper lip. His skin felt stretched tight all over his body. Styx licked his parched lips, but it was no use, even his tongue felt swollen...and so very dry. He tipped his head back against the wall and closed his burning eyes.

Concentration eluded him, and he was unable to force his fangs to recede.

Her blood called to him.

She shifted in his arms, and it took every ounce of his will to keep his arms anchored around her. Hell, who was he trying to fool? He needed a lot more than rest. He was weak as a babe. He'd be no protection for her if al-Rashid...or perhaps worse yet, another newborn...came looking for her.

Kate's pulse pounded in his ears like the cadence of native drums, calling him to feed. Dry air seared his lungs with each racing, labored breath.

*Need...to...feed...*

Leaving her now was harder than tearing off his own arm, but he had no choice. He wouldn't risk her safety again, and, if he didn't feed soon, he could well prove far more dangerous than the Rogue he'd just saved her from. With a great deal of reluctance, he eased her slumbering form from his lap and made her as comfortable as he could on the hard floor, balling his jacket up to form a cushion beneath her head. With one last hesitant glance over his shoulder, he slipped from the room and stole down the hall.

A cacophony of sound drifted down the hallway as a door was opened somewhere in the distance. The sound slowly muffled, then disappeared. Gravitating toward the sound, Styx ducked into a small alcove near a payphone as voices grew louder. A pair of orderlies wheeled a gurney past—two Human males, one tall and thin, the other short and bald—followed closely by a familiar figure. Elsie Chapman, RN.

Ah, *Dios*, he really hated to do this…but he had no choice.

Using a swift, intense call of *persuasion*, he summoned the nurse. The effort left him weakened even further, and he sagged back against the wall, praying it would be enough.

Praying she'd respond before he became the very thing he sought to protect Kate's world from.

A mindless, heartless, monster.

Elsie Chapman, RN halted in her tracks as if she'd run into an invisible brick wall. In a melodious, accented voice that reminded him strongly of the decade he'd spent deep in the bayous of Louisiana, she called down the hall after the orderlies, "Go on with ya now. Room 318. I'll be right along."

The steady squeak of the gurneys wheels paused for a moment as the orderlies peered at her curiously. When no explanation appeared forthcoming, the squeak resumed, fading into the distance. The heavy creak of rubber soles approached the alcove.

"I'm really sorry about this, Elsie," Styx soothed. She stared at him blankly.

His eyes burned, and the skin of his forehead bunched. His fangs tore longer from his gums, sharp and thirsty. And Elsie continued to stare, utterly vacant. Styx wasted no time in appeasing his need, deliberately keeping her deep in the thrall, making it as painless as possible for the unfortunate nurse. The gnawing thirst gradually receded, and strength slowly seeped into his quivering muscles. And still he drank voraciously, too close to the edge to easily draw away from her vein.

Only when her knees gave out and she sagged helplessly against him, did he realize what he was doing.

Draining her.

Horrified, Styx clamped down on the feral urge to lap up every last drop, and he pulled his lips from her flesh, gently easing his fangs from her vein.

Grateful the thirst had been tamed, thankful invincible strength had returned to his body, he sealed the small puncture wounds on the side of Elsie's neck. Offering a subliminal suggestion that she deserved a nice long vacation somewhere tropical, he sent her on her way.

"Jamaica," she muttered faintly as she plodded down the hallway. "I bet Jamaica be plum bee-u-tiful this time a' year. I gots ta git me one o' them pretty drinks with those colorful lil' umbrella's..."

Grimacing, wiping the dampness from his lips, he eased back into the hallway and darted back to the office in which he'd left Kate. She was still curled up on her side. Still out cold. Drawing her up into his arms, he strode from the office.

He didn't care how much she might rail at him later. Her shift was *over*. He was taking her home.

The corridors passed by in a blur as he raced through the hospital once more. This was getting ridiculous. He never should have allowed her to come here in the first place...at least, not without him. He'd seen more of the inside of a Human hospital tonight than he had in all his six centuries.

Cool, damp air rushed over them as he stepped

outside into the night. Kate stirred in his arms, moaning softly. Glancing down, he paused near the bus stop, his gaze searching her face for some sign of consciousness.

In the blink of an eye, Kate became a squirming, snarling, fighting bundle of resistance. Clamping his arms more tightly around her, he ignored the startled glances aimed their way and called, "Kate, it's me…Styx…you are safe, *querida.*"

She froze. Her head whipped around, bumping his chin. "Nico?"

His heart bumped, throbbing inside his chest at the sound of his name—his real name—upon her sweet lips. Big, beautiful green eyes blinked up at him in confusion. Her befuddled gaze slid over his shoulder to the hospital, dipped to their bloodstained clothing, then scoured his face. Understanding dawned.

"Nico!" Her arms wrapped around his neck, and she squeezed so hard that, had he been Human, she might easily have snapped his neck. Kisses rained down upon his face amid hysterical sobs.

Releasing her legs, he anchored an arm around her waist, pinning her to his chest. The tips of her toes dangled a full foot off the ground. He caught the back of her head with his large palm, holding her still long enough to capture her lips with his. Without preamble, he slanted his mouth and sank his tongue deep inside her mouth. Kate's legs wrapped around his waist, clamping tight.

Startled gasps erupted all around them. Unwillingly tugged back to the here and now, Styx tore his lips from hers. Bemused, she stared at him for a long moment before her situation fully sank in.

"Oh God," she panted as her feet dropped to the pavement.

And still he held her trapped against him, refusing to relinquish the feel of her in his arms.

Warm. And alive.

"Let go," she hissed.

"No...I'm taking you home."

She pushed at his arms, but he refused to budge. "Damn it, Styx. I have to go back. They need me."

"*No.*"

Energy surged unexpectedly, just beneath the surface. Ozone crackled in the air. A chilly wind swirled around them. His hands, his arms, the front of his body...everywhere he touched her...suddenly stung. Startled, he released her. Kate staggered back, clearly drained, straight into the path of an oncoming bus.

Furious, Styx leaped forward, jerking her back to safety. Back into his arms. Right where she belonged. A heated explosion of Spanish rent the air. How dare she use her magick on him like that? Dios, she was going to drive him out of his mind yet.

"No, Kate. You are going home." He tossed her over his shoulder, a conquering warlord claiming the spoils of battle. Too drained to argue, she sagged against him. Satisfied, he braced the small of her back with his hand and strode down the sidewalk, leaving shocked gawkers behind.

A few blocks later, however, she was straining against him once more.

"You can let go of me now," she muttered against his back.

He didn't reply, just kept walking.

"Damn it. Put. Me. Down." She twisted around as best as she could, batting her ponytail out of the way. "People are staring."

Again, no response. He wasn't going to stop until he had her safely behind lock and key.

"For God sakes, Styx. Someone is going to call the police if you don't put me down. How would you explain this?" When he continued on in determined silence, she thumped her fists against his back.

"Damn it, I don't know what barbaric century you're from, but men just don't walk around with women tossed over their shoulders like this."

Frustrated, he heaved a sigh and stopped. She was right. He was calling more attention to them than necessary. Bending at the waist, he lowered her feet to the ground, but he caught her by the shoulders before she could step away. He fought to control the rage pulsing in his veins, fought to be gentle with her and not crush her in his strong hands, but, by the slight widening of her eyes and the soft hissing breath she sucked in between clenched teeth, he wasn't altogether certain he'd succeeded.

"You will never, *never* use your magick on me like that again," he demanded, giving her a rough little shake. "You will never shock me or stun me again when I am trying to protect you, *comprende?*"

His nostrils flared. His burning gaze bore into hers, and, he was fairly certain, the tips of his fangs were visible as he spoke.

Wide-eyed, she nodded...just the tiniest jerk of her head...but it was acceptance.

Satisfied, he released her shoulders, but captured her hand before she could turn away. He had no explanation for it, but he needed to touch her right now. Needed physical contact more than he needed oxygen.

Kate squeezed his hand. Perhaps she needed the contact too.

Glancing around them, she frowned.

"Where are we?"

"I don't want you taking the same route to and from the hospital anymore. Your patterns are too established. It's too dangerous. Al-Rashid could have any number of ambush points plotted out by now."

"Al-Rashid?"

That's right...she didn't know yet. *Dios* help

him, he was going to have to explain what had happened with al-Rashid and him and Cole...and the harem.

"Long story," he replied, his gaze skimming the shadows around them. "One that can wait until I have you home."

"All right," she conceded.

Thankful she wasn't pushing the issue, he tugged her closer to his side. "Come on."

They started down one darkened street, turning off onto another and another. Somewhere along their convoluted route Kate skidded to a halt. She glanced around in confusion, dragging in sharp whiffs of air.

"What *is* that smell?"

"What?" Styx paused, scenting the air.

Damp earth, smog, car exhaust. Stale Human sweat, animal feces, perfume and cologne. Nothing out of the ordinary. And then he caught it...just the faintest hint of blood.

And, layered beneath...

Vampyre.

"I've never...I've never quite smelled that before." She sniffed harder, then turned wide eyes to him. "It smells...like you. Only...different. Wilder. Musky..."

Could she scent other races now? Was this some strange effect his blood was having on her senses. He'd never before given a female—or anyone else for that matter—his blood. Didn't know if there were any unusual side effects. Cole had certainly never mentioned Alex developing heightened senses.

Or could this be another facet of phasing?

Dios, how close was she to turning completely?

"It's Vampyre, Kate. You're scenting Vampyre."

Alarm surged in her eyes.

"They aren't close, that's why it took so long to catch their scent."

She sniffed at the air again, a frown puckering

her brow. "That other scent...it's sort of...sort of familiar." Then her eyes shot wide. Her mouth fell open, and her face leeched of all color. "Blood. It's blood."

"They are feeding," he stated simply. Though there was nothing simple about the way he was feeling. Everything in him screamed to go after them...and yes, he was positive there was more than one by the varying scents...go after them and kill them before they could do any more harm.

"Feeding," she gasped softly. Then her horrified gaze collided with his. "Feeding...off a Human!" Her nostrils flared and she tensed.

Before he could respond, she jerked her hand from his and streaked away. Swearing, Styx chased after her. Damn it, she was fast, all but leaving him in her dust. Adrenaline pumped through his veins, and he forced his legs faster.

The dark silhouette of a warehouse loomed ahead, and the scent of Vampyre and blood grew stronger. He caught up with Kate as she stepped up to a small door at the front left side of the building. A small, aluminum can fixture above the door spilled weak yellow light upon the top of her head and shoulders, pooling at her feet.

His hand closed upon hers over the doorknob.

"Stop," he commanded softly, wrapping his arms around her and dragging her several yards from the door.

"They're in there, Styx. I can...I can *smell* them." Her voice held faint notes of wonder and horror, but, thankfully, no hysteria. "There is a person—a, a *Human*—in there with them. We have to get in there. We have to—"

"No, Kate. You've been too weakened tonight already, first by Layla, and then by that last surge against me. You can't risk weakening yourself further. I won't let you put yourself in danger like that. Besides, it's too late to save—" He broke off, his head whipping around to peer hard at the door. *¡Mierda!* It *was* too late. "Get behind me, *now!*"

Without giving her a moment to obey...or a choice...he thrust her behind him and planted his feet, bracing himself for the fight to come. In the blink of an eye, a flurry of blurred figures burst from the building. Smiling wickedly and dripping fresh blood, looking like a trio of Valkyrie fresh from battle, they fixed their luminous, feral gazes on Styx...and on Kate.

The blood in his veins ran cold. Three Newborns. *¡Mierda!*

Styx lowered his head a bit, staring unblinking at them from beneath his brows as he let the change take him over. No way were they getting anywhere near his Kate.

"No one is supposed to be out here, this is private property." The sharp beam of a flashlight cut through the night, and Styx caught the scent of another Human. Peering past the beam of light, he watched the portly, balding man click nervously at the radio mic attached to the shoulder of his gray uniform. "Manny, be advised we got us some trespassers out here on lot seven. Manny? Manny, you copy that?"

Styx's gaze darted to the warehouse, then held steady on the Rogues. Somehow, he doubted Manny would be responding to any more calls from his partner...ever again.

The guard's light bounced away from Styx and Kate, landing on the Rogues. "Hey...what the hell's going on?"

In the blink of an eye, the Rogues descended upon the night security guard with vicious fangs and slashing claws in an unrestrained frenzy. The guard's corpulent body jerked and twitched, but the Rogues effortlessly held him immobile as they drank gustily.

Behind him, Kate gasped, sobbing softly. Her fear was palpable, seasoning the air around them...and the Rogues picked that scent up like the wild animals they were. Their greedy, glowing eyes slowly turned Kate's way.

*¡Madre de Dios!*

He couldn't tell her to hide...they'd track her scent no matter where she concealed herself. And he couldn't tell her to run, there was no telling who she might run into now. Al-Rashid? More Newborns?

A horde of frickin' Demons?

Nor could he risk her staying with him as he battled these Newborns. If one got away from him while he fought the others, she wouldn't survive. That left him only one option. Loathsome as that option might be, Kate's safety trumped all else.

Drawing a deep breath, Styx tossed his head back and bellowed into the night, "Cian O'Callaghan of the dioane Sídhe, I summon you...get your godforsaken ass down here!"

**\*\*\*\***

Ozone crackled and gale force winds swept through the side street nearest the warehouse. Kate felt the surge of energy...and the presence of magick she'd become accustomed to whenever Cian appeared...clear to her bones. Cian's wavering image solidified as he shimmered into view. He wasn't alone.

Beside him, Zack stood still as a marble statue, looking green around the gills. The moment they solidified, Cian released Zack, surveyed the situation, then he shot to Styx's side—standing firmly side by side with the male he took so much pleasure in tormenting—as a living shield with the sole purpose of keeping Kate safe.

Trembling, Kate held her hands fisted at her sides. The *quickening* surged and ebbed inside her, like a wavering presence that couldn't quite make up its mind whether it wanted to join the fight...or slink away and hide. Unreliable.

Unpredictable.

Did she dare open herself up and call the *quickening* forth? Would she be able to harness it and thereby help them?

Or would she end up blowing them all to kingdom come?

This was all too surreal. Her head swam, and she couldn't catch her breath. She'd never seen anything so violent...so cruel...as those three female Vampyre when they'd attacked that poor, defenseless man. He hadn't stood a chance, his scream of terror dying as nothing more than a strangled, wet gurgle.

Then, fast on the heels of that thought came another. One equally as troublesome.

Were *all* Vampyre like that when they fed?

Her wary gaze settled on Styx. Would he become as they were when bloodlust was upon him? She'd seen him transformed...or, at least, she thought she had. But, what if? What if he had somehow held a bit of the transformation at bay? She'd never seen him actually feeding before. What if he couldn't control himself?

And he'd made it clear he wanted her as his Bride. He'd explained all that being his *Bride*—all that *becoming* his *Bride*—entailed. Including the blood exchange. Dear God in heaven, would he turn into the same kind of slavering, sadistic beast as these females?

Shivering, she unconsciously edged a little closer to Cian.

From the corner of her eye, movement caught her attention. Zack was shaking out of his stupor. Everything from that moment on became a blur of motion and a cacophony of hisses and snarls and roars that she might never have been able to keep track of if not for her newly developing senses.

Senses that left her reeling.

Zack, upon realizing the eminent threat, vaulted into the air. Before her stunned eyes, Zack—the devil-may-care, wickedly-handsome, teasing playboy—became the stuff of the most darkest of nightmares. His body contorted in ways a Human body were not designed to bend—and she would know, after all, how many years had she spent studying the Human anatomy?—rending his expensive designer clothing until it hung in loose rags upon his bulging muscular form. His jaws elongated and vicious, sharp teeth seemed to sprout inside his widened mouth. Long, razor-sharp claws curled, poised to rip and shred, and a thick, coarse pelt sprang forth...all over his body.

Not an animal.

And yet, definitely not Human.

Howling his fury, he launched himself at the nearest Rogue. The female spun on her heel to face him, and Kate cringed...fearful somewhere deep inside for the man she'd come to call friend, despite what he may have just *morphed* into before her eyes. She'd seen those Rogues move, seen them attack. She tensed, preparing to leap to his defense.

Oh God, Zack could be killed.

The Rogue didn't last more than a slim moment. In a quick offensive, Zack was all over her. Blood splattered the pavement, and screams rent the night. The Rogue's? Hers? Kate wasn't sure. But in less time than it took her to blink, Zack slashed his way across the female's body and tore the Rogue's head from her shoulders.

The second Rogue flew across the lot toward Cian, Styx, and Kate, snarling and rabid with her wrath. Cian calmly lifted his hands to the ink-black skies, tipped his head back slightly, and inhaled deeply. Kate's skin prickled. The baby fine hairs on her arms and the nape of her neck stood on end. A strange excitement hummed in her veins.

A bolt of purple lightning cracked through the otherwise calm night sky, arcing down from the heavens, striking the Rogue. She jolted, erupting into a ball of flame. Clearly, Cian hadn't been bluffing when he'd threatened to fry Styx—quite literally—upon their first meeting. Horrified, Kate staggered back a step.

God...could *she* do that too?

It wasn't a comforting thought.

The third Rogue, apparently not having caught on that she was in over her head, streaked toward Styx. He met her head on in a brutal crash of titan proportions, and splashes of blood once more became the order of the day. But, more disturbing to her than the unbelievable carnage she'd witnessed thus far, was the fury—the utter rage—on Styx's transformed face. He'd become the very thing he fought. Feral eyes. Lethal fangs. Distorted features. Lengthened claws. Blood-soaked and fearsome.

Slowing only when the Rogue lay in a broken, dismembered heap at his feet.

Only a few moments had passed since Cian and Zack had *shimmered* nearby, and the actual fight couldn't have lasted more than a few seconds at best, and yet from the moment those Rogues attacked the Human, it seemed time had frozen for Kate.

And in that frozen space of time, her entire world had fallen apart.

The *"truths"* that she'd only begun to accept, the changes in her own body and the strange powers she wielded as well as the fantastical alternate world Styx had carefully described to her suddenly became a nightmare.

He was one of *them.* A wild...*thing*...like those Rogues. A brutal killing machine. What if he couldn't control himself and he turned on her like that? Handsome, charming Zack...*morphed* into a monster straight out of some horror flick. And Cian...her *brother*...harnessing power from the skies, calling down deadly lightning like some beautiful, vengeful god straight off Mount Olympus.

She couldn't be part of this world.

She wouldn't.

Pressing a fist to her mouth and a hand to her throat, Kate slowly backed away from them...each and every one of them. Her wide-eyed gaze darting back and forth over each one in turn. A sob escaped her. She'd trusted them. Let them all into her home. How could she have been such a stupid fool?

The soft sound of rustling clothing broke the silence. The night security guard stirred...despite the horrific wounds on his neck and chest. Slowly, he rolled over and raised himself to his hands and knees. Just as slowly, he lifted his head.

His eerie, luminous eyes fixed on her...on the wild flutter of pulse at the base of her throat. He snarled, revealing just the tips of bone-white fangs.

Without warning, Styx closed the distance and, in one violent motion, ripped the guard's head from his body.

Ozone crackled around them. Glancing down, Kate gasped. Energy orbs pulsed in the palms of her hands. Ready to explode forth. Ready to kill the creature that the security guard had become.

*Ready to kill...*

Sobbing, Kate squeezed her hands closed, spun around, and fled, running as far and as fast as she could.

Chapter 20

Cursing, Styx left Zack and Cian and raced after his female. He tore down one street after another following close behind—she didn't seem to be running with any particular destination in mind, just running to escape. He couldn't quite catch up, she was just too fast, yet she was always within sight. Humans moved on the streets around them, unable to track them, shrugging off their passing as nothing more than a strong gust of wind.

Terror rolled off Kate in dizzying waves. Even from this distance, he could smell it, and it raked at his guts because that fear was his fault. She'd watched him kill. Seen him fully transformed, fully enraged. And there hadn't been a damned thing he could have done to prevent it. Now she was afraid of him.

He'd always been gentle with her, only showing her the best side of him. And that had been a mistake. Unfair to her. He had—however unwittingly—lulled her into believing he wasn't dangerous. But tonight, she'd seen with her own eyes that he—when provoked—could be every bit as lethal and as vicious as a Rogue.

Fear gnawed a hole in his belly.

What if this changed the way she felt about him? What if she couldn't come to terms with all she'd seen tonight?

How would he survive without her?

Up ahead, Kate suddenly staggered to a stop on a deserted stretch of street, bracing herself against a brick storefront. She whirled around, catching him off guard, and jabbed a finger at him as he approached.

"You stay away from me, damn it," she ordered.

"*Querida*, let me—"

"Shut up, damn you. Just...just shut up," Kate railed, shaking with fury. "And stop calling me that. I don't want to hear any more. I don't want to see anymore. I don't want to be a part of this. I just want you...all of you...to leave me the hell alone."

"Kate, please...let me take you home. Let me help you."

"I don't want your help." Tears tracked down her cheeks, and his soul bled.

He took a step closer. His arms ached to hold her. But she shied away, glaring at him through narrowed, glistening eyes.

"I hate you," she hissed.

A splintered stake would have been less painful, for in that moment, he could see in her eyes she truly believed what she was saying. Gritting his teeth, steeling himself against the pain...both the emotional pain she'd just handed him and the possibility of another electrical jolt...Styx lunged at her.

Before the startled gasp of breath escaped her lips, he tossed her over his shoulder and began to run once more. Intermittent bursts of energy seared his shoulder and arm, the side of his neck, anywhere she touched him. He bore down on the pain and raced on, not stopping again until he had her safely inside her apartment. He kicked the door shut behind him, strode through the hallway, and dumped her on her feet in the middle of the living area. His skin burned where her body had pressed against his.

In some places, he'd lost feeling altogether.

Once she was firmly on her feet, she came up swinging.

Kate caught the edge of his cheek with her small fist. His head snapped back and to the side as pain blossomed. He gasped, blinking, stunned. Kate leaped back, cradling her fist to her chest, flexing her fingers as she glared at him.

He took a step toward her, but her eyes shot wide, and she jumped back again.

"Damn it, stop that," he barked. "You know I would never hurt you."

"You're just like them, just like those monsters out there—"

"Maybe I am," he snapped, running his fingers through his loose hair. The dark curtain of it shifted on his shoulders, shining in the light.

His response brought her up short, and she gaped at him. Obviously, she hadn't expected him to agree with her.

"Maybe I am like those Newborns, in some ways. When it comes to protecting you...to protecting the woman I love...I can—and will—be vicious. I will do anything it takes to make sure that you are safe...*anything*. I will kill any who seek to harm you, Kate. I will do anything to make you happy. You are my life now."

"Stop it. Stop saying that. I'm not—"

"Yes," he argued forcefully. "You are. No matter how you feel about me right now, no matter what you think...I *know*. You are the only thing that matters to me now. Te amo, Kate."

"How can you say that? What I think is... I feel like... I watched you *kill* that...that *thing* tonight. I watched Zack turn into a monster. And I watched my...my *brother* use some god-awful force of nature to kill another of those monsters," she yelled, visibly shaking. Oh, how he longed to pull her into his arms and soothe her. But she needed this more right now, needed to purge this from her system...no matter how much it hurt him to hear it. "And do you know what the most horrifying thing was?" She didn't give him time to answer, instead plowing on as she held her empty palms up to him. Her voice held a hysterical edge. "I could have killed him. That guard..." Her voice dropped to a whisper. "I could have killed him." Her tormented gaze dropped from the floor as she slowly lowered her hands to her sides. "I could have...I *wanted* to kill him. It was like this...driving urge, this...this *need*. I'm turning into a...a freak. A monster...and there's nothing I can do to stop it."

Never before had he seen such miserable confusion.

"Kate, it's your nature to—"

Crack.

The flat of her palm stung his cheek before he'd even seen her move. Astonished, he blinked at her, the shape of her hand throbbed with burning heat upon his cheek.

"I'm *not* a monster. I'm not a killer, damn you," she sobbed.

Styx reached for her, but she whirled from his grasp and disappeared into the bedroom, slamming the door behind her.

****

Kate stomped across the bedroom toward her bed, her abused hand cradled against her midsection. Damn him. She wasn't a monster.

*Or was she?*

No, she wouldn't believe that of herself. She'd taken an oath to save lives...not destroy them.

*And yet...*

The door exploded open behind her, slamming closed again forcefully enough to rattle the figurines on the top of her dresser. Gasping, she spun around.

And froze.

He was fully transformed. And he was furious. His eyes blazed in the darkened room. The tips of his fangs were barely visible. Trembling, she scurried across the room, cowering on the opposite side of the bed.

"Get out," she whispered throatily. "I could hurt you."

The claim was not a threat, but rather a wry caution heavily laced with fear.

Fear for him. Fear of what she might do to him without trying to.

"Not until we get a few things straight. The first of which," he muttered, then he disappeared in a blur, reappearing at her side, "is that nothing...*nothing*...will keep me from you."

Wide-eyed, Kate backed away slowly, hardly daring to breathe.

"Second," he growled, stalking her step for step. "I did not say you were a monster. And *I* am not afraid of *you*. What I was trying to say...before I was interrupted...is that it is your nature to *protect*. You saw that he was a threat...to me, to Cian, to Zack...and to numerous innocent Humans. Your instinct was to save us...and eliminate the danger to the others. You are, perhaps, more powerful than I am...or you soon will be...and that's what's got you running scared. But you don't have to be afraid, *querida*. It is not your nature to be violent. You are," his gaze turned soft, awed, but only for a moment, "without a doubt, good to the soul, Kate."

She forced a swallow. Her gaze hungrily searched his face. Yes...yes, he meant what he'd said. But he wasn't done yet. Not done speaking.

Not done stalking.

"And third...and most importantly...I will never, never hurt you. You. Know. That." Her back came up against the wall, but he continued forward. "Don't you?" he whispered softly as the tip of his nose brushed hers.

"Yes," she croaked.

His head turned, and his cheek smoothed lightly along her jaw line, his lips whispered over her ear. "You're not afraid of me, are you?"

"No," she murmured. Her chest was tight. Why was it so difficult to breathe?

"You don't really hate me, do you, *querida?*" So soft. So seductive. His hands settled on her hips, and his breath whispered over the side of her neck.

Chills of desire skated over her flesh.

"No," she sighed. "I don't hate you."

His lips caressed the sensitive curve of her neck.

Searing awareness jolted through her, and she shoved him away.

"My neck...Layla...she bit me. I lost so much blood. I lost consciousness." She glared up at him, holding him at arm's length. "I should be comatose...or dead. What happened?"

Heaving a deep sigh, Styx allowed a slim bit of space between them, though the look on his face said he'd clearly rather be doing something else than talking.

"I gave you my vein," he calmly informed her. But the intensity in his stare, the light glowing in his eyes, hinted at deep, fierce emotion barely contained.

"Your vein?" Her puzzled gaze skated over him. "I don't understand..."

"It's just like it sounds, *querida*," he asserted, the burn in his eyes growing brighter. "I gave you my vein. You drank my blood, and it brought you back."

Her lips parted, and she blinked up at him.

"You gave me your..." Her hushed voice trailed away as the words sank through her. Shocking. She rolled the words around in her head, weighing them, slowly coming to the understanding of exactly what he'd done in her defense. What he'd done to save her. Flustered, she sputtered, "And Layla?"

"Dead. You don't ever have to worry about her again."

"You killed her?" He nodded, and she licked her lips, forced a swallow. "You killed her, and then you saved me...with your blood."

He didn't say a word, simply nodded again. As if words might push her too far.

Her eyes shot wide, and she clutched at her throat. "Oh God! Am I...will I...am I going to—" She broke off, gulping.

"No," he reassured her quietly. "You didn't actually die...so you couldn't have been changed. Actually, with your Faerie blood...we're not altogether certain the change would even take for you. To our knowledge...at least mine, Zack's, and the TFRA's...you, *querida*, are one of a kind. No other Faerie has ever mated with a Human before...at least, as far as we know, none has ever conceived."

She silently processed it all, and he stood there, watching her with those unfathomable amber eyes. All this talk of parentage and blood and death had her head spinning. Surprisingly enough, the thought that she's actually *ingested* his blood didn't bother her nearly as much as she'd imagined it would...or *should*.

She glanced up at him, catching the tip of her tongue between her teeth. He'd saved her life and risked exposure at the hospital...all for her. He'd offered comfort and understanding when she'd teetered on that desperate knife's edge of despair. She'd struck him, twice. And he'd not raised a finger to her...nor a fang.

*Trust him...*

Her anger drained away.

And just like that, he was all over her.

His fingers sank deep in her hair, and his mouth slanted over hers, his tongue sinking deep. Laving.

Thrusting. Demanding. His hips pressed her back against the wall, pinning her there. The hardness of his erection strained at the confines of his jeans, bulging against her hip, teasing flutters of need deep in the pit of her stomach. Her arms crept around his waist as she yielded to him. Her hands splayed on his back.

His lips skated to her cheek, her throat.

She closed her eyes and tilted her head back as emotion swam through her veins and delicious sensations swamped her. His fangs scraped the pulse at the base of her throat, and she gasped, "What are you doing?"

A shiver went through her. Was she ready for this? Ready for him to *"take her vein"*?

As if sensing her hesitation, Styx paused. He reared up, his gaze snapping to her face. The intensity of his stare, the gruff determination in his voice shook her to the core. "I won't force the blood bond on you, Kate. And I can't force you to accept the *Sacred Vows*, even if I wanted to. But I won't be denied my mate any longer. *Te deseo...*" *I want you.* "I'm making you mine. I'll take you any way I can get you, *querida*. I'll wait for the *Sacred Vows* for now. But make no mistake. I want forever with you. Only with you."

His mouth seized hers before she could respond. Rough hands flew over her. Clothing ripped, steadily disappearing until he pressed against her in a heated, naked tangle of limbs and straining bodies. Angling his head, he deepened the kisses, devouring her with his hunger, and Kate wrapped her arms around him, eagerly yielding. Sweeping an arm beneath her knees, he lifted her high against his chest, burying his face against the side of her throat as he carried her the short distance to her bed. His breathing was little more than a ragged pant against her skin. Unmistakable urgency gave rough desperation to his motions.

His skin was hot and smooth beneath her greedy hands. His muscles bunched and rippled as he moved sinuously above her, stretching out onto the bed. Onto her. His lips, supple and scorching, plied her body with intuitive expertise, knowing precisely when—and where—to exert pressure...and when to tease. Nipping here, suckling there. The curve of her shoulder. The inner bend of her elbow. Her fingertips. Her wrist. Her collarbone. The tender underside of her jaw. Returning time and time again to the sensitive flutter of pulse at the base of her throat and to her lips, catching—savoring—the strangled sobs that escaped her.

She was on fire.

Everywhere.

Wedging his knee between hers, he nudged her thighs apart. The slightly course hair on his legs tickled her flesh as he knelt between her parted legs, leaning over her, dragging his teeth over her lower lip as he suckled it inside his mouth. His chest feathered over hers, tormenting her with the need for more contact...contact he withheld. With glowing eyes raking over every inch of her, he leaned back, his washboard abs undulating, and Kate caught her first glimpse of his impressive, straining, pulsing erection. The breath caught in the back of her throat at the sheer size of him.

Then he bent forward once more, and Kate's eyelids sank closed of their own accord and a whimper of delight gurgled free.

His large, lightly-callused hands—every bit as greedy as her own—bombarded her senses with pleasure. Her breasts came alive in his hands, nipples puckering, aching and throbbing for more of his attention. The rasp of his palms over her ribs and down across her stomach set her inner muscles quivering, and her limbs went limp.

His lips followed his hands, and he plumbed the shallow indentation of her navel with his tongue. His hands slipped farther down, spreading wide on the inside of her thighs, holding them immobile as he turned his attention to the front of her hip, and the ultra-sensitive skin where her thigh met her torso. Twisting desperately, head tossed back, Kate moaned aloud.

Styx nipped gently at the soft, quivering flesh of her inner thigh, inflaming her senses. For a split second the tiniest twinges of a sting snagged her focus. Then his hot tongue lapped at the spot, and pain turned to erotic delirium. A dark growl rumbled deep in his chest, so full of emotion, so full of hunger and satisfaction, and desire slammed through her system, heady and demanding.

"Nico…" She cried, too incoherent to form a plea for release.

One last lap of his tongue…one last hungry growl…and his mouth shifted course. As did his hands. They swept over her thighs, meeting above the soft mound of short pubic hair at the juncture of her thighs. His palms massaged for a moment, and then slowly, deliberately, he parted her. The tips of his thumbs traced a slow path down her wet folds. Then his head dipped, and his mouth claimed.

Kate nearly came up off the bed at the shock—at the utter bliss—of his mouth upon her. His tongue, his lips…his teeth and fangs…took her swiftly to peaks she'd never before known with any other. Her release exploded so quickly, consciousness winked in and out for a moment. When she regained her wits, Styx was kissing his way up her body once more, slowly lowering his weight as he progressed, settling himself firmly between her thighs. The pulsing length of his staff nudged at her slick entrance, pushing inexorably in, stretching her.

Swells of sensation quickly took hold of her once

more as he steadily pushed deeper and deeper. Every muscle in his body was locked tight beneath her questing fingers, and a fine sheen of sweat glistened on his dark, golden skin. She ran her tongue along the salty rigid of muscle running the length of his neck. He shivered in her arms, groaning as he finally thrust himself to the hilt inside her. A rolling flex of his hips gained a slim space more, and Kate could have sworn he'd touched the lip of her womb...touched the essence of her very soul.

He muttered something in guttural Spanish, his cheek pressed to the side of her throat, but she couldn't make out the words, too focused on the thickness of him filling her. She nudged at him with her shoulder, wanting his lips, needing the connection of his kiss while he was buried so deeply within her.

But he shook his head stiffly, keeping his face averted from her.

She demanded breathlessly, "Nico...kiss me..."

He pressed a close-mouthed, chaste kiss to the outer curve of her shoulder.

Frustrated, she arched against him, unwittingly grinding him inside her. He groaned and slowly began thrusting inside her. His hands held her caged beneath him, unable to move, unable to rock with him. His body was rigid. Gasping, she finally managed to push a little room between them, but still he kept his face turned away.

"What's the matter?" Cold worry was beginning to coil around her heart. Had she done something wrong?

"*Nada, querida,*" he moaned. His voice strangely hoarse, the words distorted.

"Nico, look at me," she ordered.

She didn't think it would be possible, but he tensed even more. "No...you...you will not want to see me like this. Not now... Please, Kate, just—"

"Look at me, now, Styx," she snapped, gently grasping his face between her palms, turning his head despite his reluctance.

The skin on his forehead was oddly distended, bunching in a distinctly non-Human way. His cheekbones seemed more defined. His compressed lips bulged at the corners. His eyelids remained squeezed tightly closed. He felt like a solid, sculpted chunk of granite in her arms.

Understanding dawned.

He was afraid he might frighten her.

"Show me, Nico," she pleaded softly.

Slowly...very slowly...his eyes opened.

Amber irises glowed bright around his dilated pupils...brighter than she'd ever seen them glow before. She ignored the silent plea therein.

"Show me," she insisted.

Just as reluctantly, he peeled his lips back, revealing his fangs...gleaming and lethal. She'd seen them before, of course. But never had they seemed so...so enormous...and so daunting. Even in the throes of rage, he'd not looked so fearsome.

"Kate," he rasped miserably. "I won't hurt you."

"Shhh..."

She already knew that, didn't need him to keep repeating himself. She just needed a second to gather her courage...courage for what she was about to suggest. She'd seen the Newborns in the middle of a feeding frenzy. She'd be beyond stupid not to worry that Styx might lose control too.

But she couldn't contest this suddenly overwhelming, dark need inside her. This need to give him what he so obviously hungered for. What he so obviously needed.

"*Querida*," he went on, ignoring her command. "I'm sorry, I cannot help it. If I could, I would. It's never been like this for me before. I have no control with you. I wanted to take this so slowly, wanted to seduce you, wanted to make you forget... I am so sorry—"

"Nico," she whispered, cutting him off.

Without giving herself the chance to reconsider, she reached up and traced the length of one fang with her fingertip. His eyes flared, dilated. His body convulsed. Deep inside her, his shaft jerked. A low, tormented growl slipped from his lips.

"Do you like that?" Kate murmured. "You like it when I touch them?" She caught the tip of her tongue between her teeth.

Panting, he nodded tightly, just two short jerks of his head.

She caressed the length of the other fang, and his body convulsed again. His fingers were digging into her hips, but he didn't seem to be aware. She'd have bruises, but she didn't care. Nothing else mattered but for the connection they were, even now, forging between them.

"If you...if you take my vein now, could you...could you stop?"

Had she stunned him? He gaped down at her, and she couldn't fathom the expression on his face.

Again he nodded, his ragged breath heaving in and out...seemingly incapable of speech.

"I want you to," she whispered, her voice slowly gaining strength...slowly gaining determination.

He peered down hard at her, seeming to ask with his eyes the words his lips could not form.

"I'm sure," she asserted adamantly. Steadfast.

He captured her lips with his, forcing them apart as he plundered her mouth with his tongue. His hips pumped faster and faster, plunging, withdrawing, grinding. Molten desire coursed through her veins, pooling in her core. She eagerly dueled with him, slipping past his defenses, sliding her tongue inside his mouth, tracing his fang with the tip of her tongue. He gave a strangled growl, pounding inside her now. As if the leashes of control had slipped from his hands.

Encouraged, Kate curled the tip of her tongue around his fang, and he slammed inside her more powerfully, over and over. Pain sliced across her tongue, and the coppery tang of blood—her blood—flowed into his mouth. She gasped, but he caught her tongue with his, sucking it deep. As with the nick on her thigh, the pain swiftly ebbed, replaced with euphoric, flaming need. Then the blood was gone, the sting disappeared, and he released her tongue from the suction of his mouth...completely healed from her unintentional cut. His grip on her hips eased, but only long enough for his hands to slip beneath her. He grasped her buttocks tightly, jerking her up, angling her so that his driving thrusts went deeper, faster.

Gasping, Kate pushed her hair away from her neck and tipped her head to the side, granting him willing access to her throat. An invitation.

He didn't hesitate, didn't so much as blink. His mouth descended on her skin in a rush of moist heat. The pain was sharp, and fleeting, as his fangs sank into her throat. Hot liquid rushed forth, and his tongue snaked across her flesh, lapping up her blood, seeking more, suckling her. Her breath hissed in through clenched teeth, not against the pain, but in a bid to control the shocking, powerful orgasm rocking her system.

It was no use.

She screamed his name, clutching him to her, wrapping her legs around his hips, constricting. On and on the sensations washed through her as he sucked harder, drawing fixedly from her vein. Pounding his staff inside her. He moaned against her throat. And then he was exploding inside her, pulsing, pumping hot seed deep in her womb.

His body still vibrating in her arms, he gently withdrew his fangs from her flesh and lapped lovingly at her wounds, healing them. Moving the majority of his weight slightly to her side, he collapsed on her, face buried in her shoulder, with a hefty, satisfied sigh.

Kate slipped her fingers through his hair, again and again. She'd never imagined it possible to be so content. So complete.

Her fears had all been for naught. He'd been nothing like those Newborns, lost to the bloodlust. He'd stopped feeding of his own accord. A good thing that, as she'd been out of her mind with passion, incapable of stopping him even if she'd wanted to.

"*Te amo*, Kate," he whispered against her skin.

Deep inside, she knew he'd spoken true. He believed she was his true mate. His *Bride*.

And he loved her.

"Nico," she called softly, waiting until he turned to look up at her. The changes in his face lingered, and she cradled his cheek, staring deep into his eyes. Taking in the whole of his face, and accepting each and every feature. "I'm falling in love with you too."

He blinked. His lips parted. Hope soared in his glowing stare, and his lips curved up on the most sinful smile she'd ever seen. "I'll never let you go," he vowed softly.

And then he moved over her once more, slow and easy this time. His still-hard shaft sinking leisurely into her, and he proceeded to show her exactly what he'd intended earlier when he'd said he'd meant to go so slowly, seduce her, and make her forget all else...

## Chapter 21

He trailed a fingertip down the center of Kate's silky back, smiling as he teased a shiver from her. Breathing heavily, she lay sprawled across his chest, boneless after their latest bout of lovemaking.

He'd been so appalled at his lack of restraint their first time together—so shocked by his own lack of finesse—that he'd poured every ounce of his focus and stamina into making it up to her. Judging by the number of times she'd cried, screamed, whispered and sobbed his name aloud...and the contented purrs slipping from her even now...he'd more than redeemed himself.

They'd made love into the wee hours of dawn—and well beyond—and even *he* was worn out. His grin stretched wider. *That* had never happened before. *Him*...worn out after sex. The insatiable Styx. A chuckle rumbled deep in his throat, then he sighed contentedly. He'd shown her so much last night. He had so much more to show her.

Once he got his way—once he'd blood-bonded her to him, he would have all eternity with her.

Anticipation sizzled inside him.

That was something that puzzled him, though. By rights, he shouldn't have been able to feed from her. Not anymore. Her powers had evolved enough now that that simple fact should be impossible. A Vampyre could not take nourishment from another Immortal's blood. It was physically impossible. Immortal blood was akin to poison for a Vampyre if ingested in large quantities. And yet he'd been able to ingest hers, safely. Even now, he was energized, could feel blood cells merging, regenerating. Was this some strange twist due to her parentage? Or was Kate one of a kind?

A Halfling with Human blood.

He couldn't believe his good fortune. Couldn't believe fate had blessed him with such a magnificent *Bride*. She'd been wild in his arms. As hungry for him as he was for her. Meeting him touch for touch, giving and taking pleasure with greedy abandon.

He hadn't been able to help himself. He'd nicked her thigh, the taste of her essence upon his tongue like pure ambrosia. Making him ravenous for more. But he'd held himself stringently in check. Sealing her wound before he caved to the primal urges driving him. Then she'd inadvertently cut her tongue on his fang, and his control had quaked. *Dios*, it had nearly killed him to seal the wound on her tongue and drink no more.

Then she'd actually encouraged him to take her vein.

Unbelievable.

He shivered, remembering. She'd pulled her thick, fragrant hair away from the ivory column of her neck, an unmistakable invitation if ever he'd seen one. His legendary control didn't hold a snowball's hope in hell, shattering like delicate glass before the fierce determination of this beautiful, courageous woman.

He'd seen the tempered fear in her eyes. The cautious acceptance. What she'd seen as those Newborns at the warehouse had ravaged that security guard must have frightened her deeply. But she'd overcome that fear...for him.

What's more...he saw her hunger. Hungers she could probably scarce understand.

Thank *Dios* she hadn't changed her mind, because at that point, a pack of Werewolves wouldn't have been able to tear him off her. Her blood had been just as sweet, just as addictive as he'd imagined it would be. Pulsing inside him with an intensity he'd never known. Not the power of her Faerie magick...though he could feel that too...but the power of a mate. Not the mundane existence he'd sustained from a blood host. But the sheer force of life gained only from a *Bride's* blood.

He feared he might have taken too much from her as it was. She was still recovering from Layla's attack. He should have stopped much sooner than he had. Much as he craved the rush of her blood upon his palate, he'd give her a few days to recover, even if it killed him.

Maybe he should try to get *her* to drink from *him* again. Surely it would help her recover faster. Perhaps she'd develop a taste for him, as he had for her, and it would be easier to convince her that blood-bonding with him would be a good idea.

Sighing, he smoothed the flat of his palm over the dip of her lower back, down over the gentle slope of her buttocks. He felt himself stirring against her hip...again. *Madre de Dios*, she had a great ass. And sexy legs. And gorgeous—

"Is your life always like this?"

"Hmm?" He pressed a kiss to her forehead. Closing his eyes, he rubbed his cheek against her silken curls, dragging the scent deep. He'd never smell strawberries again without thinking of this moment.

"You know, all about killing Newborns and rescuing damsels and all that?"

"No," he kissed her forehead again, moving his hand back to the small of her back. He wanted her again, but she was obviously bent on talking. So they'd talk...for now. "At least, not until I met that *diablo* Crispin."

"You're sure there's no cure?" Ah...so that was where her mind had wandered.

"I'm sure, querida…about *both* of us."

The silence stretched on as she digested that. At length, she splayed a hand upon his chest, then, slowly, she began tracing intricate patterns with the tip of her finger. "You know, by now I should be ready to accept some things are just beyond explanation. After all, what honest physician could deny that higher powers are at work every day?"

She seemed to be building up to something. By her hesitant tone, he could tell it was something important to her, and so he held his tongue, letting her get to her point in her own good time.

"I mean, how can we deny the existence of miracles?"

*Miracles?* Okay, that hadn't been what he'd been expecting. No one—himself included—had ever considered his existence a miracle.

"How many times do we, as physicians, see terminal cancer patients suddenly go into remission with no logical explanation," she rambled, continuing the teasing patterns on his skin. "And patients with vital organs damaged in accidents or ravaged by disease…they undergo transplant, and get a second shot at life. How many times do we, as physicians, dash couples hopes of having biological children of their own, watch those couples leave our offices dejected, shattered, with nothing left but their faith…only to return months, or years, later, pregnant with their own healthy miracle baby."

Her voice grew hushed, troubled. "And how many times do otherwise healthy, vital people die for reasons beyond our control?"

Styx wrapped his arms around her, inexplicably driven by the sudden need to protect her. To offer her solace and shelter. She was in no danger right now, no threat was eminent, and yet he feared for her. Feared this force that caused wounds he could neither see, nor easily heal with a swipe of his tongue and a little Vampyre saliva.

He didn't know how to fight this...this horrible regret lacing her voice.

He didn't know what was causing it.

"What happened, *querida*?"

At first, he didn't think she would answer him. He'd just made up his mind that he would distract her, somehow. But then she spoke, and his heart lodged in his throat, making it impossible to speak, to offer comfort other than the warm strength of his embrace.

The patterns grew distorted as her finger traced faster and faster. "My sister Maggie was in town visiting that week. Just her; it was one of the rare times she ever left her boys. My mother...my mother had come over, and we had an impromptu girls' night in. We'd watched an old musical, one of Mom's favorites, and another chick-flick we'd seen a thousand times before, laughing over cold Chinese take-out." Her voice dropped to a whisper. "The storm wasn't bad, but I didn't think she should be out in it. She hadn't been drinking anything stronger than iced tea...now I wish she would have. Maybe then she would have stayed. Maybe she'd..." Kate trailed off, shaking her head. "She'd scolded me, told me she'd been driving longer than I'd been alive, and I should trust her."

Kate rolled away from him then, staring, unseeing, at the ceiling. She wrapped her arms around herself, shivering. He rolled with her, cradling her in his arms, refusing the emotional—or physical—distance she tried to put between them. Kate licked her lips. Her gaze wouldn't meet his, but her hand slipped up to squeeze his forearm with gentle gratitude.

"Fifteen...maybe twenty minutes after she left, I got paged. I thought... I thought I was just going in to help out in the ER. I told Maggie I'd be back in a few hours at most, and that she should go to bed. I never imagined..." A small crystalline tear leaked from the corner of her eye. "When I got there, I suited up and scrubbed in...just like any other shift.

"Only...when I stepped into the ER, the nurses...none of them could look at me. Whispers trailed behind me as I made my way to the staff lounge. Until this charge nurse named Elsie came. She sat me down and quickly explained how they'd already paged Jeff...Dr. Stanton. I asked why, said I was already there, and that I'd help. She explained..." A tight sob caught in the back of her throat, and another tear slipped, unchecked, from the corner of her eye. Forcing a swallow, Kate pushed on. "She explained that there had been a car accident. A drunk driver had hit another car, head on, before ricocheting into a mini-van with a mother and her three children."

Styx tucked her head into the crook of his shoulder, drawing her stiff body closer into the curve of his. His heart ached, breaking for her.

"I wanted to rush out right away, wanted to get to my patients." She sniffled, and he reached behind him, grabbing a tissue for her. "Elsie was the one to tell me...tell me that mom..."

The sobs took over, shaking her slight form in his arms. Wracking, miserable, hoarse sobs. Styx held her tight, let her soak his chest, wishing to heaven he could do something to take away her pain. A long time later, once the sobs ebbed to hiccupping sniffles, she finished her story.

"Eileen took care of the mother and her children. They walked away with minor injuries. Jeff dealt with the driver. His injuries were more extensive, but he lived." Her voice turned bitter. "You ever notice how that works...the drunk driver always lives, walks away with a few stitches and the rest of his life still ahead of him."

He waited, silent, for the rest.

"They couldn't keep me from Mom's side. But I couldn't help her. I was paralyzed, standing there, watching helplessly as Stuart and his team worked over my mother." Her tone became robotic, almost emotionless, and yet the tears flowed freely now. "They clamped one artery, only to have another rupture. Her vitals were all over the board. They repaired her spleen, only to have her heart fail. I watched as, one by one, her organs began to shut down under the stress and loss of blood. They couldn't pump it into her fast enough."

And then she told him of her gift to heal...or rather, her curse, as it had failed her the one and only time she'd ever prayed for it to work. She told him of the patients she'd saved over the years, patients who'd made miraculous recoveries despite daunting injuries.

"But I was worthless for my mom. I couldn't...no matter how hard I tried to focus...I couldn't heal her. I even pushed Stuart aside at one point, first trying my traditional training, and then, when that didn't work, I tried laying my hands upon her chest...just as I did with that boy...but nothing happened. Stuart pulled me back, and he began ordering life support.

"But I couldn't let him do it. I couldn't stand the thought of hooking her up to those machines. I knew she wouldn't want that for herself. Damn me, as much as I hated to let her go...as much as it tore me up inside...I couldn't do that to her. I couldn't disrespect her that way, couldn't diminish her life. She was hemorrhaging, and her pupils were unresponsive.

"And when she flat-lined for the second time...I told Stuart to call time of death. I wouldn't let him use the paddles again." Kate tipped her head back to stare up into his eyes, and he could see what the decision had cost her. "I stood there, bawling like a child, my hands covered with her blood, and told my co-worker to call my mother's time of death."

"Ah, *querida*," he whispered. There were no words. The strength this woman—*his* woman—possessed humbled him. *Mierda*...every time her pager went off...surely it reminded her of that night. And yet she continued to answer the call.

Every time, without fail.

Without hesitating.

He would never deserve her. But he'd damned well do everything in his power to try.

"Elsie took me to my office. She pretty much central lined hot sweet coffee into me, found a pile of warm blankets and offered her shoulder until I cried myself dry. I don't know how I would have made it through those first brutal hours if it hadn't been for Elsie Chapman."

It seemed he had yet one more thing that he owed Elsie Chapman, RN. Guilt lay like a rock in the pit of his stomach. He'd be personally seeing to it that Ms. Chapman got her vacation, all expenses paid...plus some.

"By the time I calmed down, I realized that Maggie still didn't know. So I called her, asked her to come to the hospital. And I broke the news, took her in to see Mom. She spoke to Stuart, begged for answers. Wanted to know why Mom wasn't put on life support. Stuart tried to explain that she was probably already too far gone by the time she made it into the ER. He tried to... He tried to protect me, tried to shoulder the brunt of the decision. But she wouldn't listen. And when she found out that I made him call time of death..."

Kate dashed the back of her hand over her drenched eyes, smearing glistening, salty moisture across her cheeks.

"Maggie blamed me. Said I didn't love Mom

enough. That I didn't try hard enough. That I could have saved her if I'd really wanted to."

"Kate, she was grieving. She didn't mean—"

"Yes, she did. She meant every word." The turbulent, self-directed anger in her voice gave him pause. "You see, Maggie had seen my special *gift*. A few years after Dad passed away, she and I had gone swimming with friends at a creek. One of them had dove in, head first, into an area that was too shallow. The other kids went for help while Maggie and I stayed with her. I don't know why—or how I knew to do it—but I closed my eyes and held my hands over her neck. The next thing I knew, a group of adults had returned and were examining her...but she was fine. Not a scratch on her. Maggie never spoke of it, never told anyone else. But I knew that she knew.

"And that's why she walked away the day after Mom's funeral and never looked back," Kate dabbed at her eyes with the tissue, blew her nose, then tossed the tissue in the waste can beside the nightstand. When she turned her weary gaze to him, guilt and self-doubt shadowed her eyes. "She's never forgiven me for letting Mom die."

"And you haven't forgiven yourself, either."

She remained silent.

Gently, he drew her head into the curve of his shoulder, and he rocked her. He held her tight, absorbing her pain. "It wasn't your fault, Kate. Sometimes...no matter what you do, no matter what you *can* do...they still die."

Kate glanced sharply up at him. Though he'd never spoken of Eliza to anyone, never spoke of Ava, or that part of his past...not even to his best friend Cole...Styx could see Kate needed to hear, needed to understand that guilt and grief, in time, lessen.

And so he told her a story...the story of a young man tricked by a beautiful courtesan, and of that young man's friend slaughtered by that same courtesan. He told her of a young innocent girl with dazzling dreams, dreams into which a monster had tread, ignorant to the danger he'd placed her in.

And he told her of a sadistic desert sheikh...and his own part in bringing death to Tacoma.

\*\*\*\*

"Verra good, Kate," Cian called, shifting on the balls of his feet. Purple energy orbs pulsing in the palms of his hands. He fainted to the right, then lunged left, lifting his arm.

Kate's hands shot up between them, and the orb in Cian's palm erupted in a burst of brilliant shards of light. Sucking in a sharp breath between his clenched teeth, Cian shook his smarting hand, flexing his fingers. Pride swelled inside her. She was finally getting the hang of this. Learning to control these urges, these throbs and pulses of power flowing in her veins...these bursts of power that has terrified her for so long...was exhilarating.

Liberating.

She and Cian had been practicing for hours now, out here deep in the darkened forests of Pointe Defiance. Styx continued to view Cian in a suspicious light, had refused to allow him to take her anywhere alone. And, for obvious reasons, practicing this type of control was not advisable amidst Tacoma's dense population. So they'd taken a cab.

She cringed as she recalled the cabby's speculative stares in his rear view mirror. With Cian on her left, and Styx on her right, she'd felt miniscule and unnoticeable sandwiched between the two blatantly male specimens. But the dark-eyed man had continued to stare nonetheless, his enigmatic gaze slid back and forth between Cian and Styx before returning to her. Time and time again. And when his attention was on her, Kate resisted the urge to squirm and cross her arms over her chest.

His attention had not gone unnoticed.

At the driver's first glance, Styx slid his arm around her shoulders, jerking her tightly to his side. His menacing glare firmly affixed on the cabby's mirror. But Cian's reaction was the most puzzling of all. His eyes abruptly narrowed and he leaned forward in his seat, straining against the seatbelt Kate had, albeit irrationally insisted he wear. Purple energy began to pulse in the palms of his hands...until Kate unthinkingly reached over and smacked her hand down on his, palm to palm, lacing her fingers with his. His energy orb disappeared with a sizzling hiss. Grinding his teeth together, Cian leaned back in his seat; his glare centered on the back of the driver's dark head the rest of the trip.

She wondered at what Styx had said when he'd leaned near the cabby's window upon their arrival. His voice had been so low and so hurried that Kate hadn't been able to catch so much as a single syllable. Whatever it was that he'd said couldn't have been that bad, given the cabby's reaction. His eyes had widened for a moment, but then he'd simply nodded vacantly and driven away. Then again, maybe it had been...

He'd driven off without collecting his fare.

Now Styx sat on a huge boulder some five hundred yards in the distance, observing. She'd banned him from coming any closer, unable to focus on her lessons, unable to prevent him from lunging at Cian and instinctively—protectively—placing himself squarely in the line of fire every time Cian tossed one of his energy balls in her direction.

Cian dusted his hands together, smiling. A gentle breeze stirred the ends of his long, pale hair like the caress of a lover's fingers. "Verra good, indeed, lass. I believe you've got the right of it." He strode forward, and from the corner of her eye, she saw Styx tense. But he remained seated...for now. "I think it's time we moved on with our lessons."

"All right," Kate agreed. "What's next?"

"Lend me your hand, lass, and I'll be giving you your first lesson in *shimmering*."

"Like hell you will," Styx roared, the distance obviously presenting no restriction on his attuned hearing. He shot off the boulder and closed the distance in the blink of an eye, coming to stand directly between them. His fangs bared. "You aren't taking her anywhere without me, *Tinkerbelle*."

A slow, malicious smile tugged at the corners of Cian's mouth. "You think to stop me, *leech*?"

"Enough," Kate snapped.

But Cian wouldn't be denied. "*Shimmering* is a Faerie's best defense...and our best offense. It lets us move out of the line of fire, away from attack, and gives us a distinct advantage over our adversaries. Why would you hobble her this way? Why would you prevent her from learning this, prevent her from utilizing such an essential, *natural* magick?" The cool evening air swirled through his hair now, sending the low branches overhead swaying and rustling.

Styx's claws curled at his sides, and his back stiffened at Cian's caustic comments. Comments meant to imply that by doing so, by limiting her training this way, Styx somehow wished to trap her, or, worse still, that he didn't truly care for her safety.

"Cian," Kate warned.

"If you are so worried that I might *shimmer* her somewhere that you don't want her to go, then come with us." Again, that cool, malignant smile.

Kate stepped to Styx's side, out from behind the protective shield of his broad back, just in time to see all the color drain from Styx's face.

"What..." She glanced back and forth between

the two of them. "What's going on? What did I miss?"

"Nothing," Styx barked.

Cian's smirk grew. "Your Vampyre can't handle—" Abruptly Cian broke off. His gaze went oddly unfocused, and he stiffened. His head tilted to the side slightly, and his attention seemed suddenly far, far away. A hushed garble of strange voices tickled her ears, lifting the fine hairs on the back of her neck. The muted rush of sound was gone as fast as it had come, and Cian's gaze snapped back to Kate. "I am being summoned."

"Summoned?"

"The elders...I must go. Come," he ordered, holding his hand out to her. "I will take you home. The Vampyre can return to your apartment on his own."

"Home to the Isle?" Styx stepped between them once more. "No way. Kate will go with me back to the apartment."

Irritation sparked in the depths of Cian's blue eyes. "Leech, I have no' the time to argue—"

"Then you better run along like a good little boy and report in," Styx patronized. His tone turned hard, implacable. "I will see to my mate."

Purple points of light pulsed in Cian's palms. His nostrils flared as his chin dipped. "My sister—"

"Will be just fine with Styx," Kate rushed to intervene.

That muted rush of voices wafted on the wind once more, slightly stronger this time, and Cian stiffened again, his focus plainly torn.

"Go, Cian," Kate insisted. "I'll see you back at the apartment. We'll continue our lessons later."

"As you wish," Cian ground out. His head dipped on a regal nod, but his furious glower slid to Styx one last time as his body disappeared in a wavering mirage.

## Chapter 22

"I won't go," Kate snapped over her shoulder as she navigated her way along the narrow trail in the moonlight.

"Why won't you at least consider it?" Styx argued, dividing his attention between angrily glaring holes in her back and dissecting each and every shadow, examining each and every snap of twig and whisper on the wind. "At least Cole's estate in L.A. is secure. His security has dealt with this type of threat before, you know. And the place is huge...we won't be stumbling over Zack or Cian every time we turn around."

"My place is here, Styx." Kate pushed a low branch aside and stepped onto one of the hiking trails. Her sturdy hiking boots crunching dried twigs and pine needles with each step. "I have responsibilities here in Tacoma. People are depending on me. I can't just disappear without notice...without some kind of explanation. Besides, I can take care of myself."

The sound of his footsteps behind her abruptly halted, and she glanced over her shoulder. He'd stopped in the middle of the trail, fists clenched at his sides, indignant fire snapping in his amber eyes. "You are mine to protect, *querida*. My mate. My *Bride*. And, you will find, I take *my* responsibilities very seriously as well."

His mate. His *Bride*. Spoken in reverent tones, each word an endearment every bit as much as his penchant for calling her *querida*, my love, and *mi corazón*, my heart. A strange feeling shot through her every time he called her his *Bride*. And he'd been calling her that...a lot. Even after they'd spent nearly an entire night—and almost a full day—making love, those words were oddly disturbing. And that, too, was an understatement if ever there was one. She'd never imagined making love could be like *that*.

Those frightening sensations weighing on her chest and clogging her throat grew to an unmanageable burden beneath his burning gaze, a startling combination of excitement and anxiety. Elation and panic. She knew he meant every word he said, clear to the bottom of his heart. And yet, she hesitated. One thought kept swirling through her head, plaguing her mercilessly.

What if *she* didn't deserve *him*?

She'd done nothing to warrant this unconditional, all-consuming love he seemed so hell-bent on lavishing on her. She was just...just Kate. Nothing special. Certainly not someone worthy of Immortal devotion. She couldn't even control her own powers most of the time.

The good Lord knew she had no control over her heart.

She'd even admitted to *him* that she was in love with him. Cripes...she may as well have ripped her heart out of her chest and plopped it onto a silver platter for him. He'd snuck around her defenses, breeching the walls she'd been so careful to maintain for so long, claiming the territory of her heart and settling in like an invading army.

He'd alleged the connection between a Vampyre and his mate was permanent. Irrevocable. But men grew bored and fell out of love, abandoning those they'd vowed to love for the rest of their lives. Men died, leaving loved ones behind with nothing but their grief and a lifetime of memories. She'd seen it happen all the time...either of their own accord, or for reasons beyond their control...men left. Hadn't her own biological father left her mom...locked away by some meddlesome, controlling elders of his clan? Hadn't her dad—Duncan O'Rourke—died? Leaving Beth all alone...again?

In a relatively short amount of time, Kate had let this man before her become the center of her world...crazy, mixed-up world that it had become, but her world nonetheless. Stupid. So stupid.

What would become of her when Styx left? How would she survive?

Would she have completely lost her sense of self by then? Would she become one of those pitiful creatures pining for the lost love of their life?

The panic grew, nearly choking her. Turning away from him, she faced the trail ahead of her with the determination of a coward, hiding from the truth that insisted on slapping her in the face at every turn. "I'm not your responsibility, Styx," she called over her shoulder. "I'm just another of your many women. Once you go back to L.A.—back to your band and your groupies—you'll forget all about me. Once the next damsel in distress tumbles into your path, you won't even remember what I look like."

Her own words tore at her like a thousand razor-sharp scalpels, slicing her heart to bloody ribbons.

A harsh roar erupted behind her, startling the soothing sounds of the forest silent. It was her only warning before a band of bruising steel gripped her elbow, jerking her around. Instinctively her palms came up between them, flattening on the granite wall of his heaving chest. He captured her shoulders in a punishing hold, his head bent close to hers as his glowing eyes bore into her wide-eyed stare.

"How could I forget part of my very soul?" he hissed, livid. "I will say this once more...and never again will you doubt it, do you hear me? Never again will you try to diminish what is between us." He gave her a rough little shake. The tips of his fangs glistened between his parted lips. Stark white and brutal. "You. Are. My. *Bride*."

His lips slammed down on hers. His hand slid up to her nape; his fingers tangled in her hair, jerking her head back as his lips forced hers apart and his tongue plunged inside her mouth. Kate blinked up at him, dazed, as his mouth, his body commanded hers. Bark dug into her back as he pushed her up against the thick trunk of an ancient Maple. His hard body crashed into her, crushing her. A rock solid thigh moved between hers, forcing her to straddle his leg as he ground his pelvis against her. His ragged breath was fire on her skin as he dragged his lips across her cheek and down the side of her throat.

Her head began to swim. It was getting harder and harder to breathe. Harder and harder to concentrate.

Harder and harder to cling to her resolve.

It would be so easy to just give up and let herself sink. Too easy...

"Damn it," she swore, shoving uselessly at his shoulders, twisting her head to the side. "Stop it, Styx."

It seemed to take a moment for her words of denial to register for him. When they did, he sprang away from her. The lines of his face drawn tight, he raked a trembling hand through his tousled hair. The glow of his eyes cut through the darkness around them like laser beams.

"You aren't going to seduce me into submission. And I'm not agreeing to your idea of going into hiding, Styx," she snapped, her own hands shaking as she righted her clothing. "So just...just save your Casanova moves for someone else."

Great...just frickin' brilliant. Her voice wobbled

so badly even *she* didn't believe herself.

Styx's eyes narrowed, and he stiffly informed her, "Casanova was Italian."

Allrighty then. Clearly a raw nerve. But she couldn't seem to stem the reckless need to throw up barriers...in whatever form she could. Her anger. His anger. It didn't seem to matter, just as long as there was something...anything other than her unreliable self-control...to keep a little distance between them.

"It doesn't matter. You're both cut from the same damn cloth," she growled. "You don't have a sliver of self restraint." *Could he tell her words were not aimed at him, but at herself?*

"*¡Mierda!*" He exploded. "Woman, your scent is all over me...driving me damn near out of my mind." He raked his hand through his hair, paced angrily away, then stormed right back, stopping only a few short feet from her. "The fact I don't have you naked on the ground right now, writhing beneath me as I bury myself deep inside you, would be a damned good argument against your assumption about my self-restraint."

She gaped at him, unable to steel herself against the vivid images suddenly swamping her senses. Her gaze slid to the rocky trail at her feet, wandered to a large bolder in the distance, dropped to the grass nearby. The breeze was chilly. The sky above them, trees all around. There was no guarantee...even out here in the dark...that someone wouldn't chance upon them. She was, by no means, an exhibitionist. And yet the idea of making love with him out here in the heart of the forest surged excitement straight into her veins. Appalled by her own lack of control over her mental faculties, fascinated by the illicit possibilities, she blinked rapidly as heat flooded her cheeks.

"*...as I bury myself deep inside you...*" *Had he*

*meant his fangs...or his—*

"Both, damn it," he snarled, raking his hungry gaze over her.

Her mouth went dry. Her pulse hammered. Her knees shook.

Styx swore beneath his breath and stomped away once more. He prowled the narrow passage of the trail, each movement, every step a study in bewildered, ferociously contained agitation. Turmoil rolled from him in waves, and guilt flayed her.

Shocked, confused, Kate turned away.

She hadn't meant to drive him away...at least not initially. But he'd started making demands...demands that she go where he wanted her to go, do what he wanted her to do, never mind that he'd clearly only had her safety in mind. And the depth of his commitment to her...to protecting her and to caring for her...had frightened her, overwhelmed her.

And she'd lashed out.

She'd been unfair.

Contrite, she turned back to face him. But he held up a hand before she could apologize.

"Kate, it's my duty to protect you." He slowly approached, making a visible effort to suppress his temper, even though she could see it simmering just beneath the surface. "You are not making it easy—"

"I'm sorry," she interrupted. "I know...and I'm sorry. But you have to understand, Styx. I've made a commitment. To this job, and to the people I work with...and the people that come into the ER, hurt or sick. If I run away, if I hide...then *he* wins."

"*Querida*, you are Immortal...or you will be very soon." A deep sigh slipped from him. His stare was too penetrating, to discerning, and she dropped her gaze to the buttons of his shirt. "You will not be able to remain here in this city forever. Sooner or later, these Humans will start to wonder why you never grow old...why you never succumb to Human illness."

"I know that." Her shoulders sagged as she moved away from the tree she'd been leaning on and shuffled a few feet down the trail. An owl hooted softly in the distance. Leaves rustled overhead as a restless gust of wind swept through the area. "Don't you think I don't know that, Styx? But I'm...I'm not ready okay? I'm not ready to let go yet." She raked a hand through her hair, her eyes pleading with him to understand. "When I go...it has to be on *my* terms."

He remained silent, and, at length, she slowly turned to face him. He stood in the middle of the trail in a deceptively relaxed stance. Like a sleek, powerful jungle cat biding his time, savoring the hunt before it moved in to claim the prize. But the look in his eyes was one of carnal hunger. Paralyzing her with that strange, insidious thrill she'd come to associate with that particular stare, and her reluctance drained away. Ready or not, she stood at the edge of a life altering decision.

Deny the reality of her life...and continue to drive a wedge between them, making them both miserable.

Or accept...and truly *live*.

Accept, and *love*.

He waited, quiet and still, as she puzzled through her jumbled thoughts.

She'd accused him of being a Casanova. But she'd been wrong. He hadn't blatantly set out with seduction as an obvious goal...at least not obviously to her. He'd brought her no flowers. No wine and chocolates. He hadn't plied her with candlelight and all the forthright accoutrements of seduction.

But he'd seduced her nonetheless. In a thousand subtle ways, he'd slowly but surely enthralled her. A shoulder to lean on and a warm embrace after a long difficult shift. Holding her hand when she'd been afraid to walk alone. Engaging conversation and slow drugging kisses.

He'd slain her demons...and still been man enough to wash the dishes.

And he was learning to cook for her...despite the fact that he had no personal interest in Human food. She'd caught him watching the *Food Network*, on more than one occasion. Though he seemed to favor Paula Dean and Alton Brown, she'd caught him taking notes from several other shows as well. If it involved healthful, tasty nutrition for her, he was fast becoming an expert. He'd even braved Zack's teasing comments.

*"Aw, man, I didn't know you cared," Zack had joked one afternoon as Styx had sat before the television taking notes for a complicated dish. She'd told him he could use her computer since he'd left his laptop in L.A., but he'd refused, stating it was faster to use pen and paper rather than booting up her relic of out-dated technology.*

*"I don't give a rat's ass if you starve." Styx had snapped, eyes glued to the TV, even as bright color crawled up his cheeks. "This is for Kate."*

His admission had warmed her heart.

In the short time they'd been living in the same apartment, he'd gone above and beyond to make sure that she had anything and everything she could possibly want. Food or otherwise. It was as if he were trying to demonstrate that he was a good provider. As if some archaic gene were driving him to prove himself.

Maybe if he'd chosen the easy way out and ordered delivery or take out, rather than insisting on trying to cook for her...and more and more often his cooking attempts were astoundingly delicious...she might have been able to hold something of herself back. Maybe if he'd plied her with wine and roses rather than making her a cup of hot chocolate at night and cuddling with her as she'd told him about her day, she may have been able to resist.

But the real hook—the irrevocable, irrefutable magnet for her—was the fact that, despite the fact she'd already admitted she was falling in love with him, he continued to seduce her...seemed to work every waking moment at making her feel protected and loved.

Treasured and necessary.

He might not be trying—at least not blatantly so—to seduce her, but he was doing a damn fine job nonetheless. In a thousand ways, he'd shown her the depth of his commitment...shown her that his love was real, tangible and timeless. Limitless.

She might not have tomorrow with him, but she had now.

Slowly she closed the distance between them—both physical as well as emotional—and gazed up into his fathomless eyes. Just as slowly, she wound her arms around his neck and drew his head down, sealing her lips gently over his. He stood immobile for a breathless moment, and then his arms slipped around her, drawing her closer to his heat. His head angled, but he didn't ravish. Instead, he savored. Slow and easy.

*Accept...*

Kate gave herself up to his kiss, and—finally— gave her heart, without qualification, into his care. Knowing full well that once she made this commitment, there would be no going back.

*Love...*

Gently, she eased away from the kiss, though she didn't withdraw from his arms. "Nico," she whispered. Her fingers smoothed a stray lock from his temple, tucking it behind his ear. "I've made a decision."

His stare flickered confusion, then wariness. As

if he were girding himself for battle, his features tightened. "Kate, listen, I know you don't—"

"Shh," she murmured, pressing two fingers against his lips. "Let me finish." She offered him a soft smile as her decision solidified, miraculously easing the oppressing weight that had been burdening her heart. "I love you. And I *am* your Bride." She pressed her fingers more firmly against his lips as his eyes shot wide and he made to speak. "Shh," she insisted with mock-sternness. Then she ruined the effect with an achingly tender smile. "I want to take the *Vows* with you, Nico...I want to form the blood-bond. I want you...forever."

The brilliant smile breaking over his face took her breath away.

Styx tossed his head back and whooped to the heavens. His arms tightened around her, pulling her higher against his chest as he spun them in dizzying circles. Laughter rumbled deep in his chest, spilling out in warm, rich tones that melted her heart.

Then he set her abruptly on her feet and showered her face and neck with exuberant kisses.

"You won't be sorry, *mi corazón*," he vowed in a rush. "I swear...I'll make you happy. I'll—"

She caught his face in her hands and silenced him with the promise of eternity in her kiss. His hard hands flew over her then, slipping a button free here, caressing her bared skin there, his intentions clear. Styx swept his arm beneath her knees, lifting her high against his chest. His eager gaze scanning the area around them.

"Now?" Kate squeaked, stunned. She'd thought he would have at least waited until they'd returned to the apartment.

"Now," he confirmed, determination filling his voice, hardening his stare. "I won't live a second longer than I have to without the bonds between us. *Te necesito, querida.*"

Oh yes, he meant to take her...meant to claim her...right here, right now. Impetuous. Ardent. That was seduction...Styx style.

She felt like giggling. The expression on his face was akin to a small child facing a Christmas tree piled high with presents.

She glanced over as he began striding purposefully toward a small clearing just beyond two towering Big Leaf Maples. She spied his destination, a small bower, filled with soft grasses and fragrant wildflowers.

The perfect place for the beginning of the rest of their lives.

He slowly lowered her feet to the ground, keeping an arm around her waist. His palm came up to cradle her cheek. "You would do this, *mi corazón?*" Her gentle smile and small nod must not have been enough confirmation. He gazed hard into her eyes and pressed, "*Dios*, I can't believe I'm actually going to say this...going to give you this out...but, you don't have to do this...not for me. You don't need my blood to stay young. You don't have to bind yourself to me...there is no need, you are Immortal, *querida.*"

"Yes, there is," Kate argued softly. "I *want* this, Nico."

"This is for all eternity, Kate. Be sure...be absolutely certain...because once this is done, it cannot be undone. There's no going back. I'll be drawn to you, unable to stay away. Only your blood will sustain me. And our souls will be bound. If something happens to me...If I die—"

"Shh... I won't let anything happen to you," she promised, pressing the heel of her palm to his chest. His eyes widened as heat slowly seeped from her hand into his chest. A sense of well-being, of warmth and completeness rushed through him. "Trust me, Nico. I'll take good care of you."

His lips curled on a wry smile, but still he

probed, "You would belong to me forever, Kate."

"I already do," she whispered, drawing his lips to hers.

Styx undressed himself in a rush. Then, slowly, he peeled her clothing away, kissing every inch he exposed. He fashioned a bed for them from the pile of their clothes and slowly lowered her to the ground. She shivered as the chilly air touched her skin, shivered again as his heat surrounded her.

In his arms, Kate once again found the one place on earth she truly belonged. His lips claimed hers as his hands readied her body for his with tender caresses and intimate strokes. He held himself above her, his face hovering over hers. And yet he didn't kiss her.

Kate opened her eyes. Her lips ached for want of his touch. His unblinking gaze caressed her face. And the feather light, slightly calloused touch of his fingertips followed his gaze. Gentle. Reverent. Her forehead, her chin. Her cheekbones and the bridge of her nose. The line of her jaw. Her eyebrows and her parted lips. The smooth skin of her eyelid and the hollow of her cheek. The throb of her pulse at the base of her throat. It was a slow and deliberate perusal. He left no ounce of her skin untouched as anticipation built.

The angle of his head shifted and he brought his lips close...so close...his intense gaze locking on her mouth. But then he pulled back, shifting his head, bringing his lips close once more. Slowly. His breath skittered over her cheek, her lower lip, her chin. Driving her out of her mind.

Ah, at last...his head started to lower, his lips brushed hers in just the faintest whisper of a kiss. His head shifted again.

*No...*

Her nails dug into the corded muscles flexing and rippling on his back. She couldn't take this torment anymore. Lifting her head from the cushion of his balled shirt, she strained to capture his lips. With the hint of a smile teasing at the corners of his mouth, he eluded her.

Kate dropped her head back to the ground with a dissatisfied huff. She scowled her displeasure as the hunger in her grew ravenous. All she wanted was a kiss.

*Just. One. Lousy. Kiss.*

*How dare he keep toying with—*

His lips moved close again, and her train of thought...her very ability to think...went skittering out of reach. His body shifted atop her, his hips slid between her thighs. As he moved to cover her, his lips brushed her ear, and he asked one last time, "Are you certain, *mi corazón?*"

"Yes," she moaned, savoring the hard length of him as he sank, inch by hot, hard inch into her. Without warning, Styx wrapped his arms around her and rolled over until she straddled him and his broad back pressed into bunched clothing and crushed grass. She didn't feel the cool, night air whisper against her skin, only the heat radiating from the powerful male beneath her.

As she moved upon him, her body yielding to his, mastering his, she watched through lowered lashes as he set his fangs to his wrist. A burst of emotion so strong, so jolting shot through her system, bringing tears to her eyes. Suddenly nervous, she took his wrist in her hands. Licking her lips, her gaze darted to his, then back to his wrist. She forced a swallow, then brought his bleeding wrist to her mouth. The moment his blood passed her lips, she inhaled sharply through flared nostrils.

Emotion...sensation...instantly intensified.

Her body pulsed, throbbing. She drew more deeply from his vein, and with each swallow, her senses flared, emblazoned with new life. New definition. He groaned aloud. His burning gaze fixated upon her face as his free hand flexed on her hip, driving her up and down his shaft. He planted his heels, thrusting up into her harder.

At length, he drew his wrist from her reluctant lips and sealed his wound.

"Repeat after me," he coached.

Kate stared deep in his eyes, repeating him verbatim. "Your blood, my blood. My soul, your soul. I claim you as my mate. I am yours, forevermore."

A raging fever rocketed through her body. Her eyes all but rolled back in her head as she cried his name, spasming hard upon his shaft. Styx wrapped his arms around her and rolled again, pinning her writhing body beneath his. Kate wrapped her legs around his waist and gave herself over to his masterful strokes.

Her gasps and moans washed through the silence of the forest as his fangs sank into the pulse at the side of her throat. Her blood, the sweetest of ambrosias, coursed over his tongue and heat began to build in his core, melting him from the inside out. Every nerve in his body began tingling with near excruciating pleasure as he suckled from her vein, driving his shaft mercilessly in and out of her. Her legs squeezed hard on his waist as she demanded more of him, and he gave eagerly...all that he had, all that he was.

Too soon, he lapped at her throat, sealing the puncture wounds. It was so difficult to stop, so difficult to reign in the beast and temper his thirst, but he dare not weaken her too much. He wouldn't risk hurting her. She was more precious to him than life eternal. His lips pressed a delicate kiss to her healed flesh before turning to her ear. "Your blood, my blood. My soul, your soul. I claim you as my mate. I am yours, forevermore."

And with those final binding words, Styx's body

jerked. His hips pistoned, his back arched, and his body tightened as he poured his seed deep in her womb...his climax so intense as to be almost painful. Never had sensations so acute rocked through him before. He could *feel* her pulse thumping in his own veins. And the glow of her soul blinded him as it merged with his. Light to dark. Halfling to Immortal.

His Bride. His one true mate.

One soul for all eternity.

He would walk through this life alone no more.

Blood pounded in his ears as he panted against the side of her neck. He was weak as a babe...and invincible. At length, he moved to her side and gathered her close, murmuring words of love and devotion against her temple in the language of his heart as he covered her with the meager blanket of their clothing. Styx watched the moon crest high in the night sky above them, watched the diamond bright stars twinkle against a velvety backdrop. He recited stories of lovers and conquerors, of heroes and gods and goddesses, mapping out the constellations for her with each fabulous tale as the woman of his dreams snuggled close against his side.

Chapter 23

"Kate," Styx whispered against her temple. "*Mi corazón*, it is time to rise."

She murmured groggy disagreement, burying her face in the side of his neck. Her arm tightened over his waist, and she wiggled closer.

"Come, *querida*," he urged, fighting his own reluctance to move. "Dawn is still several hours away, but you are growing chilled. I must get you home, get you warmed up."

"I can think of a better way to warm up."

Her voice was husky seduction, leaving little doubt in his mind exactly what better ways she had in mind. But then she shivered, and he pushed those thoughts away...at least until later. He would see to her comfort and well-being first.

Then he would see to her desires.

A short while later, clothed once more, Styx led her down the gentle incline near a stream. Silvery moonlight dappled the ground at their feet, lending everything around them a soft, antique quality...like an old black and white film.

"Why was Cian goading you so hard about *shimmering*?"

Styx groaned. It was not easy for him to admit weakness, especially in front of his woman...and yet he would not lie to her. "The night Layla attacked you...*Tinkerbelle*—Cian," he quickly amended at her pointed glare, "*shimmered* me into the hospital. It was not a...*pleasant* experience."

He glanced over his shoulder to gauge her reaction. She worried her lower lip between her small, pearly teeth. "Do you suppose it will be like that for me too? '*Unpleasant?*'"

"It doesn't seem to bother Cian," he stated the obvious.

"Yes, but is that from practice...or is it physiological? Is there some kind of Faerie gene that makes *shimmering* less...traumatic for us?"

Damn it. Cian had been right. And the knowledge rubbed him raw. There were things he couldn't help her with, answers he just couldn't give her.

"I don't know, *mi corazón*," he replied, holding a branch aside for her. "This is something you will have to ask Cian."

"Speaking of Cian...I wonder what was so important that he had to disappear like that...not that I'm complaining." She shot him a shy smile. "But I notice he does that a lot...*shimmers* off at the drop of a hat. Is that normal?"

"I believe the Fae elders keep close tabs on him," Styx offered. "From what I understand from Crispin, your brother is a bit of a wild card. I'm betting the elders learned their lesson with your father, and are more vigilant of Cian's comings and goings."

"Hmm..."

"What?"

"Well...if that's true...sooner or later, won't those restrictions wear thin? I mean, Cian doesn't strike me as the type to put up with others telling him what to do...and when to do it...at least not for long. Won't they be risking outright rebellion if they place too many demands or limitations on him?"

Styx shuddered. Cian O'Callaghan, unpredictable and temperamental, running rampant through the Human world...unchecked and unmonitored...was, indeed, a frightening thought.

"Let's just hope they're wise enough not to push him too far."

"It shouldn't be that much farther now," Kate informed him, changing the subject as they crossed the stream and angled east. "The ranger's cabin is just beyond that rise."

As they crested the swell of land, Styx suddenly halted, throwing his arm out protectively, holding Kate behind him. His nostrils flared as he dragged in the rich scents of the forest around them. Taking her lead from him, Kate sniffed audibly behind him.

"What?" She sniffed again. "What is it?"

*Al-Rashid...*

Without explanation, Styx urged her back, across the stream and several yards farther before she dug her heels in and demanded an answer. "Styx, damn it, tell me what's going on."

"Couldn't you scent it?" She'd smelled the Newborns at the warehouse without difficulty. Why hadn't she scented al-Rashid?

When a speculative answer came to him— terrifying, paralyzing—he couldn't form words. Had al-Rashid spent so much time around Kate that she'd grown used to his scent, couldn't distinguish it as anything outside the norm?

"I didn't smell anything," she insisted.

*Ah, Dios...*

"It's al-Rashid, Kate."

"Are you sure? Couldn't you be mistaken?"

"I'm sure." Ice ran through his veins. He had to get Kate far, far away from here. *Now.* "Summon Cian."

"What?"

"*Mierda*, Kate. Do you think I *want* to do this? Do you think I want to rely on that Faerie to take you to safety?" He dragged his hand over his goatee, slipping it around to rub at the back of his neck. Bile crawled up the back of his throat, but he forced the hated words past his lips. "Summon him."

Frowning, she drew a deep breath and opened

her mouth.

Styx's hand clamped over her mouth so quickly...so unexpectedly...she gasped, blinking.

"No...don't raise your voice. If al-Rashid is anywhere nearby, he'd hear you in a heartbeat. You must..." he broke off, licking his lips, shaking his head as he tried to explain to her as best as he could, "you must *think* your command. Concentrate. Call his name in your mind, imagine his face, tell him you need help. Do it now."

"All right," she murmured, staring at him as if he'd lost his mind.

"Concentrate," he ordered.

Drawing a deep breath, Kate closed her eyes, a frown of fierce concentration digging two tiny grooves between her eyebrows.

A spare moment later, Cian wavered into view, out of breath and flushed in the face.

"What is amiss, lass?" Cian's angry gaze cut to Styx. "Did the leech—"

"Al-Rashid is close," Styx cut in.

Immediately, Cian tensed. His wary gaze scouring the area around them as he dragged the myriad scents of the night and the forest in deep.

"I do not scent him, leech. You waste my time," he muttered. "I must go back. I have...something I must attend to."

Judging by the bitter expression tightening his features, whatever Cian's *something* was...it didn't set well with the Faerie. Styx could only hope his conversation earlier with Kate hadn't been overheard by the Fates...those tricky and oft times treacherous sisters.

"He's there...or he was, not that long ago. That way," Styx indicated the small wooden structure in the distance, "inside the cabin."

Without warning, Cian disappeared. A moment later, he *shimmered* back. His face was pale...well, paler than normal.

"It is as you have said. He is no longer there. But his presence is strong. He has returned there many, many times." His blue-eyed stare pinned Styx, dark emotion swirling in their cobalt depths. "There is a female inside the dwelling."

Styx tensed. His worried gaze lingered on Kate, before slicing back to her brother. "Human...or Vampyre?"

"Neither...both," Cian answered with a disgusted shake of his head. "She is changing...but she is struggling. I do not think the female will survive."

Vicious curses ripped free of Styx's lips.

Dragging his fingers through his tousled hair, he turned to Kate. "Go with Cian—"

"But she might need medical atten—"

"There is nothing you can do for her now, Kate."

"But I could help you. I'm getting better at controlling the quickening. I could—"

"No," he barked. "You must go. I won't risk your safety this way...and I won't be able to concentrate...to do what I need to do if I'm worried about you."

Fine lines tightened at the corners of her eyes, and her lips compressed tightly. "Fine."

Before she could turn away, he reached out and caught her around the waist, drawing her into his embrace. Ignoring Cian's huffy sigh, he looked deep into her eyes and asserted, *"Te amo, mi corazón."*

He captured her lips with his own, plying them with gentle insistence until she melted in his arms. Only then did he release her.

Turning his attention to Cian, he warned, "Take her to the apartment and tell Zack to watch over her." Cian nodded briskly and held his hand out to Kate. "And Cian..." he warned with a fierce scowl. "I mean it. Take her to Zack. *Nowhere else.* Don't make me hunt you down, Faerie."

A fine muscle in Cian's jaw flexed. Bitter fire glowed in his brilliant blue eyes. "I would not take her to the Isle...not now...not even to spite you, leech. I will not let *them* anywhere near her." The acid in his tone left Styx uneasy. *Them.* A curse if ever he'd heard one. "Give me your hand, lass." Kate glanced at Styx, and then placed her hand upon Cian's. His long fingers closed over hers, the shade of their skin so close as to be identical. "Now close your eyes, lass. Picture your apartment. Think of the smells, the textures. The warmth. Now draw a deep breath."

And then they were gone.

Praying he hadn't just made the worst mistake of his life by placing Kate in Cian's clutches, Styx reached for his phone.

A single ring trilled through the phone line before the agent tersely snapped, "Crispin."

Well, hell... That didn't sound good...not from *him.*

Too bad. Styx had his own problems to deal with.

"I'm at Pointe Defiance, near the ranger's station," Styx barked. "Lock on to my phone's GPS and get out here."

"Styx," Crispin sighed deeply. "Look, I don't have time—"

"Make time, damn it." No fucking way was it going down like this. Crispin had bailed on Cole when he'd needed the agent most. No way was Styx gonna let the bastard off the hook this time.

"Styx, I've got a warehouse stacked with bodies...and not all of them are dead."

*¡Mierda!*

"Put someone else on it," Styx ordered.

"Someone else...I can't put—"

"Yes, you can," Styx countered. "I found his lair."

Five seconds of dead silence met his announcement.

"I'll be right there."

The line went dead, and Styx thrust the slim phone into his back pocket. Settling on his haunches, he eyed the cabin in the distance. Al-Rashid would return. Sooner or later. He had to. And when he did...Styx would be waiting.

The wait seemed interminable, but by his watch, no more than ten minutes had passed before he caught the scent of Vampyre. Styx turned his nose to the wind and drew deeply of the crisp breeze, all the while his unblinking gaze scoured the forest for the tiniest whisper of movement.

Crispin crouched down beside him.

"There's a female inside. He must have begun the process...and then abandoned her when it became apparent the change wasn't taking," Styx offered without any preamble. "His scent trail is a few hours old...but the saturation is constant enough to tell he's been using this cabin as his home base."

"How'd you find this place?"

"Stumbled on it, you might say," Styx murmured dryly. Crispin was ever famous for being stingy on the details...let him chew on that one for a while.

"If we go in, he'll know as soon as he comes back. The cabin will be useless as a trap later on," Crispin observed.

"There is a female inside there...suffering." *Dios*, the agent couldn't be that cold...could he? When Crispin continued to hesitate, Styx shifted his weight from one foot to the other, angling himself squarely at the agent. The space between them glowed luminescent amber. "Don't sit there and try to tell me that it would be for the greater good to leave her in there in that condition...just so you don't risk al-Rashid abandoning his lair."

"The only thing you or I could do for her is to put her out of her misery—"

"Exactly—"

"And what about all the others? If he slips away now...when we're so close to finally getting a handle on him...how many other women will suffer? How many will die? How many will change?" Crispin heaved a deep sigh, his brown eyes dull and careworn in the moonlight. "Can you live with that?"

Gritting his teeth, Styx peered hard at the cabin. Could he live with the possibility of more innocents suffering and dying?

Could he live with the certainty that he'd sat back and let an innocent female suffer needlessly?

Either way it was a lose/lose situation. One he couldn't stomach. Without a word to Crispin, Styx shot forward, a blur of motion in the still forest. The agent's furious curses fell softly in the ensuing silence. The door wasn't locked, the handle giving way easily to a quick twist of his wrist, and he was inside.

Stale sweat. Old blood.

New blood.

Terror.

Pain.

The smells were overwhelming, and he clamped his teeth down hard on the urge to gag. It was dark as sin inside the cabin, but his preternatural vision adjusted effortlessly. A soft whimper interrupted the ragged staccato of panting that filled the air. In the corner, huddled in a tight ball, the female's small body writhed and convulsed on the cold wooden floor. Her dark hair was a wild tangle, caked with blood. Her clothing—a prim, yet unmistakably feminine business suit—was shredded, streaked and splattered with blood.

Crispin appeared behind him and nudged him through the doorway. Styx stepped aside, his gaze leaving the female long enough to do a quick recon of the room. Nothing unusual. Nothing that screamed *Vampyre hideout.* As soon as he was inside the cabin, Crispin closed the door softly behind him. He skirted Styx and approached the female cautiously, murmuring in low, soothing tones. Heedless of his expensive, designer suit and his bulky overcoat, he dropped to his knees at her side.

The female whimpered again, curling tighter. She trembled violently...as if somehow sensing her torment was nearly over. Styx assumed Crispin would end her immediately, and so, when the agent merely laid his hands gently upon either side of her face, bowed his own head, and closed his eyes, Styx was at a loss.

A deep frown skittered over Crispin's otherwise impassive features. His body jerked, and his lips began to move, though no sound escaped him. As expressions slid across the female's face, they were mirrored on Crispin's as well. Curiosity. Fear. Disbelief. Pain. Horror. Shock.

And then anguish so deep, so engulfing as to consume a person's soul.

Helpless but to watch, Styx cringed as the tangled jumble of emotions passed between the agent and the female.

And then, though Crispin's expression was far from pleasant, the female went suddenly lax in his grip. A soft sigh...the sigh of one whose heavy burdens were suddenly and unexpectedly removed...seeped from between her parted lips. Her features smoothed, and her eyelids drifted languidly closed. It was as if Crispin had somehow sucked every last ounce of her suffering from her...and absorbed it into himself.

His hands slowly slipped from her face, and he tucked his palms beneath his armpits, as though his hands had been stung, his fingers singed. He doubled over, rocking himself slowly back and forth. It wasn't until that final moment...when Crispin had severed physical contact with the female...that Styx had a startling epiphany.

He'd never seen Crispin actually touch anyone before.

Not once.

Always there'd been that bland stare and evasive movement. Never a casual brush of the fingers. Even when he'd handled the dead, he'd used rubber gloves. It wasn't as if a Vampyre could contract some blood-borne disease, after all. But never had Styx witnessed Crispin actually touch someone—*anyone*—skin on skin. Ever.

*A touch empath...*

*Holy hell...*

Styx would never have guessed in a million years. No wonder Crispin was always so guarded with his emotions. No wonder he went out of his way to avoid physical contact. Styx could only begin to imagine what life must be like for the agent. Dios...how did he *feed*?

It certainly shed new light on Crispin and all his odd quirks.

Sobering, sympathetic light, to be sure.

Damn it.

The last thing he needed right now was to go and start feeling sorry for the emotionally traumatized agent. No. One thing at a time, he determined. Starting with the female.

What had Crispin done to her? She looked so peaceful now. Like a child lost in a pleasant dream.

"Is the change taking after all?" He knew the question sounded lame, but he had no other explanation. And even that one fell far short of the mark. A Newborn wouldn't have this contented, dreamy expression on her face. She'd be feral. Thirsty.

Dangerous.

"No," Crispin rasped. He sounded winded...and old. "She's dying."

"But..."

"I eased her pain, that's all...but there is nothing I can do to stop her death. She's too far gone now."

Eased her pain? It looked more like he'd somehow transferred it all into himself. Dull as his memories were of his own transformation, Styx remembered all too well that gnawing thirst. That muscle cramping, flesh burning, ear popping, brain splitting, blazing need to quench the astonishing thirst. It had been excruciating.

And *he* hadn't faced a failed transformation.

He hadn't gone through whatever it was this female must have gone through...only to die in the end anyway.

"What's happening to you?" Styx whispered. He swiped the back of his hand over his mouth. The way the otherwise unshakable agent continued to rock on the floor, hugging himself was...unsettling...to say the least.

"As long as she is alive...I will channel her...buffer her." *Christo*...every word sounded painful.

"Buffer...you mean, you are feeling *for* her?"

"Yes," Crispin groaned, hunching forward and closing his eyes.

"Well...stop, damn it. It's killing you." Styx paced away, paced back. What the hell was he supposed to do now. He'd never intended for something like this to happen. Hell, he hadn't known anything like this was even possible.

"Can't," Crispin panted. "Once there's...been physical contact...can't...sever connection...ever. Only death...can do that."

"*¡Madre de Dios!*" Styx raked the fingers of both

his hands through his hair, licked his lips. His gaze skated from Crispin to the female and back to Crispin. How long would the female last before she succumbed to death? How long could Crispin survive in his current condition?

How long did he have before al-Rashid returned?

His gaze returned to the female, and he forced a swallow. She was an innocent. She hadn't asked for this. Hadn't asked to have this curse devour her like this. She was no longer Human. But not Vampyre either. She was stuck somewhere in between...for all eternity. She would never wake up now. Never enjoy the crisp scent of a new morning, never marvel at the sunrise. She'd never return to her job...or her family, if she'd had one. She'd never taste another bite of her favorite food, nor sip her favorite wine. She'd never fall in love again, or fall out of it.

She'd never hurt again.

Crispin had ended her suffering.

And yet, Styx couldn't allow her to go on as she was. Couldn't allow her to continue to live so long as she presented a danger to others. And a danger she was, for Crispin had just explained that as long as she lived, he would bear her emotions, bear her suffering.

*Christo*...the agent was all but paralyzed with it.

Guilt all but crushed Styx as he slowly closed the distance. He placed his hands on her head, much the same as Crispin had done a few moments ago. But he didn't close his eyes. He did not bow his head. Her skin was soft beneath his hands, cold, clammy. The dark sweep of her lashes fluttered upon her cheeks, and yet she didn't open her eyes.

A small blessing, indeed, for he would bear the memory of this moment for the rest of his life. At least he wouldn't have to see her eyes pleading with him in his dreams for the rest of eternity. Before he gave himself too much time to dwell on the act lest he lose his courage, Styx gave a vicious twist and jerk, severing her head from her body.

Almost immediately, Crispin went limp on the floor.

Slowly, as if he were a decrepit old Human, Crispin rose to his feet. The lines of his face were haggard. His stare was haunted.

He glanced down at the headless corpse at his feet, then turned to Styx, his stare so full of emotion—shock, gratitude, and relief—that Styx had to turn away. The death of the female weighed upon him like a ton of bricks...but he would survive...somehow. He had not killed a Human in centuries. And, though he didn't even know her name, her death was a personal blow. He would learn to live with her blood on his hands. He had Kate now. He had a future. But Crispin's gratitude could not be borne so easily.

"Let's see if we can find anything in here to tell us where that bastard might have gone," Styx grumbled as he stalked away from the male who felt too much...and the female who would never feel again.

****

Al-Rashid drifted over the landscape, a dark shadow in the pre-dawn hours. How had Styx found his cabin? He'd been so careful to cover his tracks. Ah, well...the time for vengeance was at hand.

He'd been caught off guard when he'd seen the tall, blonde Faerie male appear. Having had no contact with that particular race before—trapped in Ava's cursed dungeon as he'd been, he hadn't had any idea what to expect. But when the Faerie had disappeared in a wavering mirage, taking his Johara with him, he'd been stunned.

He'd come close to panicking.

Where had the Faerie taken his Johara?

But then he'd forced himself to calm down, to think the situation out rationally.

The female in the cabin held no interest for him now. The transformation hadn't taken. She hadn't wanted to live badly enough. She'd let him down...disappointed him. It mattered naught what Styx did...or didn't do...with her anymore. His mind had already turned to other, more important thoughts.

Where...where would the Faerie take Johara?

He could not trace them by scent. And so he had to use process of elimination.

The first logical place to look would be her home. Sights and sounds passed by, but he took no notice of any of it. Her apartment loomed in the distance. Up he rose, scaling the side of the brick building, a rising shadow of wrath. He perched on the ledge outside her bedroom window, biding his time.

He could hear the Werewolf's muffled voice inside the apartment. Heard another, deep voice.

And then he heard the soft, melodic voice of his beloved. He canted his head, closing his eyes, focusing his acute sense of hearing on every pin drop of sound inside her apartment.

"Zack, you should go to the cabin...help Styx," Johara pleaded.

Bilious outrage pummeled him that she should debase herself to beg for help for that bastard Spaniard.

"Don't worry so much, Kate. Styx can handle himself. And he's got plenty of back-up with Crispin and Cian." A rustle of sound proceeded a soft grunt as someone dropped heavily onto a padded seat. A plastic bag crinkled, and the quick hiss of carbonation escaping a can filled the room. "Besides, I'd rather battle a legion of Rogues than face Styx if I left you here alone."

"I can call Cian back."

"Seriously, Red, you're gonna piss me off if you tell me you'd rather spend time with that...that brother of yours rather than with my charming self."

Brother? His Johara had no brother. Of whom did this Werewolf speak? It made no sense. He knew all there was to know of Johara.

"Relax," Zack coaxed. "They'll be back before you know it. Why don't you grab a brownie or something and just hang for a while?"

"I'm not hungry...God, do you ever stop eating?" Her voice held a ring of amusement now.

"Rarely. And only for a *really* good reason." There was enough innuendo in that loaded word that al-Rashid could all but see the lecherous grin, even through the brick wall separating them.

"I'm going to go take a shower," Johara called, her voice drifting closer to her bedroom.

A door opened and closed. And then another door opened inside the bedroom. Her soft humming whispered over the sound of rushing water.

All the while, he amended his plans for her, solidifying them in his mind. Had she stayed in the woods with Styx, he would have killed his nemesis and taken her there in the woods, made her his. But then the Faerie had come and taken her away, and he'd only been concerned about where she'd gone. He hadn't liked not knowing where she was at all. These last several days had been hell for him. While he didn't doubt his abilities, she'd been too well guarded to risk another Werewolf bite. Styx would be a formidable adversary as it was. And he had no idea what that Faerie was capable of.

But now was the perfect opportunity. With only the werewolf standing guard...poor excuse for a guard that he was sitting in a separate room stuffing his face...she was as good as his.

He slipped through the minute crack in the

window sash, filling the room with a darkened, ominous shadow. Just as insidiously, he seeped himself beneath the bathroom door, flowing up behind her. She stood at the vanity, hands braced on the edges of the sink, head bowed. Steam had begun pouring from the shower, but she had yet to remove her clothing.

And she reeked of Styx.

Fury boiled inside him.

She'd let him touch her.

She'd *lain* with him.

His body vibrated with outrage as he solidified behind her. His nostrils flared and his fangs pushed long inside his mouth. How dare she betray him like this? How dare she defile herself with that treacherous bastard? She wasn't worthy of the gift he could give her. *Would have* given her, he amended. Now she would taste nothing but his wrath.

"*Ya sallam*, Johara," he whispered menacingly.

Her head snapped up, and her deceitful eyes shot wide in the mirror. Her perfidious mouth dropped open and she sucked in a sharp breath. He clipped the back of her neck with the blade of his hand, and she crumpled to the floor. He broke her fall, but only to stifle the noise she might make. It wouldn't do to draw the Werewolf's attention...not just yet.

In a quick and efficient motion, he scooped her up and tossed her over his shoulder. On silent feet, he tread across the bedroom, eased the window open, and slipped out onto the ledge. Wind rushed by as he leaped from the edge and dropped the eight stories to the pavement below, landing lightly on the balls of his feet. Jostling her weight closer to his neck, he anchored a hand on the curve of her bottom and drew a deep breath.

His Johara...no, no, he corrected himself. She

wasn't his Johara...not anymore. She wasn't his jewel.

Kate O'Rourke had a lot to answer for.

His lips curved on a mirthless smile, and he stalked into the shadows, disappearing into the night like the shade he was.

## Chapter 24

Kate groaned, and slowly she forced her eyes open. Darkness. Shadows. Pounding pain in her head. Something cold and hard pressed against her cheek, and all down the length of her body. She was laying on something cold and hard...a rough floor of some kind. The air was musty, and putrid with the smells of stale sweat and blood.

She made to press her palm to her temple, and the bindings at her wrists cut into her skin. Wincing, she half-rolled, half-shimmied, wiggling into an upright position. Pain lanced up the back of her neck and split her skull open. Her breath caught as she sagged sideways, bracing her shoulder against a rough-hewn log wall. Where was she?

*That face...that gruesome, twisted face in the mirror...*

Her heart picked up speed as her eyes slowly adjusted to the darkness. A cabin. She was inside a cabin...

*The ranger's cabin...*

*Oh, dear God, no...*

"Ah, you have awakened," a deep voice resonated from the shadows.

Kate turned her head, frantically searching for the source of the voice. A subtle shift in the shadows caught her attention. Instinct urged her magick to quicken inside her. Unfortunately, tied as she was with her hands behind her back, her newly honed skills were useless. At least he hadn't tied her ankles. Maybe if he got close enough, she could score a kick somewhere vital.

"What do you want," she demanded with false bravado.

"Now there is the question, my pet," the deep voice crooned. He was mocking her. And, unless she missed her mark, he was angry.

Very, *very* angry.

"So brave," he murmured, tsking sadly. "Such a waste." His voice dropped, and his tone hardened as he separated from the shadows.

Kate caught herself pressing back against the wall at the first glimpse of him. If she pressed much harder, she'd slip right through the chinks in the wall. Stiffening her spine, she forced herself not to cower. She'd show no weakness to this monster...even if she was scared out of her mind. Her gaze skated away from him for a moment, and she took in her surroundings.

Only one door, and he stood square in the way. Three old-fashioned, wood-framed windows. She could probably throw herself through one. It'd hurt like hell, but she could do it if she had to. Nothing to use as a weapon. The room was empty, but for a lamp and the sparse, Adirondack-type furniture...and the bloodstains. She took a deep breath, as much to calm her nerves, as to lend strength to her voice. A new scent caught her attention, and she hesitated.

Styx?

Styx had been here. Not long ago...and he was gone now. But he'd been here. She drew strength from the lingering scent of him, imagined his arms around her, his lips pressed to her hair offering her courage when her own flagged.

"You brought me back to the cabin," she stated, staring unflinchingly at the Rogue. And she could see why the Vampyre race called them that...Rogues. His eyes burned brightly with an unholy, maniacal glow. His fangs never seemed to

334

quite disappear the way Styx's did. And the way his face seemed permanently contorted...a shiver skated down her spine.

"Brilliant move," he quipped conversationally, "don't you think?"

"How do you figure?" Kate watched him through narrowed eyes, feeling as if she treaded a tightrope. She would not shrink from him, nor could she push him too far. Her only hope was to keep him talking, maybe someone...*anyone*...would come to her aid.

"That bastard Spaniard," he paused to spit on the floor, as if the name had fouled his mouth, "and the TFRA agent have convinced themselves that once they contaminated my lair with their scent, I would not return here. Ridiculous, how easy it was to linger on the fringes of night as a shade and listen to them. Imagine that, '*contaminate my lair*'...as if I were some lowly, mindless animal, driven purely by instinct, with no sentient intelligence. Fortunate that I caught the scent of you near the stream before I came too close, though, or he might have caught me anyway."

"What did you do with the female that was here earlier?"

"She was gone when I returned with you. It seems your honorable Spaniard took it upon himself to end her suffering," he sneered.

He was baiting her, gauging her reaction.

"I'm sure Styx did what he felt was necessary." She schooled her features into an impassive mask, determined to give away none of the turmoil his words had sparked. Styx had killed the female? Could she believe that of him?

Yes...yes, she could. If he thought he'd had no other choice.

Maybe if she lulled this Rogue into a false sense of security, she could convince him to free her hands. If Cian could call down an electrical storm, surely she could summon one tiny little lightning bolt. And, if her luck held, she might even be able to give it a target.

"Styx is smart. And so is Agent Crispin. They'll figure out where you've taken me, and they will come for you."

"I sincerely hope that they do," he reassured her with an odd little smile. The points of his fangs gleaming like lethal beacons in the darkness. "It will be my pleasure to face that perfidious bastard at long last. But rest assured, Kate O'Rourke, we have plenty of time before he figures it all out. Plenty of time for me to show you the error in your judgment."

Al-Rashid strode forward. His smile sent a chill of dread racing through her. His arm stretched toward her, and his fingers slipped through her hair. The gentleness of his touch so at odds with the banked fury smoldering in his unwavering gaze. "You know, I am sorely disappointed in you, my tarnished jewel." The tip of his finger trailed down the curve of her jaw, pressed against the bottom of her chin, lifting her face to the moonlight filtering in through the nearby window. "I had such plans for us." He shook his head, and the look in his eyes turned sad, almost wistful. "Such grand plans."

The pad of his thumb smoothed across her lower lip, and she gritted her teeth behind her lips, just barely restrained herself from flinching away...or taking a chunk out of him.

"I would have made you my queen, Johara," he whispered, as though he spoke to a memory. "I would have treated you like a princess in a fairy tale."

Well, he'd gotten some of the story right, she reflected ironically. For in all good fairy tales, there was always an evil villain...a madman from whom the hero must always rescue the fair damsel in distress. Well, al-Rashid would certainly qualify as an evil madman, and, right now, she seemed to have fallen neatly into the role of damsel in distress...galling as that thought might be. Now all she needed was her knight in shining armor to come charging to her rescue.

*Styx...where are you?*

Kate held still for al-Rashid's touch, but she couldn't hide the revulsion in her gaze.

His eyes narrowed as he bent closer, peering hard into her eyes. His pupils dilated, and his lips moved quickly. Only the faintest whisper of sound met her ears. She'd seen Styx do this.

Was al-Rashid trying to compel her? Trying to use that vaunted '*voice of persuasion*' of which the Vampyre race was supposedly so adept?

Well, as far as she was concerned, they all needed to practice, because she didn't feel compelled to do *anything*, not in the least little way.

Arching a brow, she stared right back at him and waited.

Fleeting puzzlement flickered over his face as he drew back, frowning at her. He blinked, then dropped to one knee at her side. He leaned closer once more and gazed into her eyes with renewed intensity.

Kate heaved a sigh. "It doesn't work, you know."

He blinked rapidly, jerking back, gaping at her.

"That mind trick thing you guys do...it doesn't work on me."

"Why not?" The question seemed to have slipped free without thought, for he scowled, plainly chagrinned.

And something else became clear. He still thought she was only a Human. What would he do if he found out she was half-Faerie? Would he let her go...or would he kill her immediately.

*Half-Faerie...* What had she been thinking? The *quickening* wasn't her only power.

Closing her eyes, she battled fiercely to concentrate. She imagined the scent of her apartment, as Cian had once instructed...but the smell of blood kept seeping into her nostrils, contradicting her. She imagined the objects in her apartment, wishing with all her might that she could shimmer there.

For one slim moment, she felt the ground beneath her shift. Or maybe it had only been wishful thinking, because when she opened her eyes, she was still inside the cabin. And al-Rashid still loomed over her.

Damn it.

Why hadn't she paid closer attention? Why hadn't she insisted that Cian teach her to *shimmer* sooner?

*Okay, Katie girl, no time to lose your head. Think. You can find a way out of this.*

Unfortunately, *shimmering* wasn't working. She didn't possess any ruby slippers, and all the wishing in the world wasn't going to whisk her away to Kansas. She needed to find that level head she'd so prided herself on.

"Let me go," she reasoned softly. "You don't need to—"

Humorless laughter cut her off. His eyes gleamed bright. "I don't need to what...hurt you? Kill you?" He shot to his feet and paced away. When he reached the middle of the room, he spun on his heel to face her. "Don't you get it? You were special. I *courted* you. I gave you attention that I gave to none of the others. You were to be my first wife...my most beloved. But you gave yourself to him. To *him*, damn you. To the one male who took *everything* from me." Al-Rashid stormed across the room, dropping to a crouch before her. "You betrayed me, Kate O'Rourke. And betrayal is punishable by death."

She gasped, cringing back against the wall as he

bared his fangs, hissing righteous fury at her. Magick vibrated through her body, sizzling ineffectually in the palms of her hands. His hand sank roughly into her hair, fisting, jerking her flush against his chest, wrenching her head to the side. His breath seethed over her flesh, hot and damp, as his fangs grazed her skin.

Kate scrunched her eyes closed.

Dear Lord, how could she have been so stupid? How could she have forgotten?

*Cian...Cian, help me!*

In the space of a heartbeat, a split second before al-Rashid's fangs penetrated her flesh, ozone crackled in the air. Over al-Rashid's shoulder, she watched as Cian shimmered into view...with Styx at his side. Deathly pale, Styx staggered forward as soon as his feet found purchase, launching himself shakily at the Rogue's back.

With an outraged howl, al-Rashid dropped her into a heap on the ground and spun to meet Styx head on. They crashed into each other mid-leap, snarling and hissing. In a flash, Cian was at her side.

The room around them began to shift as he began to *shimmer* her away.

"No," she screamed, jerking and thrashing violently away from him.

"Lass—"

"Let me go," she demanded. "Get my hands free."

He hesitated, clearly torn. With a scowl of reluctance shadowing his handsome face, he turned her around, placing her between his body and the far wall, shielding her as he worked on her bindings. Behind them, the battle raged. Furniture skidded and smashed. The walls shook. Roars and snarls, growls and gut-deep grunts marked the combatants progress across the room.

At last, her hands were free. Rubbing the feeling back into her wrists and hands, Kate shoved her way around Cian, but he jerked her back against his side when the combatants rolled across the floor in their direction in a tangle of flailing limbs and gnashing fangs. Blood sprayed in a wide arc across the wall at Kate's left. Some of the crimson droplets splattered on her jeans and boots.

Purple points of energy pulsed in her palms, but she couldn't get a clear shot at the Rogue. Every time she tensed to throw an energy orb, the two hissing Vampyre rolled, unwittingly exchanging positions as fists pounded and claws shredded. Frustrated, Kate pulled the magick back. All around the cabin, the wind raged, ripping at the shingles, rattling the windows. Purple lightning arced across the skies.

"Breathe, lass," Cian coached, his hand resting lightly on her shoulder. "Focus. Feel the quickening. Channel it."

The Rogue landed a particularly vicious kick to Styx's midsection, sending Styx skidding across the floor, leaving a bloody smear in his wake. In that instant, the Rogue leapt into the air...not to attack his fallen foe, but to disintegrate into a dark cloud of shadow-mist. The shadow-mist floated across the floor, headed straight for the door.

"Now," Cian urged.

Needing no explanation, Kate pulled her arm back and hurled the energy orb into the center of the dark shadow. Her magick dispersed in a shower of purple sparks and miniature, sizzling electrical shocks. The shadow faltered, lit oddly from within. Kate hurled another orb, and another in quick succession. Heat flowed through her, wild and exultant, pulsing brighter and brighter.

"Easy," Cian soothed. His hand tightened slightly on her shoulder, and that point of contact centered her. Grounded her.

One last orb burst forth, and al-Rashid tumbled to the ground, once more a tangible target. Styx vaulted into the air, landing astride the fallen Vampyre. Al-Rashid slashed his claws across Styx's chest, and more blood gushed forth. But Styx was undaunted. His fangs gleamed, long and lethal, as he roared, grasping the Rogues head between his hands.

With a deft jerk, he severed the Rogue's head from his twitching body.

For an endless moment, Styx sat there on the Rogue's chest. Holding the Rogue's head in his hands. Then he chucked the head across the room and rose shakily to his feet. Turning, he faced Kate. Blood covered him from head to toe. Jagged wounds ravaged his flesh. His chest. His arm. His thigh. His shoulder. His cheek.

He was fully transformed...and a more ferocious sight she'd never beheld. But there was no fear in her heart, no hesitation. This was the man she loved. Her knight.

He took a wobbling step in her direction. And then his eyes went strangely unfocused, and he collapsed.

"Styx," Kate shrieked. "Nico...no..."

She jerked away from Cian and flew across the room to his side. Her hands raced over his fallen form, probing, assessing. Broken ribs. A shattered collarbone. A possible fractured femur. And too many lacerations and contusions to count.

*Dear God...so much blood.*

Her stomach lurched.

*Please...please...*

Kate placed her hand over his ravaged chest. Heat poured from her palms, and some of his smaller wounds began to mend. The bleeding slowed.

But it didn't stop.

"No," she cried brokenly. "Damn it, you fight this, Nico. Don't you die on me…"

Gently, she gathered him into her arms. Her tears fell, unchecked, on his face. "I love you…so much. *Te amo*, Nico."

Again, she tried to channel her energy into him. But it felt weak…as if she'd used it all up on battling al-Rashid.

"Cian," she shouted, even though he'd already come to kneel beside her. "Do something."

"He's dying, lass." He squeezed her shoulder, offering silent sympathy.

"No, he's not," she denied adamantly.

"He is, lass," Cian argued. "You know it…you feel it."

Kate glared up at him, and caught her breath. The pain in Cian's eyes shocked her.

"If I could spare you this loss, little sister, there is naught I wouldn't do."

"He needs blood," Kate gasped. Why hadn't she thought of this sooner? It seemed her brain was functioning a half step behind, ever since the Rogue had knocked her unconscious earlier.

Cian frowned, his gaze dropped to Styx's still body, considered.

"I can find a Human," he offered at last.

"No, that won't work…not anymore."

"What do you mean? Why not?"

"He cannot consume another Human's blood now…well, theoretically, I suppose he could still consume it, but it would no longer nourish him. We've blood-bonded," Kate reported absently, all her attention on the faint pulse fluttering in Styx's carotid.

"What?" Cian yelped, leaping to his feet.

The words pouring forth from him were in an ancient language she'd only heard on the whisper of the wind...and always in those tense few seconds before Cian informed them he was being summoned and then promptly vanished. The cadence was melodious, the lilting brogue like the sweetest of music to her ears...despite the fact that Cian ranted and raged with enough venom that she had no doubt that the words themselves were anything but PG-rated.

But she had no time for Cian's temper...or his tantrum. Styx was dying. "Would blood heal him?" She tore her gaze away from Styx's unnaturally pale face long enough to glance inquiringly up at Cian. "If I give him my blood...would he survive?"

"I do not know," her brother admitted hoarsely. His eyes burned with a new fervor, one she'd never seen before in him. He looked...desperate. "But you have no choice now, lass. You must try something. Your soul has merged with his. If he dies now...you will die too."

"Can you heal him...like I do...with your hands?" She didn't know how to explain that strange and unpredictable magick she wielded, and her question barely made sense even to her own ears.

"Every Faerie has his own individual magickal offerings. Many are passed generation to generation...kin to kin. Alas, I have no' that power, Kate," Cian acknowledged regretfully. "I can no' heal him."

Tears burned her eyes. "Okay..." She drew a deep breath and eased Styx back to the ground. His face was still fully transformed, and she'd never loved him more, never needed him more. With shaking hands, she carefully pulled his jaw open and parted his lips. If she could just slip her wrist into his mouth...and slit her wrist on his razor-sharp fangs...then gravity—and hopefully Styx's will to live...should do the rest.

But luck was not on her side. His face might be

fully transformed...but his fangs had retracted. His teeth were no sharper than hers.

A sob escaped her lips, and she dropped her chin to her chest in defeat as tears coursed hot tracks over her cheeks, falling silently on the Vampyre that she loved.

*Don't you do it, Katie girl...* Her father's voice whispered somewhere in the back of her mind, stirring her to battle. *An O'Rourke doesn't hang her head and quit. You get up, dust yourself off, and you figure out a way around that obstacle. Tear it down if you have to. That's my girl...now you go get 'em...*

She wasn't a quitter.

Kate lifted her head. Resolve gleamed in her stare as she focused all her energy, all her magick on Styx. She placed both her hands on Styx's chest, closed her eyes, and surged every last ounce of strength into the *quickening*. As if sensing her intent, Cian placed his hands on her shoulders. Heat, power rushed from her shoulders to her palms and fingertips, like a conduit.

At length, Styx coughed, sputtered. He gasped for air. And his eyelid's fluttered.

"Nico...wake up." Drained, Kate sagged against his side, held up only by sheer dint of will, and Cian's hands. She reached for Styx's face, cradled it tenderly in her palms. "Styx, open your eyes," she commanded, though her voice was feeble at best.

His eyelids fluttered again and then lifted slowly.

He blinked groggily, his eyes dilated and unfocused. Breath rasped in and out of his lungs. But he was holding on, and, for the moment, that was all that mattered.

"Styx," Kate called in a bid to get him to focus on her. "I need your help, Styx. I need you to listen to me carefully." Encouraged when his gaze landed on her, and a frail smile curled the edges of his lips, she pressed on. "I need you to...to extend your fangs. Make them longer."

His brows drew together in confusion, and he mumbled something unintelligible.

"Listen to me, Styx," she demanded, clutching at his shoulders, shaking him when he let his eyelids slip closed. Jolted, clearly still in a substantial amount of pain, he exerted the effort to open his eyes and gaze at her once more. "Damn it, you cannot go to sleep. Stay with me now. I need you to bite me...drink from me. You are hurt...badly. And you need blood. Now."

She thrust her wrist to his lips, but he turned his head away. His lips moved, and she bent close to hear him.

"Might not...be able...to...stop..." His words were sluggish, slurred. He blinked owlishly up at her and wobbled his head in denial. "Might drain you...could...kill..."

"Styx, stop it...listen to me," she pleaded, desperate to get through to him. Obviously, he wasn't thinking clearly, or he wouldn't be so concerned about draining her. "If you don't drink from me, you'll kill me anyway. You have to remember, Styx. We've taken the *Sacred Vows*. We've blood-bonded."

He blinked up at her, slightly more alert than he had been a moment ago. More alert...and definitely more alarmed.

Forcing a swallow, his gaze searched her face, and he seemed to be struggling to get a firm grasp on the situation. His weary gaze slid to Cian where he towered behind Kate, then swept the apartment.

He muttered a low curse beneath his breath.

"Cian," he croaked.

Cian growled something dark and venomous, but he went to his knees beside Styx. And even on his knees, he was still every inch the regal prince bowing before no one.

"You must...stop me," Styx rasped, his hand lifting to clutch anxiously, albeit weakly at Cian's wrist. "Swear...to me...you will stop...stop me from...draining her..."

Cian's long, narrow hands had balled into fists, and, judging by the expression on his face, he dearly wanted to plant one of those fists against Styx's strong jaw...but he nodded brusquely, instead. Kate watched as Cian's furious gaze met Styx's woozy, apprehensive stare, and a tenuous understanding seemed to pass between them, male to male, Vampyre to Faerie...the brother of a hardheaded woman to the man that she loves.

Kate urged Cian aside and thrust her bared wrist up to Styx's mouth once more. "Drink," she pleaded.

Styx licked his lips, and then set his mouth to her wrist in a small, apologetic kiss. His eyes dilated, his irises glowed, and his fangs shot long. She caught her breath, but held steady as his fangs pierced her flesh. His hands came up to grip her forearm, holding her immobile. His jaws clamped down, and the suction of his mouth increased.

The sharp flare of pain had disappeared as soon as he began to draw from her vein, even though his fangs were still embedded in her wrist. A soothing euphoria settled around her like a warm, fuzzy blanket, making her want to close her eyes and slip under, pull the blanket up over her head and close the rest of the world out. But she fought the sensation, struggled valiantly to keep a firm grip on reality. And she battled to hold his gaze.

Guilt and relief warred in his eyes.

But love glimmered there as well.

And that love gave her hope.

"That's it," she encouraged, lovingly stroking his hair away from his forehead with her free hand.

"Take all that you need, Nico. I love you." She offered him a tremulous smile and kept stroking his hair.

And Styx gaze clung to her, unblinking, as if her stare were his only link to sanity. Even when his mouth began to pull harder, and his already puckered forehead wrinkled even deeper. Even as his hands convulsed upon her forearm. His gaze never left hers.

Kate felt her eyelids begin to slip closed. The smile on her lips felt strangely dreamlike in quality. And yet she couldn't seem to pull away, didn't even have the desire to try. Everything had started to go a bit muddled around the edges. And her blood rushed in her ears...like the ebb and flow of the nighttime surf against sandy shores, growing fainter and fainter by the second. Her breathing grew heavy, until it was almost too much of a struggle to bother with the monumental effort of inhaling and exhaling.

"That's enough, Styx." Cian's voice hummed, just above the surf, but his words made no sense. "You must let her go."

Something tugged at her arm, but the suction continued.

"By Danu, you'll kill her, Styx," Cian swore from a great distance away. "Release her!"

Why had he wandered so far away? Didn't he know that she needed help...needed help to save...save Styx...

The warm blanket was just too inviting to resist any longer. With a soft sigh, Kate pulled the soft edges close around her and curled up in its blissful folds as night's dark arms reached out to embrace her.

Epilogue

Silvery moonlight glittered across the rolling surf as wave after wave crashed rhythmically upon the white sandy beach. Kate reached across his chest to set the tall glass down on the table beside the wide, swaying hammock. Droplets of cool condensation tracked down the chilled glass, dripping onto his bare skin. Her breasts, covered as they were by the tiny scrap of material that passed for a bikini, teased him, and his loins stirred to life...a regular occurrence around his *Bride*, it would seem.

They'd been vacationing—honeymooning, Kate called it—on this all but deserted little island off the coast of Fiji for almost three weeks now. And, to his vast relief and amazement, not a single moment of restlessness had intruded the entire time. Three blissful weeks of surfing and lounging in the shade. Three idyllic weeks of exotic drinks and precious alone time with his female. Three peaceful weeks without buzzing pagers and trips to the Emergency Room. Three harmonious weeks without Zack underfoot and irregular visits from Crispin.

Three glorious weeks without Cian.

Styx lifted a hand to his cheek and flexed his jaw as Kate settled herself at his side, nuzzling her head into the curve of his shoulder. Damn him if his jaw wasn't still tender. Cian had barely waited until Styx was back on his feet before knocking him back on his ass for endangering Kate that way...meaning the blood-bond, of course. Frustrated that he couldn't simply fry Styx on the spot—which would kill his sister in the process—Cian had attacked him the only way he could. With fists flying.

That had been almost four weeks ago, right after they'd returned from the cabin in the woods. And his jaw still hurt...despite the fact he'd recovered from all his other wounds without any difficulty.

That brother of hers sure packed a hell of a wallop.

"Is it still hurting?" Kate rolled her head back on his shoulder and searched his face with probing eyes. "He shouldn't have punched you like that. I was fine. You stopped in time, and there was no harm done."

He muttered a non-committal response, the memory of her pale and unconscious in his arms was still too fresh...too painful...to deal with. She'd come a lot closer to death than she'd realized, even now.

"Do you want me to—"

"No," he denied, shaking his head as he dropped his hand to cover hers where it rested on his chest. "It's fine."

She arched a dubious brow, but settled back against his shoulder with a contented sigh.

She could heal the bruise with nothing more than a pass of her gifted little hand over the tender spot...a spot no doubt still sore only due to some dark magick on Cian's part...but he wouldn't allow her to do it. A part of him still felt guilty over how close Kate had come to dying, all because he'd selfishly allowed the blood-bond between them. Perhaps this was to be his penance.

Heaven knew he'd already received the only reward he would or could ever want...the angel in his arms.

"How much longer do we have until we have to go back?" How could anyone sound so completely satisfied, so content, and yet so reluctant at the same time?

Grinning, he pressed a soft kiss to her forehead. "We have all the time in the world, *querida*. There is no rush."

A long, slow sigh escaped her. "What will we do when we go back?"

He took a while to roll that one around before answering. "Well, first off, you will continue your lessons with Cian...starting with *shimmering*. I don't want you at anyone's mercy like you were with al-Rashid ever again."

The tip of her finger began tracing distracting circles around his nipple. "Speaking of Cian...I wonder what he and Zack were up to right before we left Tacoma. The two of them were thick as thieves that last few days, come to think of it."

"Whatever it was...Crispin is in on it."

And that, in and of itself, left Styx with a bad feeling in the pit of his stomach. A very bad feeling, indeed. The last thing he needed to worry about was Crispin dragging Zack and Cian in on some foolhardy, Rogue-hunting mission. They were grown males, responsible for their own decisions, and there was relatively little Styx could do to stop them. The damnedest thing was, he'd grown genuinely fond of Zack, and Kate would be devastated if anything happened to her brother...therefore he didn't want to see either of them come to any harm.

Pushing that worrisome thought aside, he sought to divert Kate's attention. "I think we should make a trip to L.A." He nuzzled her hair, relishing the soft essence of strawberries and Kate. "I want you to meet some friends of mine."

"The ones you mentioned before, Cole and Alexandra Gunnarrson?"

"Yes," he confirmed, trailing his fingers down the arch of her back, and over the flare of her hip. "And then," he heaved a beleaguered sigh, "I guess we should make a trip to the Isle of Fae. Cian said

Aaron is eager to meet you...and the elders are struggling to keep him contained. I don't suppose we should unleash him on the world just yet, do you, *mi corazón*?"

"What about what Cian said before...about not letting me anywhere near the elders?"

"I don't think we have much to worry about there...not anymore," he assured her. "I believe the elders will think twice before interfering where you are concerned again. Angering Aaron was a mistake they will not want to repeat. And they sure as hell won't want to anger Aaron *and* Cian. Not unless they want outright war on their hands."

A soft giggle escaped Kate. "That's a frightening thought." Then her giggles subsided, and anxiety laced her tone. "What do you suppose he's like...Aaron?"

Styx squeezed her tight. "He loved your mother, *querida*. And he's mourned her loss, every minute of every day since the elders bound his magick and sanctioned him to the Isle. He might be a bit...fearsome. But his devotion to your mother, I'm sure, has carried over to you. He will love you." He kissed her forehead again. "How could he not?"

"Admit it. You're just relieved that he's given us his blessing...even if it was through Cian," Kate teased.

"I will admit no such thing." Chuckling, Styx tickled her ribs as he shifted his weight and eased her atop him. Then his laughter died and his voice took on a serious note. "I'd face a thousand pissed off Faeries to be with you, *mi corazón*. Nothing will ever keep me from your side."

Kate nibbled at his lower lip as she eased up, straddling him. The hard ridge of his arousal pressed against her through the barrier of their swimsuits. She shifted her weight, angling her hips, rubbing herself against him. Torment had never been so sweet.

"You know," she murmured suggestively, "it's awfully warm tonight. Don't you think a nice cool moonlight swim sounds good?"

Styx eyed the rippling, silver-dappled waters lapping at the pale, sandy shoreline some fifty feet away. Overhead, the fronds of a palm tree rustled gently in the breeze. The moon listed overhead, like a giant glimmering pearl. Styx wrapped an arm around her waist, pinning her to him, as he deftly vaulted from the hammock. The sand was pleasantly warm on his feet as he padded toward the water. Kate wrapped her legs around him, locking her ankles, as she met him kiss for kiss.

Blessedly cool water licked at his ankles, then his knees and hips. He didn't stop walking until he stood chest deep in the gentle waves. As his lips trailed down the side of her throat, Kate gasped softly.

"I didn't really want to swim," she whispered, arching her back, tilting her head to the side to allow him better access to her neck.

"Me neither," he rumbled against her skin.

The straps of her bikini snapped easily in his eager hands, and, after he'd loosened the string in the waistband, his board shorts washed to the shore on the next set of waves. In one deft thrust, he embedded himself deep inside her, gasping as her silken flesh closed tight around him. He moved with the waves, easing her slowly up and down his shaft. Then he turned into the waves, letting them pound and jar their motions, driving her down hard upon him. His arms were locked around her, holding her close...right where she belonged...as his mouth claimed hers, again and again.

This was as close to heaven as he figured he'd ever get. And he didn't plan on letting go anytime soon. It didn't matter where he went, or how he got there, as long as Kate was by his side. It didn't matter what name he called himself, or what profession he took up, as long as this woman loved him. All that mattered was that they were together.

Because as long as he was with her...he was home.

## A word about the author...

Always a voracious reader, Brenda Huber closed the cover on a book by one of her favorite authors and said to herself, *I can do this!* Ever fascinated by all things mythical and mystical, Brenda began penning her first novel and discovered her second great passion...writing. She lives in Iowa with her husband and two children.

Thank you for purchasing
this Wild Rose Press publication.
For other wonderful stories of romance,
please visit our on-line bookstore at
www.thewildrosepress.com

For questions or more information,
contact us at
info@thewildrosepress.com

The Wild Rose Press
www.TheWildRosePress.com